D1361998

Other books by Janelle Taylor

CAN'T STOP LOVING YOU

DEFIANT HEARTS

DESTINY MINE

FIRST LOVE,WILD LOVE

FORBIDDEN ECSTASY

IN TOO DEEP

LAKOTA DAWN

LAKOTA WINDS

NIGHT MOVES

NOT WITHOUT YOU

PASSIONS WILD AND FREE

SAVAGE ECSTASY

SOMEDAY SOON

SWEET SAVAGE HEART

TENDER ECSTASY

WILD WINDS

LAKOTA FLOWER

Janelle Taylor

ZEBRA BOOKS
KENSINGTON PUBLISHING CORP.

ZEBRA BOOKS are published by

Kensington Publishing Corp.
850 Third Avenue
New York, NY 10022

ISBN 0-7394-3688-0

Printed in the United States of America

To my youngest grandson,
Brandon Michael Thurmond,
And to his parents:
our daughter, Melanie,
and son-in-law, Jonathan

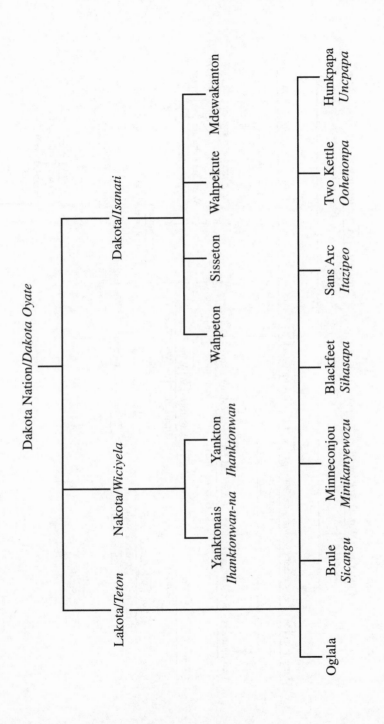

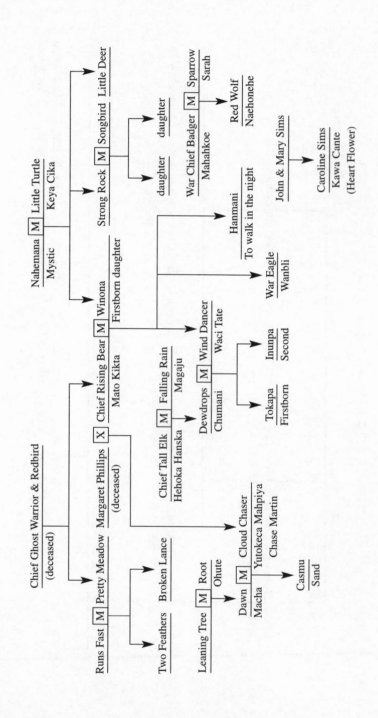

Chapter One

With his dark eyes narrowed, War Eagle lowered the field glasses his older brother's wife had given him many seasons past during other difficult and dangerous times. He studied the troubling scene that was taking place not far beyond his concealed position near his best friends: Swift Otter, River's Edge, Bent Bow, and Broken Lance, who was also the son of his father's sister. While the rest of their hunting party was busy elsewhere, they had been scouting the buffalo herd's size and movements when he sighted the grave intrusion. They had hidden their horses behind a hill, climbed it, and lain on their stomachs, checking out the situation. He glanced to his right, then to his left, all faces turned toward him with expectant expressions, for he was their chief's son, their shaman's grandson, and today's leader.

He took in a deep breath and slowly released it. He almost wished this awesome decision would not be thrust upon him, but there was only one path he could ride. He whispered, "We must gather the other hunters and attack, my friends. We cannot allow them and their weapons to reach the other soldiers. If they do, their numbers and powers will soon be too large for us to defeat."

"What of the bluecoats' treaty with the Oglalas and others?"

For a brief time, War Eagle thought about the deceitful Long Meadows Treaty that had been forced upon the Indians—ally and enemy tribes alike—near Fort Laramie in what the white man called 1851. "If the bluecoat leaders truly wanted peace with us, Broken Lance, they would not be sending more soldiers and big thundersticks into our lands. Do not forget what my second brother learned when he last rode to the forts called Laramie and Kearny. Cloud Chaser was told they had sent for their great war chief named Harney to come and punish *all* Lakotas for the death of Grattan and his bluecoats and for the daring raids carried out by Spotted Tail and Little Thunder. Did we not strike our winter camp early and come to the grasslands to be ready to hunt the buffalo as soon as the great herds gathered? We hurry to hunt and prepare our meat and hides so we can return to the sacred Black Hills to ready ourselves to meet Harney's challenge, for a bloody conflict is stalking us. Many soldiers come from far away and send powerful thundersticks to destroy us and steal our lands. Already their forts almost surround our territory. They seek to slay us as Grattan tried to do at the camps of our Brule brothers Little Thunder and Spotted Tail before the last hot season was gone."

"Should we ride to camp to ask our council if we can attack them?"

War Eagle knew the main camp was nearly a day's ride away on the White River near the Badlands, which would make another day's ride back to the soldiers' position. He looked at the son of their war chief, Blue Owl, and explained his reasoning. "If we did so, Bent Bow, they would be out of our reach before we returned or others could have joined them, and we would be forced to battle them on another sun when their number might be larger than ours." Only a few more hunts, and the drying and storing of the meat re-

mained to be done before their return to the sacred hills to
ready themselves to face an unknown destiny, but trouble
had come before the completion of their seasonal tasks. "I
make this choice for the safety and survival of our people
and allies. If it is wrong, I will offer myself up to be punished for it, even at the risk of banishment or death. The
bluecoats will be slain fast and with mercy; we do not seek
to torture them for the false words and bad actions of their
leaders."

He took another breath. "A white woman rides with them,"
he said. "She must not be harmed, for that is not our way; I
will take her captive. Do you agree with me, my friends?"

The warriors nodded. The youngest son of Chief Rising
Bear of the Red Shield Oglalas told them, "We must set a
cunning trap, my friends, and destroy this dark threat before
it can join with other evil forces and destroy us. Come, let us
gather the others and prepare to attack, for our hunting party
must become a war party to save our lands and people."

War Eagle observed the steady approach of the unsus-
pecting enemy; he had guessed their path of travel. The men
and wagons would pass along the flat area between the
grassy hills behind which his large band was scattered out
and concealed. When their targets reached an entrapping
point, the attack began. Without delay or error, the warriors
swarmed from hiding and swooped down, sending forth a
flight of arrows. To catch the soldiers by stunning surprise,
no whoops were shouted to alert them to their imminent
peril. Arrows thudded into bodies; men fell from their sad-
dles. Only a few of the blue-clad foes were able to seize their
weapons and fire them, their hasty and desperate shots missing their attackers. Two who whirled their mounts and tried
to flee found it impossible and were quickly slain. When
three soldiers attempted to charge the braves blocking the

terrain ahead, they were met head-on by warriors who could shoot multiple arrows before they could get off a single blast.

War Eagle had ridden straight for the group's leader, closing the distance between them fast. The officer no doubt realized he was in command of the assault, and he accepted the unspoken challenge. Lacking time to pull a long thunderstick from its leather pouch and prepare to discharge it, the captain withdrew a saber, waved the shiny blade above his head, and shouted profanities. War Eagle ignored the man's courage as he nocked and released two arrows with amazing speed and accuracy. He saw the officer's chest accept the sharp tips, the man's shoulders jerk in pain, and his body give way to death, slumping forward and then plunging to the ground. Without hesitation, War Eagle galloped toward his next unfortunate enemy; he could not give a foe—however worthy—a fighting chance at survival. . . .

Caroline Sims watched the one-sided battle in rising fear as soldiers clashed with bronze-bodied men clad in loincloths and moccasins, their black hair whipped about in the wind. It was as if they were demons who had been spewed forth without warning from the bowels of the earth, or perhaps from hell itself. Her ears were filled with mingled sounds of shouts and curses, gunfire, the whinnying of startled horses and the thundering of unshod hooves and iron shoes. She saw dust and broken grass flung wildly into the air, and feather-tipped shafts swishing lethally across its unseen currents. When she turned westward on the hard seat, the sun—two hours past noon—almost blinded her and made her squint as she tried to take in the terrifying scene. Tension added to the sweltering heat; her mouth and throat felt dry, but that wasn't the reason she did not faint or scream in terror. It seemed that she was trapped in a nightmare and could not move.

The driver of her wagon had been killed and had fallen to the ground shortly before the team halted its movement. As her anxious gaze darted in all directions, she realized there was no place to flee and hide, as Indians surrounded her. There was no weapon within her reach. Even if a rifle had been nearby, no doubt she would be slain before she could ready it to fire, and attempting to do so might imperil her still more. The harness ribbons had fallen to the ground between the wagon and the last two mules, so she could not seize them and send the team into a swift run from danger. In fact, she was fortunate the animals had not bolted and possibly crashed the wagon and injured or killed her.

Caroline recalled a trapper at the fort saying that Indians respected "grit and good sense," so it was best if she faced her fate revealing those traits, and maybe doing so would earn her her survival, though she doubted it. She gripped her deceased parents' Bible, which she had been holding and pretending to read during the long journey, a trick to remind the lonely and lusty soldiers that she was a lady and to imply that God would punish them if they accosted her in a crude or physical manner. As her tension increased and the early August sunshine beamed on her with unmerciful blazing rays, she climbed down from the wooden seat and leaned against the covered wagon to find shade and a cooler temperature. She ordered herself not to panic and to keep her head clear for what lay ahead. *God, help me, for I do not know what to do or how to behave under these grim circumstances.*

War Eagle guided his horse to where the young woman was standing near one of the three wagons. He was amazed she was not yelling or crying. She made no attempt to flee or to use a weapon against him or to run at him with balled fists to strike him. She clutched to her heart what he knew, from his half-white brother, to be a Bible. Her head was lowered and her eyes were closed as he heard her softly murmuring a prayer. No doubt she had heard his approach, but his presence did not halt her action. He could not see her face and expression, as the wide band of her head cover and her lower chin prevented it. He dismounted and stood before her, admiring the hair, yellow like the sun, which flowed over her shoulders. Her stance was straight; the top of her head came to his chin. Surely she was no heavier than a small doe. He noticed the way her chest rose and fell with her rapid breaths, exposing her fear, though blended with courage. Since he began each day and event with prayer, he did not intrude on her communion with her Creator. He always asked the Great Spirit for guidance and protection in all things and his existence revolved around his beliefs. He assumed it was the same for her, so he waited for her to finish.

Caroline was aware that someone was standing before her. She was confused by his silence and dreaded a confrontation. She was afraid that if she looked up at him, she would be staring into the face of the devil or pure evil. She had left Fort Pierre almost six days ago, so she was certain no rescue party was approaching. She had been told they were to cross the White River and grasslands, skirt west of the Sand Hills, reach the North Platte River Road, and travel southeast to Fort Kearny where her brother had been reassigned during her journey from the South to the Nebraska Territory.

Now, she would never see David again; and her death, added to those of their parents, would pain him deeply and he would blame himself for sending for her. What if, the horrible thought entered her mind, David's troop also had been ambushed and slain, perhaps by this same ferocious band? What if her beloved brother was . . .

No, she must not think such heartrending thoughts! Without lifting her head, she opened her eyes and saw feet clad in moccasins, long and firm legs, a loincloth, dark skin at the hips, strong-looking hands resting at his upper thighs, and a narrow waist where a beaded belt held a pouch and a knife in a sheath near a flat stomach.

Although he was not holding a weapon, her heart pounded and she assumed death was imminent. She swallowed with difficulty and forced out the words, "I am ready to die now; I have made my peace with God."

When the man did not speak or move, she slowly lifted her gaze. It traveled up a bare chest with two scars, passed muscular arms and broad shoulders, and halted on his face to find him staring at her with eyes so dark brown they appeared almost black like his long hair, or as ebony as the two slashes painted across his cheekbones. She was astonished by two things: his alert gaze—though unreadable—was not cold and hard, and he was handsome, very handsome. Unable to help herself, she matched his stare.

When Caroline realized her breathing had increased its pace, her cheeks felt hot and itchy. She looked away and saw Indians recovering their arrows and gathering soldiers' bodies and horses. She also noticed that none of the warriors were scalping, robbing, or mutilating their victims. The man near her made no attempt to attack or kill her, but she moistened her lips and—to learn her fate—asked, "Why do you hesitate? I am unarmed and there is no escape. Slay me if that is the evil you have come to do."

War Eagle noted that her eyes were as blue as the sky, large and clear, and displaying a mixture of emotions. Her lips were the color of pale sunset; her skin, not as white as the clouds. Wind played with the free portions of her hair, blowing it across her beautiful face, then away from it again. Her hair was as long as his sister's, but had a rolling shape like the grasslands surrounding them, even curly in some places like the buffalo's cape. Oddly, he yearned to reach out his hand and feel it, but knew that would frighten her even more than she already was, and it was a foolish yearning. He saw the glow on her cheeks, signs of rapid breathing, and her trembling, yet she did not beg for her life or curse him.

"Whites bring evil to our land. We must defeat them before they destroy us. Wanbli no slay enemy women and children. You no die; you come to my camp."

As she listened, Caroline's gaze widened. "You speak my language?"

To prepare for the dark times ahead, he had learned and practiced English with his first brother's wife since their joining during the land's rebirth time four circles of the seasons ago. Dewdrops had learned it from a trapper who lived with her Brule band, and she had used it to trick and to spy on the whites while riding at Wind Dancer's side against their foes. He had learned more from his second brother, who had been taught by his captive white mother and by the white couple who had stolen and raised him from eleven winters old until the last hot season when Cloud Chaser returned to them and earned his way back into their lives and band. "I speak white man's tongue little," he told her. "It wise to know enemy's ways and words."

"But I'm not your enemy, and I didn't come here to bring evil."

"You white-skin; white-skins, enemies; make war on us."

Caroline grasped his matter-of-fact tone and expression. Since her parents' tragic deaths in Georgia last year, she had learned—sometimes with reluctance and at the hand of a cruel fate—how to take care of herself in difficult circumstances. She knew she must use all of her skills, strength, intelligence, and courage to survive. After considering his words, she replied in a gentle tone, "But I don't even know you, and you don't know me. Why do you want to kill an innocent stranger who has not done you any harm? Is . . . Wanbli your name?"

He nodded. "It mean War Eagle. Son of Rising Bear, chief of Red Shields. We Oglala. Lakota. Dakota. What white-skins call Teton Sioux."

She had heard the words *Oglala, Lakota, Teton,* and *Sioux* from the people at Fort Pierre and from the soldiers before and during their journey from there to Fort Kearny: allegedly fierce warriors who were hated and scorned by her traveling companions, warriors who believed they were "the so-called rulers of this vast domain." It wasn't a good sign that he considered all "white-skins" as enemies. Yet, he was talking to her, a mere woman, a foe. . . . Perhaps she could reason her way out of this grave situation, despite the slaughter that surrounded them.

"I'm Caroline Sims," she began. "I came here to meet my brother at Fort Pierre, but he was sent to Fort Kearny before I arrived. These soldiers were escorting me there. Why did you murder them, and why are you going to capture and harm me?"

War Eagle found himself impressed by her wits and behavior; it was as if she were using three of the Four Virtues that he and his people honored and practiced: Courage, Wisdom, and Fortitude; perhaps she revealed the fourth— Generosity—on other occasions. "You should not come to our land; we at war here," he told her. "Soon, we ride for my camp."

"No, I die here or you let me ride back to the fort." She spoke with false bravado before she could stop the demand from leaving her lips. She watched his body stiffen and his gaze narrow and darken at her words. *That was stupid and reckless; now you've provoked him to anger!*

War Eagle placed his hands on his hips, glared at her, and warned in a stern tone, "You come easy way or hard way; choice yours, woman."

Caroline studied him for a few minutes, then realized it was foolish to defy him. If she did so, he could become riled and violent, and he could turn her over to his men to be . . . "I will come with you, War Eagle, but if you try to harm me, I will fight you to the death."

War Eagle grasped her true meaning—forcing her to his

mat—which was not something he would do. "Your choice wise, woman."

Forcing herself to use a polite and soft tone, she corrected him. "My name is Caroline, not 'woman,' War Eagle."

He touched her shoulder with one hand and said, "You woman." He touched his chest and said, "I man. Why bad to call you woman?"

With his men working quietly, and with her back pressed against the wagon, his body filling her view, and her mind on matching wits with his, she briefly forgot about the gruesome sight encompassing them. "It's the bad way you said it, War Eagle." She lowered her voice and said gruffly, *"Woman,* like an insult. My name is Caroline."

He knew the word *insult,* for he and his people had been ridiculed many times by whites and enemy tribes, and he hated being mocked and belittled even by a foe. For a reason he did not understand, and while being drawn unwillingly to her blue gaze and gentleness, he complied with her softly spoken request. "Ca-ro-line. It hard word to speak."

"Speak it faster, as one word, not three. Caroline," she said again with a half smile. Perhaps she could trick him with southern charm!

"Caroline," he echoed, and watched a full smile capture her mouth and a sparkle like sunshine dancing on water fill her eyes.

"That's good. Thank you, War Eagle."

As she smiled again, he surmised she was impressed by him. He scolded himself for being even slightly tempted by her beauty and favorable manner, and for standing there talking with her as if they were friends. He must not allow her to touch his heart and mind in a forbidden way. He summoned a stoic expression and firm tone as he commanded, "No more talk. It wise to be silent; woman not speak orders to man. If you speak or do bad and shame me before others, I punish you; that our way."

Caroline grasped the sudden change in his mood and the

warning tone of his voice. Perhaps, she reasoned in haste, he was embarrassed and alarmed—even vexed—by his brief softening toward her, the "enemy." Perhaps Indian women were viewed and treated as lowly and servile beings, as in the Arab countries. For certain, something repellent had assailed him. Minutes ago, he was being genial and kind; he had almost grinned and shown a sense of humor during the amusing name incident. Now, he was acting distant, brusque, and intimidating. She cautioned herself to silence, feigned respect and obedience. For now, that behavior seemed wisest, unless he attempted to ravish her; then, she would fight him to the death with her bare hands! She had not lived to the age of nineteen and guarded her chastity so strongly to come there and be ravished and humiliated and permanently entrapped by what the soldiers had called "savages." Until a moment ago, she had not believed that word described him; now, she wasn't certain. She hoped that all he wanted was a slave to serve him and his family, just as unfortunate blacks did for their white masters. For now, she must bide her time until she could escape or be rescued. . . .

War Eagle stepped to the rear of the wagon and looked inside. Just as he had expected, the cloud-colored blanket covered a cannon whose fire—he recalled from past experience—roared like thunder during its use; it was a symbol of the white man's encroachment, greed, and impending plans. The awesome weapon must be destroyed so it could not be used against his people or their allies. He knew the hard object could not be chopped to pieces with stone or even the white man's iron hatchets, but he could place it where the soldiers could not find it. After today, a least there would be fewer weapons and men to battle them.

He returned to where Caroline awaited him, her head lowered again. "War Eagle tie hands? Yes? No? You be good? Bad?"

When she lifted her head, her gaze revealed sadness and reluctant compliance. He knew he was to blame for the losses of her joy and spirit, but he quelled his strange reaction.

Caroline saw his momentary wince as if he felt guilty about hurting her feelings and intentionally frightening her, yet, she knew he could neither apologize nor explain the motive for his sudden sternness. Perhaps he only had corrected his prior slip toward her and was putting things back in the proper order for their captor/captive relationship before they joined the others for departure. Though she had seen his other side and could not forget it, she knew it was perilous to defy or to befriend him before his band. "I will be good, unless you try to harm me."

War Eagle was aware of her intense scrutiny. He reasoned that she was thinking over her situation and accepting it. "Get possessions from wagon. We ride for camp."

Caroline nodded her gratitude and obedience. She climbed aboard the wagon to gather what she could carry easily on a horse, which didn't include her two travel trunks. She flung them open, grabbed a fabric bag, and stuffed simple clothing and a few of her favorite things inside it: the Sims family Bible, several photographs, and a rag doll her mother had made for her as a child. She didn't gather frilly dresses and hats or satin slippers or thick petticoats, as they would be unsuitable in her new surroundings and role. She hated to leave her belongings behind, but she could take only so many items with her, and those must be practical ones. She rushed because she didn't know how much time he would give her to make her choices.

At one point, she glanced back at the cannon that was bolted to the wagon bed. She remembered that he had looked inside, so he knew it was there—a weapon of great power and destruction, and perhaps the reason for his attack. War, she mused, was a costly, cruel, and sacrificial event that men believed they must engage in from time to time, no matter how much suffering and loss their families had to endure. Could she blame him and his people for trying to protect themselves and their lands? She pushed those grave matters aside and returned to her selection task.

When she uncovered the black dress she had worn at her parents' burial, she clutched the wrinkled garment to her heart, closed her eyes, fought back tears of renewed grief, and took a deep breath. If only they were still alive, and if only that unscrupulous and greedy banker had not snatched away her own and David's inherited property—home, furnishings, land, stock, even her mother's best jewelry—to cover a large and alleged overdue loan she could not pay, or if only the grim news had reached her brother in time for him to take an emergency leave to thwart that man's evil, or if she had accepted William Crawford's proposal, she would still be in Georgia, safe and free.

Despite her dire straits after her many losses, she could not bring herself to marry William. He was considered by most females to be a good catch, but she did not love or desire him, and she had not believed he would be a good husband or father for her children, regardless of his social status or exceptional looks or charming traits. So she had packed her remaining possessions and left the South to begin a new life in the West with her brother. Now, that chance at a fresh start was also lost to her, unless she could find a way out of this predicament.

Predicament, her mind scoffed, *that's a mild word for the trouble and danger encompassing you!*

Caroline realized she could not change the past, and must deal with a difficult present. In a way, she had that same wicked banker to blame for her current crisis; if he had not, due to "a generous heart and nature," allowed her to keep enough money for her journey, she would not be here today. No doubt the grasping beast had done so to be rid of her as fast as possible before others could learn of his actions and view him in the same dark light in which she did!

Caroline put aside the dark dress and those unsettling thoughts and went back to her task. After it was finished, she replaced the dislodged items and fastened the trunks; why, she did not know. Perhaps it was with the hope that they could be recovered later. She tossed the bulging satchel to the grass and climbed from the wagon, her heart pounding as her unknown fate loomed closer.

War Eagle stood a short distance away, facing her and talking with several of his men whose backs were to her. She assumed he was their leader and was giving them their final orders. She could not prevent herself from staring at him. Strands of ebony hair were tossed about by the prairie wind, as if an enchanted Mother Nature's fingers were playing with them; the top and side sections of his hair were secured at the back of his head with a leather strip. His features were bold and appealing, accurately proportioned for the size and shape of his face. Even the black slashes on his prominent cheekbones looked sensual on him. He had compelling dark eyes, full lips, and even white teeth. She would guess him to be a little over six feet tall and at the ideal weight for that height, and his age, near hers. His muscular body looked strong and well honed; his flesh, sleek and almost unmarred. She couldn't guess how much of his skin coloring was due to his Indian heritage or how much was obtained from years spent outside, and now the slowly lowering sun seemed to enhance its dusky shade. When he had stood near her, he had smelled of fresh sweat and animal scents; an odor neither overpowering nor unpleasant. He was the perfect image of a man to be in charge of others and important decisions. He was indeed handsome and virile and no doubt stole the hearts of many females, even if he had a wife and children.

A wife . . . If one existed, was she being captured to become her slave? If so, how would that woman view and treat her? What would a wife think and feel about her husband bringing another female, a stranger, an enemy, into their abode? From the tepee she had been shown outside Fort Pierre where "friendlies" and "beggars" camped, those hide dwellings had only one room, offering no privacy. At those dismaying thoughts, apprehension filled her. *Please, dear Heavenly Father, don't make this situation any more difficult than it already is.*

War Eagle saw Caroline slyly watching him and patiently waiting for him, though he concealed that knowledge from her and his friends. He finished speaking with the others, then rejoined her at the wagon, along with his best friend from camp, Swift Otter, who was also a Sacred Bow Carrier. That small group of men were among the highest-ranked warriors in charge of his people's protection and the most prominent in battles. He glanced at the fat pouch on the ground, then looked at her. "You ride with War Eagle. Swift Otter carry possessions. Come, we go."

Caroline watched the warrior pass his weapons to his friend, no doubt to put them out of her reach for his safety; they could be tossed back to him if danger approached. Then, he leapt upon his horse with great agility and extended his left arm to her. She grasped it and found herself hauled up behind him. As she had ridden horses and even a mule since childhood and sometimes double-back with her brother, in one lithe action she had tossed a leg over the horse's rump and taken her assigned place. She straightened the bottom of her dress, grateful it had a full skirt to aid her movements and to allow her to retain modesty. She slipped her arms around his waist, knowing that was expected and necessary to avoid being thrown off during their ride. She realized how close that made the contact of their bodies and how his bare flesh felt warm and smooth to her palms.

Since much of his height was in his long legs, she could peer over his broad shoulder. She saw his friend mount his own horse with her bag and nod that he was ready to travel. As their journey began, she noticed that three Indians were driving the wagons away; others were leading army horses with soldiers' bodies strapped across them; the rest of the large group waved to their companions and rode in a different direction.

To keep her wayward thoughts off the man before her and her unknown fate that loomed ahead, Caroline viewed the vast landscape of grassland and rolling hills; in many spots, large buffalo grazed in massive herds that stretched out farther than she could see. It was an awesome sight and distracted her for a while.

Soon, they reached a lovely river and followed its tree- and bush-lined banks until it veered southwestward. She, her captor, and Swift Otter continued along the water's course, but the wagons and bodies were taken onward in a westward direction. The largest number of warriors had not rejoined them, but she didn't know why. She wondered how far away his camp was, as the hot August sun began to set.

War Eagle glanced to his right and watched part of his band heading onward to Makosica. He knew why they were traveling to the area known by Indians and Whites as the Badlands; some of his party were going to shove the cannons, other weapons, and wagons over its steep bluffs in places where the army could not retrieve them. The soldiers would be buried in winding canyons there, their final resting places covered with rocks for concealment. Even if the slain bluecoats were found, he knew arrows with telltale Red Shield markings had been removed, and would be used again during future hunts or battles. The mules and horses would be released to roam the grasslands, as far away as his men could lead them in the passing of one sun, as it would be perilous to keep those animals in or near their camp. The remainder of his party was running a large herd of buffalo over all wagon and horseshoe tracks so that no revealing trails could be sighted and followed; then, they would return to the big hunt, which had been halted earlier to carry out those tasks.

As for him and Swift Otter, they were returning to the main encampment to relate those deeds to their chief and people, and to leave Caroline there while he and his friend rejoined the hunting party for a few more days. He could not surmise what his father and the council of Big Bellies would say and think about his attack, or what they might do to him for it. Yet, he was certain his oldest brother, Wind Dancer, who was to become their next chief, would have taken the same protective action. As to Caroline, once more he could not guess what the reactions to her would be. Surely they would agree he had no choice but to capture her after the lethal attack on her traveling companions, and he was sure his father and the council would not order her death.

War Eagle felt her soft arms around his waist and the way her body pressed close to his bare back. He could not help wondering what she was thinking and feeling. She must be afraid and worried, maybe plotting an escape or praying for a rescue, though neither would happen, as he would not allow it. He was impressed by her continued display of courage and obedience and was relieved that she did not provoke him to use force on her for defiance.

War Eagle did not have to look back at Caroline to see her face. His mind's eye could envision it with ease and detail, her coloring so different from his and his people's. She was beautiful and tempting, just as Cloud Chaser's white mother must have been to their father long ago during one night of weakness on Rising Bear's part when the chief was consumed by grief and loneliness over the loss of his beloved mate to the Pawnee. But Winona had been returned to them by the Great Spirit, and Omaste—Margaret Phillips—had been taken by death. If his mother had not escaped her cruel captors many seasons after she was taken by them and was believed to be dead, he and his younger sister would not exist; and perhaps Omaste would still be with their father, tending his two brothers. Would Rising Bear, chief of the Red Shield Oglalas, have made Omaste his wife if Winona had never returned? Somehow War Eagle knew that would never have happened. It had been difficult enough for his father to accept having a half-white son. That had taken place last summer, and only because Cloud Chaser had proven his worth and loyalty to them, proven his Lakota blood was stronger.

Those thoughts compelled War Eagle to ask himself why he hated the whites so fiercely when his father had mated with one, although only once. His second brother was half white, one of his best friends, Red Wolf of the Cheyenne, was half white, and Red Wolf's mother was all white, as was the girl behind him. It was obvious to him that he did not detest all whites, just most of them, and in particular, the soldiers, their leaders, and greedy hunters and settlers. Perhaps it was easy to accept Cloud Chaser because he almost looked pure-blooded, and Red Wolf did not hint strongly at possessing enemy blood. If more of their race were like those three women, peace would be possible with them. But they were not. They craved all that the Indians possessed, craved their destruction so they might feel safe in stolen lands. War was inevitable.

What about Caroline? What will happen to her in our camp when—not if—war with her people comes?

Rising Bear's third son did not want his mind to dwell on that oddly troubling thought, so he dismissed it. He glanced at Swift Otter and said in their language, "It grows dark soon, my friend, and we still have a long way to ride. We halt here and finish our journey on the next sun. There is no need to reach our camp while it sleeps. There is much for us to reveal, so we should be rested."

"That is true and wise," Swift Otter said.

War Eagle reined in his horse and slid to the ground. "We camp here," he said as he extended his arms upward to Caroline.

Caroline became tense at the thought of what might loom ahead during the night with the two warriors. Even so, her cold and quivering hands clutched at his hard forearms as she was assisted down by his grip on both sides of her waist. He released her instantly and turned to tend his horse.

Her mind shrieked, *What now?*

Chapter Two

Caroline summoned her courage. "May I be excused?" she asked. She could tell from her captor's baffled look that he did not understand the meaning of her query. "Visit the bushes," she said and pointed to them.

War Eagle nodded permission, then warned her, "You run, I chase, punish. It name *leja.*"

Caroline nodded. Embarrassment burned her cheeks as she committed that Lakota word to memory. She went behind the dense greenery growing near the river's bank and relieved herself in a hurry; though for some reason, she trusted him not to intrude on her privacy. She noticed that he had used a matter-of-fact, even slightly affable, tone of voice. She rinsed her hands in the river, dried them on the hem of her dress, and awaited his next order.

The two men sat down on the grass beneath a large tree, their horses grazing and drinking in contentment nearby. She watched the men retrieve food from leather pouches and begin to eat, occasionally sipping water from strange bags. She took a seat on the grass not far away, close to the edge of the tree's remaining shadow. When her stomach growled in hunger, she placed a hand over it to muffle the sound. She glanced around as the men ate and drank and talked in their language. Although she yearned for food, she did not ask for it; she was uncertain about the way a captive was treated and should behave to avoid injury or death. It seemed best to remain as still and quiet as a mouse trying to go unnoticed by a ravenous hawk circling overhead; or in this instance, a war eagle.

As she gazed at the river, her heart and mind ached to know her brother's location and condition. Was David alive or dead, wounded or unharmed? If alive, he couldn't possibly know about her grim fate. When he learned about it, what action would he be allowed to take, if any? Surely somebody would come searching for them when they failed to reach Fort Kearny on schedule. But what would have happened to her by then, and would she be found and rescued?

Caroline's thoughts were interrupted when War Eagle nudged her shoulder with a gentle touch. Startled from her reverie, she looked up at him. The handsome warrior appeared to tower over her, yet neither his stance nor his expression seemed menacing. He held objects out to her.

War Eagle passed her the water bag and said, "*Mni*. Drink. *Wasna*. Eat," he added. As he gave her the second object his keen senses noted that she appeared alert and wary but not terrified, and that pleased him. An odd warmth spread through his body as she gazed up at him with wide blue eyes. He had never experienced such strange alarm and tension, even during stealthy raids and perilous battles, as he did at that moment when unwanted desire claimed him. She was nothing more to him than an enemy captive, but a mysterious and potent force drew him to her. He knew he must not surrender even slightly to those sensations; he must resist them with all of his might. He must not dishonor himself and his rank or be cruel by taking her for the mere release of physical urges. He warned himself to put a safe distance between them as fast as possible so as to resist her unnerving magic.

Caroline accepted the offerings, fearing to reject them and

offend him; and she needed her strength for what loomed ahead. She nodded and said, "Thank you."

After the warrior rejoined his friend, she sniffed the unknown food, bit off a piece, rolled it around on her tongue, chewed, and swallowed. She was surprised and gratified to find its flavor pleasant. It seemed to be some kind of bread with dried nuts and berries. As she sipped from the Indianstyle canteen, she committed the two new words to memory: *mni* for water and *wasna* for bread or food. Since she would be a captive in his camp until she escaped or was rescued, she should learn all she could about his culture, ways, and language. She had heard only bad things about Indians from the soldiers and most of the settlers she had encountered at Fort Pierre during her short stay there, but were they all true? If not, which ones were accurate?

As she ate and drank, Caroline called those people's opinions and assertions to mind. Especially during her five-day journey with the soldiers who were compelled to travel slowly due to heavy wagons, she had overheard many things. The men had talked and laughed about spoiled meat, insect-infested flour, skinny cattle, inferior blankets, and a lack of or sorry condition of the annuities promised to the "Injuns" in the Laramie Treaty of 1851 in exchange for peace with the whites and with enemy tribes and for permission to cross certain areas of their lands. They had jested about giving Indians more whiskey to dull their brains and weaken their bodies and spirits, and bringing in more diseases to slay them as with past epidemics. They had revealed their greed for the fertile land so perfect for ranches and farms, for roads and for more forts to be built for protection. They had joked about enslaving Indians and teaching them to pick cotton and tobacco and sending them to the South to work on plantations or driving them northward into Canada where they could starve and freeze or become the problem of the Canadians. They had ridiculed "redskin" customs, beliefs, rituals, and appearances. They had bragged about how the army was going to whip the

Indians so badly they would "be running with their tails between their legs like dogs and licking their wounds for years
to come," if they allowed any of the "savages" to survive.
They had talked of total conquest, subjugation, humiliation,
destruction of Indian villages and way of life, eradication,
and outright slaughter, even of "squaws, breeding brats, and
gray-heads."

If such grim atrocities already had occurred and more—
worse—were planned in the near future, Caroline asked herself, could she blame the Indians for their defensive and
retaliatory actions? Whites were deceiving them, encroaching on their lands, bringing in weapons—as with those cannons and crates in the wagons with her—and more soldiers
for an impending assault; so it was natural for the Indians to
assume they were being challenged to war.

What, she wondered, was the truth? No doubt both sides
believed they were in the right. How did David feel about his
role in the gruesome matter, and what horrible orders had he
been forced to carry out since coming to this territory? *No,
don't think about such awful things!*

Caroline watched as War Eagle built a small fire, no
doubt to provide light during the blackest phase of the new
moon. Perhaps he only wanted to make sure he could keep
her in view all night. He needn't worry, she told herself, as
this was not an opportune time to risk an escape. She could
not get far without a horse, and she could not flee afoot in
total darkness. To attempt such an obviously futile feat
would only serve to provoke him against her. She watched
him gather some items and walk toward her, an animal skin
draped over one arm. She was surprised when he unfolded a
buffalo hide and motioned for her to lie on it.

"Sleep. We ride to camp on new sun."

Caroline thanked him and handed him the two pouches.
She watched him nod, then rejoin his friend and lie down on
the thick grass next to Swift Otter's furry mat, implying he
had given his to her. She told herself she should be grateful

to War Eagle for not slaying her on sight, for not harming her so far, and for being generous—even gentle.

Caroline settled down on the soft hide, her back to the men and facing the river. She didn't want to think about the disturbing fact that she was lying on his *bed*. She had seen the way he had stared into her eyes for a few moments, then averted his gaze as if she made him as apprehensive and confused as he made her. What if he found her appealing as a woman? When they reached his camp, would he keep her as his slave or give her to another to avoid temptation? If so, how would that person treat her? Since he had shown her such kindness so far, Caroline prayed she would remain with War Eagle; yet that thought troubled her.

She tried to discard such thoughts and go to sleep, but they continued to race across her restless mind; and the location he had chosen for camping was a busy one. Crickets, frogs, other nocturnal insects, and birds created loud and almost competitive noises. A few animals came to the river to drink not far away. The horses moved about and swished their tails. The fire crackled and popped from feasting on dry wood. She smelled its smoke, along with the fragrant scents of wildflowers and crushed grass blades, and the odor of horse droppings when the seemingly incessant wind changed direction and blew toward her. Fatigued, she eventually became accustomed to the sounds, sights, and smells and slumber overtook her. . . .

Caroline was awakened when her shoulder was nudged as she lay on her left side. While her senses were still groggy, she rolled to her back, took a deep breath of fresh air, and opened her eyes to a now familiar sight, War Eagle's arresting face. He knelt beside her and spoke to her in a mellow tone.

"We ride soon. Eat. Drink. *Leja*."

Caroline sat up and rubbed heavy lids. She could hardly

believe she had gone to sleep and slept so deeply. The sun was rising in an untroubled blue sky and birds were singing in the trees and bushes along the riverbank. A pleasant breeze wafted across her. She concluded it was going to be a lovely, but hot, day, one filled with unknown things. After he returned to his friend's side for his morning meal, she knelt by the river to bathe her face and hands, doing the task slowly since she dreaded joining the intimidating strangers.

As she reached for the hem of her dress to dry her hands she heard a terrifying noise to her right and froze in alarm. Without turning her head, she glanced in that direction and saw a large snake atop a nearby log. Its fat body, triangular-shaped head, a pit on each side, and evil-looking eyes told her it was poisonous; the multiple rattles on its tail exposed that fact. Within easy striking distance of her, it seemed to stare menacingly at her as its forked tongue flickered in and out of its mouth. She knew the snake detected her presence, perhaps viewed her as a threat, and would strike if she moved to escape or to attack it.

Suddenly an arrow thudded into the viper's head, pierced both sides, and pinned it to the log. That action caused its body to thrash about wildly in a futile attempt to free itself, Caroline's wide gaze retraced the shaft's path and she saw her captor standing about fifteen feet away as he lowered a bow, then walked toward the imprisoned snake. She watched him cut off the viper's head and rattles, the latter of which he kept.

"You hurt?" War Eagle asked.

Caroline shook her head, still too frightened and shaky to speak. She saw him nod understanding and rejoin his friend. She remained there for few minutes as she calmed herself, wondering if he had been spying on her or simply had heard the snake's warning sounds. As she settled her frayed nerves, she refused to glance at the bloody creature. Unable to avoid the inevitable any longer, she joined the men and thanked her captor for saving her life. He kept silent and only nodded again.

When War Eagle gave her more of the same food she had eaten the night before, she consumed it without delay while he recovered his sleeping hide and readied his horse for departure.

Then the final leg of their journey began.

After a couple of hours of riding, Caroline saw an encampment looming ahead, countless tepees with poles jutting skyward from each of them. Even at that distance, she saw many people—women, men, and children of various ages. She trembled and tightened her grasp around War Eagle's waist as if seeking protection and courage.

War Eagle felt and heard her reaction to the sight beyond them. Before he realized what he was doing and could halt himself, he placed one hand over her interlocked fingers, stroked them, and whispered over his shoulder, "You not fear; we not slay or harm enemy women and children."

Relieved, Caroline laid her cheek against his back, took a deep breath, closed her eyes, and murmured, "Thank you, War Eagle, but I'm still afraid of what's to come."

"Fear good; make you obey and no be punished."

His tone of voice had altered from compassionate to almost stern as they reached the sprawling village. The two warriors—amidst the stares of their people—wound their way between tepees to a large clearing. During their passing, all work and play ceased. Caroline saw some women and men whispering to nearby companions. A few motioned toward them as they talked in low voices. Some ran past tepees, no doubt to spread the news of their arrival to others who had not yet seen them. Dread caused her heart to beat faster as she realized she was totally surrounded by, and at the mercy of, The Enemy.

A buckskin-clad crowd gathered around, most with expressions of curiosity and confusion. As some of the dark-haired females openly stared at her, Caroline released her hold on the warrior's waist and rested sweaty and shaky hands on her thighs. Four males stepped close to her captor's horse and studied her for a minute: two slightly older than War Eagle appeared to be, one at least twice his age, and an elderly man with gray hair and a serene aura. When the middle-aged man spoke with War Eagle, she assumed him to be their leader, perhaps his father. She lowered her gaze and focused it on the back of her captor's waist. All she could do was await her fate, as she could not understand their language. *Be still and silent; don't do anything to offend or provoke them against you. Please, God, guide me and protect me.*

In Lakota, Chief Rising Bear asked his third child, "Why do you and Swift Otter return to camp without the others, my son, and bring a white woman with you? Was there trouble during the hunt?"

War Eagle remained mounted so everyone could see and hear him. "Yes, Father, we battled with bluecoats on the past sun, but no Red Shield was lost. We slayed them, but I spared her life, as is our way."

Rising Bear replied, "It is not our way to take white captives, my son."

"I could not leave a helpless female on the grasslands alone to die or be found and abused by an enemy band or found by other soldiers, for she would tell the white-eyes who did that deed, which would endanger us."

The chief nodded and praised him. "That is true and wise. We must call the council together so you can reveal your news to us. Take the woman to our tepee and leave her with your mother and sister."

War Eagle nodded. The crowd parted for him to do as his father, their chief, had commanded. He guided his horse to the side of the largest and most highly decorated tepee, situated in the inner circle in a place of honor. He dismounted and helped Caroline to the ground, then handed his reins to a young boy who took charge of the horse. "Come," he told her and led her to the waiting women near the tepee's entrance. He pointed to the oldest one and said, "Mother, Winona," and to the youngest and said, "Sister, Hanmani. I go. You stay."

Caroline nodded understanding and compliance before he left on foot. She looked at the women who gazed at her, thankfully without loathsome expressions. She pointed to herself and said, "Caroline."

Hanmani, who was astonished by her youngest brother's action, said, "Sit," as she motioned to a rush mat nearby. "I give you water."

"You speak English, too?" Caroline asked.

"Speak little. Know more. Not Mother. Not Father. Brothers, yes."

Caroline was relieved that at least some of them knew her language, as that would help her understand their orders and learn their tongue. She took the assigned seat and sipped from the water bag the young girl handed to her. As she returned the bag, she smiled and said, "Thank you, Hanmani," and saw the girl nod. She watched the two women return to their tasks nearby, working with buffalo hides and meat drying.

At that time, she thought it was best to hold her silence until she was spoken to, though they seemed to ignore her presence and chatted amongst themselves in low voices. She saw an Indian man pause and stare at her from across the center clearing; there was something intimidating in his frigid expression, narrowed gaze, and stiffened body, which she found alarming. Who was he? And why, since she was a stranger and a mere woman, did hate and repulsion seem to emanate from him like an evil force? *Relax, Caroline, don't surmise the worst until you know the truth. . . .*

* * *

When the men gathered in a group beyond the tepees and sat down on the grass to listen to the report, Rising Bear asked, "Why did you attack and slay the bluecoats, my son?"

After War Eagle explained his deed and motives, Runs Fast accused, "You will call down the white war chief's anger upon us, as with the Brules."

"Have you forgotten, my uncle, the great white war chief Harney and other white leaders blame all Lakotas for what the Brules did to Grattan and for their many raids before and after that battle? They do not listen when they are told Grattan was the first to attack and spill blood or that other bands are not to blame. They use Grattan's death as a reason to slay all Indians and take our lands. They do not speak the truth or honor their treaty with us and our foes. We must attack all small parties of bluecoats and destroy their powerful weapons before they join as one big force against us."

Runs Fast debated, "The whites and bluecoats are many; more will come to replace them, and they will bring more of their powerful weapons. Arrows, lances, and war clubs are weak against the giant thundersticks."

War Eagle looked at the husband of his father's sister and agreed. "That is true."

Before he could continue, his uncle challenged his words. "So why do you call down their anger upon us with your attack?"

Using great restraint to master his annoyance and a calm tone to conceal it, War Eagle repeated his motives and went on to say, "While they receive word and journey here, that will give us more suns of peace and more suns to prepare for the great battle that is certain to strike at us before the cold season, for Harney will reach our lands soon as my brother Cloud Chaser learned during his visit to their forts." He reminded them, "My war party removed the arrows with Red Shield markings. They pushed the big thundersticks over the bluffs of Makosica. Some buried the bluecoats' bodies there in Mother Earth, as is their custom and where they can not be found. Others drove buffalo over their trail and ours to conceal them before they returned to the great hunt. Even if such signs are found by their scouts, they will not know who did that deed. If you doubt my cunning, we can put out false signs of the Crow to lead the bluecoats to our enemy and to blame them, as we did long ago when I followed my brother Wind Dancer and his wife, Dewdrops, during their sacred vision quest."

War Eagle then asked Wind Dancer, "Since you will become our next chief, my brother, what would you have done if you had been our leader on the past sun?"

Wind Dancer replied, "I would have ridden the same path as you did. My head and heart tell me you showed great courage, cunning, and wisdom. It is much easier and safer to destroy small bands of soldiers than to defeat a large force of them after they unite to attack us."

"That is true," Two Feathers agreed, "but I say the white girl must die as the bluecoats did. It is too dangerous for her to live with such secrets."

"No." Cloud Chaser hastily refuted their cousin's cold and cruel words, "It is wrong to slay a helpless female."

War Eagle tensed in dread as he watched Two Feather's expression harden with determination, for the breach between his second brother and cousin was a long, deep, and hostile one.

"A *white* female is what you mean," Two Feathers said. "Your feelings run in that direction because you are half white and have a bond to her."

War Eagle was stunned by his cousin's display of antagonism, as the man had kept such bad feelings concealed for almost a year since Cloud Chaser had earned his way back into their band.

Cloud Chaser stiffened. "That is false, Two Feathers. I have proven that my Oglala blood and bond is strongest. I speak against your words because it is not the Red Shield way to kill women and children, be they white or Indian enemies. If

War Eagle agrees, I will accept the white woman into my tepee to help Dawn with her chores and the tending of our son. I will prevent her escape, so she will not endanger us."

Two Feathers argued again in favor of her death, claiming she would spy on them, flee, and reveal their location or tell of War Eagle's grave deed to the soldiers. Or, he reasoned to sway others to his side, white soldiers could sight her in their camp, which would provoke an attack on them. He loathed and distrusted all whites, and he had even hoped Dawn would lose the half-breed child she had carried, but those prayers had gone unanswered and his hopes for victory over his rival had been defeated.

Even the infant's name—Casmu, meaning Sand—exposed its inferior and mixed bloodline, for its flesh was paler than a true Oglala's. He refused to accept the reason why the child was given that name, his birth coming upon a sandy stretch of terrain, as it was their custom to choose something close by during a baby's arrival. Somehow and in some way, he must be rid of his foe . . . and take Dawn as his mate!

War Eagle made a difficult decision and revealed it. "Cloud Chaser speaks true of our ways, Two Feathers. I vote she lives. If others agree, I will give her to my second brother and his wife as a gift."

Nahemana now spoke. "My grandson speaks wise on this matter. I say she must not be slain and must live in the tepee of Cloud Chaser. Who votes with me?"

Since their shaman was well respected and deeply loved, the council and other warriors—even those who agreed with Two Feathers—concurred with Nahemana as did Chief Rising Bear.

War Eagle sighed in relief and from gratitude to his father and grandfather. From the corner of his eye, he saw Two Feathers scowl and study him closely. He resolved he must say and do nothing to let that defeated man learn of his forbidden feelings for the white girl, as his cousin would surely seek ways to shame and harm him for her presence there, for winning their verbal battle, for helping Cloud Chaser defeat him once more. He wished the conflict between the two men did not run so deep and strong, but it had been that way since his half brother's birth. He worried that one day it would come to a lethal battle between them, as Two Feathers refused to bury the sharp hatchet between them. If only he knew why Two Feathers detested Cloud Chaser so much, he could settle the rivalry, but the man's motivation remained a mystery to him. At least his cousin had not been allowed to harm Caroline for revenge. He wondered how she would feel about being given away to another.

With the decision made, everyone must honor it, as was their custom. The impending hostile situation with the soldiers was discussed for a while longer; then the group dispersed to return to their chores.

War Eagle asked Cloud Chaser to go with him to their father's tepee to fetch Caroline, as Wind Dancer was busy speaking with other warriors and their father about their impending return to the Black Hills. "Did I do wrong to bring her here?" he asked.

Cloud Chaser shook his head. "No, you could not leave her there alone. You know her fate if Crow or Pawnee had found her or bad white men who sneak and hunt buffalo on our lands. And it was too far and dangerous to take her back to the fort. You did what is best for us and for her. She will be safe in my tepee, and she will help Dawn with our baby."

Cloud Chaser's response pleased War Eagle and caused him to smile. "That is true, my brother, for she is strong, brave, and wise. She gave me no trouble during our journey. Her name is Caroline. She is the sister of a bluecoat; she came to this territory to join him."

Cloud Chaser glanced at him in surprise. "You spoke to her in English?" He also noted a strange softening of his brother's voice and expression when War Eagle spoke of the white girl.

"Only a little. She had to grasp my words to obey them."

"She was afraid?"

"Yes, but not weak with tears or bad with her tongue and actions."

"That is good. She—" Cloud Chaser halted before they reached Rising Bear's tepee, as he sighted Caroline sitting on a mat near the entrance. Her appearance shocked him for a moment. "She favors my mother."

War Eagle also paused to reply, "Yes, she has sky eyes and sunny hair and pale skin. Does it pain you to be reminded of Omaste?"

"A little," Cloud Chaser admitted. He had loved his mother, who died when he was young. "She is pretty."

"If you say so, I believe you. Come, you must take her to Dawn."

Cloud Chaser was almost amused by War Eagle's offhanded reply. He suspected that his youngest brother was well aware of the girl's beauty and wanted to get the lovely girl out of his sight, perhaps to escape temptation. Was it possible a *white* girl could affect him in a physical way? If so, that would certainly present them with a grave predicament. . . .

Cloud Chaser approached the wary female, who stood immediately and clasped her hands tightly before her waist. "My name is Cloud Chaser. I am the brother of War Eagle," he said, motioning to the man beside him in case she did not know her captor's name. "You will live and work in my tepee." When he witnessed her alarmed reaction, he rushed on to explain, "You will help my wife with her chores and with the tending of our baby. If you obey and do not try to escape, you will be safe with us in all ways. In time, perhaps you will be happy in our camp if you allow yourself to do so. Do you agree to my words?"

"Do I have a choice?" Caroline asked in a polite and careful tone.

"No, but it will be easier on everyone if you agree and behave."

"How long will I be held captive here?"

"Until there is peace with the white man."

"In other words, forever; am I correct in my observations?"

"You are an intelligent and brave woman, Caroline, or so my brother told me, and from what I see and hear." Cloud Chaser watched her glance at War Eagle in surprise. A gleam of relief and gratitude shone in her blue eyes. "Come, I will take you to meet my wife and infant son. Dawn will teach you what you must do. In our tongue, she is called Macha, which means Dawn."

"Will you teach me your language? You speak English very well."

Without explaining why that was true, Cloud Chaser said, "If you want to learn our language, we will teach it to you. Come."

Before Caroline followed Cloud Chaser away, she glanced at War Eagle once more, baffled by this turn in events. He had allowed his brother to do all of the talking, but he had observed her closely during their conversation. "Good-bye, Wanbli, and thank you."

"Why thank me?" the warrior asked, though he surmised the reason.

"You know why."

From inside his parents' tepee not far away, and while keeping out of sight, Two Feathers observed the meeting at Rising Bear's tepee. During the short talk between Cloud Chaser and the girl, he witnessed the expressions on the captive's and his younger cousin's faces. There was no doubt in his mind that she was beautiful and tempting, even to him. What unattached man would not want to throw her upon a mat to appease his cravings? *So,* he mused, *perhaps War Eagle finds you desirable and it frightens him, just as you find my cousin good to look upon and be with. Perhaps those reluctant feelings will be useful to me.*

Two Feathers reminded himself he had not given up on

his two bold plans—to possess Dawn and to become the next Red Shield chief. If he was right about War Eagle's forbidden desires, all he required for success was the death of Wind Dancer and Cloud Chaser. War Eagle would shame himself over the white woman and lose his right to that rank. *No matter how hard War Eagle battles his great hunger he will yield to it one sun, just as his father yielded to Omaste's evil magic long ago and shamed himself. Perhaps I should silence my protests against her and allow War Eagle to dig himself a deadly trap, or perhaps I can provoke him into doing so. . . .*

Chapter Three

Rising Bear took a stroll beyond the camp with his wife's father to talk in private with the shaman. "I fear nothing good can come of holding a white woman captive, so why did you speak for her to stay here?"

In a gentle tone, Nahemana reminded him, "Do not forget, our chief, Cloud Chaser came from your union with Omaste. Was she not a good woman though her skin was white, and was not the birth of your second son by her good? I believe it was the will of the Creator for you to mate once with her to bring forth the seed that has done many great things for us."

"That is true, Wise One, but I sensed a strange hunger in War Eagle for her and it worries me, as it will trouble others. I do not want him to suffer as I did over a forbidden bond with a white woman, for she is unlike Omaste was. Omaste was given to me; War Eagle captured this girl. Omaste was a friend to us; that girl is an enemy, and could be a danger to us."

"My grandson did not keep her for himself, my chief," Nahemana said. "He gave her to his second brother and Dawn as a helper. Even if he has feelings for her, how do we know the Great Spirit did not place them within his heart and head for a purpose? Wakantanka often works in mysterious, and sometimes painful, ways. Many troubling thoughts have come to me during this hunting season; I sense large peril not far ahead. On the past moon, I prayed to the Creator to send us a sign on this sun; and War Eagle brought the girl to our camp, a female with hair that glows like the sun. I say it is wise to allow her to live with us for now."

"If what you say is true, Wise One, I will not intrude in the workings of the Great Spirit, but I pray it is not so. If the Creator speaks other words to you and she must die or be freed, whisper them into my ear first."

"It will be as you say."

While they ate the midday meal and Macha breast-fed their infant son with her back to them for privacy, Cloud Chaser asked Caroline about herself. He needed to learn all he could about her and what she knew, if anything, about the army's war plans. Besides, he could think of no valid reason to be cold or cruel to an innocent female.

Caroline decided it could do no harm to reveal the losses of her parents and property and her trip west to join her brother. She related her grim information as the man listened and watched intently. Afterward, he offered her sympathy . . . then made a provocative statement.

"Such tragic losses should help you grasp how Indians feel about the white man's encroachment."

"Why did your brother attack us?" she countered. "We did nothing wrong or threatening, unless it's a crime to cross your lands. We were taken by surprise and all the soldiers were killed. Why?"

"Your brother is a soldier. What did he tell you about the troubles in this territory? Why did he come here to help your people steal our lands and to slay us when whites have plenty of land elsewhere?"

"David didn't tell me anything about this kind of trouble and danger. If he had known it was so bad, he wouldn't have allowed me to come and be imperiled like this. He's a good man. He joined the army for two reasons: he wanted to see the West before he settled down and took over the plantation for our father, and he wanted to escape the pain of the woman who broke their betrothal. All I know about the hostilities was told to me by soldiers during my short stay at Fort Pierre and the five-day ride across the grasslands before I was captured."

Cloud Chaser nodded. "Did they tell you the white leaders are sending their best general here to subjugate or destroy us? They plan to attack as soon as he arrives at Fort Kearny, where your brother was sent. That's what those wagons were for that War Eagle attacked and destroyed with just cause; and those men were slain before they could join forces with the other soldiers to attack us."

Caroline was alarmed. "Is there no hope for peace between the whites and Indians?"

Cloud Chaser shook his head. "In September of fifty-one, Indian nations in this territory were tricked, bribed, and coerced into signing a treaty at Fort Laramie to evoke peace between Indians and whites and between enemy Indian nations. It failed because some nations or tribes refused to sign and because whites didn't keep their side of the bargain. This current trouble started last August over the simple killing of a stray cow that wandered into a Brule camp and was slaughtered and eaten. A soldier named Lieutenant Grattan went to their camp to recover the cow or to arrest and punish the slayers. He took many men and even cannons with him, and a drunken and abusive translator. Naturally the Brules felt they had done nothing wrong and refused to surrender their friends to be punished for a foolish reason."

Cloud Chaser observed her closely as he continued. "The soldiers fired first and killed the chief, the very man who had been chosen by the whites as the head chief of all Lakotas for the treaty council and signing, a man of peace who was once a great warrior. The Brules killed the entire unit while defending themselves and their camp. Some raided the American Fur Company, others raided at Fort Laramie to replace the animals slain and to retaliate for lost lives and for damage done to their camp. But the owner and workers at Bordeau's Trading Post were not slain. Nor was Private Cuddy, the one survivor of the battle; he and others told the officer at the fort what happened, but their words changed nothing. Your government and army blame all Lakotas for those deeds and plan to punish us all, though we were not involved in that battle or those raids. Remain silent for now and I will speak more after I wet my throat."

Cloud Chaser took a deep breath and a few sips of water and said, "Let me explain about our nation so you can understand my meaning better. Our nation is called the Dakotas; it is like a giant tree with three huge branches: the Dakota, Nakota, and Lakota. Each branch has many small tribal limbs, with the Lakota, which is often called the Teton, having the most, seven. Each tribe has many bands, like leaves on the limbs. We belong to the Oglala tribe and the Red Shield Band. The Brules are also Lakotas, Tetons. They are our allies and friends, but we are not of the same limb."

"Why are you called Red Shields?" *Does it signify blood, death?*

"In years long past, band members carried red shields to represent the earth color of the sacred racetrack," Cloud Chaser explained. "The tall black ridge of the first rim of our sacred hills far away parts the grassland from a valley where red dirt forms a near circle around the inner mountains. Long ago, The People and animals began to hunt, slay, and eat each other, destroying the harmony between them. The Creator was displeased, so He commanded the animals to race around the red trail to learn if they would be predator or prey in suns to come. A *halhate,* a magpie, raced for The People; he used trickery and won, so man earned the rank of hunter and animals, the hunted. To show their victory, hunters carried red shields to remind the animals of that great race. Many seasons following that time, warriors were told to make different shields during their vision quests."

Caroline found that story interesting but it wasn't what she needed to learn. "Why is the army so convinced all Lakotas are to blame for the Grattan incident? Why doesn't your father or the other chiefs explain matters to them?"

"They see all Indians as the same, as the enemy. They have been told of their mistake, but it does not matter to them. It gives them an excuse to attack us and take our lands. To do so is like punishing the French for evil deeds done by the Spanish because both peoples have white skin."

"But the soldiers said Lakotas are carrying out raids and killings." *So did you earlier,* she thought, but didn't remind him of that.

"Some raid stages so soldiers will have no pay and supplies and will become disgruntled and perhaps leave. Horses and goods are stolen to feed people and to use for escape after destructive attacks on their camps."

Caroline queried, "May I ask you a personal question?"

"Yes, but I might not answer it."

She hoped she was not offending him when she asked, "Are you an adopted son to the chief? Are you white or part white, and is that why you speak such excellent English?" *And look a little mix-blooded?*

Cloud Chaser did not think it was smart to tell her about his parents and his birth. "I am the blood son of Rising Bear. I was born and lived in this land until I was ten, when I was attacked and wounded by our enemy the Crow. I was found by a white couple traveling in a wagon to Oregon. While unconscious, I was taken there with them and was reared by them. I didn't know how to return home and was told my band had been slain. When I became a man and learned the truth, I returned to my family and people. I am Oglala by birth."

Caroline didn't doubt him, but sensed there was far more

to his story. "Is that why you hate whites, for stealing you and deceiving you?"

"No, for they were good but misguided people who yearned for a son and believed their God had sent me to them." That was all he would tell her; he felt it was not smart to expose too much about himself to her.

"We did not start this war," he went on. "We did not travel to your lands to steal them. When white trappers and traders first came to this territory, they were greeted in friendship. More and more came. Greed was born in them and sprouted swiftly. They made themselves our enemies. But enough talk of such dark things."

Caroline realized he wanted to change the subject, so she asked, "How old is your son? What's his name?"

"He is two months old and is called Casmu, which means Sand. My wife is Macha, which means Dawn." He smiled at his beloved as she looked around when he spoke her name. "I am Yutokeca Mahpiya, Cloud Chaser. If you wish to learn our language, I will teach you. I warn you now, Caroline, it would be foolish and dangerous to dupe us, disobey, or escape."

"I understand, and I'll do as I'm told. What do you want me to do? Where will I—" She halted as her captor ducked his head and entered the tepee, carrying her fabric satchel in one hand, and glancing at her with a strange look.

War Eagle spoke with his half brother in Lakota. "I come to bring her possessions. They were on Swift Otter's horse. Does she obey you?"

A confident Cloud Chaser nodded as he said, "I believe she is a good woman and will give me no trouble. Does that please you?"

"Yes, for I would not want trouble to come from my action."

Cloud Chaser saw how War Eagle looked at the captive. He also saw Caroline gaze at the younger warrior, then blush and lower her eyes. "Trouble will come," he told War Eagle, "but it will not be caused by your brave deed. It was generous of you to allow her to bring her possessions with her."

"I allowed her to bring only what could be carried with us. The rest of the hunters will return on the next sun. When the third sun rises, Father says we will strike camp and leave for the sacred hills. There, we will prepare for war with our enemy."

"I wish peace could come this season, my brother, but it will not be so with the white war chief riding to our lands to challenge us."

"That is true," War Eagle agreed. "What words did she speak to you?"

Cloud Chaser told him, then added, "She knows nothing of use to us in the coming conflict."

"Do you think she would reveal such words if she knew them?"

Cloud Chaser pondered this, then nodded. He wanted to question War Eagle's thoughts and feelings about the girl, but decided it was unwise; he needed to do all he could to draw War Eagle's perilous attention from her. "Did Father order out more scouts to watch for signs of trouble and for the camp's protection?"

"Yes, and I ride to obey him." War Eagle smiled at Macha when she turned and greeted him. "Casmu grows larger and stronger each sun. He looks at many things with keen eyes. Soon, my brother will have a shadow trailing him," he joked with a grin.

"That will please him," Macha said. "One sun, you will know such feelings, for you are a man now and should seek out a mate."

"I have much to do before that sun rises. I must help drive the enemy from our lands and protect our people."

"You are strong, so you can do both tasks at the same time, as do your brothers. I have seen young women watching you with desire in their gazes."

War Eagle ruffled Casmu's dark hair, grinned, and said, "I

ride before you choose a wild female for me when I am not ready to tame one."

"If she loves you as I love Cloud Chaser, no taming will be needed."

"Help me, my brother, for your wife seeks to push me into a trap."

Cloud Chaser chuckled. "If the right woman shares that trap, you will be happy there with her, as I am happy in mine."

"I did not know men viewed unions as traps," Macha said. "Why have you not shared that secret with me before, my husband?"

Caroline listened to the genial exchange, though she could not grasp their Lakota words. It was obvious to her that they were a close-knit family, and that all three had forgotten her presence for a while. From their cheerful tones, expressions, and gestures, she surmised they were joking about something or someone, perhaps having to do with the child since their attention mainly seemed focused on the baby. During the men's earlier talk, she had heard her name mentioned several times. She wished she knew what had been said. For certain, the warrior who had captured her was difficult—impossible—to ignore. She found herself wanting to stare at him, talk with him, learn everything there was to know about him. She watched him tousle the infant's ebony hair for a second time, then depart without even glancing in her direction.

Cloud Chaser passed her the satchel, which she accepted with relief and joy. He asked which items she had selected from her belongings to bring with her, perhaps in an attempt to learn more about her. She opened the bag and said, "I have no weapon inside," in case that thought had entered his mind. "Only clothes, photographs of my brother and parents, a rag doll my mother made for me as a child, and our family Bible. Would you like to examine the contents?"

"No, but show me the photographs."

Caroline handed the prized objects to him, and prayed he would not keep or destroy them. She watched him gaze at the two pictures for a long while, especially her brother's, before returning them. After thanking him, she inquired, "Where shall I put my satchel?"

Cloud Chaser pointed to an area near the colorful dew cloth, an added interior layer for deflecting rain and smoke to the outside and to beautify the dwelling.

She stood and placed her belongings where instructed, noticing how clean and orderly the tepee was kept by his wife. *A home.* . . . Would she, Caroline fretted, ever have her own home? A family? Freedom? True love and happiness? At present, those longtime dreams looked bleak. Yet, she must not lose faith in God or herself and become despondent or reckless. She must make the best of the situation until it changed.

Caroline told Cloud Chaser what she had been thinking about his wife and added, "She's also a good cook; the meal was delicious. How do I thank her in your language?"

Although Macha spoke some English, Cloud Chaser had instructed his wife to conceal that ability so she could glean information on the sly. "The word is *pilamaya* for *thank you*. Good food is *woyute waste*; it translates to *food good*. Our sentences are different from English. The main word comes first. Speak to her before I tell you more."

Caroline realized Cloud Chaser had learned a lot while living with the whites which might be advantageous to her during her predicament. She smiled at Dawn and said, *"Pilamaya, Macha. Woyute waste."*

Macha smiled and nodded her gratitude. She listened as her beloved husband taught the white female a few Lakota commands for communication during their chores. She was amused as Caroline repeated them until she could speak them correctly. She was proud of her husband for his keen wits and kindness. She had never been sorry or ashamed for fleeing with him during the last hot season or for becoming his wife under the white law before joining to him in their custom. It had been a long, hard, and perilous task for him to earn his way back into their band, but the Great Spirit had blessed them in countless areas. She yearned for peace to return to their land so they could have safety and harmony again, but she feared it was not to be, at least not during this or the coming season. She also feared for her husband's safety and survival, as he was the one who rode to the forts to spy on the bluecoats, placing himself in great danger each time he carried out that brave and cunning deed. With the rising of each sun and moon, she prayed for all she loved to be protected from harm. Her thoughts were halted when Cloud Chaser said he had chores to do and that Caroline was ready to help her with her tasks. She watched him rise, send her and Casmu an adoring smile, and depart to join other men.

Macha said, *"Uwo,* Caroline," and motioned for her to come.

That night, a weary Caroline lay on a buffalo hide assigned to her as a sleeping mat. Hers was positioned near the back edge of the tepee, with the couple's unrolled in the center, between her and the entrance, along with the infant's cradleboard where the baby slumbered in serenity. Considering how hot it was during the day, she was surprised and pleased by how cool and pleasant it was at night on the vast grasslands and near the river, and especially inside the tepee. A refreshing breeze wafted into the dwelling and swept upward to a wide-spread ventilation opening, creating a steady and soothing airflow. Outside the tossed-back flap was a small fire to provide light during the dark new moon's phase, as it would send forth too much unneeded heat if burning inside.

She was tired and drowsy, as she had worked hard after her long ride. After Cloud Chaser left them alone, the baby had been laid on an animal skin beneath a wooden stand topped with branches to provide shade. She and Macha had tended to his needs whenever necessary and had kept watchful gazes on him. She had helped the Indian woman cut buffalo meat into long thin strips and suspend them over high and sturdy racks to dry for preservation. They had fetched water from the river and gathered scrub wood and buffalo chips as fuel for a fire to cook the evening meal, a stew of fresh meat and wild vegetables, that simmered for hours.

Other than War Eagle's mother and sister and Macha's mother, no other women approached them during their labors, as if it were forbidden or perhaps her presence was repulsive. Only Hanmani had half smiled at her during those two visits. Other women, mostly females around her age, observed her for brief periods. From their expressions, she concluded that they were vexed by her presence, or by her capture by the handsome War Eagle. A few times, she caught some of the men glancing at her, but for the most part, they ignored her, which suited her just fine.

After they had eaten at dusk, she and Macha stored the tools for their tasks, checked on the meat's safety—from wild animals, she supposed—tended the baby, unrolled the mats, and lay down on them. For a short time, she had heard the couple whispering as they snuggled together. She didn't know what they said, but it was evident they were deeply in love. She couldn't help wondering how long it would take them to resent the loss of their privacy. What would happen to her when that dreaded day came? Would she be given to another family, endlessly passed around from tepee to tepee, perhaps left in the wilderness to die alone, or be returned to her captor?

Caroline took a deep but quiet breath to quell those harsh concerns.

Stop worrying and get to sleep! You'll probably have a longer and harder day tomorrow, so you need your rest.

The next day was filled with those same chores and more. She watched as the rest of the hunters returned with loaded travois from their final task, and the women set about to handle the meat and hides. They rode into camp shortly before the return of the braves who had taken the wagons away, which evoked another gathering of the men present to speak with them.

During the hottest part of the day, she and Macha washed clothes in shade provided by trees growing along the river's bank and spread them out on bushes to dry.

Later, at the water's edge, she and Macha gathered rushes to make backrests and sitting mats and trays for carrying items. During each trip to and from the tepee, Caroline caught furtive glimpses of War Eagle as he talked or did tasks with other men.

As the August sun sank into the horizon, they foraged the surrounding area for greens and dug up bulbs to be used in their next few meals. She learned which plants were edible, which ones to avoid, and which ones were used for medicines and dyes. She was amazed and impressed by how the Indians used the wild offerings of nature for survival. She also discovered that nothing from the great hairy beasts they slew went to waste. Horns became weapons and tool handles, drinking cups, and diggers. Hooves became glue. Hair was fashioned into balls for children and other items. Bladders and stomachs made excellent water bags and supply pouches. Hides would be turned into tepees, clothing, and shoes. Sinew provided thread for sewing. Bones became tools and weapons. The meat was the main source of their nourishment, especially in the winter when snow covered the ground and many animals migrated to other locations. Of course, other creatures were slain for those same uses, but the buffalo was their main provider for survival. Now, she understood why the Indians were so concerned about white men slaying the beasts only for their hides. It was clear to her that stopping those hunters would go a long way toward peace.

* * *

As War Eagle furtively observed Caroline while she did her chores, just as he had done yesterday, he wondered if she hated him and viewed him as a "savage," a fierce "hostile," as most whites did. Surely she was frightened by and distrustful of them, of him, even though she had given him a gift of gratitude for the snake rescue. He touched the *pezutaozuha* suspended around his neck where he had placed a white circle the size of his two thumbnails. Carved in black upon what Cloud Chaser told him was "whale ivory" was a scene with a big fish, a strange boat, clouds, and water. His brother had said it was called "scrimshaw" and had been done by the chief of a boat that captured huge fish called "whales," which swam in the big waters far away. A yellow circle on its top revealed it had been suspended on a thong of some kind and worn around her neck after her brother gave it to her long ago, according to what she had told Cloud Chaser. He was amazed she had parted with it, but it must have been the only possession she had with her that was an appropriate gift for a man, and she had felt compelled to thank him for saving her life and for bringing her to a camp of good people. But did that alter her feelings about them? About him?

Neither he nor they had mistreated her, but perhaps she was being obedient and even friendly to Cloud Chaser and Macha only to avoid punishment or death. He tried to study her in closely guarded secret, as he did not want others alerted to his interest in her. He could not help desiring her. With her sunny hair and sky-colored eyes, she was beautiful and alluring. Cloud Chaser's mother had those same colorings and agreeable traits when she was their father's captive long ago. Perhaps some white females possessed great magic and could not be resisted, which would reveal why their father had taken Omaste once when he was suffering in a weakened state and she was comforting him. Perhaps because Caroline was forbidden territory made her a stimulating and tempting challenge.

War Eagle remembered during the last hot season how Cloud Chaser had said that Macha made his heart "sing loud." He himself had jested, "I do not know of such feelings to this moon, but they must be powerful, for your eyes glow with flames like the fire's and your voice becomes soft as the rabbit's fur when you speak of her."

He had not understood such emotions at that time, but since meeting Caroline, they had become as clear as mountain stream water to him. His second brother had advised, "Allow Wakantanka to choose your mate for you as He did for me and Wind Dancer and your spirit will soar as ours does and you will find great happiness and victory in your joining." Yet, no Red Shield or other Lakota woman had drawn him as this white girl did. She made his heart "sing loud," though his mind rebelled.

Had the Creator guided him to that location so he could find and lay claim to Caroline? How could a white woman be chosen as his mate? Why did his spirit soar as the eagle at one time and then plummet to the earth? How could he, son of the chief, grandson of their past chief, grandson of their shaman, a great warrior, a hater of bluecoats and white encroachers, desire one of the enemy? How could he take one into his life, arms, heart? Cloud Chaser's final words to him filled his ears as if he were hearing them spoken again: "If we allow the Great Spirit to guide our steps, War Eagle, we must be willing to walk the path He chooses for us and at His pace. It was the same for Wind Dancer; Dewdrops walked into his life and heart when he did not expect such a glorious event. Perhaps it will be the same for you."

War Eagle knew that he must not dishonor himself. He must not allow his strange hunger for Caroline to increase, though it was gnawing at him from head to foot. What if it drove him wild and senseless, and made him reckless and weak? No, it must not! It could not, for they were foes and strangers; and he was too strong-willed, a man of great pride and honor. How and why did she affect him so strongly?

Should he throw away the gift in his medicine pouch or return it to her? A stimulating and distracting hunt was what he needed! He went to ask Swift Otter to join him, as the deer would be foraging nearby at dusk.

On the third evening in the camp, Caroline saw a warrior approaching, the same man who had worried her with his hateful stares upon her arrival. She quickly averted her gaze to the two rabbits roasting on spits over a fire beside the tepee. Macha was inside feeding her baby.

Cloud Chaser, who was sitting on a rush mat near the entrance as he worked on his weapons, looked up and watched his cousin nearing him. He noted that the man's expression was stoic and his stride was purposeful. He could not imagine what inspired the unusual visit and was shocked when he soon learned the reason for it. He greeted the man in wariness.

Two Feathers announced, "I have come to trade for the white woman. I will give you two of my best ponies for her."

Chapter Four

Cloud Chaser put aside his weapon and stood so the man would not be looking down on him. Being several inches taller, that action made him feel more confident for their impending debate, one he was resolved to win. "She is not for trade, my cousin. You hate whites, and you talked against her when she came."

"Others did not accept my words of warning and our shaman spoke for her to live and stay, so I must side with them as is our custom."

Custom, Cloud Chaser's mind scoffed. *It is our law that the majority vote must be honored by everyone, even those who opposed and voted against it.* He was certain the decision stuck in his cousin's craw, and the man was up to spiteful mischief. "Why do you want her?"

"My mother has no daughter or son's wife to help her with her tasks and she grows older and weaker with each passing season. I have watched the white girl; she works hard and obeys. If two ponies are not enough, name how many you want for her."

Cloud Chaser struggled to conceal his anger, positive the

man was lying. He repeated, "She is not for trade. Dawn has need of her in our tepee."

"Your mate is young and strong, but my mother is not. How can you, the son of our chief, refuse to help Rising Bear's sister when she is in need? Where are your Generosity and Wisdom? Are you cruel and selfish?"

So, you cunningly fling two of our Four Virtues and insults into my face to provoke me to sell her to you! If I did, you would surely abuse her to spite me! He locked gazes with his rival and stressed, "She is not for trade. Your bad words to me shame you, my cousin, for I have proven them wrong."

"Do you refuse because it would anger War Eagle?"

Once more, Cloud Chaser was astonished by the man's bold words, as it was unlike Two Feathers to also insult his own full-blooded cousin. "If my brother had wanted her to serve him, he would not have given her to us."

"Perhaps he did so to save face when she calls to him as a woman."

Cloud Chaser grasped the man's meaning—unbidden lust for Caroline. "Why do you speak such harsh words of your cousin and my brother?"

"If they are untrue, why do they anger you?"

Cloud Chaser refuted, "Your insults and sly plans are what anger me."

"I go now, but think on my words and large offer," Two Feathers told him and sauntered away.

Macha, having overheard the exchange from inside the tepee, joined Cloud Chaser and said, "His deed and heart are bad, my husband, for he knows it is not our custom to trade away a gift from another."

Cloud Chaser placed his arm around her waist. "That is true, my wife. He still hates me for being part white and for stealing you away from him."

"You did not steal me from him, for he had no claim on

me. I do not know why he wanted me to join to him, for he does not love me."

He reminded her, "He desires you as a woman and he wants to injure me. He has hated me since we were children. I prayed such bad feelings would leave him and we could have peace between us. For a while we had a truce but he has broken it. Why, I do not know."

"Surely an evil spirit dwells within him. After we eat, you must find your brother and warn him of your cousin's mischief."

"That is wise and I will do so."

"Be wary of Two Feathers, my husband, for he is evil and dangerous."

Cloud Chaser looked into her worried gaze. "I do not trust him. Fear not, for soon his evil will be exposed to the others as it has been to us."

"I hope so," Macha said. "For his hate of you does not weaken, and I fear it."

"Do not forget that the Great Spirit watches over and protects us. He will allow no harm to come to us. I will—" His words were interrupted politely by Caroline when she told him the rabbits were done cooking. He nodded and relayed the message to Macha, who joined the captive at the fire.

As they ate, Caroline yearned to question Cloud Chaser about the warrior's visit. She suspected that the conversation had included her. She had sensed a potent and alarming aura emanating from the other man, and she perceived the two men were enemies or fierce rivals. She didn't know why, but she found the other brave intimidating, as if he were a lethal threat to her. When she could restrain her gnawing curiosity no longer, Caroline asked, "Is the man who visited earlier another brother or a close friend?"

Cloud Chaser paused before answering. He was impressed by the clever way she was trying to glean information. "His name is Two Feathers. He is the son of my father's sister, my first cousin. I have two brothers and one sister. Wind Dancer is the oldest, twenty-eight by white man's counting, and will become our next chief. He is a great and much-honored warrior. War Eagle is the youngest and is a high-ranking warrior, a Sacred Bow Carrier. I am twenty-three. My sister, Hanmani, is seventeen. Two Feathers is not my friend; we have battled with words and actions since we were small boys. He came to trade for you."

Terror filled Caroline. "He wanted to buy me from you?"

"Yes. He offered many ponies."

"Why, when he looks at me with such fierce hatred in his eyes?"

"He said he wanted you to help his mother. She is Pretty Meadow, sister of my father. She has no daughters and her two sons have no wives to help her with chores. He says you work hard, and she needs you."

Caroline's heart began to pound in dread. She gaped at Cloud Chaser, then sent Macha a pleading look. No, she could not become that repulsive's man slave! "But you refused, didn't you?"

"Yes, because you have been obedient and respectful and a great help to my wife and son." He saw and heard her give a deep sigh of relief and she closed her eyes for a few moments as if in grateful prayer. "And because he spoke against sparing your life when War Eagle brought you here." He saw her blue eyes widen as that grim fact settled in. Of course there were more personal reasons, but he could not reveal them.

Caroline felt herself trembling. "He wanted me . . . killed?"

"Yes. He said he feared you would escape and tell the soldiers our secrets, or you would be sighted in our camp and we would be attacked."

"But you didn't believe him?" she asked, sensing there was more to the matter than he was telling her.

"I cannot read what lies hidden in another's heart or head."

"But you didn't believe him?" Caroline pressed for confirmation of her suspicion, as he had given a clever and uninformative response.

Cloud Chaser thought, *You are intelligent and perceptive, but there is much I cannot tell you.* "I did not think either would happen, so you are not a threat to us. My father, our shaman, the council, and other band members said you could live and stay. But if you deceive us, escape, and betray us, you will be recaptured and slain for our protection and survival."

Caroline could imagine how most Indians felt about the white invaders, especially if an impending war with *her* people was a dark reality. For her own "protection and survival," she must not give them any reason to mistrust or fear her. "I won't try to escape."

"Would you swear it upon your life and honor and your God's Bible?"

"Yes. Even if I were tempted to escape, Cloud Chaser, to try it would be foolish and dangerous. Besides, it's impossible, so why take that risk?"

"I pray you speak the truth, for all of our sakes." *And especially for mine, as I would be the one ordered to track and slay you.*

As Caroline ducked her head to leave the tepee to fetch water for the night, she almost collided with War Eagle. She felt his hands grasp her forearms to steady her when she tottered in midstep. Regaining her balance, she backed up to allow his entrance. As they straightened their bodies within the abode's confines, their gazes met and locked briefly. "I'm sorry, Wanbli, I didn't see or hear you coming." In his now familiar behavior, he nodded acceptance of her apology. Strange sensations raced over her at his nearness.

War Eagle recovered his scattered wits in haste. He knew that he made her nervous, but he was not sure why. Under the guise of talking about their departure tomorrow, he had wanted to observe her with his brother's family, away from the eyes of Two Feathers and his people. Before he could speak, Cloud Chaser stood and told him they needed to take a walk.

At a discreet distance, Cloud Chaser revealed the news about Two Feathers' offer to trade for Caroline. He witnessed how shocked and dismayed his brother was and how his expression softened when he was told of Caroline's terrified reaction.

War Eagle said, "She has many wits and skills and she senses much. It is good you told her of your conflict with our cousin, but not the whole truth about it. I do not believe Two Feathers seeks the white girl in trade as a helper for Pretty Meadow. Our father's sister is not old or weak. It worries me our cousin watches Caroline on the sly. Why does he think I desire her as a woman? Have I behaved in such a manner?"

Cloud Chaser asked, "What are you thoughts and feelings about her?"

"She possesses a strong but gentle spirit. She is brave, wise, and skilled. She is obedient. She can be trusted not to escape and endanger us. Is that not true, my brother, from what you have seen and heard?"

"That is true, War Eagle, but what of her as a woman?"

"I must not look or think upon Caroline as a woman."

Cloud Chaser noted that he spoke the female's name in a tender tone and with a sad look in his eyes. "Why?"

"She is white, a captive. I am Oglala. Red Shield. Son of a chief."

"Do these things prevent thoughts and feelings about her?"

"I have told you what I think and feel. Why do you dig for more?"

"Is there more to reveal but you wish to keep it buried?"

"I wish she were not here and had not been with the soldiers."

Cloud Chaser surmised that War Eagle had answered too quickly, even falsely, out of desperation and denial. "Because she does evoke strange and unwanted thoughts and feelings?"

War Eagle lowered his head as he took a deep breath. "At times strange thoughts enter my head and strange feelings tug at my heart, but I do not know why or what they mean. She is unlike all women I have known."

"Is that why you gave her to me and Dawn, to escape her temptation?"

"Yes, and to save her life. She is a good woman, and it is wrong to slay her. But there can be nothing more between us."

"Only the Great Spirit can make that choice, my brother. Do not forget I carry white blood and I am joined to a Red Shield. Many others, including her parents, resisted our union and viewed me as an enemy. What if the Great Spirit placed her in your path as He placed me in Dawn's and placed my mother in Rising Bear's for a short time?"

"What if an evil spirit did so to shame and defeat me?"

"If that is so, the truth will be revealed soon. Until that sun rises, War Eagle, do nothing to harm her or turn her against you. But guard your secret and honor fiercely, as many will oppose such a bond. Do not forget you are next in line to become chief if our brother dies or is slain."

War Eagle knew Cloud Chaser did not have to tell him that many would not want what they viewed as a lowly white captive to become his mate and weaken their chief's blood-line, just as both knew that the "tainted" blood Cloud Chaser carried would prevent him from becoming chief even if War Eagle and Wind Dancer were both slain. But why were they even speaking about such an impossible feat? Why had he foolishly exposed such private thoughts and emotions? Had he done so before others, or was their cousin only guessing at that possibility, perhaps only using such words as a ploy to coax Cloud Chaser into a trade? Why was his second brother seemingly encouraging such a perilous bond? It would be a great loss of face if he took Caroline as his woman, mate or not, if the Great Spirit did not clear that tangled path; and he could not imagine why the Creator would choose her for him.

Cloud Chaser was thinking much the same and scolded himself for what he had said and done, as it could be terribly wrong and hazardous for his brother to accept and follow his reckless advice. Perhaps it was her resemblance to his beloved lost mother or Omaste's gentle spirit that was guiding him in that direction. No matter, he must say and do nothing more to promote such a relationship. It would be easier for both of them to avoid the risky matter soon, as they were striking camp tomorrow and leaving for their winter location in the sacred hills.

"We must go to our tepees, my brother. There is much to do before our journey begins on the next sun. I am happy you alerted me to the bad scent of trouble. I will watch our cousin as a hawk during our long ride."

"As will I, War Eagle, for he remains my enemy for some reason."

"Do not worry, my brother, for I will not allow him to use me and my captive to injure you. If he tries to sway others against you and her, I will take Caroline to another band to prevent trouble. Perhaps to Red Wolf's camp, for his mother is white and would accept her. She would be safe in their tepee." Yes, perhaps his Cheyenne friend was the answer he needed.

At sunrise the following morning, Winona and Hanmani began to take down Rising Bear's tepee, the signal for others to do the same with theirs. It was time to leave the grasslands.

Caroline helped Macha remove the lodge poles so Cloud Chaser could use them to make a travois for hauling the couple's possessions. As he did so, the two women packed the home's contents and piled them outside. They collapsed the tepee, then folded and loaded the strong hides that formed the dwelling's walls. They added sleeping rolls, sitting mats, a backrest, cooking items, clothing and sewing pouches, Caroline's satchel, fresh water, food, and all other belongings to the heap on the travois.

During the past few days, Caroline had caught her captor watching her. He seemed to be intrigued by her, though he tried to conceal his stolen glances. She had studied him on the sly this morning as everyone worked on their chores, as Cloud Chaser's tepee was close to his father's where War Eagle lived and had been helping his family since sunrise with their preparations for departure. She had seen him loading his many weapons, and already had been warned it was forbidden for a female to touch them. There were two magnificent mounts nearby that were his personal property—his buffalo horse and his war and riding horse. It was obvious to her that both were well tended and that strong bonds existed between man and creature, which greatly impressed her.

She was amazed by how efficient, swift, cooperative, and hardworking the band was. She witnessed their enthusiasm about the seasonal move, as if they were filled with joy and energy. Families labored together in harmony. Youths aided childless elders with their tasks. Teenage girls tended small ones and babies while their mothers or aunts were busy.

A strange recollection entered her mind. Long ago at her friend Clara's wedding party and honoring a southern tradition, she had taken a slice of fruitcake and wrapped it in a lacy handkerchief. For amusement, she had placed it beneath her pillow that night to see if she actually would dream of the man she would one day marry; and it hadn't been William Crawford who "visited" her! She quivered as she remembered dreaming of a tall and muscular man with his back to her, long black hair grazing the lower portion of his shoulder blades, his bare torso a coppery shade. Was it possible, Caroline mused, that dream man could be . . . No! Dreams were not real, and visions had never called on her! Yet, it was an odd and provocative coincidence, if happenstances existed. *Why,* she scolded herself, *are you even thinking about such ridiculous things? Stop it now!*

After everything was secured in place, Macha mounted a gentle mare that would pull the dragalong, Casmu's cradleboard strapped to her back with the infant sleeping safe and snug inside.

As the sun rose higher and the day's heat steadily increased, Caroline stood beside the heavily loaded cart awaiting the signal to move out, as she was to walk beside it. Many others would be afoot, so it was not only because she was a lowly slave that she was not allowed to ride one of Cloud Chaser's extra horses. She came to alert when Macha called her name and motioned for her to follow as the long trip got under way, with families falling into line in preassigned positions. She saw Macha wave to her husband, who left to travel with his father at the front of the column.

The chief, shaman, war chief, and Big Bellies left first with their families close behind them. The highest-ranking band members were next, among which were the Shirt-Wearers and Strong Hearts Warrior Society. Then, the rest of the braves from various societies left the area. Guards encompassed the large group, men who were heavily armed and on alert for daring raids by enemies, be they Indian or white.

Caroline knew from what Cloud Chaser had told her that he and his brothers could locate themselves in several places by their own choice. Wind Dancer could travel either up front with the chief or with the Shirt-Wearers, or with the Strong Hearts. War Eagle could journey with his father or the Sacred Bow Carriers. Cloud Chaser could travel with his father or with the Strong Hearts. Wind Dancer had chosen to be near his parents and grandparents for their defense in the event of trouble, as protecting their chief was important to him for many reasons. War Eagle was riding at an advanced distance with the other Sacred Bow Carriers, as it was their duty to act as scouts and guards and to be first to challenge any threat. Cloud Chaser would rejoin his wife and child later. She didn't know what those warrior ranks meant, but her owner had promised to explain them to her later.

As she trudged along, wearing her sunbonnet to shield her face from the blazing sun, Caroline wondered if Cloud Chaser had told War Eagle about their cousin's offer to trade for her and what had he thought about it. She had promised Cloud Chaser she would not try to escape, yet nothing would prevent her from attempting it at any risk if she were sold to Two Feathers! She could imagine no worse fate than to become that cold man's slave.

Besides, Caroline encouraged herself, when she and the soldiers failed to arrive at Fort Kearny soon, a search party would be sent out to find them. Even if she and the men were expendable, surely the canons and other weapons were not. The army would have to locate and rescue her if only to learn what happened to the soldiers and supplies. *Just be careful and bide your time; help will come soon. But when it does,* her heart queried, *what will happen to these people? To Cloud Chaser, Dawn, and Casmu? To War Eagle? A massacre?* As she glanced at the people around her and thought about how they had not mistreated her, she realized she did not want to be responsible for their deaths. Yet, how could she prevent the army's retaliation for the attack on them? Time, that was what the Red Shields needed, time to get out of this area before a search was on and the grim evidence of their deed was discovered. But how many days or weeks of safety did they have, and would a generous Mother Nature conceal those telltale signs before they could be found? She did not know, but despite her circumstances, she prayed for their survival.

At that same time in Kansas Territory, General William Harney and his infantry and dragoons were leaving Fort

Leavenworth for Fort Kearny to begin what was already being called "the Great Sioux Expedition."

At the end of the first day of travel and while they were eating, Cloud Chaser tried to explain his people's government to Caroline. "Our chief is like your president. He leads us and has much power. The council, as with your Congress, can change his orders if they believe he is wrong in a matter, though that rarely happens. They are called Big Bellies; they are made up of our present and past chiefs, shamen, and the best warriors who are too old or disabled to fight. The council makes our laws and gives instructions. Twelve Shirt-Wearers who are chosen by the Big Bellies carry them out, as with your lawmen. Wind Dancer has been a Shirt-Wearer for many years. In big matters, all warriors have a vote; and the majority rules. No one can go against the vote or he is punished. But most heed the words of our chief and council and vote as they do. The warrior societies are our army, our soldiers. As in your military, there are ranks, and the leaders of them are their officers. In our band, the best warriors belong to the Strong Hearts and Sacred Bows. The shaman is our spiritual leader and is in charge of all events. He is Winona's father and is named Nahemana."

Caroline was surprised to learn of their democratic ways, and she had witnessed how religious and family-oriented they were. So much for their being uncivilized and insensitive as alleged! "What are the Strong Hearts and Sacred Bows? You and your brothers belong to them, isn't that right?"

"Strong Hearts are skilled and fearless warriors who take the Four Virtues to heart; they defend our camp, take care of those in need, and show other braves the best way to behave. Wind Dancer is a Strong Heart, as I am, as is Two Feathers, though I believe our cousin is unworthy of that rank for many reasons. The Sacred Bows lead in battles with our enemies and are last to leave the area. They must show great courage, cunning, and stamina and they must attack a foe in every fight. War Eagle, his friend Swift Otter, Broken Arrow, and Two Feathers are the four Sacred Bow Carriers. Our other cousin Broken Lance is a good warrior and is unlike his brother."

Caroline did not want her mind to dwell on the perils of War Eagle being a Sacred Bow Carrier. Nor did she want to think about Two Feathers. Besides, she needed to learn all she could about these people, and fast. She asked, "What are the 'Four Virtues' you mentioned?"

"Courage, Generosity, Wisdom, and Fortitude, which means to be able to endure discomfort and pain in body and spirit, and the ability to show patience and self-control during times of strain."

He had described himself and War Eagle perfectly. "You said Wind Dancer would become the next chief. Does leadership always pass from father to son?"

He nodded. "Unless a son proves himself unworthy of that rank."

"What if a chief doesn't have a son when he dies or is slain?"

"A new leader is chosen from among our best warriors."

"So if Wind Dancer was slain, you would become chief?"

"The second son is next in line unless he is unworthy."

Caroline thought Cloud Chaser had looked and sounded odd for a few moments before and during his response. For certain, he had learned a great deal during his life in Oregon, as he knew English as well as she did! "I think you would make a good chief; you're a kind and wise man."

Cloud Chaser smiled. "Your words are generous, but Wind Dancer is best for that rank."

"I haven't met him yet. Will I?"

"If you prove yourself worthy of that honor. Finish eating now, for we must rest soon. Tomorrow will be a long, tiring, and dusty day. We—" Cloud Chaser halted as Two Feathers approached, scowling. *"Taku ca yacin hwo?"* He asked the man what he wanted.

In Lakota, Two Feathers scolded, "Why do you speak with the captive for so long? It is offensive to hear the white tongue in our camp. You must save that . . . *skill* for when you scout the bluecoats."

To perturb the man, Cloud Chaser feigned a calm he did not feel at that time. "I speak to her of our laws and ways so she can obey and not offend. Do not give me orders, my cousin, for I know what is good and bad."

"If that is true, you would trade her to me."

"It is true, my cousin," War Eagle said as he joined them. "The girl was a gift to my brother and his wife and must not be traded to another. That is our custom so why do you challenge it? Why do you seek to provoke him and cause trouble and bad feelings? That is not the way of a Strong Heart or Sacred Bow Carrier or a Red Shield warrior. If her presence angers you, speak to me of that matter, for I am the one who captured her and brought her to our camp."

Two Feathers frowned at War Eagle for taking Cloud Chaser's side against him again, and for daring to scold him before others. "It would be good to break our custom this time. Your brother carries white blood, so it is bad for a white to live with him and remind others of that weakness."

"Cloud Chaser has proven his Oglala blood is strongest. He did so many times during the last hot and cold seasons. Why do you insult him and seek to injure him? To treat him in that way insults and injures all in my family, and it shames you in our eyes. Go, pray, and cleanse yourself of such evil, my cousin."

War Eagle saw Two Feathers lock challenging gazes with him for a short while before the rebuked man stalked away. Each of them had spoken in lowered tones, but some were observing them in curiosity, as each campsite was spaced from others to allow ample room for sleeping mats, horses, travois, walking, and cooking-smoke dissipation.

War Eagle hunkered down, looked at Cloud Chaser, and said, "It is settled for now, my brother, but not for long. Be wary of him, as some evil force lurks within him, and I do not know why or how to slay it."

Cloud Chaser nodded in agreement, then told his brother what he had been explaining to Caroline. "If part of what Two Feathers said is true, I will speak less and more quietly to her in the suns ahead."

"That is wise, but it is good for her to learn much about us."

"Takuwe?" Cloud Chaser asked why.

"To help her obey and show respect. If she becomes a friend to you and your mate, she will not want to escape or betray you."

"That is true and wise. Do you want to eat and drink with us?"

"Mother has filled those needs. I must go, for night comes swiftly."

"Thank you, my brother; my heart leaps with joy over your help."

"You would do the same for me or Wind Dancer." War Eagle made certain he did not even glance in Caroline's direction during his visit or his departure, as he furtively glimpsed Two Feathers watching them.

After her handsome captor left, Caroline summoned the courage to whisper, "What did he want tonight?"

"You," Cloud Chaser replied, knowing to whom she referred.

"Why is he so determined to have me?" she asked as her quivering fingers toyed with the dried fruit and nut bread in their grasp.

"When I learn that secret, I will share it with you. I warn you again, Caroline, do nothing to show defiance or disrespect to me and others. We must not speak so long and openly. We must not forget our ranks again."

By "ranks," she assumed he meant as owner and slave, as enemies. "Does that mean we cannot be friends?"

"Not this soon. First, you must prove yourself to me and

others. And my people must get used to you being among us."

Caroline noted how he looked at the ground as he spoke, as if he were embarrassed. "Is that what your brother told you to do?"

"It is my decision, a wise one for all of us. No more talk tonight."

Hurt and dismayed, Caroline did not speak again, but she mentally berated Two Feathers for his interference and spitefulness, as she blamed him for this change. She realized their peoples were in deep conflict; soon, at war. It seemed obvious Cloud Chaser was entrapped in a predicament concerning her. She must do nothing to shame or disappoint or anger him. And she must keep a close eye on his antagonistic cousin who appeared resolved to have her either dead or in his tepee.

As for War Eagle, he had ignored her completely.

Chapter Five

By the time the long and wearying journey ended, War Eagle was annoyed and alarmed by his cousin's offensive behavior. At least he was relieved those actions had been carried out only between them during the final few suns before they reached this location today and set up their winter camp. For a while after his warning and scolding on the plains, Two Feathers had controlled his words and conduct, especially before others, but as they had neared their destination, he had begun to make cunning remarks and eventually to tease War Eagle with bluntness about Caroline.

On one occasion as they scouted ahead together, Two Feathers had grinned and said, "Cloud Chaser's captive makes a man's shaft grow hot and hard within his breech cloth. Why did you not keep her to relieve your own fierce urgings?"

War Eagle recalled how he had frowned at the insidious jest and scoffed, "You watch her enough to know she works hard and obeys. Even if she belonged to me, why would I want to cause her pain in her body and heart and stir defiance? That is rash and cruel, and it is not our way. She has not earned such mistreatment."

"She would be a good mate," he persisted.

"How so, my cousin, when she is white and an enemy to you?"

"She does not behave as our enemy and works hard, as your words told me and as I have seen. Why should her white skin trouble me or others when the white blood of your second brother does not?"

"Cloud Chaser is Oglala, Red Shield, son of our chief. It is different."

"Is that why you did not keep her, she is a pale-skin and an enemy? Or did you fear you could not fight her magic and win that battle?"

"I had no need for a captive. My mother had no need of one, for she has my sister to help her. Four living in our tepee is plenty."

"But Cloud Chaser cannot be alone with his mate with her there."

"It is the same in all families where others share a tepee. When desire burns within a husband and wife, they find a way to be alone."

"They could be alone if the white girl becomes my mate and shares my new tepee. Surely Cloud Chaser would be pleased to have her gone, for she must remind others of his mixed blood."

"You do not seek to help my brother, and you speak false when you say his white blood does not offend you, for you show such bad feelings to him many times and they are wrong. You must purge yourself of them. Speak no more of such things, for such foolish talk stirs bad feelings within me toward you."

War Eagle worried that Two Feathers would become bolder with his remarks, speak them before others, and create trouble. He must not allow his cousin to cause dissension in their band during the grave times ahead, or provoke bad feelings toward Caroline after those hostilities increased. He had a grave decision to make, one he must discuss with Cloud Chaser—but after he talked with his grandfather. . . .

*   *   *

As they ate an early meal, Caroline asked Cloud Chaser, "What will happen when soldiers come looking for our missing party and find those men's bodies and the wagons? Will they trail us and attack your camp?"

"Do not worry, Caroline, for a great herd of buffaloes was stampeded over the tracks made by the wagons and horses, so there is no trail for soldier scouts to find and follow. The wagons were shoved over steep bluffs in a location called the Badlands by whites who visited it while hunting and collecting bones of ancient creatures years ago. Many of its canyons are unreachable from the top or bottom, so the army cannot recover those weapons even if they are sighted. The remainder of your possessions are resting there; perhaps they can be retrieved one day, as we know many secret paths into such places. The soldiers' graves were concealed by stones, and their horses were released far away. I hope it will not injure your heart or anger your mind and provoke defiance to learn no rescue is coming."

Caroline knew she had underestimated War Eagle's intelligence and foresight. "But won't the army blame the Lakotas for those disappearances in their territory?"

"Probably, since they blame all Lakotas for anything bad that happens in this area. If a large troop nears our camp to search it, our scouts will warn us of their approach, and you will be hidden from them. If a miracle occurs and a real treaty is made, you will be released to return home. Until that day comes, you will live among us in peace, so accept that fact."

Caroline was not provoked by his last statement, as he had spoken it in a gentle tone and with a pleasant expression. "I've already promised you I'll be obedient and respectful, unless I'm mistreated. If I'm abused, I will try to escape. Surely that's understandable."

Cloud Chaser eyed her honest expression and countered,

"As I have promised, you will not be mistreated unless you are bad or try to flee."

"Then, we have a bargain we can both honor."

Cloud Chaser nodded in agreement and returned to his meal.

As Caroline ate, she reflected on certain episodes during the long journey to the lovely and serene location. It was so different from the immense grasslands, now yellowing at the end of summer, a gently rolling terrain that had seemed to go on forever until abruptly terminating at the Paha Sapa. A verdant forest of mainly pine, spruce, and hardwoods swept up into picturesque foothills that continued upward into mountains of black spires, awesome pinnacles, and rugged ebony peaks. The winter village was situated amongst sheltering trees and boulders for protection against harsh weather during the cold season, a river flowing beyond the lengthy stretch of tepees for a fresh water source. She had sighted many animals nearby, so fresh game was abundant.

Cloud Chaser had explained their yearly routine to her: break camp in late spring, travel to the grasslands, hunt buffalo during the summer and preserve rations for the harsh winter, and return to this or a nearby location in early fall. He had said they normally gathered afterward with other tribes and bands for an annual trading fair, but it had been canceled this year due to the brewing trouble. Her owner had given her more language lessons, and she had worked hard to learn as much of their tongue as possible.

She recalled meeting his oldest brother, Wind Dancer, the future chief's wife, Chumani, which meant Dewdrops, and their three-year-old son, Tokapa. She had been impressed by that warrior who had treated her with respect but reserve. She remembered working with their seventeen-year-old sister, Hanmani, who was best friends with Macha and was pretty, kind, and genial. She had seen but not spoken with River's Edge, Dawn's twin brother, a handsome and appealing man who was still unattached and living with their parents. The same almost could be said of Broken Lance, their cousin and the younger brother of Two Feathers, whom she had tried to ignore and avoid during their travels.

The most unsettling meetings, Caroline recalled, were with Chief Rising Bear and the shaman Nahemana, powerful and esteemed leaders of the Red Shields. Neither had spoken to her directly, but both had studied her intently while visiting with Cloud Chaser along the way on two occasions. Although she had not understood the conversations, there was something about each man that had commanded her respect and evoked her curiosity. Oddly, Cloud Chaser did not favor his parents, grandparents, or siblings. In fact, he did not even look like a full-blooded Indian, which struck her as being strange since he had told her he was the birth son of the chief.

That which dismayed and intrigued her the most was how she caught herself covertly watching and thinking about War Eagle, as if she could not control an enormous interest in her fascinating captor.

To distract herself from more thoughts of him and to cool the warmth that came to her cheeks, she looked at the baby who was sleeping on its cradle-board. Positioned over the infant's head was a low three-pronged stand from which was suspended a "dream catcher." The small hoop of interwoven sinew—with fluffy breath feathers, colorful wooden beads, and intricately carved miniature animals dangling from its weblike surface and from its willow ring—was supposed to ensnare and destroy any bad dreams that tried to enter the child's mind while he slept, allowing only good ones to slip through a tiny hole in its center. She wished the Indian myth were true and she had one to hang over her head at night to halt near-nightmares about Two Feathers finding a way to coerce her from Cloud Chaser and Dawn, and to halt horrible dreams about her beloved brother lying dead and unburied somewhere, victim of another Indian attack. What, she worried, was her fate, her destiny? Surely it wasn't the tragic life of a slave. . . .

War Eagle met with his grandfather in the edge of the forest to explain his dilemma to the shaman whom he loved, respected, and obeyed without question or hesitation. After he finished the dismaying tale involving his cousin, he said, "I do not know what path to follow, Grandfather, to find what is best for all concerned. What do you think I must do?"

Nahemana laid a gnarled and gentle hand upon War Eagle's shoulder. He smiled and urged, "You must follow the tuggings of your heart, my grandson, for surely the Creator placed them within you. If He did not, and the path you have chosen to ride is not His will, He will send you a sign to stop traveling it. If it is meant for the white girl to live with Red Wolf's family in the Cheyenne camp, you will encounter no danger or hindrance in your path. If one appears, you must halt and return home."

"Was I wrong to bring her to our camp?" he was compelled to ask.

Nahemana shook his head and smiled again. "I do not believe that is true, my grandson. I believe she was sent here for a purpose. What it is, I do not know, for Wakantanka has not shown me that answer in a dream or a vision. But deep within me, I feel and think she was placed among us for a good reason."

War Eagle was confused. "Do you say that reason has passed? Is that why you tell me to leave with her and head for Red Wolf's camp?"

"I believe you must follow the urgings in your head and heart. But leave before the sun rises and do not tell Two Feathers of your journey, for she is not to fall within his greedy and sly grasp."

"Why do you say such words, Grandfather?"

"We do not want him to stir up trouble. I believe he seeks

the girl only to injure your second brother, and that is wrong. If he tries to follow you, I will order him to remain in camp."

"That is wise and true, Grandfather, and I will obey your words."

"Have you spoken to Cloud Chaser on this matter?"

"I go to speak with him soon, but he will agree it is best."

As War Eagle left, Nahemana took a deep breath and lifted his gaze skyward. *Guide him and protect him, Great One, for he is lost in a forest of unknown emotions and her loss will pain him deeply. She has touched his heart in a mystical way and he battles that truth fiercely. If there is to be a bond between them, You will find a way to bind them together, just as You did with his half-white brother and Macha. What is destined to be, no man can prevent. If he tries, he is punished or slain. I pray You do not allow my second grandson to suffer greatly before the truth is revealed to him and us.*

Shortly before dusk at the river and while they had privacy, War Eagle related his dismaying decision to Cloud Chaser as they tended their horses. When he finished, he asked, "Do you agree, my brother, for she now belongs to you? If you object, I will not take her to Red Wolf's mother. Speak the thoughts that are strongest and largest in your head and heart."

Cloud Chaser was surprised by that discovery; yet, it was not totally unexpected. He had not known how War Eagle would deal with the serious matter, but he had been convinced his brother would find a way to handle it wisely. He suspected how difficult the decision was and felt empathy for the other man.

"Do as your grandfather says. I think it is wise for all involved if you take her to live in Red Wolf's camp where she will be safe from our cousin's wickedness, for surely it will continue to grow worse. If it is not the will of the Creator, He will block your path as our shaman told you. I am to be one of our camp guards this night, so you can slip past my position without alerting others to your leaving. I will tell Caroline to pack her possessions and be ready to go with you when you come for her. You must leave when the moon is straight over our heads, for it enlarges to full cycle soon and will provide enough light to guide you. When the sun rises, if Two Feathers learns of your absence, you will be far away. Nahemana will not allow him to follow and halt you."

War Eagle realized—with the positions of their tepees, his own and those of Cloud Chaser and Two Feathers, and with his brother standing guard tonight—that sneaking away should be easy. "That is a good plan."

Cloud Chaser smiled and reminded him, "During the last hot season, I was the one sneaking from camp during darkness with Dawn at my side."

"That is true, but things were different for you and her. You rode away to prove yourself to us and to claim Dawn as your mate."

Cloud Chaser countered with a grin, "Yes, but I was helping her elude the greedy grasp of our cousin, as you now do to protect Caroline. That is good; yet, it is strange how such actions and deeds match. You will find victory and joy, as did we," he said with confidence.

How so, War Eagle's heart scoffed, *when she who steals your heart and troubles your spirit will be far away and lost forever? That is true and good,* his mind retorted, *for no union between you two is possible, and she will be a great temptation if she remains nearby. If you can endure the pains of the Sun Dance and find victory in the Sacred Bow Race, surely you can abide her loss and find triumph elsewhere.* "I hope so, my brother," he finally responded, "for soon we must war with the bluecoats, so no other worries should steal our thoughts and distract us from our duty."

As soon as those words left his mouth, War Eagle realized that ignoring the flower of his heart would be the hardest challenge he had ever faced. If only that task were a physical one, it would be easy to confront it with courage, stamina, skills, and resolve; and he was confident he would succeed. Kawa Cante, Heart Flower; it described her perfectly, for she had taken root within his chest, entwined herself around his pulse of life, and grown larger and stronger and more beautiful each day. What or who would pluck her lovely bloom? he fretted; and would doing that deed slay her? Make him bleed to death? *Hear me, Great Spirit, for I need Your help and comfort in the suns ahead.*

Cloud Chaser saw how Caroline gaped at him as he revealed what would take place during the night. "Do not worry; you will be safe and happy in the Cheyenne camp. He takes you to the mother of his close friend, Red Wolf. She is the wife of Badger, their war chief; she is white, but not a captive. She is a good woman. You will like her and respect her. She is called Sparrow, for she is small and sings much in a good voice."

Caroline was stunned and panicked by the unexpected news that she was being sent—no, taken—to strangers. Had she done something terribly wrong, committed an unforgivable act, or accidentally offended the chief or shaman or another important person during the long journey? Whatever the mistake was, it couldn't have occurred today, as she had worked diligently since their arrival at midday. She doubted that Macha was jealous of her or hated her and wanted her sent away. As for Cloud Chaser, he was too much in love with his wife and was too honorable to have lustful cravings for her or for any other woman, so it couldn't be to get rid of a temptation. The couple had said and done nothing this afternoon to indicate displeasure with her or to even hint at what was about to happen. After those thoughts whirled through her mind at high speed and provided no explanation, she murmured, "I don't understand. Haven't I been obedient and respectful?"

"Yes, but—"

Though rudeness was unlike her, Caroline interrupted, "Am I being sent away because of your cousin?"

"Yes, for Two Feathers seeks to make trouble for us about you."

His reply verified her suspicion, but evoked more questions. "What kind of trouble? Why does it matter what he says and does? You're the chief's son, the shaman's grandson. Surely you have more power and respect than he does. I thought you told me a gift couldn't be given away, and I was a gift from your brother," she reminded him.

Cloud Chaser frowned, unsettled by the predicament and his cousin's spitefulness and touched by her fears and pleas. "With just cause, the deed can be done. Trouble is trouble, and I cannot explain more to you."

Caroline realized all of her hard work to learn Lakota would profit her nothing in the Cheyenne camp. Yet, since Red Wolf's mother was white, she could communicate with her, and learn another Indian language. But how would she be viewed and received there? Here, she felt safe in Cloud Chaser's protection and had hope for a future release. There, she didn't know what to expect. She recalled that everything seemed fine until his walk and conversation with . . . "Is this exile War Eagle's idea?"

With the hope of preventing Caroline from hating and losing respect for his younger brother, Cloud Chaser said, "Yes, but it was a necessary and wise decision, and will be good for all concerned. Soon, Lakotas will be at war with the army, with your people, with your brother. We must not have dissension among us when that bloody sun rises."

"What will your people say and think when I'm sent away?"

"I cannot predict the words and actions of others, but I will find a good and true way to explain this deed."

You speak, but reveal nothing! Try another path to obtain clues. "How will Two Feathers behave when he learns you refused to trade me to him but you sent me to others, and on the sly, under the cover of darkness? Won't that look odd? Be offensive? Angering?" *Please, change your mind!*

"It does not matter what my cousin says, thinks, or feels. The choice is mine, and I have made it: you go to Red Wolf's mother as her helper."

Caroline realized he was being contradictory and befuddling. If his cousin had no importance in the matter, why and how was Two Feathers the cause of it? Even so, it was futile to argue with Cloud Chaser. Perhaps the motive was to separate her and War Eagle for some reason. . . . Whatever the truth, she wasn't going to be told the entirety of it, so she must resolve herself to her new fate and hope for the best. "I'll pack my belongings and be ready to leave when your brother comes for me during the night. Before I go, I want to thank you and Dawn for being so good to me. I know it must have been hard at times since I'm considered an enemy to your band."

"You are not our enemy, Caroline, and we will miss you and your help. If this were not necessary for harmony here, you could stay with us. Do not be afraid, for you will be safe in Red Wolf's camp; that I swear on my honor."

She nodded acceptance of his final statement. Regardless of the fact he had said earlier, "I cannot predict the words and actions of others," she knew he was being sincere. Yet, her distressed mind retorted, *And your brother will be safe here with me gone. Isn't that part of the dilemma? Or have I read too much into his furtive observations of me? Besides, what could come of such a mismatched relationship? Become his "squaw," as the soldiers called such women? Give up everything I am and know for a nomadic existence, take on such a hard and perilous life? No, it's impossible and foolish. We're from two different races, cultures, upbringings, religions, and more. Worst of all, our peoples are enemies and we're heading for war.*

Maybe her imagination was just running wild because of that weird dream following Clara's wedding and that silly act of placing the fruitcake beneath her pillow. Yet, it was a strange coincidence that her dream man looked like her captor from behind. How could she explain dreaming about an Indian when she had never met one, although she had seen sketches and photographs of eastern band members during history classes at school? And why did this particular man so enchant her? Caroline realized she would have a long and close study of War Eagle beginning in a few hours. She could not guess what he or she would say or do along their journey when they were alone and—

Cloud Chaser interrupted her rambling thoughts when he suggested she take a nap after packing her possessions. The first leg of the ride would be long and a sleepless night awaited her.

Caroline agreed, then countered, "I would rather take a bath and put on clean clothes first if that's permissible, since I don't know when I can do so again anytime soon."

Cloud Chaser nodded. "I will watch Casmu while Dawn takes you to a private spot in the forest. But you must hurry, for dark comes soon."

"I will, and thank you, Cloud Chaser, for everything."

"You are welcome, Caroline. Now, get your things and hurry."

While she fetched what she needed from her satchel, Cloud Chaser related her request and his agreement to his wife.

Macha whispered to him in a sad tone, "I wish she did not have to go."

"As do I, my wife, but it must be this way."

"You are right, but it pains my heart to hurt her and to lose her. I pray the Great Spirit will protect her from all harm in the Cheyenne camp."

"As do I, my wife. She is ready. Go and return quickly."

* * *

At a secluded section of the stream, Caroline stripped and bathed in a hurry as ordered. She rushed to wash her hair, knowing it would dry soon in the August heat. She was glad she had retrieved the remaining bar of French soap from her trunk, a gift from her parents at Christmas, and knew it would not last much longer. For now, its fragrant scent clung to her blond hair and her skin.

Perhaps, Caroline admitted to herself, she was spoiled by her upbringing back South, but she dearly missed long and soothing tub baths and freshly laundered garments, a colorful and fashionable variety of them. She missed shopping strolls, visits with friends, musicals, plays, and other activities. She missed having a chamber pot and an outhouse, a stove, real dishes and utensils, books, needles for sewing, oil lamps, private rooms, privacy itself. Most of all, she missed her parents and her brother and freedom.

Tears filled her eyes as she thought of those losses. After her parents' deaths, she had been afraid and confused, but—with faith in God and solace from friends—she had coped with her anguish and survived. After the surrender of her home and land, she had managed to abide that harsh misfortune and move onward toward a fresh start with her brother. After her capture, she had learned to accept yet another intimidating deviation in her life. How many more changes and losses, unwilling sacrifices, must she endure? How much anguish and how many challenges must she confront before she was free and happy and belonged to herself again?

"Ceye sni he," Macha told her in a gentle tone.

Caroline took a deep breath to regain control of her emotions. She turned and said, *"Slolwaye sni,"* revealing she did not understand.

Macha wished she could speak to Caroline in English to comfort her, but she had promised she would not. She pointed to her own eyes, trailed forefingers down her cheeks, smiled, and shook her head, indicating she had coaxed her not to cry.

Caroline wiped away her tears, forced out a smile, and told Dawn she was good-hearted and thanked her. *"Macha cantewaste. Pilamaya."*

Macha smiled and returned the kind words. "Caroline *cantewaste."*

Caroline stepped from the water and dried off using the thin blanket Macha passed to her. She donned clean garments, combed her damp hair. *"Winyeya manka."* She told the woman she was ready, finished, as Cloud Chaser had taught her en route to the camp.

Caroline was surprised when Dawn gave her a quick embrace and said, "Macha, Caroline, *kolas."* She smiled, as she did consider Dawn a friend and was happy the woman felt the same way about her. *"Han, kolas,"* she concurred—*Yes, friends*—as she gave the woman an embrace. She wished she could say more but a language barrier prevented sharing her feelings.

Now that Caroline was dressed, War Eagle watched the scene and listened to their genial exchange from his concealed position. While sneaking in the forest to hide journey supplies to retrieve later, he had come upon the women by accident. Not wanting to frighten or embarrass them or provoke them to think he was spying, he had remained still and silent to prevent exposing his presence, as he knew they would finish and leave soon. Though he had tried not to peek at the bathing female, the scene had been too tempting to resist. He had committed that offense only once, if he did not count his initial glimpse of the naked woman.

At the first look, his breath and self-control had been stolen for a short time. It was as if he had lacked the will and strength to turn away from the glorious sight. She was beautiful. Her waist was small and her breasts were ample. Her arms and legs were sleek and strong. He could imagine how soft her unmarred skin was and how enjoyable it would be to touch it, even more so to place his lips on hers and to share a union on a sleeping mat while his hands roamed her body. It would be a great and joyous victory to win that coup for himself, but it could not be; and strangely that reality pained and frustrated him. He had jerked his gaze from the forbidden sight and stared at the ground for a while.

Then, some powerful force had pulled his gaze back to her, and he had been unable to resist it, despite what he believed was a fierce struggle on his part. As his enthralled gaze caressed her from sunny hair to water-enclosed calves, he tried to surmise the potency and source of her large magic and appeal. He somehow knew it was more than her looks and the excitement of challenging the unknown and taking an enormous risk that drew him to her. What else it was, he did not know. *Are you good or bad, Heart Flower? Have you been sent by the Creator to test my skills with the Four Virtues, or to give me joy, or for some purpose to help us win our battle with your people? Or were you sent to me by an evil spirit to shame and defeat me? If you are evil, I must slay you, for I am the one who found you and brought you to my people. But I pray you are good and live, even if I cannot have you.*

He had averted his gaze once more and had not peeked again, even when he heard Macha comforting her. He had not looked until Caroline said she was ready, and then Macha had embraced her and she had done the same in return. It had seemed to him as if Caroline was being as sincere as the wife of his second brother. His keen mind had shouted that surely an evil spirit did not weep, did not look so sad about leaving friends, could not smile with such honesty in her sky eyes and on her lovely face. Surely she could not be an evil *wicagnayesa,* for such a wicked trickster could not fool him so easily.

War Eagle watched the women depart, waited until they were out of hearing and seeing range, and completed his task. Perhaps, he reasoned, the Great Spirit had urged him to learn more English from Chumani while traveling to their winter camp so he would be prepared to communicate with Caroline better when they faced the dark event looming ahead. But why, he wondered, would that be important to the Creator? Or was it only important to him, a selfish desire? *Soon, I will learn the truth about you, when we are alone. . .*

Chapter Six

Near midnight while the camp's inhabitants were asleep except for guards scattered out in all directions beyond its perimeter, War Eagle sneaked from his family's tepee without arousing his parents and sister and went to Cloud Chaser's dwelling. He found Macha and Casmu slumbering peacefully, but Caroline was waiting for him just inside the shadows of its entrance. She arose from a sitting mat and nodded that she was ready to go. He lifted the satchel from the ground to carry it to make certain it created no alerting sounds during their stealthy departure. He peered outside and listened with keen ears to check their surroundings for any indication of possible discovery, then signaled for her to come with him. They slipped into the nearby forest and retrieved the hidden supplies, then made their way to where his large Appaloosa and another smaller horse were secured to bushes. He helped her mount and watched her settle herself on the blanket that covered the horse's broad back. He grasped the tethers of both animals and guided them away on foot.

As a precaution against falling off, Caroline clutched the mane as she had done many times during childhood bareback rides. She had not spoken to War Eagle and had done her best not to make any noise. He looked mysterious and tantalizing in the light of a two-thirds moon. He was clad in moccasins, leggings, loincloth, and vest, all in sienna-colored buckskin and all unadorned, if she didn't count the fringe work. The top and sides of his ebony hair had been gathered and secured behind his head with a short binding. What she had learned was a medicine pouch was suspended around his neck on another thong, one containing what he had chosen as protective charms. A sheathed knife hung from a plain belt around his narrow waist.

In fact, she recalled from past sightings of him in only a loincloth, his entire body was sleek and agile with visible well-toned muscles. His flesh appeared darker than usual beneath the moon's caressing light, as did his deep brown eyes when he looked at her. He was an example of near perfection in a man. She didn't know if it was being so close to him or making a furtive escape or both that caused her heart to beat faster. She could not surmise what might happen if they were exposed and halted.

When they reached Cloud Chaser's guard position, War Eagle related his gratitude and farewell in sign language and saw his second brother respond in like manner to maintain their silence and secrecy. He leapt upon his horse's back and, still holding her mount's tether, left the area in a slow and cautious walk. After reaching a safe distance, he passed the leather strips to Caroline and motioned for her to follow him.

It did not take long for War Eagle to realize she was a skilled rider, and obedient to his order for silence and caution. A surge of excitement coursed through him at being alone with her, while sadness and anger nibbled at his mind to think of her lost forever. He could not help remembering her own sadness and tears at the stream, and how he had yearned to comfort her as Macha had done.

No, he must not give Caroline comfort by holding her in

his arms and telling her not be afraid because he would protect her from all harm. But, he reasoned, was taking her to
Sparrow the only way to do so? He wished he were convinced of that so he would not be so troubled by it. Should
he plead with Wakantanka to intervene on his behalf, beg the
Creator to find an honorable way for him to keep her as his
woman? Would it be showing shameful weakness and self-
ishness to ask to be blessed or rewarded in such a manner?
Yes, for it was up to the Great Spirit to decide when and how
a man should be honored by Him. At present, he needed to
push such tormenting thoughts aside; he must not allow
himself to be distracted.

By the time they halted for their second break, the first
soft glow of dawn was beginning to chase away the darkness. During their first stop, they had not spoken—just dismounted, sipped water, and allowed the horses to rest and to
drink from a stream. She guessed they had been traveling for
about six hours, but their pace had been slow during the
night to avoid accidents such as a horse stepping into an unseen animal burrow or hole from a rotted tree stump. They
had journeyed through many patches of woods and a dense
forest, crossed several meadows of tall grass and wildflowers,
ridden over many low rolling hills, and skirted higher ones.
They had flushed birds in ground or bush nests and had spooked nocturnal animals foraging in the woods or grazing in the
meadows or drinking at streams. From the moon's angle during their movements, she knew they were heading north-
westward from the eastern side of the Paha Sapa's rugged
but beautiful range. She did not know where the Cheyenne
camp was or how long it would take to reach it; and she did
not ask him since he wanted to maintain silence between
them for security reasons. But on that stop, she did ask to be
excused. *"Leja?"*

War Eagle glanced at her lovely face with pinkened cheeks and gave permission for her to enter the bushes nearby. *"Han."*

To Caroline, he looked as if he had been about to say more—no doubt to warn her not to attempt an escape—but had changed his mind. She assumed it was because he realized he could trust her not be reckless, and she wouldn't be.

Perhaps, she thought, she could coax or trick or scare the Cheyenne into releasing her. Or perhaps she could earn her freedom in some manner. Or she could find a way to escape after she procured their trust and wasn't watched as closely as she would be upon her arrival. In the event the latter was possible or was provoked by mistreatment, she was making a mental map of their route, just as she had done from her capture point and from the encampment on the grasslands. She was glad she had a good memory.

Upon rejoining War Eagle, she knelt by the stream to wash her hands and to refresh her face with cool water from the nearby mountains. She was aware that the stoic warrior was watching her, openly this time, and she wondered if that meant anything special. . . .

"We go, *Wi* come," he said, pointing toward the rising sun.

Again Caroline mounted with his assistance. Although his help was unnecessary, she said nothing to discourage it, and she deduced he knew that fact and chose to ignore it for an unknown reason. Each time, he had lifted her up on the horse's back as if she weighed less than one of her fancy evening gowns with many yards of satin and ample adornments, items now resting in a canyon in the Badlands. Every time his hands had gripped her waist or brushed against an arm or a leg, quivers had raced over her body and a strange warmth had spread across every inch of her. On occasion, their blue and brown gazes had met, to be averted quickly or to lock for a few moments. It was as if they wanted to say or do something impetuous and intimate but both lacked the courage. If, she mused, something physical—a kiss or an embrace—occurred, would it change anything between them? She didn't know.

Late that afternoon and following a midday halt to eat and rest, War Eagle became worried about possible perils ahead. Soon, they would cross the edge of Crow territory, the Lakota's fierce enemies. He hoped he was right about the Bird People not being in that area during this time. He knew the Long Meadows Treaty near Fort Laramie four hot seasons ago forbade enemy tribes and nations from warring with each other. They ware supposed to be allowed to pass through each other's territory without being attacked and slain. Still, sneaky raids and slayings happened and were concealed from the army's knowledge. He also knew the Crow mostly honored their treaty with the army, as the Bird People liked trading with them and liked receiving the goods called "annuities" for keeping the peace with whites and bluecoats. If they kept up their current pace and confronted no trouble, they should reach the Cheyenne camp when the sun was high overhead on the next day.

That meant he only had this evening and tomorrow morning to spend with the captivating woman who rode slightly to his left flank. He ordered himself not to think about her or about losing her, to concentrate on the path ahead to sight any Crow or other hazard before reaching it. He was tired, but he had gone without sleep for two days on many occasions and could rest and drop his guard after they entered Red Wolf's camp. He had allowed Caroline to sleep for a short time after their meal, knowing she was in need of that kindness since she was not a trained warrior.

She had smiled and thanked him for his generosity and good deed, which made her beauty and great appeal more noticeable to him. Despite his constant cautions to stay alert, several times he had caught himself gazing at her as she slumbered. He had craved to stroke her sunny hair, to caress her soft skin, to press his lips to hers, to take her as his woman in all ways. It had been a fierce struggle to restrain his desire and to focus on his duty and remember his sense of honor. He—

Caroline felt compelled to intrude on what she deemed were serious thoughts since her captor seemed oblivious of what was chasing them from their rear. She called his name and told him to *look*, "Wanbli, *iho!*" She saw him rein in his mount and turn toward her in haste. As he did so, with amazing speed and agility, his weapon was in his grasp and ready to use if a threat was approaching them. She repeated, *"Iho,"* as she motioned to the dark sky behind them, which indicated that violent weather was stalking them. She knew that summer thunderstorms struck swift and harsh in this territory, so she wanted to seek cover as quickly as possible.

Thunder rumbled behind them and slate-colored clouds moved nearer as if in a hurry to overtake and assail them. Strong gusts of wind began to whip about the grass and wildflowers as if threatening to yank them up by their roots, and to shake trees and bushes as if furious at them for some offense. Lightning, singular and multibranched streaks, flashed to their rear and almost overhead. Loud booms of thunder came in their wake; the time separating those two forces of nature revealed how close the dazzling bolts were.

War Eagle studied the ominous sky in haste just before a lightning bolt was seemingly hurled downward like a flaming lance and struck a large tree. The severed top half of the tall pine crashed to the earth and obstructed the trail ahead of them. He heard Caroline shriek in surprise, and the two horses pranced and whinnied in agitation. Since he was familiar with this area, he knew where to find safety. "Come. *Inankni yo!"*

Caroline did not delay in following his lead and obeying his command to "hurry." She had never liked bad storms. She remembered being terrified of them as a child after she saw a man killed by a brilliant strike of lightning like the one that had felled part of the huge tree not far beyond them. She recalled how she had snuggled in her mother's arms, hidden her face against a comforting chest, closed her eyes, and covered her ears with her small hands until it ended. This storm alarmed her, since they were in the open and it was surrounding them fast. Her tension and fears increased as she coaxed War Eagle to go faster and find adequate shelter before they were injured or drenched.

What if God is intervening and saving you? What if your captor is slain and you're freed? You could take the horse and supplies and join David. Yet, as she looked at War Eagle's broad back and recalled that he had never mistreated her, she realized she didn't want her freedom at that enormous price. It pained her to think of his death and saddened her to think of never seeing him and many of the Red Shields again. As if he sensed she was thinking wicked thoughts, he half turned and looked at her, their gazes locking for a few moments. Shame flooded her entire body and she had the urge to apologize, but she did not.

War Eagle misread the expression on her pale face and in her wide blue eyes to mean great fear and a plea for comfort and protection. He could not help murmuring, *"Kopegla sni yo,* Kawa Cante. Come," he added in English and hoped she had not grasped his careless slip.

After he turned forward and continued downward, Caroline stared at his back. Had she heard and understood him correctly? Had he intentionally meant to say, "Do not be afraid, Heart Flower?" Surely not. Yet, from past lessons, she knew what those first three Lakota words meant, and she was certain Macha had pointed to a flower when she said *"kawa."* She knew *"wastecante"* meant *good-hearted* and *"waste"* meant *good.* That had to mean *"cante"* was *heart,* even if it had come last because they were joined to form one word. She had learned that adjectives came after nouns, as the Paha Sapa, Hills Black, for Black Hills. Verbs came after direct objects and nouns before prepositions. Many of their language rules were reversed from hers. She was glad Cloud Chaser had spoken English so well and had taught her those differences.

You're mistaken; you must be, she told herself. *Perhaps Dawn was referring to that particular kind of flower, one with yellow petals, and the color of your hair simply reminded him of it. Since your name is so hard for him to say and Indians often choose names from nature, he probably just called you something easier and more familiar to him. Forget it, silly girl!*

After they reached a place with large black boulders scattered about and a broad and high cliff behind them, War Eagle leapt off his Appaloosa and helped Caroline dismount. "Go," he told her as he pointed to a spot where a thick ledge jutted from the dark wall of solid rock. As Caroline ran in that direction, he tethered the horses in a dense area of trees where he hoped they would be safe from harm. He grabbed the supplies and ran to join her as rain started to come down in large and fast drops.

Caroline bent over, ducked her head, and scrambled beneath the overhang, which was about four feet from the ground. The shelf was wide and deep enough for two people to share close confines in an emergency, and this certainly qualified. She pressed her back against the rock, drew her legs to her breasts, and tugged her skirt behind her calves. She hugged her knees to her chest where her heart thudded in anxiety as the storm's fury increased. She watched War Eagle toss in the supply and water pouches, duck, and take a seat beside her. Within minutes, a deluge of water was coming down.

To prevent thinking about the handsome man whose virile body was touching hers in the snug space, Caroline stared at the impenetrable and noisy curtain of liquid that poured over the end of the ledge and sealed them off from the assailed world. The depth and downward angle of the shelf and gentle slope of the ground prevented water from flowing into the shelter, though splatters on the hard ground bounced toward them and dampened his leggings, her skirt-tail, and their footwear. She saw shiny reflections on the lambent veil when frequent lightning flashed outside and she heard the grumblings of thunder as if it were a hungry and angered beast. She listened to the sounds of rain beating down on the overhang, hard earth, and nature's greenery. Despite the fact they were enclosed and it was summer, the small area did not get stuffy from a lack of airflow. In fact, the deluge created cool and soothing sensations and a delightful smell of freshness.

Suddenly the ferocity of the storm increased, although Caroline had not thought that was possible. A bolt of lightning shot down near their location and sent forth a thunderous *crack,* which caused her to jump and shriek in fright. Uncontrollably she whirled sideways, flung her arms around his waist, and buried her face against his chest as she trembled.

Without thinking, his arms embraced her of their own volition and held her against his body as he murmured again, *"Kopegla sni yo,* Kawa Cante. War Eagle protect. Great Spirit shoot Fire Arrows. Wakinyan flap wings, make . . . noise," he said after his mind sought the right word as Cloud Chaser and Chumani had taught him.

"What or who is Wakinyan?" she asked to keep him talking to distract herself from the storm and his tantalizing appeal. With her cheek now resting on his chest, she heard the steady beat of his heart, which seemed a little fast for normal. . . .

"Thunderbird. He good spirit. No fear him. You safe."

Caroline was surprised and confused—and aroused—by his gentle manner and comforting overtures. For now, he was being compassionate, and that behavior and his tender tone encased her in a warm glow. "I'm afraid of bad storms, but I feel safe with you. Thank you, Wanbli, for being so kind and generous. How long do storms last out here?"

War Eagle comprehended the gist of her words and they pleased him, just as their contact enflamed his desire. "Great Spirit say . . . how long."

"After the storm is gone, we'll ride to the Cheyenne camp?"

Assuming the fallen tree in their path was a sacred signal from the Creator to turn back and to keep her, he replied, "No. Grandfather say return to camp if sign come from Great Spirit to turn back."

Caroline's shocked mind ventured, *He discussed you with Nahemana?* Was the shaman, she wondered, the person who had suggested she be sent away to maintain harmony in their camp and between relatives, not War Eagle? Yet, it sounded as if Nahemana . . . She lifted her head and looked at him in bewilderment. "But I thought you were taking me to the Cheyenne camp. What sign are you taking about?"

"Fire Arrow strike tree, tree fall, path closed. It mean, go back."

She surmised that he believed his God had placed a barrier in their path and they should not go around or over it. He was taking her back home with him? But what about his reasons for sending her away? "What will Two Feathers say and do when I return?"

All he did was shake his head as if to respond he did not know, or as if it no longer mattered to him after receiving a divine sign from his God.

Caroline knew there was another angle to be considered and she broached it. "When war comes, I could endanger your camp by being there; I wouldn't want to be responsible for suffering and deaths." Besides, she had a better chance of freedom and rejoining her brother in the Cheyenne camp, didn't she? "You must not take me back to your camp."

War Eagle was touched by what he thought was her concern for their safety and survival. "What mean . . . *re-spon-si-ble?* What mean . . . *suffering?"*

"Responsible means . . ." Caroline paused to think of how to explain those words to him, then began by touching her chest and saying, "I caused bad to come." She spoke slowly to give him time to mentally translate or to reason out her words. "Responsible means soldiers come and attack your camp to rescue me, to punish Red Shields for attacking soldiers in the wagons and stealing me. Suffering means injuries, wounds, deaths, burn tepees, destroy food, shoot with . . . thundersticks. Do you understand?"

"War Eagle understand." She would blame herself for causing the soldiers to attack them. She was wrong, as an attack would come whether or not she was among them, and he doubted the bluecoats would know she was their captive before they did so. Yet, it warmed his soul to hear that concern worried her. Macha was right at the stream: Caroline was good-hearted, unlike the enemy white-skins who wanted their land and wanted them slain or pushed out of this territory. "Man, woman born to live, die; it Great Circle of Life. War Eagle no fear ghost ride to Creator. Good man, woman return to Wakantanka. Spirit of bad man, woman not go to Him. War Eagle obey Great Spirit command; He say you go back."

As he gazed into her blue eyes and sensed her lingering concern, War Eagle finally admitted to himself that Two Feathers was not totally to blame for his decision and action; he had feared Caroline's potent effect on him and had been desperate to end it by separating them, to sacrifice her to save himself and his honor. Now, he knew that losing her would not accomplish that.

As she observed the man in such deep thought, Caroline murmured, "I wonder what it would be like to kiss you."

Grasping the gist of her words, War Eagle asked, "What *kiss* mean?"

Caroline blushed and averted her gaze, shocked and embarrassed by her slip. When he pressed for an answer, she looked at him and explained, "It means to touch my mouth to yours," as she placed fingers first on her lips and then on his, then lowered her quivering hand to his chest. She watched him stare at her for a few moments before he reacted.

War Eagle's left hand cupped her jawline to prevent her from lowering her head again as he bent forward and meshed their lips, his right arm still cradling her against his body. He wanted, needed, yearned, to know how it would feel to "kiss" her and could not resist her unintentional invitation to do so. He had meant for the action to be short and light, but when she responded and his self-control weakened, the kiss became long and profound and tender. Every part of him came alive with desire and delight. His emotions took flight and sang as joyously as a colorful songbird. Within his head, his thoughts were only of her, of this heady experience, and this awesome coup. Within his body, a sensual hunger for her increased at a rapid pace. Within his heart, her lovely flower bloomed and pervaded his senses with her special scent of passionate submission. Within his soul, he somehow knew he had seen, smelled, touched, heard, and tasted an intrinsic part of his destiny. Every part of him urged him to take and savor each moment and sensation, the exposure and outpouring of their innermost feelings. Yet, something he could not grasp, perhaps the voice of the Great Spirit, whispered to him not to go beyond kissing and embracing and he was compelled to obey.

As for Caroline, when she had witnessed his imminent intent to sate her curiosity and perhaps his own, she had lacked the will and strength to pull away or to protest. She feared, whether she returned to his camp or was taken onward to the Cheyenne's out of self-defense, this would be the only chance to discover why and how he affected and enchanted her so deeply and strongly. She wondered where she had gotten the courage—no, boldness—to tempt him with a kiss.

War Eagle realized their desires were increasing to a hazardous level. As with the fallen-tree signal, they could travel this reckless path no longer and must return to the way things had been between them before they kissed and revealed their feelings. He must behave as if he had been doing nothing more than sating her curiosity, performing a generous deed. With great difficulty, he released his hold on her and leaned against the rock behind him. As he gazed forward, he said, *"Magaju* go fast. We ride soon."

Caroline took a deep breath to calm her tension and tremblings, to quell her wayward passions. The magic and intimacy of the moment were gone, shoved aside by him, and that was for the best at this stage of their relationship. She glanced beyond their sheltered position and nodded. Whether *"magaju"* meant *storm* or *rain,* both were leaving the area at a steady pace. She straightened her dress and body, lifting and hugging her knees. She realized how easily and quickly she could have submitted to him, surrendered to wild and wonderful passion, and that astonished her, since they were almost strangers and were enemies of a sort and she had been reared as a lady. She had never experienced such feelings or weakness with any of her past beaux, not even with William Crawford when he had courted her. Why, she mused, did she experience them with this particular man, one out of her reach?

When War Eagle noted how late it was, he said, "Night come soon. We camp here. I go tend horses."

"Do you need help making camp?" she offered as she realized he had been speaking better English since they reached the winter campsite.

"No. Stay." *I need to be alone,* and he supposed she did, too, for them to recover from their reckless lapse.

Caroline watched him leave the shelter and make his way toward the horses. Under these new circumstances, she wasn't sure how she should behave. She imagined it was best to ignore the incident as if it had never happened, which is what she was certain he would do. She still was amazed that he had kissed and embraced her, held her for so long, comforted her during the storm, and wasn't acting ashamed or angered or as if she had lured him into evil. She also was amazed—relieved and grateful—that he had not taken advantage of the situation and had not tried to force her to submit to him. Shouldn't that tell her he was not a savage or a lusty beast, that he was a gentleman? Tell her that he possessed kindness and integrity? Tell her that he might have good feelings for her and did not want to harm her in any way? Even if those assumptions were accurate, what did it matter in their situation? It mattered greatly to her, she decided, what kind of man he was.

As a nearly full moon rose in a now clear sky, Caroline curled on her side on a bed of black rock, the buffalo mats too wet to lie on for sleeping. Earlier, War Eagle had made it obvious to her that she was to stay beneath the ledge tonight while he camped with the horses in the tree line. He had brought her food and water, then left her alone to pass the night.

She rolled to her stomach and rested her head on her folded arms. The surface beneath her was smooth and flat, but it was hard and uncomfortable. A cool breeze wafted over her, fresh-smelling after the rain. She heard nocturnal animals, birds, frogs, and insects sending forth their own sounds and songs. She doubted she would get much sleep tonight, though she was fatigued from their long ride. But it wasn't only fatigue that kept her awake, it also was thoughts of the man nearby and what she had shared with him today.

She remembered how it had felt to kiss him, to be in his arms, to hear his soothing voice, to view his handsome face, to perceive his desire for her, and to lose herself briefly in the wonder of . . . what? Love? Passion?

Caroline recalled how her hand had wandered over his broad chest and fingered the Sun Dance scars located there, one over each breast. Cloud Chaser had told her about that awesome ceremony when he was explaining their customs, rituals, and beliefs. She could not imagine the full extent of the physical pain he had endured and survived, or a warrior's fear and anguish that he might fail in his sacred task. She knew it was done as sacrifice, an offering of flesh and energy—his very life if need be—to Wakantanka, as a show of gratitude for blessings and to achieve total unity with his Great Spirit and heritage. She reasoned that it required enormous strength, courage, willpower, prowess and immense love and faith to accept such sufferings. No, her mind refuted, to actually create them by being pierced willingly and bound by those fresh wounds to a pole, by allowing himself to be tormented as he chanted and danced and struggled to jerk free, and to endure pain without flinching or screaming or ceasing until the thongs ripped away and victory was won.

He and his family must have been very proud of him that day. Cloud Chaser also had told her that a warrior's honor, "his face," was one of his most important possessions and he worked hard not "to lose" it. She wondered if "saving face" was the only reason War Eagle would reject her, as it surely wouldn't be because he didn't want her as a woman. She couldn't be mistaken about his behavior earlier. Or could she? . . .

In the edge of the forest, War Eagle was having a restless and difficult time trying to ignore the woman nearby so he could get to sleep. He was not worried about an enemy slipping up on them as he dozed lightly when away from the safety of their camp. He had been foolish to expose his feelings for Caroline and to allow her to reveal hers for him. If he was not reading her signs wrong, she desired him as a man and did not look upon him as a "savage" or "hostile" or an enemy. Yet, how could he allow that to matter to him? How could he, a high warrior, a Sacred Bow Carrier, son of the chief, grandson of the shaman, grandson of the past chief, take a white woman as his mate without appearing weak and sacrificing his honor? If there was a way, only the Great Spirit knew it, as he did not.

The next morning was pleasant beneath a serene blue sky. They had eaten, loaded their supplies, mounted, and left the secluded and enlightening setting. They had communicated mostly with motions and nods and had tried to avoid looking at each other any more than necessary, as if their hearts carried heavy burdens or they feared a repeat of yesterday's lapse in their appointed roles as enemies.

They rode for what Caroline guessed to be two hours before they halted at a stream for the horses to drink. She was impressed by his care of his animals. To elude his temptation for a while, she excused herself in the bushes and was slowly returning to his side when trouble struck. Suddenly she found herself seized from behind, a hand over her mouth, a knife at her throat, and elbows somehow imprisoning her shoulders and arms. A man spoke to her in a whisper in a language she did not comprehend. "I don't understand," she told him when he slightly moved his hand from her mouth. Before she could scream for help, his strong and dirty hand was replaced.

"You white-eye. Why you ride with Red Shield? No yell or I kill. You no fight, be quiet, obey, yes?"

Caroline nodded. He lifted his hand but pressed the blade to her neck in warning.

"Talk, white woman. Why you here?"

"I'm a captive of the Red Shields."

"If that true, why you no bound? Why you walk free?"

"I had to . . . be excused, visit the bushes. Please don't kill me. My brother is a solider, so you'll be punished if you harm me. Release me and I'll tell you what you want to know. I won't scream or fight you."

The warrior ignored her and yelled, "Wanbli! *U wo!*"

Caroline realized her captor knew the warrior she was traveling with and had ordered him to come to their location. It did not take much intelligence and perception to realize he was an enemy and that she and War Eagle were in jeopardy, or perhaps only she was in peril. She watched her traveling companion step from behind a large tree and reveal he was already nearby. She listened to them speak, but could only grasp a word here and there.

"What do you want, Crow dog?" War Eagle scoffed as he glared at the foe who held Caroline captive and in danger and who glared back at him.

"I have your woman, son of Rising Bear. Throw down your knife or I will cut her throat and you can watch her bleed and die before I slay you. Yield and I will set her free to return to her people."

"She is a lowly captive; she means nothing to me," War Eagle bluffed. "You do not need to use her to challenge me. I will fight you. Come, I am ready to do battle with a coward who hides behind a woman."

"You lie, Lakota dog. If she was a captive, she would be bound and injured. Must I cut her many times before you speak the truth? Throw me your knife or she dies." War Eagle knew the Crow brave would slay Caroline if he refused. He had no choice but to do as ordered to save her life.

As War Eagle withdrew his knife from its sheath and tossed it to the ground between them, a shocked and frightened Caroline shouted, "No! Don't give up your weapon! He'll kill you!" Her blue gaze widened in rising terror as the man she loved took several steps backward, away from the discarded knife, his arms hanging by his sides in submission. It was apparent to her that he was endangering his life to save hers. Didn't he realize his humiliation and sacrifice were for naught and their enemy would probably slay both of them now that he was disarmed?

Chapter Seven

The Crow warrior shouted for War Eagle to move farther away, which he did, slowly and without taking his gaze from his adversary.

Caroline wished she could understand what they were saying when the two men argued following her outburst. Since the enemy behind her knew English, he must have grasped what she had yelled to her companion, which foolishly exposed her concern and affection for him.

The challenger whose left hand was either painted or charcoaled ebony—the latter she guessed from the horrible taste on her lips—did not cover her mouth with it again, but he ordered her, "No speak!" as he shook her. Then, using his body, he urged her forward until they reached the discarded weapon, which he kicked backward with one foot, out of the Red Shield's reach and temptation.

War Eagle reminded him, "Release her, for I gave you my weapon."

"You spoke false. She is your woman. She tried to save you."

"She is not my woman, Black Fist. She is only a captive.

I was taking her to the Fire Hearts Cheyenne camp to trade her to War Chief Badger."

Black Fist pointed out, "You ride away from Badger's camp. You lie."

"The storm forced me to take another trail to his camp. A fire arrow struck a tree and it fell across the path and many rocks rolled down the hills and closed the opening between them. If you do not believe me, we will ride there and I will show you that the path cannot be used."

"If you speak true, why did she seek to help her enemy live?"

"She called out to me because she fears your capture more than she fears me. She knows it is not the Red Shield way to harm women, even helpless enemy females. That is not true of your people. Do you break your word to me and dishonor yourself? Do you forget Crow have a truce and treaty with the whites and army? If you hurt or slay the sister of a blue-coat, it will call forth the soldiers' wrath on your camp."

"They will not know Black Fist killed her, for the dead do not talk."

That boast told War Eagle that the man had lied and had no intention of letting either of them live, just as he had suspected. "I do not die fast or easy, Crow dog. I gave up my weapon to fight you with bare hands. I do not want her death to call forth soldiers on my people. I say Black Fist shames himself before the Great Spirit if he slays a lowly and weak female who is not my woman."

He had a second knife concealed behind him in his belt, but he had to get closer to them to use it. First, he needed to get Caroline released from the man's tight grip, and get her a short distance away. He tried not to think about how she had warned him and had revealed her good feelings for him once more. He had to save—

When Caroline felt the intruder's grasp loosen and deduced he was distracted by his quarrel with War Eagle, she summoned the courage to use a defensive action her brother had taught her long ago. She elbowed him in the stomach as hard as she could while she simultaneously stomped his foot with her laced ankle boot. Her gambit worked; the foe's lungs let our a *whoosh* of air as his body jerked forward, wobbling on an injured foot, and released her in painful surprise. Without delay, she slammed her elbow into his jaw while he was doubled over and sent him stumbling backward before she darted toward her companion for protection. She almost collided with War Eagle before he agilely side-stepped her as he took swift advantage of his enemy's briefly disabled condition by running forward to attack the man. As she stopped and whirled to observe the impending action, her gaze took in the knife stuck into his waistband, revealing he was not unarmed after all.

War Eagle reached his challenger before the man recovered fully. He lowered his left shoulder and rammed it with great force and strength into the Crow's chest, causing the man to stagger backward to the ground, roll over and bound to his feet, then shake off his dazed state. When Black Fist yanked his knife from its sheath, War Eagle grinned as he retrieved his concealed weapon. He saw the Bird warrior's eyes widen in surprise at that cunning deceit, then narrow and harden in hatred. "Come, Crow dog, fight me as man. You no longer have a woman to hide behind."

"You are sly, son of Rising Bear, but I will defeat you and slay you. Before I slay your woman, I will take her upon the ground with much pain."

"You speak of the woman who attacked you and freed herself," War Eagle scoffed in ridicule. Just as he presumed and hoped, that insult angered his rival and provoked him to charge in a rage, as he knew a warrior could not think clearly and act wisely when agitated.

Caroline watched as the enemy ran at War Eagle with his blade held high and threatening. She saw her handsome captor dart aside at the last moment and slice across his opponent's waist as he did so. Blood flowed down the enemy's exposed hip and leg, for the wound was deep and long. The two warriors began to move in a circular pattern as they studied each other, their dark gazes locked in mortal combat. When they halted and glared at each other, their feet were set apart, their knees were flexed and ready for fast movements, their arms hung loose before them, sharp knives held in tight grips. She knew they were assessing each other's strengths and weaknesses, waiting for the perfect moment to strike a stunning or lethal blow. They began to dance in and out as they slashed at each other. It was War Eagle who seemed to be the superior warrior; his prowess was undeniable as he nipped at his competitor's flesh and created new injuries while he sustained only one minor nick on his right forearm.

War Eagle knew he could not allow himself to be diverted or slowed for even a brief time; such an error could cost him his life, and Caroline's. He knew a wounded and desperate foe was dangerous and unpredictable, but the excess pride and draining wounds of Black Fist would be his undoing. He did not play with his rival, as he wanted this battle settled soon and in his favor. If he did not make a mistake, he would be granted his wish, as the Crow was tiring fast from the many slashes and loss of blood. He could tell from the way Black Fist now moved that his muscles were getting taut and cramped.

Caroline did not move or do anything to break War Eagle's concentration. She was positive he would win. In the flicker of an eye, War Eagle lunged at his antagonist and threw him to the ground. He leapt upon the man's prone body, straddled it, and struggled to disarm him as his opponent squirmed for freedom. As they scuffled about on the grass and dirt, she turned her back as she saw War Eagle lift his left arm and start to bring down his knife toward the disabled man. She heard a thud, then took a deep breath and turned toward the scene where War Eagle now stood and gazed down at his dead challenger. She watched him lift his head skyward and close his eyes for a minute. She assumed he was giving a prayer of gratitude to his Great Spirit.

War Eagle lowered his head and looked at Caroline, whose still-worried gaze was locked on him. She nodded as if to say she was happy he had won and was relieved the fight was over.

"Go to horse. I come soon," he said.

Again she nodded, then left to go to where the horses were tethered to await him. He was unconcerned about her going alone, as he was convinced she would not try to flee, just as he was certain the Bird Warrior had been traveling alone. If not, the enemy's friends would have pounced upon him by now to slay him in revenge. He gathered the Crow's weapons, took a small scalp lock from the top front of the dead brave's head, and retrieved the fallen man's horse. Those were battle prizes he would take home for this coup, one that she had helped him obtain with her daring deed. Relieved he and Caroline were safe, he headed to join her at the horses.

Caroline looked up at him as he approached, leading an unfamiliar horse with weapons and other possessions secured on its back. He tethered the animal near their mounts and turned to face her and spoke.

"I go bathe, I return soon. You guard camp. Gift for coup. You brave, cunning. You help defeat Crow. Black Fist bad; he attack Lakota camps, raid, kill. He dead, spirit gone. This protect you from enemy."

Caroline eyed him with astonishment as he handed her an unadorned belt with a beaded sheath dangling from it, no doubt taken from his defeated adversary. "You trust me to have a weapon?" she asked in amazement.

"War Eagle trust Caroline," he replied, *but do not prove me wrong.*

She watched him head down the riverbank until he was concealed from view by bushes and other lush vegetation. Yes, he needed a bath, for his flesh was splattered with his foe's blood and dirt from their fierce fight. But was he testing her by giving her a weapon? Was he seeking to learn if she would use it against him for revenge or to disable him for flight, or on herself to end her captive life, or for protection if she tried to escape? Did he think she hated him enough to take the first action? Despised her existence so much she would flee it in death? Or was he giving her a sly opportunity to escape to her brother and people? How could she guess what that befuddling warrior was thinking and doing? She could not. It had seemed as if he was surrendering to his challenger to save her life, but he had not been weaponless as she and the Crow were led to believe. Perhaps he simply had wanted to outsmart the enemy and obtain a chance to defeat him. He had her bewildered, probably right where he wanted her to be. *Well, my mystifying captor, when you return and find me patiently waiting here and I don't attack you while en route home, either you will be pleased to discover that your faith in me is justified or you'll be shocked and disappointed that I have obeyed you and thwarted your clever ploy. I wonder which will be the truth and if I can discern it from your reaction. . . .*

War Eagle thought it was wise to prevent a show of pleasure and relief when he saw Caroline sitting on a fallen tree and gazing at the lovely scenery nearby. He had hoped, prayed, and believed she would be obedient; and he was glad his judgment was accurate. He joined her and sat down beside her, noting she had tied Black Fist's belt around her waist with the sheath grazing her right hip. If trouble appeared again, she would be able to defend herself. She deserved the gift, as part of the daring and victorious coup was hers. His family and friends back in camp would understand and accept his action and motive after they heard the thrilling story of the Crow's defeat and how she had initiated it. They, too, would realize she had been willing to risk her life or an injury to save him, marks of a friend and worthy of the honor he had bestowed on her. When she turned her head and looked at him, he grinned. "Face black from enemy hand. I wash. Come." He grasped her hand, guided her to the river, and indicated she was to kneel beside him.

Caroline did not flinch as he used water and a piece of soft leather to remove the dark smudges from around her mouth.

He scowled and said, "No good; it stay."

"It needs soap to take it off. I have some in my satchel, my pouch."

"What *soap?*"

"I'll show you. Wait here while I get it." She retrieved her bag, placed it on the ground, withdrew the dwindling bar, and rejoined him. She took the wet leather swatch from his hand, lathered it, and stared to scrub off the charcoal with some type of oily base, probably animal fat. She did not protest when he took over the task. His touch was gentle and he used only enough pressure to wash away the dark smears.

War Eagle smiled after he finished. "Gone. *Haipajaja,*" he said as he gestured to the soap in her hand, and grinned when she repeated the word correctly but with difficulty; then she also grinned in amusement. "Caroline hurt?" he asked as he lifted her arm and checked her elbow where a bruise was forming from the two hard blows she had given to his enemy.

"It's fine, just a little sore," she responded during the examination. When he looked confused, she clarified, "Hurt, little. Heal, soon. Thank you. *Pilamaya.*" She expressed her gratitude once more in his language. She noticed his right forearm was still bleeding. "You're hurt. I'll tend it." When he did not protest by word or action, she tore a strip of cloth from the bottom of her dress, then separated it into two pieces. She dipped one in the water and washed the wound. Though it was not long or deep, it continued to bleed at a slow and stubborn rate. She used the second piece to wind around his arm, then secured it in place with ties ripped from its edge. "There, that will keep out dirt and keep away insects."

"What *insects?*" he asked, recognizing the other English word.

Caroline glanced around and pointed at several different kinds in the air and on bushes, flowers, and the moist soil of the riverbanks. "Insects."

He nodded understanding and translated, "Insects, *wabluska.*"

"*Wabluska,*" she echoed, and he nodded again.

War Eagle lifted his arm and looked at the neat bandage. He smiled and thanked her.

Caroline smiled in return, delighted they were talking and relaxing with each other. Could they, she wondered, become friends? Become more to each other? Was it foolish and futile to make that effort?

Their gazes remained locked following his last word and an exchange of smiles. It was as if they were communicating without speaking, relating their own feelings, and each searching for indications that the other felt the same way. It was as if they were entangled in a private domain and lacked the strength and willpower to escape those irresistible and strong emotional vines that sought to bind them together. For a while, all they did was look at each other with soul-deep yearning, then, each leaned forward—drawn together by a potent force—until their mouths touched and they embraced.

They kissed with eagerness and joy, their lips performing a magical and arousing dance. Their bodies enflamed, tingled, and trembled with rising desire and blissful sensations. As if one being or with one purpose, they eased from the log to the grass with War Eagle lying half atop her, their mouths never parting or ceasing their passionate task. As one of his hands played in her blond hair and the other caressed her face and neck, Caroline's hand wandered over his broad shoulders and back beneath his vest. Each savored the other's touch and their own rovings over warm flesh.

War Eagle's right leg was between her thighs. His loins ached with eagerness to possess her, and his heart urged him to do so. At that point, his mind was too clouded by her and his cravings to think clearly. All he wanted at that moment was to make her his completely.

With Caroline, it was the same. Her wits were dazed by him and fierce desire. Awesome pleasure washed over her and a ravenous and unfamiliar hunger chewed at her. Never once did she think, should she, could she, surrender totally to him. It was as if the ability to reason with clarity and caution had been ripped from her brain, leaving her vulnerable and susceptible to his enchanting summons to yield.

Yet, as they kissed and caressed, a wise and kind spirit was watching over them, one who knew this was not the time and place for such a special union, a bonding experience on the highest level. . . .

A large buck bounded across a shallow section of the river, bolted up the bank, and halted only a few feet from them. It shook its head with a ten-point rack and snorted loudly before it dashed away across the terrain.

The noise the animal created startled War Eagle and Caroline, who jerked apart and sat up in haste. Both gaped at the majestic creature as it stared at them for a few moments before its swift departure. Then, they turned to face each other. He looked dismayed and Caroline blushed.

War Eagle spoke first, his voice husky. "We go. Danger here."

Caroline guessed what he meant by those words—the peril of runaway passions—and nodded agreement. *"Cantesica,* Wanbli," she apologized as Cloud Chaser had taught her to do when she made a mistake.

War Eagle eyed her worried, pleading expression and it tugged at his heart and conscience, his sense of great honor and courage. He refused to allow her to take the blame for his reckless actions. Although it was her big magic that had evoked them and enthralled him for a time, he was not angered by her deed. He was the man, the warrior, the captor, the one who should have been in charge of the situation and either prevented it or halted it sooner. If the Great Spirit had not sent the forest warrior to warn him to awaken from his forbidden dream quest, he would have claimed her as his own. Too, during his rash distraction, another enemy could have attacked and slain them as they mated in wild and wonderful abandonment. The woman who had sneaked into his heart and thoughts and stolen them with ease returned him to reality when she spoke in a quavering voice.

"I'm ready to ride. Shall we go now?" she implored, anxious to flee his indiscernible silence and probing stare.

"No be sorry. We weak; hunger strong. No more kiss, touch. Yes?"

Whether his "Yes?" asked if she concurred with his opinion of their breach—relapse—of proper conduct in their roles of captor/captive and his assertion of their character flaws, or it was meant to coax her compliance to his softly spoken commands, she nodded and said, *"Han."*

War Eagle took a deep breath and held it for a while to slow his racing heart. After he released it, he said, "We go."

They gathered their things, repacked and loaded them, and mounted. This time, Caroline grasped the horse's mane and swung up onto its back before the warrior could assist her. As she situated herself and positioned her dress, she realized he had a broad grin and an amused gaze.

"Kawa Cante ride good. Cloud Chaser, Dawn, be happy you return. We go," he repeated, and leapt upon his Appaloosa's back. Then he headed homeward to hand the sunny flower of his troubled heart over to his brother again.

Caroline followed, staring at his back as he sat tall and straight on the animal as the proud and honorable man that she knew him to be by now. She realized, and was certain he was aware, he had made another slip of the tongue, which probably had provoked his ensuing frown and rush. She was astounded and elated that he had not punished or berated her, and had not appeared enraged or insulted by their show of desire for each other. Having been told at Fort Pierre that Indians were very "superstitious," she was glad he had not seemed to believe she was evil or had cast a wicked spell on him to lead him down a dark path of shame and defeat and enthrallment.

Caroline admitted there was a great deal she did not know and many other things she could not explain about the Indians, but she was learning more every day; and most of those discoveries were contradictory to what she had been told and had overheard. In her opinion, the man riding just ahead of her was not a savage or a churl. He was a man of immense integrity, courage, compassion, and intelligence. Except for his cousin, he was close and intensely loyal to his family, people, and lands. He lived his religion every day, beginning with prayer. He was more than worthy of his ranks as the chief's son, a Sacred Bow Carrier, and a small-band leader. He was a warrior of great prowess, a superior figher and protector. He was handsome and virile, strong and gentle. He was the epitome of what she wanted, needed, and admired in a man. She could not deny that she desired him, yet, she could not, must not again, forget he was beyond her reach, as painful as that reality was, and no matter that he might also feel the same way about her, however reluctant he was to admit that fact. Have him, she could not. Except in her dreams. . . .

War Eagle was thinking and feeling much the same as Caroline, whom he could not seem to force from his heart and thoughts, hard as he tried. She embodied everything he wanted, needed, and desired in a female. She was beautiful and alluring, and she possessed countless good traits. She had an appealing mixture of strength and gentleness. He enjoyed being with her, talking with her, watching her, hearing her, smelling her, tasting her. She made every part of him come alive with excitement and joy. He could not deny he loved and desired her.

But she was white; he, Red Shield, the future chief if death stalked and overtook Wind Dancer. Even if Caroline dressed, spoke, and lived as an Oglala, the colors of her sunny hair, sky eyes, and pale skin would shout that truth to everyone who looked upon her. She was viewed as one of the enemy, a captive, a woman out of his reach; those facts angered and frustrated him as a man who had never feared or hesitated to challenge even seemingly impossible odds and risks in battles, raids, or in contests with fellow warriors.

He must not allow either of them to show such bittersweet weaknesses before his people, especially before Two Feathers, who might seek to shame him to the point of dissension or lethal conflict. The motive for that sudden spitefulness, he did not know. Hard as it would be, he must ignore and evade her. From this sun forth, he vowed, she could come to him only in his dreams. . . .

Upon their return to camp and without saying a word or even glancing at each other, a cautious War Eagle left an equally discreet Caroline at Cloud Chaser's tepee with Dawn. Both knew they were being observed by people who were curious about her departure and surprising return with him.

Afterward, he handed the three horses' tethers to a young brave who had hurried forward to take the animals for tending, a way of showing honor to their chief's son and practicing the Virtue of Generosity for when the youth became a full-fledged warrior. Without delay, War Eagle went to meet with his father, brothers, and grandfather.

After the five men gathered in Rising Bear's tepee and Winona and Hanmani gave them privacy, War Eagle revealed the stirring events that happened during his absence and his motive for leaving camp with the white female, only omitting his private feelings for her. The shaman nodded in accord when he related the elderly man's advice before his departure. "After the Fire Arrow struck down the tree and blocked my path, I felt it was a sign to turn back as Grandfather told me to look for when I spoke with him before leaving with her."

"To return was wise, my grandson. You have done well to see and obey His will," Nahemana praised him. "The Great Spirit has not shown me the reason, but my heart and mind tell me He has placed her among us for good purpose. The Great One has spoken; she is to remain with us."

A disturbed Rising Bear asked, "Why does Two Feathers crave her so fiercely when he hates whites? Why does he seek to shame you and to injure Cloud Chaser? After my second son proved himself to us during the last hot season, a truce was made between them. Why has he broken it?"

War Eagle shook his head and responded, "I do not know, Father, but his hatred for Cloud Chaser has returned, if such bad feelings ever left his heart and head. Perhaps he insults me and craves the captive in an attempt to harm my second brother in a sly way. When he saw me return and walk to your tepee, he followed me in anger. It is not our way to quarrel among families or with our people or to go against the council's vote, which was for her to stay with us unless the Great Spirit said otherwise. Two Feathers does not honor those ways, but he will not tell me or Cloud Chaser why he feels and acts as he does."

"That is true, Father," Cloud Chaser concurred. He related the many conflicts and harsh talks with his cousin following Caroline's arrival. "Even she senses there is trouble in him and questioned me about it. She fears the manner in which he watches her. She has worked hard for me and my family, and she shows no hatred or disrespect toward us or our people."

"That is true, Father," War Eagle said. "She begged me not to bring her back to our camp, as she feared we would be

attacked for her rescue. She has many good feelings for
Cloud Chaser, Dawn, Casmu, and others who have been
friendly to her and she does not want them harmed or slain
because of her presence among us."

"And she helped you defeat Black Fist," Wind Dancer
noted.

"I will talk with Two Feathers," Nahemana decided aloud,
"for he will not speak falsely to a shaman, the Great Spirit's
sacred messenger. If he is bold and evil enough to try to deceive me, I will see it in his eyes and hear it in his voice. This
conflict must end before it causes trouble for our people. I
will tend this task soon, after I pray for guidance."

"That is good," Rising Bear agreed with the shaman's
idea.

War Eagle motioned to items lying near him and said, "I
give you the weapons and horse from our fallen enemy, my
father. I will ask Mother to place the Crow's hair lock on my
war shirt."

"I thank you for these gifts, my son. Your battle with
Black Fist was brave and cunning; he will no longer raid us
or slay our people or our allies."

War Eagle asked his family, "Was it wrong to give the
white girl his knife and sheath?"

"No," Rising Bear replied, "for she earned them with her
courage, help, and cunning. Perhaps she saved your life; perhaps that is why she was sent to us and why you were evoked
to leave camp with her. Your skills are many, but if you had
been alone and he sneaked up on you, you could be lost to us
this sun. I thank the Great Spirit for your life and her help."

Wind Dancer said, "It is good for Grandfather to settle
the conflict between Cloud Chaser and Two Feathers, for
danger rides toward us at a swift pace. While you were gone,
my brother, a messenger from Red Cloud came to us with
bad news. Agent Twiss, who took the place of Broken-Hand
Fitzpatrick after he joined his Creator, has sent word to the
bands of all Lakota tribes saying White War Chief Harney

will reach Fort Kearny in a few suns, then ride into our lands. Twiss warned all Lakotas who are good and want peace with the whites to move their camps to the other side of the Kampeskawakpa, the flowing waters they call Platte River. Those who do not move will be viewed as enemies, 'hostiles,' and will be attacked."

The astonished War Eagle asked, "How can Agent Twiss and War Chief Harney command us to leave our land when the edges of our territory were chosen by the white leaders who made the Long Meadows Treaty four circles of the seasons past? Is this a trick to steal our lands? If all Lakotas move and surrender these grounds, even for the passing of one season or less, many whites and bluecoats will cover them as flood waters. It will be a long and bloody fight to push them out and regain them."

Wind Dancer, Rising Bear, and Nahemana had been present at that "Big Council" near Fort Laramie in September 1851 where ally and enemy nations gathered in one enormous group to hear the army's proposal for peace, to assess their strengths and weaknesses, and to see which friends and which foes voted to either accept or refuse their offer. None of the five men had forgotten that two of their fiercest enemies had not attended; nor had some of their allies; so the Laramie Treaty had not prevented all aggression upon other tribes, soldiers, settlers, or passing emigrants. Even some who had signed the agreement had not honored it.

Since the whites had demanded and selected one chief to represent and sign for all Lakotas—Brave Bear of the Brules, who was now dead, slain by Grattan in a foolish dispute over a strayed and slaughtered cow—Rising Bear had not put his mark to the paper and had not agreed to their terms, their ridiculous demands; nor had he or his band accepted any of the annuities given in exchange for a vow of peace with all other Indians and with all whites, compensations that were too often of inferior quality and lesser amounts than promised.

Yet, their own band had lived and hunted in their assigned territory and had fought only in defense or retaliation for evil deeds committed by enemies of either skin color. They had not leaned toward large and violent warfare until they were given no choice following Grattan's "massacre" and the raids and slayings by certain Brules and a few small Oglala bands, for which all Lakotas were being blamed and punished, despite knowing the truth from Cloud Chaser's glorious deeds last summer.

After those memories had galloped through each man's mind, Wind Dancer answered for the others, "What you say is true, Wanbli, so we must soon battle them, for they are sure to challenge and attack us."

Rising Bear added, "Our council talked and voted after we were given those words. As with our best allies, we will wait to learn what their war chief will do when we do not abandon our lands as ordered. We fight only if he attacks us. While we wait, we will prepare for defense and assault."

War Eagle asked for clarity, "If the soldiers attack only those to blame for the deeds of the Brules and the few Oglalas who live among them, will we fight with them as allies or will we honor the old truce?"

Rising Bear said, "Only the Great Spirit knows and sees all, my son. We will follow His command when He sends it to our shaman."

Nahemana told them, "I will go into the sacred hills alone to pray and to seek a vision to learn if the Great Spirit is ready to reveal His plans to me. On the next sun, I will prepare myself in the sweat lodge. When the second sun rises, I will leave. After I return, I will speak with Two Feathers and I will tell you of that talk and of my vision."

"That is good, Wise One," the chief said, and his three sons nodded in accord. "We will gather and speak again after Nahemana returns to us."

Wind Dancer stood and said, "It is time for the evening meal. I must return to my family. Dewdrops will be eager to hear the news. She will be happy our brother is safe and the white girl was brought back to our camp."

As Cloud Chaser also rose from his sitting mat to head home, he said, "As is Dawn, for Caroline is much help to her and with our son. Do not worry, Father, for I will show courage and patience in the conflict with Two Feathers. I will not allow him to provoke me to fight or to quarrel harshly before our people. I will treat him as if I do not see or hear him, or I will smile and laugh as if he jests when he attacks me with bad words."

"That is good and wise and cunning, Cloud Chaser, and I thank you."

War Eagle, who remained seated in his family's abode, said, "I will do the same as my brother with our cousin. We must not allow his evil to flow over us as a flood and drown us."

As Rising Bear glanced from man to man, he smiled and said in a voice made husky with strong emotion, "There is much pride and love and joy in my heart for my three sons. Together you will guide and protect our people during the dark suns ahead, as will the Great Spirit and our shaman."

During the evening meal while dusk settled in on that area, Cloud Chaser related the grim news to Caroline.

She stopped eating to question him further. "How can the army order you off your lands or justify an attack on the Red Shields and other bands who aren't to blame for what those . . . other Indians did?" she asked, relieved she didn't spit out "bloody renegades" in her moment of distress. Besides her grave concern for these people and for War Eagle, she was worried about David and other innocent whites who would be ensnared by a vicious war.

"To the whites and their government, an Indian is an Indian, an enemy, and we are all at fault for troubles in our territory. The Indian agent, the commanders at Forts Laramie and Kearny, and the white government in Washington have been told what happened here and who is to blame for the raids and retribution strikes. They also have been told that in some situations, the guilty ones were whites dressed as Indians. One white gang was captured while committing a deadly robbery on a stage and they had proof that gang was responsible for robbing and slaying soldiers on another day." He knew those facts to be accurate, as he had been involved in those incidents and had written those informative but futile letters last summer, though he did not reveal those events to her.

"The truth does not matter to them; for if they accept it, they have no justifiable reason to make such demands on all Lakotas or to attack any band at random. As for the raids and slayings done by the Brules, many had just cause, as with the lethal assault on Lieutenant Grattan and his troop at the end of last summer."

Caroline had studied history and geography during her school years. She had read every book she could get her hands on and had learned the historical events affecting her country and others around the world. She was familiar with the topics of conquest and subjugation, the greed or need for freedom and expansion, for seemingly unstoppable progress. America wanted this land from ocean to ocean, from Canada to Mexico. The Indians were situated in the near center of that desire and were challenging it, so war seemed certain, just as both sides believed they were in the right. From what she had learned, the Indians were many, skilled, and resolved; but the whites far outnumbered them, had better weapons, and were determined to take control of territory they already considered theirs.

Caroline decided that Cloud Chaser was not wrong in his suspicions and assessment of the matter. She hated to think of her brother being a party to such nefarious history, and she could not imagine David doing the kinds of things that would be required for victory over the Indians. "I'm sorry it will come to war between our peoples, Cloud Chaser, but it sounds as if you spoke the truth. I dread to see what will happen in this territory and to your band since peace is impossible. It almost makes me ashamed to be white. I suppose it makes you regret the years you lived among them. Since you did and you learned so much from and about us, don't you realize the whites have more people and weapons than the Indians do? You will be going up against a mighty force. How can you possibly win?"

"I have told my people and our allies the things I learned while I lived among the whites and during my journey homeward and from soldiers at the forts near our territory, as did the ten chiefs who traveled to Washington with Agent Fitzpatrick after the signing of the Long Meadows Treaty four years ago." He did not include the eleventh chief, who was so overwhelmed and depressed by what he saw—their awesome numbers, their powerful weapons, and their "magic" possessions—that he took his life upon returning home.

"No matter the odds against us or the perils we will face or the sacrifices and sufferings we might endure, does a man of honor not have to battle for what he believes is right, for what belongs to him? Does a man of honor not fight to protect his family, home, people, and lands? You are a good woman and have much honor, so would you not do and feel the same?"

Caroline was pleased by his opinion of her, but it did not affect her honest response. "A man or woman of true honor could do no less."

Cloud Chaser grinned and added, "You are also a woman of courage and intelligence, for you speak wise words and feel things deeply." *There is no doubt my youngest brother knows such things and is drawn to you.*

As she smiled and nodded her appreciation, he changed the subject. "It is good you encountered and defeated Black Fist of the Crow. He was a fierce raider and slayer of Lakotas. The black upon his hand was the symbol of his name, one he held high and shook in warning and taunting many times in the past. You and my brother have stilled it forever, and we are grateful. Wear Black Fist's weapon in great pride, for you earned it with your courage and cunning, and for saving War Eagle's life."

Caroline wondered if the last part of his sentence was Cloud Chaser's conclusion or if War Eagle had said so during the men's meeting. "I didn't save his life. He fought and killed his enemy."

"If you had not been there or you had not distracted our foe, who is to say War Eagle would still be alive? Accept the honor he has given to you, and the gratitude of our people for your brave deed."

Those feelings and statements surprised Caroline and made her wonder exactly what his brother had told them about the incident and her. She was certain he hadn't mentioned their intimate lapses, nor would she. That thought reminded her to ask, "What does *kawa* mean?"

A baffled Cloud Chaser replied, "To flower. Why?"

"While we were traveling here from the grasslands, Dawn pointed to a flower and said that word. I thought it meant *flower* but I wasn't sure."

Cloud Chaser surmised there was more behind her query than simple curiosity. Perhaps she was trying to change the subject from war or from his brother and that was the first thing to come to mind to use as a distraction. "Flower is *wahca*. She must have meant she had to wait for them to flower before plucking them. Many are used for dyes, medicines, and in cooking. Did she pick them while she talked to you?"

"Yes, and put them in a pouch. I suppose she was trying to explain what she was doing but I didn't know enough of your language by then to grasp her meaning. Thank you for clarifying it for me." After Cloud Chaser smiled and nodded and focused his attention on the remainder of his food, Caroline's mind translated War Eagle's past words: *To flower in the heart.* Did his slip mean she had taken root in his heart like a lovely flower? Or was there a plant called heart flower, perhaps a yellow one or a blossom with that shape so he had given her a nickname or an Indian one since he had said hers was hard to pronounce? Somehow she didn't think so, as a heart flower should be in a shade of red.

She recalled Dawn's genial greeting upon her return and reflected on the talk she had just shared with Cloud Chaser. Did those actions and words mean she was earning the band's respect, even friendship? If so, how would that affect her relationship with War Eagle? Just because he found her desirable as a woman did not mean he had affection for her. Yet, she could hope and pray something special had happened between them. . . .

On the second day after their return, War Eagle watched his silver-haired grandfather—with the aid of a walking stick—head slowly on protesting bones into the forested foothills. He knew the shaman would continue onward until he found an elevated site with a level surface, perhaps a black boulder near a cliff's edge, a secluded spot where he would fast, pray, and seek a sacred vision. With the aid of a peyote button in the small medicine pouch suspended around his neck and in full view of the Great Spirit, the holy man would be granted a revelation.

War Eagle respected and was awed by Nahemana's mystical powers. He knew the day would come when his grandfather's weakening body would rest upon a decorated *wicagnakapi* built of hardwood and constructed on a lofty hill land high off the ground to protect it from scavengers. Nahemana's body would be clad in his finest Elk Dreamer array and se-cured inside a buffalo hide. There it would remain until the forces of Mother Nature claimed it, as his spirit would al-ready be with the Creator. He dreaded for that sad day to come, but it was inevitable; it was a natural part of the Sacred

Circle of Life. Neither he nor his grandfather feared death, though both wanted to walk and breathe upon the earth as long as possible.

Although he had great faith in the shaman and the Creator, War Eagle closed his eyes for a short time and prayed for Nahemana to succeed in his quest and to be safe while doing so. As soon as he finished, he wondered if the Great Spirit would reveal anything about Caroline and, if so, what would it be? What would he do if the Creator revealed that her task among them was done following the battle with Black Fist and the exposure of his cousin's lingering evil, and she must leave? Now that he knew there was a strong bond between them, could he part with her forever? Even if he could not take her as his mate, at least she was nearby and gave him happiness. Would this be the first time in his life when he could not obey the command of his grandfather and the Great Spirit? He prayed that was not true, for he knew what defiant refusal would cost him. . . .

On that same day to their south, General William Harney arrived at Fort Kearny to initiate his campaign against the dreaded Sioux.

Chapter Eight

During the afternoon of Nahemana's departure day, news spread fast in the camp that Chumani—beloved wife of Wind Dancer, their next chief—had gone into labor with her second child. Being a Brule from a band far away, Dewdrops did not have female family members there to help her with that arduous but thrilling event, so Winona joined Chumani in her oldest son's dwelling to assist with the delivery and to take care of the newborn. An excited and proud Wind Dancer went to his father's tepee to await the arrival of his next child while the men worked on their weapons and talked.

During the night, Macha was summoned by Hanmani to help Winona, as the girl was not a wife and a mother and was unskilled with the tasks to be done. Too, Chumani's best friend from her tribe who had joined to her husband's best friend of the Red Shields could not come, for Zitkala was taking care of her sick daughter, who was three, the same age as Tokapa, Chumani's son, who was with Little Turtle, his great-grandmother.

After the two females and Cloud Chaser talked, Casmu

was placed in Caroline's care before the three left the tepee in a rush. She positioned his cradle-board close to her buffalo mat to be sure she would hear if the almost-three-month-old infant awoke and needed tending. She wondered what was happening in Wind Dancer's abode. She also realized that Cloud Chaser and Macha had revealed great faith in her by leaving their cherished son alone in her care. Their action told Caroline they trusted her not to abandon him to escape while everyone was either distracted or asleep. That conclusion pleased her, and she vowed she would not fail in her duty to them.

When the time came for Casmu to nurse the next morning, Macha returned long enough to feed him, cuddling and singing as she did so.

It was obvious to Caroline from the way Macha clung to her son and from her expressions that her new friend was deeply concerned for Chumani. After she took Casmu from his mother, who kissed his face many times and stroked his head of dark hair before hurrying outside, she saw Macha whispering to Cloud Chaser beyond the entry flap before she left again and he returned to the tepee.

Caroline tended Casmu, rewrapped him in his bundle, and secured him in the cradle-board as she had been taught to do. Cloud Chaser watched over him while she fetched fresh water and gathered wood nearby. After building a fire, she prepared their first meal of the day, dried-nut-and-berry bread called *wigliun kagapi* and roasted strips of deer, which Cloud Chaser had slain and butchered during the night while he was too restless to sleep.

As she carried out her chores and later as she and Cloud Chaser ate near the fire beside the tepee and with Casmu resting close by, Caroline noticed War Eagle's occasional glances at her, though she pretended not to see him. She admitted to herself that she could not evict him from the special rooms inside her head and heart where he had taken up residence during their enlightening journey together. She could not forget his irresistible kisses and embraces, his tender gazes and enticing tone of voice, his rescue from the violent storm and fierce Crow warrior, his gentle manner, a lack of violation and abuse by him and mistreatment by his people, his enormous appeal, his seeming desire for her.

Yet, those emotions and occurrences could lead them nowhere, as the path before them was obstructed by too many uncrossable hurdles, especially for him. She could not help wondering if he was as sad and disappointed about their mismatch as she was. She also could not help wondering what he would do if the obstacles were removed by some powerful or divine force. Even if War Eagle desired her as a woman, even liked and respected her, could he ever want more from her than friendship or servitude? If so, could she give up all she was and knew to become his? *No, Caroline Sims, don't even attempt to swim in such dangerous and unknown waters, as you're sure to drown!*

At midday when Macha returned to nurse and cuddle her son, Caroline observed a scene between husband and wife that was similar to the one she had witnessed earlier. Although she was not included in their exchange of words during that hasty visit, Macha did thank her and smiled.

Caroline sensed the woman was becoming more worried and frightened for Chumani with the passing of every hour. She was asked—not ordered—by Cloud Chaser to continue her "good and kind" care of their son until Macha's task was finished. Caroline deduced it was a bad sign that the baby remained in the womb this long, especially being a second child. Although she had no child of her own, she empathized with Dewdrops, who must be scared and exhausted after laboring unsuccessfully for many hours. She liked Wind Dancer's wife, who had been amiable and courteous to her. She prayed again for the woman's safety, and for the struggling infant who could not seem to find a way or the strength to enter this world.

When Macha arrived in late afternoon to nurse her son, Caroline felt compelled to inquire about Wind Dancer's wife and child, telling them how much she liked Chumani and was concerned about the delay in birth. Cloud Chaser told her the baby refused to leave its mother's body, though the top of its head had been showing since that morning. Since Nahemana was far from camp on a vision quest, the shaman—who knew much about medicine ways—could not provide advice or send forth prayers and healing chants.

Caroline told him, "I would be honored to take Dawn's place so she can feed Casmu and get some rest before she collapses from exhaustion. In the white man's world, Cloud Chaser, a doctor sometimes makes a cut in a woman's private region to allow a large baby to come forth, if that is the problem. Since its head is showing, it isn't positioned wrong in the womb. If things continue like this much longer, both Dewdrops and the child could die, will probably die, or suffer great injuries. I've seen many babies being born on our plantation and I've helped my mother deliver a few of them. When a baby couldn't get free of its mother's body, we summoned the doctor and he did the special cutting and sewing while I assisted him. It worked every time. Also, my mother's father was a doctor; he allowed me to watch him work on the sick and injured many times, even help out on occasion. I learned a great deal about medicine and surgery from him."

Cloud Chaser eyed the white woman intently and decided she was being honest. "Can you do this cutting and sewing to save their lives?"

Caroline wondered what would happen to her if she failed and both died or suffered painful complications or received permanent injures. She could be slain, could be horribly tortured before death. She recalled that her maternal grandfather had been murdered by a crazed drunk after his wife's death following surgery, for which the man had granted permission after it was too late to save her. Even her grandmother had been killed when she went to her husband's aid. "I think I can," she murmured in brief panic, then vanquished her cowardice. "No, I'm certain I can do it. I have a small medical kit in my satchel; it belonged to Grandfather. It contains what I need. Except for a scalpel, so I'll need a sharp knife. The blade should be sterilized in a hot flame and then cooled in clean water."

Cloud Chaser studied Caroline again before he decided she could be right and was capable of performing that unusual task. After having spent twelve years in the white man's world, he knew about their good medicines and healing skills. But could he convince his brother about their powers and persuade him to trust her with the lives of his two loved ones? "I will speak with Wind Dancer. If he agrees, I will return for you."

Caroline was pleased and even surprised by Cloud Chaser's favorable reaction, but winning over Wind Dancer would be harder, if at all possible. Too, the chief and/or his wife could object and prevent her assistance. Or Chumani could refuse the strange and painful procedure. In the event Cloud Chaser succeeded, she should ready her kit and herself. She looked at Macha, who was nursing Casmu, and said she was going to be excused. She saw the weary woman look up, smile, and nod permission.

Caroline left the tepee and walked toward the dense forest nearby. Before she entered the tree line, War Eagle approached her.

"Tuktel yati hwo?" he asked just to hear her voice and to view her face, then repeated his query in English. "Where you go?"

She halted, looked at him, and said with pinkening cheeks, *"Leja."*

He nodded and said, "I stay here. Let no one come to forest."

As she warmed from being near him and experiencing his kindness, Caroline thanked him for guarding her privacy and hurried into concealment. She thought it unwise to stop and talk with him or even smile at him in public, so she merely glanced his way and thanked him again in passing. She returned to the tepee, fetched her satchel, retrieved her soap, and scrubbed her hands. She withdrew the medical kit, undid its fasteners, and checked the contents, feeling relieved she had brought it.

She turned toward the entry when she heard footsteps there and saw Cloud Chaser returning alone, and assumed his family had refused her help.

"Wind Dancer says he does not know about such female things, but he begs you to save his wife and child if you possess such magic and skill. I will take you there," he said as Hanmani entered the tepee. Cloud Chaser looked at Macha and asked in their language, "Do you want to remain here or do you want my sister to keep Casmu while you join Winona and Caroline?"

Macha replied, "I will go to help them with Dewdrops."

Caroline did not grasp all of those Lakota words, but she heard the names mentioned and wondered why Cloud Chaser had not said *"ina,"* for *my mother,* when he spoke of Winona. That seemed strange to her, but she lacked the time to ponder that mystery as Cloud Chaser told her to follow him and Macha, which she did, carrying the precious medical kit.

When they reached the other tepee, Caroline saw Wind Dancer waiting for them outside where he had a fire going and a knife resting on a flat rock with its blade in the flames. From his hunkered position, he looked up at her, studied her as intently as Cloud Chaser had done earlier, then took a deep breath before he stood and faced her.

"You possess large medicine magic and healing skills?"

Caroline responded, "I know many of them, Wind Dancer. I believe I can deliver the baby and save their lives. I pray I have not waited too long to offer my help, but I feared it would not be accepted and would anger you."

The future chief nodded understanding. "The knife is ready."

Noting how well he spoke English, she said, "Cool it in the fresh water and give it to me." She also was aware that Chumani spoke good English, having learned it from a white trapper before she met and married Wind Dancer. That would make it easier to give her explanation, instructions, and comfort. No doubt she and Cloud Chaser were the ones who had taught the others to speak it, and—for some reason—War Eagle was learning more of it fast, though it may have nothing to do with her. She put aside thoughts of her heart's desire to concentrate on the hazardous problem at hand.

Caroline took the knife by its elk-horn handle, sent Wind Dancer an encouraging smile, ducked her head, and entered the tepee. She glanced back and saw Macha lower the flap and lace it in place for privacy, though the interior was stuffy. At least the opening at the dwelling's peak allowed some fresh air to enter and some hot air to escape. Her gaze went to Chumani, who was on her knees beside a sturdy stake that had been driven into the ground. During a contraction, Chumani gripped it and bore down hard to expel the child. As Chumani struggled in vain, Caroline saw her bite on a stick. She surmised that action was supposed to prevent screams and to calm tensions. She noted a carved wooden bowl with steaming water, sweet grasses, and herbs of some kind, which held several more sticks being readied for use when needed.

Caroline smiled and nodded a greeting to the watchful Winona before she approached Chumani. She knelt beside the woman, whose anxious gaze met hers. "I have come to help, Dewdrops. What I must do will hurt, but it will allow

your child to escape your body. You must lie on your sleeping mat for me to do my tasks."

"I will lie on a blanket to not stain our sleeping mat. Use
your magic and skills to save our child," Chumani urged, her
dark eyes teary and puffy and their white areas red-streaked
from too many hours without sleep.

"Tell Winona to get the blanket, for I do not speak your
language well enough and might say the wrong words." She
waited while Chumani spoke with Winona, who fetched and
spread a blanket on the ground in the tepee's center. After
Chumani lay down on her back and her garment was lifted to
her breasts, Caroline placed items she would use on a clean
white petticoat that she had brought with her. Chumani told
her the unused deerskin nearby was for catching the baby
and wrapping it in following its birth.

Caroline was compelled to wait awhile before taking action because another fierce contraction seized the woman
who strained, grunted, and bit hard on the treated stick, fail-
ing once more to achieve victory. During those difficult minutes, Caroline recalled she had been told that before Chumani
joined Wind Dancer, she had been a warrior and hunter for
her people. Cloud Chaser had said the mate of his brother
possessed much courage and prowess. Riding at her husband's side against both Indian and white foes, she had done
many glorious and daring deeds for his band, risking her life
and captivity many times during those great adventures.
Chumani had been honored with the name and rank of "Vision
Woman," for her coming and coups had been foretold in one
of Nahemana's sacred visions years ago; then, were fulfilled.
Even so, Caroline observed that presently Chumani was
shaky, pale, sweaty, weakened, fatigued, and frightened. She
knelt between the woman's parted and raised thighs, quelling
embarrassment because the situation was serious. Indeed the
top of the infant's head was showing, which meant it was
trapped in the birth canal and had been so for a long time. "I
must use my hand to learn what is wrong, but I will be care-

ful," she told Chumani, who nodded permission and braced herself.

As gently as possible, Caroline inserted two clean fingers to examine the child's crown and hopefully to surmise the problem. It was evident the baby's head was large and Chumani's flesh refused to stretch or even tear to give it enough space to exit. "Did Wind Dancer tell you what I must do so the baby can escape your body?"

"My husband said you must use a knife to free our child. He said you must sew up the cut you make as I sew two skins together. It will hurt, but I will bite the stick. I will be still and silent. Do what must be done."

"I must tell you, Dewdrops, when a baby's head is trapped for so long in this way, it has a . . . strange shape when the child is freed. Do not be afraid or worried, for it will change before the next full moon. It may be tepee-shaped for some time, but it will soon become round," Caroline explained, choosing words she hoped Chumani understood, and knowing the moon had been full only a few nights ago. When Macha lifted Chumani's head after the woman nodded and gave her something to drink, Caroline asked what it was and hoped it wasn't some unknown herb that was slowing delivery.

Chumani swallowed ad said, "Willow bark to help soften the pain."

From days with her grandfather, Caroline was familiar with willow bark tea treatment so she relaxed. "Are you ready to do this task?"

Chumani took a deep breath and nodded. She replaced the softened stick between her teeth and ordered herself to stay motionless and quiet. Never had she been so afraid and uncertain in her life, not even during the many daring rides she had made against their enemies four summers past. She closed her eyes and prayed for her child's survival, even if that victory demanded the sacrifice of her life, though she also prayed it would not.

Caroline lifted the knife, slipped her fingers between the

child's head and mother's body, and was amazed how easily and quickly the reddened flesh gave way with the sharp blade. Blood ran forth but she could not use the alum powder as a styptic at that point, as it could get into the child's eyes, nose, or mouth. She laid aside the knife and, when a contraction started, told Chumani, "Push hard, Dewdrops; the opening is larger now."

It required only one more contraction and bearing down for the baby's imprisoned head to find freedom. As she had witnessed doctors doing, with haste and care, Caroline removed the torn veil and wiped the infant's eyes and mouth with a cloth ripped from her petticoat. Without much delay and with another determined push from Chumani, Caroline caught its slick body as it almost gushed forth in eagerness to show itself at last.

After she placed the newborn on Chumani's warm frame, Caroline moved aside so Winona could take over to cut the umbilical cord in a certain way as was their custom, and as she had been told to do by Cloud Chaser as they approached Wind Dancer's tepee. As she awaited the passing of the afterbirth, Caroline watched the older woman leave several inches of the lifeline attached to the baby, then strap it down to the newborn's stomach using a leather strip around its waist until the excess fell off. After showing the girl to Chumani, Winona took the infant aside to clean and bundle it.

As soon as the placenta was expelled, Macha cut off the remaining umbilical cord and laid it on a piece of bark so Winona could prepare it in their custom. She placed the afterbirth in a pouch and laced it snug, as it would be buried later in the forest and covered with heavy rocks by Winona, to be reclaimed by Mother Nature, who was thanked for the use of that gift.

Caroline used fresh water and strips from her petticoat to bathe and dry Chumani's loins. She removed a cork stopper from a small glass vial and sprinkled white alum powder on the incision to halt the bleeding so she could see to insert the stitches. She chose the curved wire needle instead of the straight one and prepared it with the Chinese suture thread that was called "silver wire 1/4 ounce silk." She held up the needle and allowed Chumani to view it while explaining what she was about to do. "I will work as fast and gently as I can, Dewdrops, but it will hurt and I must be careful to do it right. The loops I'll make are called stitches; they remain in your body for seven suns while the cut heals. On the eighth sun, I cut the ties and remove the *hahunta,*" she said, using the Indian word for thread.

As soon as she nodded comprehension and permission, Chumani braced herself for the piercings of the tiny and sharp-pointed bow. As the white woman did her task, Chumani thought of the cuttings and piercings her husband had received on his chest from the shaman's knife and the eagle's talons in preparation of his Sun Dance ritual. She winced at the pain, but did not jerk or flinch. This event was something she must endure with courage and prowess, even gratitude for what it had achieved. Her child was alive and safe, and soon she would be healed. To distract herself from the prickings and tuggings, she watched Macha tend her daughter, who was crying now, a joyous sound to her ears. She hoped her beloved husband was close enough to detect those cries, as they would tell Wind Dancer their baby had been born thanks to Caroline. And thanks to his brother for capturing the white girl and bringing her to their camp. Already Caroline had helped save War Eagle's life and now had saved that of this precious little one nearby. Mutely she prayed to the Great Spirit who had enabled such events to happen and such blessings to be received.

Chumani's gaze traveled to a humming Winona, who had prepared the cord with preserving herbs and other things from nature. She watched the child's grandmother coil and insert the umbilical cord inside a leather tortoise that—as was the custom—Winona had made for the baby to wear around its belly until age two, when it would be attached somewhere on its clothing. A second leather creature—a sand lizard—would be secured in full view on the cradle-board to dupe any evil spirit who might try to steal the child's lifeline, as a sand lizard was fast and cunning and difficult to catch.

She saw her husband's mother rock her body back and fort as she sewed shut the insertion opening along the edge of the tortoise's shell. Her gaze returned to the white female as she murmured she was "almost finished."

Caroline clipped the length of silk thread following the last stitch. She washed her bloody hands in the water holder nearby. She sprinkled on a little more styptic, then replaced the cork stopper. She put the needle into the water to wash it, planning to boil it later to thoroughly cleanse and sterilize it. She helped Chumani put on a female breechclout, inserting into its crotch a folded section of material from her petticoat that was filled with cattail down and crushed buffalo chips to absorb the blood that would flow for a few days. Then, Chumani was assisted to her sleeping mat.

As Caroline completed her tasks, Macha cleaned up the birthing area. Her work finished, she praised Caroline for her skills and bragged about Chumani and the infant before she left to tell Wind Dancer and the others the good news. Afterward, she would tend her son and get needed nourishment and long-awaited sleep. Besides, her best friend since childhood would be eager to visit Dewdrops, as Hanmani must present her with a cradle-board, for it was the custom for sisters of the parents to make it. Dewdrops had no sister, so Hanmani had made cradle-boards for the children of both brothers. Such a deed was done to show a sister's love, respect, and pride toward the parents, and to display her many skills.

Chumani lay on her right side, smiling and teary eyed as she looked at her baby, who was nestled against her. Her fingers tenderly stroked the girl's pudgy face and thick dark hair. Her gaze roamed the infant's large head, which did have a conical appearance. She recalled Caroline had said it would go away soon, and she believed the woman who had wrought this magic.

She looked at the white captive, who was watching them and smiling. "You are a good woman, Caroline," she said. "I thank you for this gift of life. You will be called a friend by me and my husband. When I am healed and strong again, "I will make you a gift of thanks. This daughter will be named Inunpa, for she came *Second* to me and my husband." Before anyone could speak, Chumani jested, "I would call her Comes Hard or Friend Brings Her, but her name was chosen many full moons past if she entered this land as a female."

Caroline noticed how relaxed and cheerful Chumani was as she talked and joked as if they were indeed friends. She smiled and said, "She is a beautiful daughter, Dewdrops, and I am honored to be your friend." She did not say that friendship and words of gratitude were enough thanks for her, as she had learned it was bad manners to refuse a gift. As she watched mother and child cuddled together, she felt a mixture of emotions and sensations: calm, elation, relief, pride, and envy. She also was stimulated and awed by the wonder of this miracle and her important part in it. Surely it was to her benefit being the one who had saved the lives of the wife and child of the Red Shield's future chief, the brother of her heart's desire.

Even so, to capture War Eagle's attention, respect, and affection was not why she had helped Chumani, nor was any attempt to better her role in the camp a reason for doing so. Yet, it would please her if those things happened as result of her help today. Perhaps, her excited mind imagined, her deed would prompt her release. But that freedom would have a heavy and painful price, the loss of War Eagle forever. *How, her heart queried, can you lose what you do not possess, will probably never possess?*

Caroline thrust those troubling thoughts from her mind as Hanmani entered the tepee and approached them. She watched the young woman kneel, gaze almost reverently at mother and child, and smile in apparent joy.

In Lakota, Hanmani said to Dewdrops, "I bring you a cradle for your daughter. May it give her many seasons of happiness, protection, warmth in winter, and good dreams on every sun and moon. You suffered long and hard, my sister, but she is with us now, and I thank the Creator."

The grandmother lifted the bundled infant and secured her in the highly decorated and skillfully crafted cradle. She tied the leather sand lizard to a piece of the top section, then replaced the baby by its mother, which was the signal to summon the father and the family to view the child.

Hanmani leapt to her feet to beckon the others. She noticed Caroline standing at a distance to give them privacy during this special event, or perhaps awaiting the command to leave. For a brief time, she could not help remembering that the mother of her heart's desire also was white—Sparrow, mother of Red Wolf of the Cheyenne, friend and ally of her brother War Eagle. Nor could she forget that Cloud Chaser was half white, and she loved him as much as she did her other two brothers. She smiled and said in English, "Thank you, Caroline."

Caroline smiled, and said, *"Pilamaya,* Hanmani." As the men—Rising Bear, Wind Dancer, and Cloud Chaser—entered, she wondered what she should do now—go or stay, speak or keep silent. She was surprised when the father halted in front of her before approaching his wife and newborn.

"My heart feels great joy and pride in your deed," he said. "I thank the Great Spirit for sending you to us. You are a woman of much honor and skills. I thank you for saving my mate and child. It is good you are here."

An emotional lump entered her throat and played havoc with her speaking, but Caroline finally managed to say, "Thank you, Wind Dancer, for trusting me and allowing me to help them. Both will be well and strong very soon. Your

knife," she said as she held it out to him, and he accepted its
return with another smile before joining his wife.

Wind Dancer was handsome, tall, muscular, kind, and intelligent. With numerous coups painted or beaded on his
tepee—horses, weapons, and certain garments—he was a
man of enormous courage and prowess. From what Caroline
had witnessed so far, he was loved, respected, and obeyed by
his people. There was a regal air and majestic look about
him, no doubt the results of years of training and practice to
become the next chief. She felt as if she was in the presence
of a man who would be a great leader. She noticed that his
father did not join or speak to her, but Rising Bear looked
her way and nodded before he focused his attention on his
family. But Cloud Chaser did join her for a few words.

"You did a brave and skilled deed, Caroline. Everyone in
my family is grateful to you for saving their lives and ending
their suffering. Perhaps this event was why you were sent to
us and why the Great Spirit did not allow War Eagle to take
you to the Cheyenne camp. Most of our people will feel and
think the same way. I wish this good deed could earn you
your freedom, but this is not the time for you to leave us with
war approaching. If we spoke for your release, some would
resist it in fear of you revealing our strength and my brother's
past deed to the soldiers. I am sorry."

Caroline replied in matching whispers, "Don't worry,
Cloud Chaser; I didn't perform this deed to earn my freedom. I understand your people's hesitation and reluctance to
release me. In their position, I would feel and do the same
thing. Besides, Dewdrops will need me to remove the stitches
in a week; and, with soldiers on the move, I wouldn't know
where to find my brother. I'm probably safer here for the
present. But thank you for believing in me and becoming my
friend. Is it all right if I leave now? I'm sure your wife needs
my help so she can get some rest."

"You are kind, Caroline. Return to my tepee and help

Dawn. Then, you must also rest. I doubt you got much sleep last night."

As she started to depart, Chumani halted her for a moment as the new mother smiled radiantly and thanked her again; so did a grinning Wind Dancer and Hanmani. As for the chief and his wife, Rising Bear and Winona simply nodded. The actions of War Eagle's family pleased and elated Caroline, but she wondered where he was and why he hadn't come to visit the new baby. Perhaps it was because she made him uneasy. No doubt he would come to visit as soon as she was gone.

Caroline learned the reason for his absence as she exited and headed for Cloud Chaser's tepee. She saw War Eagle and two braves—his friend Swift Otter and Dawn's brother River's Edge—returning to camp from a hunt, that fact apparent by the large buck lying across another horse. She saw him look at her, his expression one of confusion and surprise as she departed from his oldest brother's dwelling, alone. Her body warmed from head to feet as she averted her gaze and continued onward to join Dawn. Dusk was closing in fast and she had chores—fetching water and wood, cooking, and eating—to do before night came.

War Eagle leapt off his horse and asked his friends to tend it for him while he went to check on Chumani's condition, promising to return soon and help them skin and butcher the animal. As he hurried in that direction, he truly was concerned about his brother's wife and unborn child, but he also wanted to learn what Caroline had been doing there.

War Eagle was stunned to discover what had taken place during his absence. His heart and mind filled with pride, elation, and astonishment as he listened to the stirring tale of Caroline's deed. He was surprised and overjoyed when his family thanked him for capturing her, for not taking her away, and for the Great Spirit guiding him to her on the grasslands. He looked at the newborn girl, bundled securely so that all he could see was her face with ample cheeks. He glanced from Wind Dancer to Chumani to the infant, realizing how happy and fulfilled the couple was. The sight flooded him with yearnings for his own wife and child and tepee. Yes, he wanted those precious things . . . but with a forbidden woman, a white female whom he could no longer deny that he loved and craved beyond measure. . . .

After the short visit and as he departed to return to his friends and their task, War Eagle wondered if he should go to Cloud Chaser's tepee and thank Caroline, as he was tempted to do. Just to look upon her up close, to hear her voice, to see her smile, to let her know he was not a cruel enemy would be nourishing to his spirit. As his gaze touched on a watchful Two Feathers, he decided a visit was unwise. Yet, he vowed he would find a private time and place to speak his gratitude to her, perhaps even find a cunning way to capture another kiss. . . .

Nahemana returned to camp on the third day after his departure and sought out Two Feathers upon arrival. He asked the young man to walk with him in the cool forest so they could speak in private. The son of the chief's sister obeyed him as expected and required by their law. Nahemana took a seat on a large rock and motioned for the warrior to take the smaller one beside it, compelling Two Feathers to look up at him. The shaman glanced skyward, closed his age-clouded eyes, repositioned his aching body, and took a deep breath.

"Why do you seek me out on this sun, Wise One?" Two Feathers asked. "What evokes your delay in speaking? Did the Great Spirit give you a message for me?"

Nahemana locked his gaze with the other man. "Yes, firstborn son of Pretty Meadow and Runs Fast, Wakantanka showed many things to me and sent a sacred owl to whisper in my ear while I fasted, prayed, and chanted. You have lived for twenty-two circles of the seasons upon the face of Mother Earth. You have become a Sacred Bow Carrier and a

Strong Heart member. You have battled and slain many enemies, gathered many coups, protected your family, and provided much game and possessions for them. The Creator has blessed and protected you in many ways. Why do you seek to cause trouble among our people in a season of conflict and coming war?"

Two Feathers gaped at the shaman. "What do your words mean?"

"When Cloud Chaser returned to us during the last hot season, you battled his acceptance fiercely and with much hatred. After he proved himself to us with great prowess and by risking his life many times, you agreed to make a truce with him, to have peace among all members of our past chief's bloodline. You do not honor the ways of your grandfather, Ghost Warrior, who now lives with the Great Spirit. You show disrespect to his son, our chief, your mother's brother. That is wrong; it is bad; it must halt."

"How do I do such things, Wise One? What did Wakantanka say?"

"Once more, you seek to shame and injure Cloud Chaser. You pull War Eagle into your quarrel with the second son of our chief, grandsons of Ghost Warrior, creations of Wakantanka. He and the spirit of Ghost Warrior are displeased; they worry your bad feelings will bring conflict among us at a time when we must band together tight and strong to defeat our enemies. You must cease distracting War Eagle from his duty as a Sacred Bow Carrier. You must halt distracting Cloud Chaser and Wind Dancer from their ranks of Strong Hearts. You must stop seeking the white captive in trade, for the Great Spirit placed her among us for a good purpose, one that cannot be fulfilled in your tepee. You must cleanse yourself of such weakness."

Two Feathers was angered by the scolding and suspected the old man spoke from what the sons of Rising Bear had told him, and not from what he had seen in vision. He was convinced no message had been sent to him by Wakantanka or Ghost Warrior's spirit. Yet, he could not, must not, call the shaman a false speaker, as all others believed he spoke the truth at all times, so he remained silent and watchful, and consumed by ire.

"I am weak and tired from my vision quest and journey. I must go to my tepee and rest. Remember my words and obey them."

"I hear your words and I will do what is right and good, Nahemana," *but what I think is right and good for me.* Two Feathers watched the slump-shouldered man rise and depart with difficulty, using a walking stick cut and carved for him by Wind Dancer. The vexed warrior scowled to himself, displeased by this turn of events, this intrusion on his life by their shaman who was blinded by his grandsons and a half-breed. Just as Cloud Chaser had intruded on his plans last summer when he stole Macha from him, and when he tricked Wind Dancer and War Eagle into turning against him!

If only his mother had been born a man and born first or he had come from the seed of Rising Bear, Two Feathers fretted, he would be the chief's son and be next in line to become the Red Shield leader, a rank he craved. Rising Bear did not deserve to hold the highest rank in their band, for he had shamed himself with a white woman—a captive—long ago; Cloud Chaser was proof and a constant reminder of that weakness and evil.

My love and respect for our chief was slain long ago when he dishonored himself. When Rising Bear leaves Mother Earth, if Wind Dancer falls to an enemy's blow and War Eagle shames himself with his new white captive, I will be next in line as Ghost Warrior's grandson to become chief, for Cloud Chaser's tainted blood will not allow him to tie on that bonnet. I will be the one to lead our people against the enemy and defeat them. I must not allow Nahemana's false words to kill my dream. But I will not ask to trade for the white girl again. I will let her ensnare War Eagle in a trap for me. Then, Wind Dancer will live no more, just as my first mate lives no more to trouble me. I will become chief; that is my true destiny.

Nahemana went to the chief's tepee to meet with Rising Bear, Wind Dancer, Cloud Chaser, and War Eagle to reveal his talk with Two Feathers and his shocking vision. Later, he would relate that message to the council.

After the five men gathered there, the shaman was told of the child's difficult birth and of how Caroline had saved them with "big medicine and magic."

"It is good the Great Spirit sent her to us to carry out such deeds," he said. "If He had not guided you to her and you had not obeyed His commands to capture her and to keep her among us, War Eagle, you, Dewdrops, and the baby could be dead on this sun and many would be mourning our losses. The Creator often works in mysterious ways to protect His loved ones. Did more happen while I was on the sacred hills seeking His guidance?"

"There is nothing more to reveal to you. Tell us of your vision, Wise One," Rising Bear coaxed as he perceived deep concern and even hesitation in his wife's father. What, he worried, had the shaman been shown that was so alarming that he dreaded to reveal it?

Chapter Nine

Nahemana looked at the anxious chief, nodded, and said, "I saw a scene of great destruction and suffering, *Zintka-togleglega* clad in their finest blue feathers chased and encircled a large flock of *Ihuhaotila,* but the enemy's shouts were not as that bird's call; they were shouts of hatred and scorn and revenge. The *Ihuhaotila* tried to flee them, but the jays were too many and too strong, eager to swoop down on the brown-clad sparrows and slay them. The birds changed into bluecoats and Lakotas, and a fierce battle followed. Soon, many Lakotas lay dead or badly wounded. Mother Earth cried as she drank their blood, for it tasted bitter in her mouth. The grass and rocks were painted red with it against their wills, and the blades hung their heads in sadness and shame. I heard many death chants from warriors who were entrapped by countless enemies, their quivers empty of arrows, their lances and knives and war clubs useless against the bluecoats' long firesticks and big thundersticks. I heard women wailing for their losses, and children crying in pain and fear while the jays sang in victory."

"What does the vision mean, Wise One?" Rising Bear asked in dread.

Nahemana shook his head. "I do not know why I was shown such a fierce event, for I saw no Red Shields among them."

"That is good, is it not, Grandfather?" Wind Dancer asked.

Although he knew what his grandson meant, the shaman said in a gentle tone, "I do not know, but the death of any Lakota is bad."

Wind Dancer concurred, "That is true, Grandfather. Does the vision mean Red Shields must not battle the soldiers or we will die as they did?"

"That was not revealed to me during this vision quest."

War Eagle sensed another hesitation and suspected there was more bad news to come, so he asked, "What more did you see, Grandfather?"

As Nahemana's troubled gaze traveled from man to man, he said, "A betrayer walking among us, but his face and body were not exposed to me. They were concealed beneath a black wolf's head and flowing hide. He was stalking his prey among us, but his target was kept hidden from my old eyes and ears. I spoke with Two Feather upon my return, but I do not know if he is or will become that cunning enemy." The shaman went on to relate that conversation and his impressions of their baffling family member.

"Do you think my cousin spoke false to you, Grandfather?"

"Yes, Wind Dancer, for some evil clouds his eyes and mind this season. Though its source was hidden as an underground stream, I felt anger flowing beneath his surface, and he doubted my words. He said he would 'do what is right and good,' but I fear he does not know or accept what is truly honest and pure. I fear that a powerful dark force lives within him; it troubles and misguides his spirit. If he does not resist and slay it, he will be consumed and destroyed, and others may become ensnared in that battle."

Rising Bear said, "That will injure my sister's heart and stain his family's honor, so we must pray to Wakantanka to clear his eyes and mind."

"That is wise and true, my chief and friend," Nahemana

agreed. "But first, Two Feathers must be willing to change, to obey the Great Spirit."

Cloud Chaser said, "I will try to make peace with him once more to avoid trouble among our people. He may not accept my offer, for his hatred of me runs deep and strong, as the underground stream you spoke of."

Nahemana told him, "If he refuses peace, the Creator will punish him. Obey our laws and ways, Cloud Chaser, and no blame will fall upon you. All will see it is you who lives by the Four Virtues, not Two Feathers."

After Cloud Chaser nodded and they talked for a while longer, War Eagle asked, "Did the Great Spirit reveal anything about the white captive who saved the lives of my brother's mate and child and who fought Black Fist with me? Has she fulfilled her purposes for being placed among us? Did Wakantanka say to keep her here or to release her for her good deeds?"

"I was shown and told nothing about her, my grandson. But if the Great Spirit was finished with her, He would have told me to free her."

War Eagle tried not to expose his elation at that news, as this was too soon to reveal his feelings about her, even to his family. But his mind leapt with joy and excitement that Caroline would remain near him and that she was working her way into his family's and many of his people's hearts with her good ways and deeds. He hoped and prayed she would become as acceptable to them as she was to him, as he would approach her that very sun if things were different for and between them. But if that time came, he mused, did he dare to claim her as his mate? What would he have to do and sacrifice if he did so? Would Kawa Cante agree to join with him? Or would it be impossible for a captive to love and accept her captor, a captor whom she had witnessed slaying her people and who must battle them again? And how long would it be before he had answers to those important questions? *I must win you, Heart Flower, for your roots have spread throughout my body and every part of it loves and desires you.*

The day after General William Harney began his march up the North Platte Road, a feast in Chumani's honor took place in the Red Shield camp which was nestled against their sacred Black Hills for the winter. As was their custom the event was held on the fourth day after a child's birth and prior to the Naming Ceremony. The three sons of Rising Bear and some of their friends had hunted for fresh game to be served at the celebration. Winona, Macha, Hanmani, Zitkala, Pretty Meadow, Caroline, and other women had roasted and stewed the various meats and prepared other foods and breads to accompany them during the meal.

Chumani, the honored guest, had chatted with the busy women as they carried out their tasks in cheerful efficiency. Both she and the baby were doing fine, and everyone in camp knew the reason why—the white captive's medicine skills. Many of the people had expressed their gratitude to Caroline for saving their lives, which pleased Chumani greatly.

As the people ate and talked and congratulated the parents and presented the Vision Woman and new mother with gifts, Caroline watched them from a distance at Cloud Chaser's tepee where she tended Casmu. It was evident to her how close the band and families were and how special children were to them and to the continuance of their bloodlines. Using care not to be obvious, she observed War Eagle with his family, friends, and other band members. Each time she caught him slyly glancing in her direction, sheer delight washed over her. He was a unique and irresistible man. She yearned to be kissed and embraced by him again, countless times, to spend time with him, just talking or taking a stroll. She craved to get to know him better, and for him to do the same with her.

How long, Caroline fretted, would her existence continue in this state of painful denial of her heart's desire, in this state of not knowing what would happen to her tomorrow or next week or next month or next year? Would she spend the remainder of her life as a captive in Cloud Chaser's tepee with War Eagle just out of her reach? Would she be forced to watch him court, marry, and have children with another woman, with one of his own kind? How could she endure such anguish and defeat?

Stop feeling sorry for yourself, Caroline; pity never helps anything. Eat the food Hanmani brought to you and study the in-progress lesson you're viewing. You just might learn something valuable and useful.

As soon as everyone finished eating Caroline watched Cloud Chaser approach her with a grin on his face. She listened in surprise and befuddlement as he told her to join them at the gathering, at Chumani's and the shaman's requests. He retrieved Casmu in his cradle-board and guided her to the crowded area where she stood with the chief's family and next to Chumani. She remained quiet and alert as she observed the giveaway ritual to honor the newborn. Cloud Chaser had told her earlier it was the custom to give various gifts to relatives, friends, the poor, and high-ranking men and women of their band to show honor to their newborn child and as a way of practicing Generosity. She also knew Chumani and Wind Dancer's family had been making or collecting *wicaku* for months as they awaited the baby's birth. Sometimes a gift would be a horse, blanket, pouch, prime hide or fur, jewelry, knife sheath, moccasins or garment, headband, or weapons taken from enemies during raids or battles. Before the feast started, she had helped carry and pile the presents on a blanket, and had admired their beauty and quality as she did so.

Last, Chumani turned to Caroline, placed a thong around her neck, smiled, and said in English, "To honor and thank you, our friend, for saving the lives of Dewdrop and our daughter." Then, she repeated the words in Lakota for their people to understand.

Murmurs of *"Han"* and *"Heyapi"* filed the air as many agreed or added their gratitude with words of "Yes" and "It is said." Many even smiled or nodded at Caroline, who returned those kind gestures.

Caroline looked down at the necklace that rested near her heart and touched it in awe. It was a leather medallion with a right hand painted on its center and suspended from a softened leather strip. She had learned that sign language—index and middle fingers touching and lifted with the thumb and the other two curled toward the palm—meant friend and friendship. Near the edges were painted smaller symbols for Dewdrops, Wind Dancer, Red Shields, and a blue eye for her. She looked at Dewdrops, smiled with misty eyes, and said in an emotion-strained voice, *"Pilaymaya,* Chumani."

"It is good," the woman replied and smiled once more.

As the family was positioned for the Naming Ceremony, Caroline did not know if she was supposed to leave or stay until the shaman gently grasped her arm and guided her to stand beside Macha, who was next to Cloud Chaser, then Hanmani, then War Eagle, and the others. It had been difficult, but she had conquered the urge to glance at her beloved when she received the gift and when she walked past him moments ago. Yet, she was all too cognizant of his close proximity and almost intoxicating appeal. Just as she was aware of Two Feathers presence not far away. She had glimpsed the offensive man watching her several times today and—from the corner of her eye—as she followed Nahemana to her current position. No doubt he was angered by the honor and attention she had received. She didn't know why she allowed him to intimidate her so much and so often, as she was safe from his evil clutches under Cloud Chaser's protection, and surely now under that of his family, which included the chief and shaman. She also didn't know why she was being permitted to stand with the head family unless it was because this event would not be taking place if not for her. Still, she was only a lowly captive, one of the enemy. Or was she? . . . If her role had changed, she had not been informed of it. For now, she must quiet those troubling thoughts and observe the event, even though she could grasp only a word here and there.

In his right hand, Nahemana held a long white feather with snowy tufts attached to its quill and held a thick rock with a hollowed-out center in his left one. Slowly burning herbs and sweet grass in nature's container sent forth grayish fumes, which were captured by a mild breeze and swirled about as they drifted upward. First, the shaman prayed to evoke the presence of the Supreme Being, Mother Earth, and other good spirits. "Tunkashila, Maka Hun'ku, Woniyawaste, we summon you to watch this sacred ceremony. Tunkashila, we thank You for those who have lived before us and for all they taught those who came after them. We thank You for those to be born on future suns and moons who will carry on our customs and bloodlines, those who will love and serve You after we live at Your side. Those who stand here in Your sight thank You for sending them to walk upon the face of Mother Earth and we thank Her for allowing us to do so. We thank You for your many blessings, guidance, and protection. Hear and watch us on this sun."

Afterward, he said more prayers as he used the eagle feather to wing smoke—the breath of the Great Spirit—over the infant. "Tunkashila, we thank You for this child who battled hard to enter the world You made for us, and she will be called Inunpa, for she came Second to our chief's son and mate. We ask You to give her strength, courage, and good skills to serve You, her family, and her people with. Guide her and protect her in all things."

He wafted smoke into Chumani's face and said, "Dewdrops, be a good mother to your daughter. Teach her all she must learn to become a good woman and Red Shield."

Chumani—who was still weak and sore from her ordeal, but filled with joy—smiled and nodded, wishing her parents and grandparents could be there for this special ceremony and happy event, but they were camped far away with their Brule band, as her father was their chief.

Nahemana sidestepped to Waci Tate, used the feather to propel wisps into his face, and said, "Wind Dancer, be a good father to your daughter. Protect her and provide for her needs."

He approached Rising Bear and Winona, guided smoke into their faces, and said, "Our chief and his mate, be good grandparents to this child."

Caroline saw the older couple nod that they would do as commanded.

After repeating those actions with War Eagle, Hanmani, Cloud Chaser, and Macha, he told them, "Help Inunpa's parents and grandparents teach her to be a good Red Shield," and all four nodded that they would obey.

To all others present, Nahemana commanded, "Family and friends of Wind Dancer and Dewdrops, help them to carry out the Creator's will."

Then, to the surprise of some present, the shaman stepped before Caroline, swept grayish wisps into her face, and said, "Tunkashila, we thank You for sending this white woman to live among us. We thank You for showing her how to save Inunpa's life when she was too weak to enter this world. Open Ca-ro-line's heart and mind and teach her who and what we are so she will understand and be loyal to us in the dark suns ahead."

Caroline was relieved she did not cough when the smoke was urged into her face and up her nostrils, as she feared that would be an insult to them and their Great Spirit and would place a dark cloud over her and the ceremony. Tears did dampen her eyes, partly from the smoke and partly from deep emotion, and she hoped everyone blamed the latter if the moisture was sighted. She smiled at the gentle-mannered shaman and nodded, though she only grasped some of his words. Once more, she told herself she must work harder to learn their language and customs.

Nahemana looked from one family member to the next and then at the crowd as he finalized the ceremony. "It is done; she will be called Inunpa of the Red Shields. May she be protected and guided by her people and by the Great Spirit until she joins Him many suns from this one."

War Eagle's heart surged with happiness and pride for his brother's victory and for Caroline's inclusion in the stirring event. His spirit soared as high, free, and powerful as the sky creature from whom he had been given a name during his vision quest upon entering manhood. He saw her leaving the area with Cloud Chaser and Macha, but did not approach her because his cousin was watching him with a scowl. So far, he had not been given an opportunity to speak to her alone, but soon he would seek one so he could thank her and praise her for her good deeds. After he reaffirmed that decision, he wondered how such behavior would affect her.

As War Eagle returned to his family's tepee, his mind was flooded with remembrances of their meeting, their ride to the summer camp after her capture, their journey toward the Cheyenne camp, and their intimate moments beneath the ledge during the storm and near the riverbank after the battle with Black Fist. He wanted to share the latter again with her. He yearned to hold her, kiss her, stroke her hair and flesh, and possess her fully. Would he ever be given the chance to do so? If not, this ache within him would increase. Some sun and in some way, he must have his heart's desire, but when and how, he did not know. . . .

Shortly before dusk, Caroline asked if she could take a gift to Inunpa. She showed the rag doll she had made during the last few days to Cloud Chaser, who smiled and gave his permission. She had used the remainder of her demolished petticoat for its head, body, and stuffings. Macha had given her a yellowish oily substance from the buffalo's gall to dye multiple strips almost the color of her own hair. She had used skills her mother had taught her long ago and supplies from her travel repair kit for sewing them into place. She had removed two blue buttons from the bottom of a blouse to give it eyes the shade of hers. The rest of its facial features—nose, mouth, eyebrows, and lashes—had been stained with other dyes from nature. Its dress had been made from a piece torn from the same garment from which she had made a bandage for War Eagle following his fight with the Crow enemy. "I named her Friend Brings, for I helped bring Inunpa into the world. Is it an acceptable gift, or will it be insulting because the doll is white?"

"It is a good and generous gift, Caroline. Dewdrops and Wind Dancer will be pleased and honored. Inunpa will enjoy playing with it when she is older, and it will always remind her of the white woman who saved her life."

"Thank you, Cloud Chaser, and I'll return as fast as possible."

In Wind Dancer's tepee, Chumani took the doll from Caroline and studied the excellent workmanship as she was told its name and the reason why Caroline made it. She smiled and said, "It is good, my friend. I will wrap it in a fur and keep it safe in a pouch until Inunpa can play with it."

Wind Dancer took it from his wife's extended hand and looked at the doll with sunny hair, blue eyes, and white skin. "It is good and generous, Caroline. Thank you for the gift and for the lives of Dewdrops and Inunpa."

"I'm the one who is grateful to you and your people for being so kind to me. I hope everyone here will realize I'm not an enemy to be hated and feared. I will not try to escape and I will not betray your people to mine. I only hope my being in your camp does not provoke an attack on it."

"Do not fear a bad deed, for soldiers do not know you live

among us. If they ride to our camp, it is not to fight for your return. It will be to destroy us and steal our lands. You will not be blamed or punished for their evil."

"Thank you, Wind Dancer, and I'm sorry about the wicked things my people do to yours; they are wrong. You are a good man and will be a good chief for your people. I must go and help Dawn before it's dark outside."

Wind Dancer only nodded with a pleasant expression, but Chumani spoke to her again before she left their tepee.

"Go with our thanks, my friend. We will talk more on a new sun."

In Cloud Chaser's tepee that evening as they ate their last meal of the day, he related to Caroline what the shaman had said to her during the Naming Ceremony, and what Nahemana had said to the others present.

Caroline was surprised to hear those words, and they pleased her. Yet, she decided not to comment on them. Cloud Chaser's mood appeared somber, and she wondered if her lack of a response disturbed him. To check out that possibility, she murmured, "Your father and mother were so proud and happy today."

Cloud Chaser's mind had wandered during her silence as he thought about the doll Caroline had made and given to Inunpa, a doll with the same colorings of his own mother, who had missed Casmu's birth and Naming Ceremony. He had not asked his father if he had been given such a ceremony, but he suspected there had been none due to the circumstances of his conception—one encounter between Rising Bear and Margaret Phillips, who had come to be known as Omaste, meaning *Sunshine* for her golden hair. Yet, that unintentional sharing of a mat had resulted from his father's grief and loneliness and perhaps his manly needs during the difficult time when Winona was a captive of the Pawnee for two years and was feared dead or lost to him forever. He had been named Cloud Chaser at birth, not given a childhood name, which usually was changed during a brave's vision quest upon entering manhood as with his brothers. He remembered his mother telling him that she had selected it, not his father. Despite his mixed blood, he had been reared as Rising Bear's son until he was taken far away by the Martins, a year after his mother was lost to him. He could not help wondering if his life would have been different if Winona had not escaped and returned and Omaste had lived and perhaps become Rising Bear's wife.

In the midst of those recollections and thoughts, Caroline's query crept into his mind. "My mother is dead. She died—" Suddenly he realized what he was saying and halted, scolding himself for his distraction and slip.

A startled Caroline asked before she could stop herself, "Winona isn't your mother? How so? You said you were not adopted. I'm confused."

"My mixed bloodline will not help you escape your fate as captive."

"I don't follow your meaning, Cloud Chaser."

He looked at her with a stoic expression and used a firm but harsh tone to close the matter as he stated, "I am the blood son of Rising Bear, but not Winona; that is all you need to know about me."

Caroline did not apologize for asking about him, but nodded obedience to his implied command not to pry any further. From his tone of voice and expression, he was troubled by his slip of the tongue and by something that had happened in his past. She knew he had been captured in this territory at the age of ten and had been reared in Oregon by an elderly white couple until the age of twenty-two. He had returned to his people last year, but there was more to his story, to his history, to his birth than he would reveal. Many questions filled her mind. Who was his mother? When and how had she died? What did he mean by "mixed bloodline"?

And why had he said it "will not help you escape your fate as a captive"?

Without looking at Cloud Chaser and while pretending to focus on her food, Caroline called his image to mind and studied it. Was it possible her owner was part . . . white? That his mother had been a white captive? Had Rising Bear taken a second wife or simply . . . mated with her? Perhaps, if she had guessed right, that incident was a shameful secret, one kept hidden in a box that she must not attempt to unlock and peek inside. If her deductions were accurate, her mind continued to reason, it would explain his appearance, that strong hint of *whiteness* in him, despite his long brown hair and mostly Indian features. It also would explain—wouldn't it?—why War Eagle had chosen his second brother to be her owner, a man who would understand and accept a white woman in his tepee. After all, Chumani already had a son of three years and was heavy with child number two when she was captured, so Dewdrops—who spoke English—could have used her help more than or as much as Macha. . . .

Perhaps, Caroline reasoned, it would be smart to test his feelings toward her and learn if he wanted her out of his sight now that she had discovered his closely guarded secret. "Would you like for me to stay with Dewdrops for a few days to tend the baby so you and Dawn can have some privacy for a while? I've been living and working underfoot for a long time and you two have been married for only a little over a year."

Cloud Chaser grasped her meaning from her lowered gaze, flushed cheeks, and strained voice. "That isn't necessary, Caroline, but I thank you for your generous offer. A man and wife do not . . . touch each other on the sleeping mat until their child is two years old. It is believed that doing so may harm the mother's milk, and it would be unwise to create and carry another child until the other one is weaned." To change the subject, he queried, "Did you have black captives?"

"What?" she asked, baffled by that question.

"You said you lived on a plantation and helped deliver babies there. From what I learned while I lived among the whites, they used slaves to work their land, black captives from far away across the big waters."

Caroline realized he would talk about his existence with the whites, but not about his strange birth. She told him, "My father did not believe in slavery. He hired men to work our land and hired a woman to help Mother in our home. Those who had families were allowed to live in small houses Papa built near the edges of our plantation. That gave them and us privacy."

"So you think it is wrong to capture and enslave a person?"

Caroline hoped, considering her situation, it wasn't a trick question that would insult him and entrap her with her answer. "Yes."

Cloud Chaser smiled. "It is good you are honest. Red Shields do not capture or trade for slaves, Indian or white. But we cannot refuse one as a gift from another band or tribe member; to do so would offend and wound the giver. You were captured and are being held here because you could be a threat to us if you told your people what you witnessed with the soldiers. We do not want the army to know Red Shields carried out that attack, but it was necessary for our protection and survival. Even if you promised not to do so, the soldier chief could force or trick the truth from you. We do not make you labor hard for us. Your chores are to earn you a place to live and eat."

"I understand your motives and believe what you say, Cloud Chaser. It gave me great joy and pride to help Dewdrops with her baby, and I was honored by my inclusion in the Naming Ceremony and by Dewdrop's gift to me. I view you and your family and most of your people as my friends. I wouldn't do anything intentional to harm any of you. I don't want revenge."

"Not even on War Eagle who captured you and killed the soldiers?"

Caroline's heart skipped a few beats at the unexpected mention of his name. "No, because I understand he had no other choice. I view him as a friend, but I do not know if he views me in the same way."

"That is good, as I do not want you to hate my brother for doing his duty to us. But if you did, I would understand and forgive you."

"That's very kind of you, Cloud Chaser. How did you and your brothers get your names? You mentioned something one night about vision quests. How do they work?" *I want to know more about War Eagle and your band.*

"I will tell you in a short time. First, I must speak with Dawn."

I suppose she is wondering what we're saying, especially since you behaved so oddly minutes ago. "Tell her I'm trying harder to learn your language so I can talk with her. Friends should be able to communicate."

He sensed that this was not the time to reveal his wife's secret, but soon that secret must be told.

As the couple conversed for a while, Caroline could not help noticing the love shining in their eyes. It was evident to her that their bond was strong and deep. In her opinion, it was the same with Wind Dancer and Chumani. The brothers were lucky to have found and married such good women. And she was lucky that Dawn was not a jealous or insecure female, considering the amount of time her husband spent with another woman, a white woman, a young woman. Yes, she liked Cloud Chaser and thought he was handsome, but it was his younger brother who had stolen her heart. If only they were as perfectly matched as the other two couples were. . . .

Cloud Chaser broke into her mental roamings when he was ready to speak, and she listened.

"I will tell you about vision quests now. From the time a

boy is old enough to understand such things, he is taught our customs, history, and laws by his father, grandfather, uncles, shaman, male relatives, and the old ones. He must learn them and obey and practice them. He is trained to hunt, ride, shoot, fight, and track in many ways, sometimes in games with other boys or with playthings. He must learn to show courage and wisdom, to know when to be patient or to act swiftly, to endure hardships, to suffer in silence when necessary, to protect and provide for his family and for others in great want. He must not risk injury or sacrifice his life foolishly, but he must fight to the death if need be. He must do and say nothing to stain his honor, or that of his family or of his people. When he has learned such things and is old enough, he goes into the hills alone after purifying himself in the sweat lodge. He must choose a high and open place beneath the sight of the Great Spirit. There, he fasts, prays, and chants until he is given a sacred vision. Sometimes it takes only a day or two, but it can take as many as four or five."

As Cloud Chaser sipped water, an intrigued Caroline asked, "What if a vision doesn't come or he gets too weak to continue?"

"It is better to die trying or not return to his people than to fail in his task. My first brother's vision told Waci Tate he was to 'dance with the wind;' that means he is to live and ride in freedom, to challenge the powers and dangers of the unseen forces of nature and man, and to soar on its currents as a man above other men. He has done such deeds many times in the past; he has danced around our enemies, often like an unseen wind, and blown them away from our lands. He is a superior warrior and will be a great leader after our father is gone. My name, Mahpiya Yutokeca, means 'to chase the clouds.' I am meant to challenge the powers and dangers of the unseen forces of nature and man, which often lurk behind clouds of many sizes, kinds, and colors. I am to chase them away so I and my people can live in freedom and pride. I did so many times last summer and will do so again when your people bring war to our lands."

Cloud Chaser did not give her time to refute his last words, though he doubted she would attempt to do so. "My second brother, Wanbli, was shown a vision of himself standing on the edge of a high cliff at sunset. His hand was lifted toward the sky, and a war eagle, the most powerful and awesome sky creature, flew down and perched upon it without ripping his flesh. The spirit bird looked out over our lands, sought out enemies with his keen gaze, and guided my brother to them by speaking within his head. He is meant to soar in freedom and greatness, to be swift and deadly when he swoops down on our enemies and captures them in his sharp talons. As with Wind Dancer, he is a superior warrior and a skilled party leader. He has earned and deserves the rank of Sacred Bow Carrier. If evil slays Wind Dancer, Wanbli is next in line to become chief and will be a good one."

Caroline was perplexed by his last statement since Cloud Chaser was the second son, but she did not ask for clarity. Besides, her thoughts and emotions were running wildly in another direction. What she had heard about her captor caused her mind to sing happy songs and her body to quiver and burn with scorching desire. She could envision the scene that Cloud Chaser had described, her heart's desire standing tall and proud and brave upon a jagged precipice with a giant bird of prey perched on a balled fist with both silhouetted against a blazing sunset. His bronze frame would be shiny and sleek beneath the fading sun's glow. His long dark hair would be blowing in the wind. His gaze would be intense. What a thrill it would be to run to him and be embraced in those strong arms! To have his potent gaze engulf her. To press her mouth to his and kiss him countless times. To feel his hands caressing her and to sink to the black stone and make passionate—*Caroline Sims! Stop thinking such things!* She swallowed and remarked in a hoarsened voice,

"From what I have seen and been told, the Great Spirit chose perfect names for each of you."

Cloud Chaser realized he had made another careless slip, which was unlike him. Yet, Caroline must not have caught it or she would have queried him about not being next in line as chief. Perhaps she was thinking about War Eagle, as her blue gaze had softened and gleamed as she listened to that part of his revelations. He suspected she was enchanted by his younger brother, just as he suspected War Eagle was potently drawn to her. He wondered what, if anything had taken place between those two during their journey together. For certain, no matter how sly they were, he had seen them stealing looks at each other. What would happen and what would others say and do if War Eagle laid a claim on her? He did not want to think along those perilous lines. "It is late. We must sleep soon. Finish your tasks and prepare your mat. We will talk more on another day."

"Thank you, Cloud Chaser, for teaching me your language and for helping me to understand your people and ways. I'll work hard to learn more, to learn all you'll share with me. And thank Dawn for her patience with me and for allowing you to spend so much time teaching me things."

He was compelled to translate her words to his wife, who smiled and nodded. He was tired tonight, and he hungered for that special closeness with Dawn. He could hardly wait until the necessary span of time passed so he could make love to her again. Even so, she was his life, his heart, his spirit, his destiny. He was the luckiest man in the world to have her. If the time came, he would lay down his life for her and their son. Peace, mercy, how he wished and prayed it were possible, but he doubted it! If only most whites were like his mother, his adoptive parents, Sparrow, Caroline, and some others he had met, it would be possible. Sadly that wasn't the fact, and a bloody war between the two cultures was inevitable, and soon. . . .

* * *

War Eagle was glad a large dark cloud concealed the half-moon above so his stealthy presence near his brother's dwelling would not be seen by others. Yet, he had been unable to resist the urge to hear her voice and hopefully to grasp her words. Now that they were taking to their sleeping mats, he would sneak away to his own. As he had listened to Cloud Chaser and Caroline talk, his heart and mind had soared with joy and relief. How he wished he could be the one teaching her their language and ways, and sharing a tepee with her. His emotional and physical hungers for her grew larger and stronger each day, and the pains of denial gnawed ravenously at him like a starving wolf's empty belly in winter. As with that wild creature and a discarded bone with a little meat still attached, he could force himself to settle and be grateful for even tiny scraps of attention and time from her during these difficult days of separation. Dare he take the enormous risk of reaching out and laying claim to her? The hindrance was, he would not discover the effects of that decision upon his family and people, upon his rank and honor, until it was too late if their reactions were unfavorable. Whom could he ask to advise him, someone who would keep his secret?

What must I do, Great Spirit, for I love and desire her as my mate? Is it wrong to take her as one? Why did You send her to tempt me if I cannot have her? Why did You not allow me to part us if we cannot be together? I am wise in many ways, but not about this matter. I have the courage to face whatever comes from claiming her, but first I must know it is right and good to do so. Only You possess that knowledge. I beg You to share it with me or with Grandfather so he can tell me what I must do. Give me a sign to tell me which path to walk, for I must not shame myself, my family, and people. Show me if I can have the flower of my heart.

War Eagle quietly entered his family's tepee where they were asleep. He lay down on the mat that his mother or sister had spread out for him in its appointed place. He closed his eyes and hoped it would not take long for the Great Spirit to send him an answer about Caroline. Then, he prayed it would be the one he yearned for and needed as much as the air he breathed and the food and water he consumed for survival. . . .

Chapter Ten

"Hello, Caroline. Where you go?"

"Hau, Wanbli. *Contanka on can. Hanyetu ecaca uwo."* She greeted him and told him she was going to the forest for wood as night was coming soon.

"I come, protect. Go," he said and motioned for her to continue so she could finish before darkness. If someone saw them together, he had a good reason for accompanying her into the woods this late: her safety from predatory animals and any foe who might be lurking and spying near camp.

"Pilamaya." She thanked him as they entered the dense tree line. She was surprised when he talked to her as she gathered scrub wood in a hurry to use in the morning, just as she was baffled by his concern and behavior.

He leaned against a large tree and revealed in a casual tone, "Next sun, War Eagle to scout white war chief's trail."

Caroline jerked upright. "Wanbli *hinhanna kin heyab iya yo?"*

War Eagle's heart leapt with joy to see how much it disturbed her to learn he was leaving camp tomorrow to spy on the soldiers. "Yes."

Caroline was astonished by how fast and easy the Lakota words for "It is dangerous! Too many white soldiers are with the white war chief" flooded her head and spewed out her mouth. *"Okakipe yelo! Nina ota ska akicita un ska akicita itancan." Including my brother.* "Wanbli *zuya?"* She asked if he was going to attack them, to make war on them.

War Eagle wondered if she was worried about an attack on her people, or if he might be harmed or slain. He hoped it was the latter. "I scout, no fight. Many bluecoats. Many firesticks. Scout with Swift Otter, River's Edge, Cloud Chaser, Broken Lance."

"Hiya Waci Tate, hiya ozuye, hiya Wiyaka Nunpa?"

"No Wind Dancer, no war party, no Two Feathers." He translated her words as his response, and noted her mention of his troublesome cousin. *"Zaptan* scout," he said as he held up five fingers since he did not know that word number in English. Suddenly he grinned, then chuckled.

"Taktokanun han he?" She asked what he was doing as she patted her mouth and pushed her lips into a smile.

"Caroline Lakota *ia.* War Eagle speak English. You know much." Yes, she had learned much of his language, a great deal more of it recently, which was true of him with English. Even if she did get some words out of order at times, he always grasped her meaning.

She smiled, then laughed softly. "War Eagle speaks good English."

"Caroline Lakota *waste ia."* He returned the praise and smiled again.

"I do not know how to say this in Lakota: I will be happy to teach you more English so you can speak with whites or soldiers if necessary."

He guessed all except one word. "What . . . nes-see-sary mean?"

"Cin." She spoke the word for *want, need, to desire.*

"Good task when War Eagle return," he agreed. "Thank

you." He was pleased by her generous offer; it would serve him well to be able to know what the whites were saying when he spied on them or any soldiers he confronted.

For a while, they were silent as she gathered more wood and placed it in the leather carrying-sling.

As she worked, War Eagle watched her. He could not forget what he had overheard last night as he listened near Cloud Chaser's tepee, nor his thoughts and prayers ensuing at that stirring event. She moved easily and gracefully. He wished he could reach out and touch her. He got so much joy out of just speaking to her, hearing her voice and laughter, looking at her, and spending time with her.

Caroline sensed War Eagle's constant gaze upon her, for it was potent and arousing. Did he realize how he affected her? Was his temptation accidental or intentional? Was he trying to attract her attention, evoke her affection, heighten her desire for him? Whether he meant to or not, that was exactly what he was doing! How and why was she being drawn to this particular man, one so unlike her, her very captor! She belonged to Cloud Chaser and Dawn, but War Eagle still had a say-so in her fate, as proven by his attempt to take her to the Cheyenne camp. Did his control extend to being able to recover her if he so desired?

As Caroline picked up the last piece of wood, she sighted a lovely and fragrant night-blooming flower nearby and plucked it. She placed the bloom in the sling, turned, and handed it to War Eagle. "Thank you for protecting me, Wanbli. *Wakan Tanka nici un.*" She saw him take the flower, glance at it, then fasten his alluring gaze to hers; and she could not look away.

War Eagle was moved by her action and last sentence: *May the Great Spirit go with you and guide you.* If he was not mistaken, she was just as flooded by love and desire as he was. She was standing so close. Unable to halt himself, he lifted his empty hand and allowed its fingers to brush a stray lock from her flushed cheek. Without breaking their gazes, his head bent forward and he fused their mouths, and was thrilled to his core when she responded.

Caroline lacked the willpower or wits to refuse his intoxicating kiss. Her arms slipped around his waist and she leaned against him, suddenly feeling weak and trembly. She felt his arms embrace her; then, he pulled her closer—if possible—to him. After a long, deep, and stirring kiss, his lips wandered over her hot face and across her neck. He pressed them to her hair, upon each closed eye, and on her left ear where she felt the heat of his breath. She quivered in rising need, and was shocked it did not alarm her. To crave the man one loved was normal, but she could not lie with him unless they were married. Yet, she somehow knew that would be a glorious and fulfilling experience, one she hoped to share one day in the future. Despite her intentions, she was soon swept away by the flood of passion.

War Eagle felt charged with energy and strength, with joy and pride, with hope and pleasure. *"Niye mitawa,* Kawa Cante," he murmured before kissing her a final time. He must not risk them being found like this, hard as it was to halt their closeness and revelation of feelings. *"Nisnala ya yo,"* he told her. *You go alone,* before someone came searching for her.

Caroline looked up into his handsome face and saw him smiling down at her. She read the desire in his eyes and saw how rapidly he was breathing. It was getting dark, so she surmised he was sending her back to camp without him so no one would know they had been together, and perhaps to give him time to quell his ardor. She smiled and nodded compliance. She told him to be careful. *"Itonpa.* Return soon."

War Eagle nodded and used one hand to urge her toward camp before he changed his mind about their parting and his caution. As she walked away with the loaded sling suspended over her back, he raised the crushed blossom to his nose and smelled its sweet scent. He recalled his final prayer words from last night: *Show me if I can have the flower of my heart.* Had the Great Spirit answered him this soon and in this manner? With all of his being, he hoped so. He untied the thong of his medicine bundle and placed the special coup inside it, and smiled in victory. . . .

As Caroline left the tree line, she was happier than she had been in a long time. Surely he loved and wanted her, as he had whispered, "You are mine, Heart Flower." Perhaps he hadn't meant to do so or didn't realize he had spoken loud enough for her to hear him, but she had. Now that their mutual feelings were exposed, what would happen between them?

When she entered the tepee, Cloud Chaser looked at her and said, "I was about to come look for you, Caroline. It's almost dark, and danger could be lurking about in the night." He noticed she was smiling and humming upon her return, but she halted both actions as he spoke to her. Her eyes seemingly glowed, as did her cheeks; and she quickly averted her gaze as if she had been caught doing mischief. He would think she had been running except she was not breathless, not even breathing hard. He had a strong feeling that something unusual was up with her. He wondered, *But what?*

As she put away the sling filled with wood, she said, "I'm sorry I worried you, but it's such a lovely and calm time of day that I got distracted and worked slowly. It will not happen again." *But I had to spend time with War Eagle because he's leaving tomorrow and, heaven forbid, might never return. Please, God, protect him from all harm; and protect David from all harm. Please don't let them challenge each other in battle. I couldn't bear it if either killed the other or if either was slain in this war.*

"Is something wrong, Caroline?"

"No, why?"

"You looked strange, sad, for a moment."

"I was just thinking about my brother, who must also be worried about me. Do you think I could send him a message that I'm alive and safe?"

"I will think upon your request, but it will be a hard task. We do not know where he is, and contacting him could endanger us."

"You're right, Cloud Chaser, and I don't want to imperil anyone here."

"I cannot make you a promise, but I will do your deed if possible."

"Thank you, Cloud Chaser; you're a kind person. I—"

Caroline's words were interrupted when War Eagle called out for her owner to join him. Her head jerked in the direction of the entrance flap and she saw him standing beyond it. Actually, she saw him from the chest down, as his neck and head were concealed by the tepee. But even a half sighting was sufficient to spark the embers of her smoldering passion to life again. She struggled hard to prevent exposing his effect upon her.

Cloud Chaser told his brother he would join him soon, then said to Caroline, "We will talk again later. I must speak with War Eagle."

As the men walked away to seek a private spot to talk, Caroline busied herself helping Macha with Casmu and with spreading out the sleeping mats. She was glad they had eaten early this evening and was elated it was almost time for bed. She could hardly wait to drift into slumberland where she could visit the man she loved. . . .

"Something troubles your spirit, my brother?" Cloud Chaser asked.

War Eagle nodded as he took a deep breath. He was worried about leaving Caroline without close protection in camp from Two Feathers. He wished he could take their cousin along so the evil-ensnared man would not be there to intimidate her with his stares and presence. But he could not allow Two Feathers to distract them from duty and alertness with his spite toward Cloud Chaser, whose presence and special skills were needed on this particular mission. He did not know what his second brother would think or say on the strange matter, but he related that concern to him.

Cloud Chaser was not surprised by that revelation, as he had suspected there were strong feelings between those two people. He did not know if a serious relationship between them was possible or wise, but he was not the one to make that decision or to face that great challenge. He remembered how difficult it had been for him—with his half-white blood—to lay claim to Macha as his wife, but it would be harder for War Eagle—who was second in line to become the next chief and was full-blooded Lakota—to take a white woman—one of the enemy—as his mate. His heart went out to his younger brother, who might be denied his desire forever and for what War Eagle might endure if he attempted to travel that obstructed path regardless of the perils, sacrifices, and consequences. He said, "I will ask Wind Dancer to look after her during our absence. Bent Bow is to hunt fresh game for Dawn and Caroline and to protect them if peril strikes at our camp. Do not worry, for they will be safe in our brother's and our friend's care."

"My heart thanks you, for I am sure Two Feathers will harass her while we are gone. He will try to do so cunningly, and she might tell no one."

"You fear for her safety and feelings because you love and desire her?"

Before he could halt himself, Ware Eagle admitted, "Yes."

Cloud Chaser smiled and said, "I am happy and proud you trust and love me enough to share this secret with me."

"On this moon, you are the only one who would understand my trap and feelings. What must I do and say, for you have learned the truth?"

Cloud Chaser inhaled deeply through his nostrils and exhaled the spent air. "I do not know how to advise you, my brother, for this matter is a heavy one." He related what he had thought earlier, then added, "Perhaps our people would accept her in your life, for she has done many good deeds since coming to our camp. But the impeding war with the whites could cast shadows over her and many might resist a bond between you two. Two Feathers is certain to cause trouble for you and her. He hates and distrusts me for my white blood and for stealing Dawn from his grasp, and he will feel even stronger about Caroline's enemy blood and for my refusal to trade her to him. I do not know which path to tell you to walk, for either will demand much from you. I will tell you: no matter the sacrifices and perils, I had no choice except to walk the path toward Dawn, for she is my destiny, my true love. If you feel the same way about Caroline, you must journey toward her."

"What if taking her is not the will of the Great Spirit?"

"Ask Him to guide you to the path you must walk."

"I have done so many times, but I do not know if He sent me the sign I prayed for on this sun." War Eagle related what had happened between him and Caroline on the trail toward the Cheyenne camp, during their return ride, and in the forest earlier. "Could the flower she picked be a sign?"

Cloud Chaser was surprised to learn how far things had gone between them. Then, he realized he should not have been, for the clues had been there for him to grasp. He grinned and confessed, "It was much the same with me and Dawn before we fled our camp during the last hot season so I could prove myself worthy of her and of becoming a Red Shield and Rising Bear's son again. We sneaked many visits together where we shared kisses and embraces and special words. Often Hanmani would stand guard for us, for she knew of our feelings and believed we belonged together, and she did not want Two Feathers to ask for her best friend in joining. I will guard your secret and meetings until it is the right time to reveal your feelings to our family and others.

Until this current conflict with the soldiers and whites is settled, that time is not here. You are certain Caroline feels as
you do?"

"Yes. She does not respond out of fear for her safety and
life."

"Are her love and desire strong enough to give up her
world and ways for you, to turn her back against her people,
against her brother? You know what she will be called by
them and how she will be treated if they steal her back from
us. Is she willing to have her hand held in the fire with yours?"

Would she, War Eagle wondered, endure such shame and
anguish? Did he know her well enough to answer that question in her stead? "I have not asked her to join me. I have not
asked her about her feelings for me. I have not told her I love
and desire her and want her for my mate. I did not think the
time had come for speaking such things to her. But she has
much cunning and wits, so surely she has grasped them."

"You show wisdom with your caution and delay. Allow
more suns to pass while she becomes more acceptable to our
people. After we return from our journey, we will choose
what you must do about her."

"That is good and wise, my brother, and I thank you."

After Cloud Chaser returned to his tepee, he told Caroline,
"I ride with War Eagle and others at sunrise to learn the
plans and location of General Harney and his troops. The
council met today and chose us to carry out that task. We do
not leave to ride against them, for they are too many and too
strong for a small party to challenge. While we are gone, our
friend Bent Bow, son of the war chief, will hunt fresh meat
for you and Dawn and will protect you if our camp is attacked by enemies. If Two Feathers tries to harm or harass
you, go to Wind Dancer and tell him of such trouble, and he
will handle it for you. Do not let him frighten or injure you.
I trust you, Caroline, so I know you will not attempt to es-

cape during my absence. Do all you can to help Dawn and Casmu, and be good and respectful to our people."

"I will obey your words, Cloud Chaser, I promise. Thank you for telling me what to do about Two Feathers if he causes us trouble," she told him, though she suspected, hoped, that idea was War Eagle's. "Be careful."

"I will be alert and take no unnecessary risks, and so will my brother and our companions. If the Great Spirit so guides me, I will seek out your brother and study him. If he seems safe, I will speak to him about you."

Caroline smiled and thanked him. "I would be forever grateful, Cloud Chaser, but do not speak to David if it endangers you and your people. Perhaps you could . . ." she began, then asked, "Do you know how to write English?" After he nodded, she smiled again and suggested, "Perhaps you could slip him a note telling him I'm safe and alive without speaking directly to him and letting him see your face and learn who has me captive."

Cloud Chaser grinned, then chuckled. "You are as smart and cunning as War Eagle said. That is a clever idea. Go to sleep now if you want to get up early to watch us ride away."

Caroline smiled and nodded, before she took to her buffalo mat. Lying on her right side and facing away from the couple, she nestled her cheek against the soft fur and let her joyous and inquisitive mind roam for a while. So, they had talked about her. What had they said? More importantly, what had War Eagle said about her? Had he revealed their actions and feelings to his brother? If so, what had Cloud Chaser thought and felt and responded? Was that why he had told her to "be good and respectful to our people," so she could win them over as friends? Was that why he thought she might want "to get up early to watch us ride away" so she could see War Eagle for a last time before a lengthy absence? If he was in the know, it didn't appear to disturb, offend, or anger him. Unless, Cloud Chaser believed, hoped, it was only a passing fancy for his brother. Could that be true in more than one way? Was War Eagle only temporarily intrigued by a forbidden temptation?

With the aid of a small fire providing light, Caroline rolled to her stomach, turned her head, and sneaked a peek at the couple on the other side of the tepee. They were cuddled together and whispering too softly for her to overhear their words. Perhaps, she reasoned, he was telling Macha about his talk with War Eagle. Or maybe they were only saying bittersweet farewells. If secrets were being exposed over there, surely she would guess the truth tomorrow or soon, according to Macha's gazes and behavior. For now, she had best get to sleep or she'd slumber through her love's departure.

Caroline stood close to Macha and held Casmu while the couple said good-bye and embraced for a final time, their strong bond evident in the ways in which they looked at and touched each other. She smiled and nodded at Cloud Chaser when he told her farewell and asked her to take good care of his wife and son during his absence. He mounted and took his place with the other riders: Swift Otter, her beloved's best friend; River's Edge, also a friend and Macha's brother; Broken Lance, their first cousin and brother to her nemesis; and War Eagle, the man who had stolen her heart with ease and speed. All five men glanced at her and Macha and the men's parents, who were nearby to observe their sons' partings. She wished Cloud Chaser good luck and coaxed him to be careful, then glanced at War Eagle to let him know those words also applied to him. She saw her beloved give her a slight nod to reveal he had grasped her unspoken message. Then, the party of five walked their horses out of camp to avoid disturbing those who might still be asleep this early. Sadness and worry tugged at her heart and mind as they vanished from sight, off to scout the "enemy," Harney's massive forces.

As she and Macha reentered the tepee, Caroline prayed

for everyone's safety and survival. *Please, Heavenly Father, forgive me if it is wrong to have such love and desire for this particular man. You know these are good people, so protect them from the greed and misunderstandings of mine. I beg You to find some way to evoke peace between our two cultures. If there is any way I can help bring about harmony, please show me how to do so.*

As Caroline did her morning chores, she was aware that autumn would make its vivid presence known in a few weeks. She wondered what would happen when winter followed that colorful season and this area—as she had been told at Fort Pierre—was assailed by heavy snow and strong winds. Surely, she reasoned, soldiers could not travel the countryside in such harsh conditions, so the Red Shields would have a reprieve from their threat. Unless, her troubled mind refuted, General Harney was so determined to crush the Indians that he would take any and all risks to do so.

Caroline called to mind things Cloud Chaser had revealed to her. Why, she fretted, had Lieutenant Grattan foolishly and recklessly provoked the Indians into a new conflict last August over the slaughter and devouring of one stray cow when the majority of the tribes and band in this vast area had agreed to peace with ally and enemy alike only four years ago? Didn't her government and the army realize Grattan had drawn first blood when his nervous men had fired on friendly Brules, slaying the leader they had appointed as the head chief of all Dakotas? Didn't they know Grattan took two cannons and a drunken and insulting interpreter with him to demand either the cow's return or the brutal punishment of those who had slain and eaten the sorry beast? Didn't they understand that the Brules were only defending themselves and their home when they retaliated? Why would a great man like Secretary of War Jefferson Davis send in General William "By God, I'm for battle—not peace" Harney to handle what was being called a "bloody uprising" that must be quelled at any price and action? How could they order every Indian—men, women, children—to leave their land—a territory designated to them in the Laramie Treaty or they would be viewed as "hostile" and in peril of being slain or captured and sent far away?

Cloud Chaser had told her that Harney was closing in fast with a force of thirteen hundred or more heavily armed soldiers, including cannons, with orders to punish the dreaded "Sioux" and "restore order." He said the War Department was humiliated and infuriated by Grattan's "massacre" and held all Dakotas to blame for that incident and other deeds, even though only certain Brule bands and a few Lakota allies were involved in them. He said the government and army feared that unless punishment was swift and hard, worse trouble and more deaths would ensue. She had to concur with Cloud Chaser that the cow's loss had been only an excuse for Grattan to intimidate, ridicule and attack the Indians. Now, Grattan's loss was being used as another excuse to subjugate or exile the Indians from these lands.

It was an injustice and a tragedy, Caroline decided, one that might be prevented if the two sides would talk and an understanding could be reached, but she somehow knew that would not happen. Just as she knew her people were wrong in this grave matter. She hoped and prayed their cruel and antagonistic actions would not taint her currently good image in the Red Shields' eyes and spoil her accomplishments there. Yet, it would be only human nature for at least some of them to turn against her. . . .

War Eagle and his small band headed southward toward Ash Hollow on the North Platte River to parley with Spotted Tail and Little Thunder, who were camped there according to the messages they had received recently. Their task was to learn if any bands had moved out of the specified Lakota territory as ordered by General Harney through Indian Agent Twiss. If so, they wanted to know which bands, where they had gone, and why they had agreed to the white war chief's unreasonable demand. They also needed to ascertain Harney's location and strength, and future plans if possible.

As they journeyed over flat terrain or rolling hills covered with grass, wildflowers, scattered trees, and scrub bushes, they saw or encountered rutting buffaloes and herds of pronghorn and intermingled deer. With the sacred Paha Sapa to their right, each knew the leaves of hardwoods growing in abundance in the black mountains and its foothills would be putting on their colorful garments soon. Various grasses and wildflowers would either die or sleep as the bears until Mother Earth renewed her lovely face, most of them to slumber beneath blankets of snow. Spirits of fallen flowers would drift skyward to form the bands of rainbows whose edges kissed the ground one final time before rejoining the Creator to beautify His surroundings and those of Dakotas who had been summoned into His presence. Days were warm now, not hot; and nights were cooler, often enticing small fires to ward off a chilly one. Yes, the next season was approaching at a steady pace.

After those perceptions were noted by War Eagle, he thought about Caroline, her mute message to him, and her close proximity to his spiteful cousin. He wished Two Feathers was like Broken Lance, but the two brothers were as different as the buck and the badger. He admitted he would miss Caroline greatly, but he must not allow such feelings and needs to distract him from his duty or provoke him to rush to complete it to hurry back to her. For now, he must think of his people and their allies, not the woman who had captured his heart as surely as he had captured her body.

Four days after War Eagle and his companions left camp, Caroline went to Wind Dancer's tepee and removed Chumani's stitches. After the task was completed, one mildly embarrassing for both women, Caroline smiled and said, "You are healed, Dewdrops. I will turn around while you use your white man's mirror to see for yourself."

Chumani retrieved a "magic glass," which she had purchased at Fort Pierre four summers past when she performed a brave and clever deed of spying there. While Caroline was turned away from her, she positioned the mirror and visually examined her private parts. She looked at the captive's back and said, "I am ready. You said the cut flesh would rejoin. You said Inunpa's tepee head would grow round as it should be. You spoke true words. You have great medicine skills, Caroline. You are a good friend. Thank you."

"I thank you, Dewdrops, for trusting me and making me a friend."

After she checked on her newborn daughter who was sleeping nearby, Chumani revealed, "Grandfather wishes to know your medicine skills."

Caroline was confused. "I thought you were from a Brule band far away. I did not know you had family in camp. Who is your grandfather?"

Chumani laughed and explained, "My husband's family became my family after we joined. Nahemana is now a grandfather to me. If you learn our tongue better, you can speak with him about healing skills."

Caroline was surprised by that news, as the shaman was considered sacred and wise. He actually wanted to learn something from a captive? As she allowed that suggestion to settle in, she said, "You speak English well. Cloud Chaser said a trapper taught you long ago."

"That is true. He lived and trapped among the White Shields for many circles of the season. He was white, but a friend to my father. Before his family died and he came to our land, he was a teacher in a white man's school. He taught me English so I could speak with any whites who came to our camp after he left. For years, we had what he called 'class' almost every day. I learned how to speak and translate English, but I cannot read or write such words. Cloud Chaser does that task for us, for he knows all ways of English. If you learn Lakota, you can teach Nahemana the great magic you know, and he can teach you his healing skills. If you become as one of us, when Grandfather's eyes, hands, and head cannot do healing skills, you could become our medicine woman. With war coming fast and our shaman growing older and weaker, you can help those who are sick and injured."

Caroline was amazed by the woman's proposal. If what Chumani said was accurate and if she was accepted by them in such a rank, would that make a relationship with War Eagle permissible? "Is that possible for a captive? Would others trust me to treat them?"

"All know what you did for me and Inunpa, and we are family of the next chief who trusted you and allowed you to save our lives. If you become as one of us and Nahemana says it is good, it will be so."

Caroline's heart raced in excitement and elation. "How do I become as one of you? Become an adopted Red Shield?"

"Only the Great Spirit knows such secrets and magic. If it is the Creator's will for you to join our band, He will make it happen."

"How? When?" Caroline asked, eagerness flooding every part of her. Once more she was given Chumani's first sentence as an answer. Would their Great Spirit, she mused in earnest, be generous and compassionate to a white woman? Was Wakantanka her own God and Creator in another form? Would praying to the Lakota deity be wrong, wicked? She did not know for certain, and white ministers might disagree, but she felt deep inside that God and Wakantanka were one and the same Divine Being. Even so, it was to God whom she prayed for guidance, help, and victory.

As she returned to Macha's tepee, Caroline felt a near-overwhelming sense of impending doom that almost halted her in midstep. She glanced about and saw no threat to her; even Two Feathers was not in sight. She hoped and prayed it wasn't a mental message from God telling her not to wish for a goal she could never obtain. . . .

Far away on September 2, War Eagle and his small scouting party steadily rode from the north toward their destination on Blue Water Creek, while General Harney and his massive force advanced from the southeast on the same location and target with much different plans in mind. . . .

Chapter Eleven

At five o'clock in the evening on September 2—a Sunday—General William Harney and his massive force reached Ash Hollow on the North Platte River. Advanced scouts reported that the encampments of Little Thunder and Spotted Tail—plus those of a few Oglala, Minneconjou, and Cheyenne—were sprawled on the left side of the snaking bank of Blue Water Creek, which traversed a long valley with rocky bluffs, rolling hills, ravines, sandy draws, an abundance of grass, and various trees and scrubs. To their advantage, the outriders related that the "Injuns" had no lookouts posted and were unaware of the army's arrival only a few miles away in the hollow. Harney plotted his shrewd strategy, divided his troops into various companies, and ordered those groups to take positions at both ends of the canyon for a surprise assault at predawn the next morning.

Ordered to be careful so as not to alert the Indians—estimated at about 250 by the stealthy scouts—to their presence, the soldiers ate a cold supper of near-tasteless rations, washed down with fresh water. Even if they had been allowed to build fires to cook a hot meal and brew coffee, the sudden thunderstorm that struck the location would have extinguished their flames. Most took cover fast beneath either a "shelter half" or a poncho.

As soon as the deluge halted, fog engulfed the area, keeping everything and everybody wet with its heavy moisture and stealing their visibility range. Those who could get to sleep under such conditions stretched out on their bedrolls and cursed the "infernal dampness" and "devil darkness" before succumbing to restless slumber. Each knew that in a few hours, they would be up again, mounted, and heading for a fierce battle that some might not survive, even though their numbers were far greater, they had new long-range rifles, and possessed the valuable element of surprise. . . .

Earlier and west of the valley's north entrance, War Eagle and his party had been compelled to halt their journey when the unexpected storm struck with the fury of an enraged grizzly. They did not have much farther to travel to where their two allies were supposed to be camped according to the last message they had received. Even if the bad weather ceased later, the Red Shield warriors knew there would be no light to guide their horses' steps for the rest of the way, as the moon was wearing her black face for about five nights, which made it perilous to proceed in darkness.

As they tended their horses and made camp in the shelter of dense trees and large boulders, War Eagle was drenched by the torrent of rain. The wind was brisk. Lightning flashed in rapid succession, and peals of thunder followed its brilliant path. He scowled in worry and said to Cloud Chaser, "It is as if the Great Spirit sends thunderbirds to slow our approach and to warn us of danger ahead. Even *Hanhepi Wi's* face is hidden from us so we cannot use her glow to continue our ride if the rain halts soon. It is as if the Creator, Mother Earth, the Good Spirits, and all forces of nature are troubled on this dark sun. I feel something is wrong, my brother, but I do not grasp their warnings. Do you sense messages are being sent to us?"

Cloud Chaser stopped his task, checked the tempest's frenzy, and replied in a somber tone, "Yes, but my eyes see and my ears hear nothing to tell me peril is coming soon to challenge us. Even so, it will be wise for us to share times standing guard while the others sleep."

War Eagle nodded in agreement. His agitated thoughts took rapid flight to their camp far away, and he wondered if something could be terribly wrong there. Surely, he reasoned in dismay, the Great Spirit and His Helpers were not telling them to turn back and return home fast, as the Creator knew it would take days to reach Paha Sapa, too late to challenge any imminent threat to their loved ones. Besides, if the message they had received recently was accurate, the white war chief and his forces should be heading for Fort Kearny or Fort Laramie, and could not have had the time to reach their winter encampment. No, the foreboding hints must have to do with an event to happen soon and probably in this area. Perhaps they would gather important and enlightening information from their allies on the next sun, or Cloud Chaser would gather it when he rode to Fort Laramie as a white man to scout for news after their meeting with the Brules.

Aware there was no action he could take tonight, War Eagle chewed on strips of dried meat and sipped water as the rain ceased and a heavy fog surrounded them. Trained to endure harsh weather and discomfort without complaint, he settled down on his wet sleeping mat. He rolled to his left side, closed his eyes, and summoned Caroline's image.

He envisioned her lovely face smiling at him, her blue eyes aglow with love and desire. As surely as he inhaled the Creator's air and walked upon the face of Mother Earth, she was his one weakness, if his matching love and desire were a debility. So far, he could not think of anything he had done or said because of her or their feelings which could be viewed as a flaw or had impaired his prowess and duty. Yet, he must make certain he did not allow his craving for her to shame him or to cause him to fail in his ranks. *If the good deeds she has done were not to show me and others she is to live among us until she breathes no more or the flower she gave to me was not the sign I prayed for, Great Spirit, give me one soon so I will know whether to advance on her, even at a slow pace, or to retreat from her forever.*

Just as dawn began to expose its first traces of light, War Eagle and his companions were awakened not by Swift Otter, who was on guard, but by the ominous sounds of gun-fire that seemed to echo off the cliffs in the valley. The dis-turbed warriors leapt to their feet and seized their nearby weapons, bringing their keen wits to full alert. The sinister noises continued as all gazes were drawn to the bearing of their destination.

War Eagle, the leader of their assignment, ordered, "Come, let us seek a high place to search out this trouble with Dew-drops' magic eye."

In a hurry to investigate the matter, they gathered and loaded their belongings and rode to the base of a chosen bluff, as wet ground prevented telltale dust clouds. Quickly they made their way up its westward slope, sneaked through a narrow cleft to an advantageous point, and flattened themselves on their stomachs so their presence would not be noticed.

War Eagle used field glasses, loaned to him again by Wind Dancer's wife, to study the situation in the canyon. The "magic eye" had been a gift to Chumani's father from a white trapper friend long ago and had been given to her after she became a female warrior and hunter following the slaughters of her first husband and small son by the Crow. The looking glass had been used by him four years past dur-ing one part of the sacred vision-quest journey with his older brother and Chumani, who had chosen him, Zitkala, and Red

Feather as their helpers during those awesome adventures. Those had been exciting, challenging, and victorious events in his band's history; and they had been painted upon their tribal record hide. Now, more deadly ordeals confronted them; a grim one, today. . . .

War Eagle scrutinized the startling scene below their position, and a lengthy view of the canyon and action was good from that elevation and with the white man's spyglass. He told the others what was happening where the camps of Spotted Tail and Little Thunder were situated. Groups of soldiers were attacking them from all directions and had most of the Brules and their friends cut off from escape. He saw a tall man with snow-colored hair growing around his mouth and along his jawline sitting astride his horse on a hill, one who War Eagle surmised was the menacing white war chief. He saw some of their allies taking cover in the bluffs' caves or behind rocks or trees or in ravines. He saw frightened women trying to grab children and supplies to flee the massive threat but soldiers were bearing down on them too fast for them to achieve their goals. Many females were cut off from their little ones who stood crying and flailing their arms in terror. Their agility and swiftness long gone, old ones simply stood in the open and awaited their ends, soulful death chants leaving their mouths. Panicked Indian horses whinnied, snorted, stomped, and jerked at thongs around either their necks or their hobbled front legs. Many of the unsecured animals with long leather strips dangling to the grass as they grazed and drank raced off in several directions to elude the unfamiliar sounds of gunfire. Seasoned warriors and braves-in-training darted about fetching more weapons and trying to defend their families and camp; but their bows, arrows, lances, and war clubs made little headway against the harrowing weapons of the soldiers who could fire from a long distance away from their targets.

Soldiers galloped toward the bluffs and underbrush-dotted

crevices and spat forth countless bullets into those hiding places, causing some Brules to leap up and run in panic. The bluecoats fired rifles and pistols and slashed with sharp sabers as they galloped around and between scattered tepees, slaying unarmed people as well as resisting warriors who had been taken by surprise and with terrible odds of at least three to one from what War Eagle could determine. He told his companions Little Thunder had seized a white cloth, secured it to the top of his lance, and was waving it wildly in the air. No doubt, he reasoned, the Brule chief was shouting over the combined noises for mercy and truce.

As War Eagle watched and passed words to his party, for a time the grim action ceased as Harney met and spoke with Little Thunder, Spotted Tail, and a few others of high rank, though the general refused to shake hands with Little Thunder, who withdrew his offering. But the chiefs and warriors must have been given impossible-to-meet demands and, when they saw soldiers still riding to close the circle more tightly around them and their bands, the parley halted abruptly and the Brule leaders retreated at a rapid pace. Soldiers fired on them, but missed their fleet targets, expert horsemen who swayed side to side to dodge the bullets.

Once more, the fierce and lethal fighting ensued. Some tepees were torched, perhaps to force dwellers outside. Cooking stands and weapon stands were knocked over and trampled. Drying garments were yanked from wooden racks and thrown to the ground. Indians of all ages were clubbed with gun butts or cut with sabers; many were shot in the back or head with iron balls. Red became a vivid color as blood flowed from countless wounds on the injured or finally halted on the slain. Desperate attempts to flee were renewed as the Lakotas and their friends tried to make an opening and guard the flank of their women and children who were heading toward the north end of the lengthy canyon. But, War Eagle spied in dismay, many bluecoats were coming from that direction, indicating that Harney was clever and well prepared for this onslaught. Worse, it appeared as if the white war chief was bent on total death and destruction. . . .

War Eagle slowly lowered the field glasses and took a deep—though not calming—breath before relating those atrocities. "They are outnumbered, my friends, and their weapons are weak against those of the bluecoats. They did not have time to prepare for battle or defense before Mad Dog struck without warning. But we would only lose our lives if we rode to help them, for they are surrounded, and the white war chief has the big thundersticks with him. We must live to battle these cruel enemies when they strike at our camp soon. Do all agree we stay here to live to fight another sun?"

After the four nodded, he passed the field glasses to his brother to watch and report for a while, as the wanton slayings of their allies below and their inability to give them aid angered and pained him, and stung his pride.

It did not take long for Cloud Chaser to grasp the depth of and reasons for War Eagle's strong feelings and the sharing of the grim observation task as he now studied the carnage and razing. He sighted Spotted Tail and his warriors, even his young nephew Crazy Horse, battling with all of their might to give their band and their allies time to flee or to seek cover, although concealment seemed to offer no protection on this dark day. It was evident to Cloud Chaser that General Harney, as War Eagle said earlier, had planned cleverly by positioning companies of infantry, cavalry, artillery, and dragoons in many different locations, as most of the cornered Indians were cut off from freedom or survival. His heart surged with elation as he saw some eluding the sly trap by running up a dry ravine; then, his joy vanished as he saw them stalked and cut down. A few scurried for concealment among rocks and trees or in shallow caves, darting between groups of soldiers, who followed them with eagerness, or with resolve to carry out their orders.

As Cloud Chaser scanned the north end of the setting to see if or how many Brules and others were sneaking through Harney's line there, he saw a man whom he was sure he recognized. As if his mental message, *Look up here at me,* were heard and obeyed for a minute or two, he focused on that soldier's face and surmised from the photograph he had seen in his tepee that it was David Sims. He watched in amazement and elation as the sandy-haired man checked for witnesses before motioning for three women with infants or children to hurry past him into a dry wash. When two braves ran into view as soldiers pursed them on horseback, he was positive that David Sims fired *over* the Brules' heads on purpose. He watched that particular man for a short time and decided that David was only pretending to attack the Indians. Without delay, he reported those stirring incidents and his impressions to the others, revealing how he knew the white man's identity.

War Eagle hoped he had heard his brother correctly. He murmured for confirmation, "Caroline's brother helps our allies live and flee?"

Cloud Chaser answered, "That is true, for my eyes saw him do so. He is like his sister; he does not hate Indians or want them dead. He seeks to help our kind here as his sister does in our camp and in my tepee."

War Eagle's heart pounded with excitement and pride as a glorious ray of sunshine slightly brightened the gloomy day. Perhaps this was the sign he had been seeking from the Great Spirit. . . . "That is good. She will be happy to hear such things and to learn he lives and is safe." As he saw his friends nod and smile in approval, he was positive they would relate such big news to their people, making her more acceptable to—

Cloud Chaser knew his brother was distracted from the harsh reality below them. But he understood why the younger warrior felt and reacted as he did: love and desire for his captive and the hope that one day they could have a special relationship, a bond and union like those he, Cloud Chaser, shared with Dawn and Wind Dancer shared with Dewdrops. He recalled War Eagle's strayed attention to the action in progress when he said he saw Spotted Tail, Crazy Horse, Long Chin, and Red Leaf—brothers of slain Chief Brave Bear— Little Thunder, and some of their band members evading Harney's snare and obtaining freedom. But maybe not for long, he feared, as he saw dragoons in hot pursuit, slaying the rear guards or slow movers with ease. Other soldiers began to check the motionless bodies and round up prisoners. He heard the bugler sound the recall order, but knew some companies were probably out of hearing range and would keep up their quest of total victory for a while.

"Do you say we track our allies and speak to them on this matter?" Cloud Chaser asked their party leader as he gazed into the canyon.

His decision made fast, War Eagle responded, "Yes, let us ride, my brother and friends. We must find and talk with our allies. We will tell them what we saw and why we could not help them battle the enemy this sun."

River's Edge remarked, "They will know we could not help them, for they could not help themselves and were forced to flee this strong enemy."

War Eagle said, "That is true, my friend, but I do not want them to think we were too weak or afraid to ride to their defense. Sometimes a man's thoughts are clouded when he suffers such great losses and shame. His mind must clear before he understands and accepts that we could not take such a futile risk, for five warriors would not have changed this sun's defeat. But we can tell them what we observed and reveal the number and strength of the white war chief's forces and actions, for we had the eagle's view of the sneak attack and saw more than our allies could in the valley."

As the other men listened and nodded, War Eagle continued, "Harney did not speak false or overlarge words in his warning threat through the mouth of Agent Twiss; he attacks

Lakotas who do not surrender their lands and leave them so his people can steal them. The bluecoats are many and have powerful weapons, so we cannot help our allies rescue the captives, or make such a rash attempt ourselves. This white war chief is cunning; he will camp and wait nearby to see if others return to lay the slain ones on death scaffolds or to gather their bodies to do so elsewhere. To try either deed would be foolish and deadly, for it would be riding into a trap."

After those conclusions entered his mind, War Eagle altered his prior decision. "I must change my words. We will track and speak with our allies later, for we must remain here for a time to learn all we can about this sly and cruel enemy leader. We must see if he slays the captives or sends them to one of the forts. If they are kept alive, perhaps we can join forces with more allies and free them."

"To band together and attack a fort is to make war on them."

War Eagle replied to the unseasoned but trained and skilled warrior, "We did not strike the first blow, my cousin. They made war on Lakotas."

Broken Lance reminded him in a respectful tone, "That is not what the white leaders and soldiers believe; they think they retaliate for the slayings of Grattan and his followers. That was in Agent Twiss's message."

"Has Cloud Chaser not told us what he learned at Fort Laramie before the past winter came? My brother said the white leaders far away were told both sides of the Grattan battle, but they choose not to believe the truth. They choose to forget Chief Brave Bear and other Brules were slain before the first arrow was fired in defense. They choose to forget only Brules and a few Minneconjou friends fought against Grattan on that sun. They choose to attack *all* Lakotas and to order us off our lands. Even if we do not attack them, Broken Lance, if we stay on our hunting and camping grounds, they will attack us. Even if we do not strike the next blow, we must defend our lives and our territory, my cousin, for they were given to us by the Creator."

After Broken Lance agreed he was right, War Eagle said, "Swift Otter and I will soon go scout the bluecoat chief's movements. When he halts, I will hide and watch Mad Dog while Swift Otter returns for you, my brother and friends. But if we are seen and captured, do not risk your lives to rescue us. We will find a way to escape their grasp."

It was midday when the Red Shields saw the weary-looking dragoons return with a few captives, and the massive force made ready to leave the body-strewn area. By then, wagons had been loaded with wounded women and children and with four dead and four injured soldiers. Within a short time, the rolling travois were rumbling down the canyon toward the river, three bluecoats with minor wounds riding on horses beside them. The remaining prisoners walked close behind the wooden conveyances, their heads hung in dejection and with some women trying to comfort frightened little ones or assist the aged. Already many vultures were circling overhead, waiting for safety before they swooped down on that tragic site.

War Eagle and his party knew the land scavengers—mainly wolves and coyotes—would be arriving soon to claim their share of the offerings, for the scents of death and blood were in the air. The Red Shields wished they could put the bodies out of the birds' and creatures' reach in caves sealed with rocks, but the cunning and determined Harney had posted lookouts on several hills, no doubt to watch for such a deed.

War Eagle said, "Come, Swift Otter, we ride to trail our enemies."

*　*　*

War Eagle and Swift Otter had watched as General Harney and his troops halted and began to set up camp near the mouth of Blue Water Creek and within sight of Kampeskawakpa Waziyata, the North Platte River. The visible wagon ruts on the Mormon Trail on the north side and those of the Oregon Trail on the south, which cut into the face of Mother Earth and scarred it, exposed the crossings of numerous white settlers and other wagons for the passings of the last nine and twelve circles of the seasons. As soon as it was evident to them that the soldiers would travel no farther, Swift Otter had left to retrieve the others.

War Eagle admitted to himself while he waited for his companions that several Indian bands or small parties of braves had raided a few of the cloth-covered travois and had wounded or slain some of those people. But the soldiers and other whites had wounded or slain Indians for various reasons, and evildoers had stolen the furs and hides of Indians or cheated them in trading. Yet, the majority of whites had passed through or crossed their lands unharmed and mostly ignored; and on the whole, the treaty had been honored by the bands of most tribes. His people did not punish the Pawnee for misdeeds by the Shoshone, nor one band of the Crow for the evil actions of another. As Cloud Chaser had said, the whites did not punish the French for wrongdoings by the Spanish, or declare war on an entire nation for the "crimes" of a few men or a small group of people. Yet, the "Americans" were starting a war on *all* Lakotas for the offenses and alleged bad deed of Little Thunder's and Spotted Tail's Brules and some of their friends.

How, War Eagle wondered, could whites—if there were many good ones among them like Caroline and David Sims, Red Wolf's mother, and Cloud Chaser's mother and adoptive parents—accept and explain such a contradiction? Was Good not stronger than Bad? Was Good not always victorious over Evil even if the battle between them was long and hard and often painful? What about their Creator and His laws, the ones that those called "Spanish missionaries" said commanded them to not—

War Eagle ceased his mental roamings and glanced behind him when he heard muffled sounds and saw his companions coming to join him so they could all watch the camp of the bluecoats to see what action they took next.

From another high vantage point not far away, the movements in the camp were visible to all five men without the aid of the field glasses. For the present, they saw that the captives were being held in a group that was encircled by soldiers, about seventy women and children, as the warriors were either dead or had fled with other survivors. They heard sorrowful wailings of mourners and groans of the wounded, though those sad sounds were low at their distance away. To their astonishment and joy, the saw some soldiers and a man Cloud Chaser called a "doctor" tending wounds. A few were laid beneath brush shelters to keep them out of the sun, and all prisoners were being offered food and water.

"These bluecoats and their leader are strange. Why do they slay and injure, then help those they have harmed badly?"

War Eagle replied, "I do not know, River's Edge. Perhaps they seek to trick the Lakotas with false kindness so they will reveal where the others have fled or they will give the bluecoats no trouble as captives."

Cloud Chaser added, "Or perhaps they fear the good people among the whites will turn against them for cruel deeds, for many will believe it is wrong and evil to slay women and children. Or perhaps a few of the soldiers have good hearts as with Caroline, her brother, and those who adopted me."

War Eagle said, "We will watch to see what happens to our allies. We must learn if the white war chief's thirst for revenge has been quenched by the blood of the Brules or if he will still attack all Lakotas as he threatened. If he wars against all of us, we will have no choice except to battle him." He touched the small medicine pouch suspended around his neck and hoped the magic tokens he had collected over the years and the scrimshaw circle and dried flower were good luck charms against the enemy's evil. If Harney was sated and turned back, he could go home and see his heart's desire. . . .

After dark, countless campfires were visible to the observant War Eagle and his party; that is, until another violent thunderstorm with brilliant flashes of lightning and a torrential downpour occurred. To the Red Shields, it was as if the Great Spirit was showing His anger at the slaughter and destruction He had witnessed earlier that day. For safety, they hurried to bluff caves to seek shelter from the bad weather. There, they ate and four slept while one stood guard nearby, though they doubted any soldier scout would be out riding in the fierce storm.

Early the next morning, War Eagle and his party watched as the captives, after they were given food and water, were gathered into a herd like buffalo or pronghorn and were led down the well-worn trail toward Fort Kearny. The prisoners afoot followed wagons that were loaded with the injured and all were surrounded by a heavy guard as they departed. It was a unit much too large and powerfully armed for five men to attack to free the captives, and the surviving members of their families probably were far away by now and trying to recover from a stunning defeat and loss of their food supply, tepees, and other possessions. Even so, the remaining force numbered in the many, many hundreds. That told the Red Shield party that Harney was not satisfied with his punishment of the Brules and was not returning to Fort Kearny and to wherever he had come from before being sent there. It was evident by his actions that the white war chief intended to continue his scourge on all Lakotas.

While the other three men stayed behind to observe Harney and his troops, with great caution and stealth War Eagle and

Swift Otter left and skirted the army's sprawling position to see what the unit of soldiers had left to do in the Indian camps, as they had ridden in that direction. Since it was not the Red Shield way to mutilate slain bodies, they hoped the same was true of the bluecoats, as that would be a grave and challenging offense.

After secreting themselves in the westward bluffs, the two warriors watched most of the soldiers search the camp while a few others did the same with the surrounding area, as if they were making certain no survivors were hiding nearby and none of the escapees had returned for their dead or belongings. As soon as the smaller group completed its scouting task, they rounded up Indian horses grazing here and there and herded them down the canyon. The Red Shields saw vultures and crows circling overhead and coyotes and a few wolves lurking in the underbrush and rocks, probably frightened off by the soldiers' approach before their own arrival.

Using the field glasses, War Eagle grimaced as he saw the condition of the scattered bodies; numerous scavengers had been working on them yesterday and during the night. Even if their remains had not been properly prepared for their final journey and put upon scaffolds, he decided, surely the Creator had summoned their brave spirits to His sacred location. War Eagle closed his eyes for a minute and prayed that their souls were at peace now, and he prayed nothing like this would happen to his people and Caroline.

He sighted soldiers collecting weapons, winter food supplies, buffalo robes, clothing, and other possessions. Some were tossed onto a wagon and others were thrown into a heap, which grew larger with more additions to it. Tepees were pulled down and added to the pile, their lodge poles left where they had fallen. Then, to his astonishment, men flung something like water on the mound and used "magic fire sticks" to set it ablaze. He noted how fast the flames licked at and consumed or ruined the things amassed there, cruelly destroying months and years of hard work by his allies.

War Eagle could not help but recall how the vision-quest party, led by Wind Dancer and Chumani, had used "magic fire sticks" four summers ago during some of their raids and tricks, after she had traded for them at the Pierre post before it became a military fort three full moons past. It was obvious to him that the soldiers were keeping—stealing—the meat and other foods, horses, robes, weapons, and other things for their use or as war prizes or to use in raiding. It also was apparent that the crafty and brutal Harney had made sure any returning Brules would be left with nothing to sustain their lives during the harsh winter looming ahead. Unless, War Eagle reasoned, the survivors hurriedly carried out another buffalo hunt or pleaded with allies for replacements or raided forts and homesteads for their needs, or they surrendered as the fierce slayer desired.

After he related those observations and conclusions and suppositions to Swift Otter, he said, "Come, let us join our friends and reveal these evil acts to them, and learn what has happened while we were gone."

Cloud Chaser pointed out one event to his brother and friend upon their return. Harney had buried his dead men in "graves" near the mouth of the river, within sight of anyone traveling on the two settler trails. *Hante* trees growing on the bluffs had been cut, hauled to camp, and carved into the shape he wanted. The cedar marks had been painted white; then, the soldiers' names, ranks, and death "dates" had been painted on the wood in black. Cloud Chaser said the troops had gathered where some had dug long and deep holes in the face of Mother Earth, listened to their leader speak and pray, and said farewell to their companions as was their custom.

War Eagle glared at the raised mounds, as bluecoats did not belong in the ground on their territory, and not while scavengers were picking clean the bones of their allies not far away! Surely Mother Earth and the Great Spirit were angered by those two incidents. He told Cloud Chaser, River's Edge, and Broken Lance what they had witnessed in the valley. He read the signs of matching anger burning within them, for their expressions and stiffened bodies exposed such truths to him. "We will stay and grasp more about these enemies. We must learn their weaknesses to use against them on the sun they swoop down on our people and camp. After we know which path they ride, we will seek out our suffering allies and reveal the dark deed to them. Then, we will ride to our camp to tell Father and our people all we saw here. It is past time for him or one of the chiefs of our allies to summon the Seven Council Fires of the Lakota together."

Cloud Chaser locked gazes with War Eagle and nodded. "Your words are strong and true, my brother. Harney and his soldiers have come to challenge us to the death or to defeat, so we have no choice except to meet them on the battlefield. But we cannot fight alone, for they are too many and their weapons are too powerful. It is time for the seven tribes of the Lakota branch to gather, smoke the pipe, and speak of war, for we cannot yield to such evil. Lakotas must band together to strike at them as one mighty force or all tribes will perish one by one." Even though he spoke those word and believed they were accurate, he hoped and prayed something would happen to quench the army's thirst for "Sioux" blood and to sate their hunger for revenge in the name of the undeserving Grattan. He knew that once an all-out war was declared, it would be a long and bloody and costly episode, as both sides would be compelled to fight until one side was defeated. Aware from his existence among the whites for twelve years and from what he had learned while spying on them at Fort Laramie last summer, he feared the Lakotas—even banded together—stood little chance of being the victors. Yet, he thought with a happy heart, they had the Great Spirit on their side. Then, his troubled mind refuted, *So did the Brules yesterday. . . .*

*   *   *

On the following day in the Red Shield camp, Two Feathers rode into camp, carrying a weak and injured female across his lap. Many crowded around his horse and viewed her in astonishment and suspicion. . . .

Chapter Twelve

From where she was working at Cloud Chaser's tepee with Macha and Chumani while their three children napped beside them, Caroline realized that something important and shocking was taking place not far away in the clearing. She saw many people gather around Two Feathers after he rode into camp and halted there to talk to them from his horse. The tethers of a second animal that carried a doe were dropped to the ground. She eyed the female who was sitting across his lap and almost snuggling against him with her dark gaze wide as if she feared the Red Shields. It was obvious the young woman was injured, as there was blood on her garment and a bandage around one forearm and her head. Although the pitiful creature was dirty and her dress had rips on a shoulder and near a thigh, it was obvious she was pretty and was Indian. "Who is she, Dewdrops? Do you know her?"

Chumani gaped at the woman in disbelief as she murmured in English, "She is Wastemna, daughter of our past war chief."

Caroline was intrigued and stunned by Chumani's reaction to the woman's return. She noted that Chumani's gaze was narrowed and chilled, her tone was cold, her body was rigid, and her fists were balled so tightly that her knuckles were white. She glanced at Macha, who stared wide-eyed at Two Feathers' burden, but her reaction to the event was not as strong as Chumani's. She whispered, "What happened to her? She has not been in your camp since I came. Was she captured by an enemy?"

"She was banished four years ago for trying to slay me and for many other bad deeds. She was forced to leave our band as punishment. She was told never to return. It is wrong for her to enter our camp and our lives again."

Caroline was astounded by that news. She surmised that since Indians were nomadic and did not have jails and prisons, exile was the penalty for the crime of attempted murder, even of their future chief's wife. Perhaps they were more civilized than her people believed, as they could not bring themselves to execute even a guilty woman. "Why did she try to kill you?"

"She desired Wind Dancer and I had joined him. She wanted me dead or tricked into returning to my people so she could have him. Hanmani and Dawn learned of her evil and exposed it. She is not Sweet Smelling as her name says; she is tainted with evil and stinks of it. She shamed herself and her parents, and she ensnared her mother in her bad deeds. Buffalo Hump was a good and cunning war chief, but he could not allow his wife and child to leave without him for their protection and hunting. They left to join another band and we have not seen or heard from them since they rode from our camp long ago. Why does she return and alone?"

Caroline realized Chumani did not expect her to answer that query, as it was asked more of herself than of another who was ignorant of the matter. "It is strange, Dewdrops. Doesn't she fear punishment for her defiance?"

"Her boldness is too large and she has many cunning ways. Perhaps she thinks she can trick us into allowing her and her parents to return. See how she tries to look afraid, weak, and hurt. Such things are false and sly. She proved she fears little when she tried to slay me or turn me against my husband and the Red Shields and to turn them against me. Winona was almost slain by one of her bad deeds, but I saved my second mother's life. Two Feathers shows he is unwise and cruel to bring her here."

Before she could reason if it was smart or rash, Caroline suggested, "Perhaps Two Feathers has turned against Wind Dancer as with his brothers and now seeks to injure your husband in some clever way, just as he seeks to wound and shame War Eagle and Cloud Chaser. Will he be punished for disobeying your law?" *Perhaps be exiled and put out of my hair. . . .*

"I do not know. Two Feathers is a great warrior and comes from the bloodline of their past chief, his grandfather. I will watch him closely for bad deeds against my husband, and I will watch Wastemna with eagle eyes until she is sent away once more."

"I will help you watch them, Dewdrops, my friend," Caroline offered.

Chumani glanced at the white female and smiled. "That is good and I thank you. I will ask Hanmani and Dawn and Zitkala to do the same."

Caroline noted that while they were talking in whispers, others joined the crowd around that scene: Rising Bear and Winona, Nahemana and Little Turtle, Wind Dancer and his best friend, Red Feather, Hanmani, War Chief Blue Owl, and Pretty Meadow and Runs Fast, the parents of her nemesis. Neither she, nor Chumani, nor Dawn spoke as they observed the incident, as they could hear little of the discussion taking place too far away from them.

After a while, a stimulated Hanmani joined them in a hurry to relate the astonished news. She revealed that Two Feathers had found Wastemna, hurt and hiding, while he was out hunting alone. The concealed woman had sighted and signaled to him, and he approached her and learned that her parents had been slain by a Pawnee raiding party. Wastemna told him they had wandered about the territory since leaving camp because no ally would accept them because of their banishment. Wastemna had said that when her father saw enemies coming, Buffalo Hump had forced her to hide while he and her mother battled with two warriors. She had been injured when she disobeyed to help them. Her father had slain one Pawnee and she had slain the other, but her parents died from their wounds. Two Feathers tended her injuries and brought her to camp with him.

Hanmani whispered, "She pleaded with Father and the others to be allowed to return or to be slain, for she cannot survive winter alone. She said she had suffered much for her evil. She pleaded for our forgiveness and for mercy."

The seventeen-year-old girl went on to tell the women that Two Feathers had reasoned that since Wastemna was alone and helpless, injured and hungry and had no possessions to survive the coming winter, had helped slay two of their enemies, and begged for forgiveness for her past wickedness, she should be allowed to rejoin their band. When others had protested and reminded him of her serious offense, he had argued that the Four Virtues were Generosity, Courage, Wisdom, and Fortitude. He had pointed out that sending her away in her condition was not honoring those traits, and it required the use of all four to allow her to remain with them. It was decided that Wastemna would stay in the tepee of Blue Owl until the council met, talked, and voted on her fate.

Chumani said, "You saw and heard her up close. Do you believe her?"

Hanmani took a deep breath as she considered the question. "I do not know, my sister. Does the fawn not lose its spots? Does the snowshoe rabbit not change its color from brown to white in winter? Does a hard bud not become a soft flower? Does a dark cloud not drift away and the sun return? Does the buffalo calf not lose its reddish hide and become brown when it is grown? If Wastemna has changed, it would be wrong and cruel to send her away alone to face certain death. Perhaps she is bad no more, for she has endured much suffering and pain in four circles of the seasons."

A suspicious Chumani, who vividly remembered the woman's past evil, refuted, "Perhaps her heart has grown harder, colder, and darker."

"If that is true, my sister, she will expose herself to us. Is it not best to allow the Great Spirit to test her, and to punish her if she is still bad?"

After the wife and sister of Wind Dancer went silent, Caroline asked, "What happened, Dewdrops? I could not grasp all of Hanmani's words, for they were spoken in haste from her excitement."

Chumani related what Hanmani had said and her own response. She went on to reveal what had taken place years ago with the ex-war chief's daughter. "I do not trust Wastemna, my friend. Is that wrong of me?"

Caroline knew the Bible said to forgive those who had done evil against you and she supposed that a person could alter from bad to good, but she placed a hand over her heart and said, "If I were Dewdrops, I would feel and think the same way. If Wastemna has changed, let her prove it to you."

Chumani smiled and said, "Thank you, my friend, for you are wise."

Even the gentle-spirited Hanmani nodded in concurrence. "I must go help Mother with our tasks. Do not worry, my sister, for I watch over you as I did long ago."

Chumani smiled at the girl in gratitude. "I must go to my tepee, for there is much talking to do with my husband before he meets to vote."

After the council met and voted, Hanmani hurried to Macha's tepee to tell her best friend that Wastemna would be allowed to stay with Blue Owl and his wife at least during winter if she committed no new offenses. The two talked for a while, as that decision surprised both of them.

Not long after Hanmani left, Caroline and Macha saw Two Feathers approaching them near dusk as they returned from fetching fresh water.

"Ye sni ye." Macha whispered for Caroline to stay with her, as she did not want to face that man alone, and feared he still lusted after her.

"Toniktuka hwo?" Two Feathers smiled and asked how Macha was doing. He did not even glance at the white female nearby.

"Mantanyan." Macha told him she was fine and tried to appear calm.

Two Feathers said he had slain a large doe and was sharing part of it with her because she needed fresh meat since he had noticed Bent Bow's offering yesterday was small. As he spoke, he set down a hide, loosened its ties, and showed her a big hunk of game. He told her she also could have the hide for making herself or her son a garment during winter.

Macha knew, just as she realized that Two Feathers knew, she could not refuse his generosity or it would shame her. *"Pilamaya."*

"Ake wancinyankin ktelo." He told her good-bye and he would see her again. He added, if there was more she needed, to summon him to get it.

Again Macha was compelled to feign appreciation and to thank him. *"Pilamaya."* Wanting him gone fast, she lifted the bundle to go inside.

As Caroline attempted to follow Macha, she had to pass the repulsive and menacing warrior, who gave her a look that made her cringe and her steps almost falter, though Black Fist's knife sheath was secured around her waist, an enemy blade she had not wanted to use to deliver Inunpa last month. If it was possible, she fretted, his frigid gaze stripped her naked and flogged her to a bloody pulp before ravishing her.

Before she could avert her gaze, she saw him send her a wicked and threatening sneer. She hurried past him, ducked, and escaped into the tepee. Although she heard him leave, she turned and peered outside to make sure he had. She realized she was shaking and breathing fast. She wished he didn't intimidate her so much, but he possessed the power to do so. She had no doubt his heart and soul were as black as the new moon rising!

Macha asked, "What is wrong, Caroline? You look afraid."

Since she did not know how to explain her perceptions in Lakota, all she could say in that language to partially get her point across was, "I fear Two Feathers. He is bad."

"Han, sica iye." Macha quickly agreed as she prepared to breast-feed Casmu. *You do not know how bad I think he is, for I believe he killed his wife and tried to blame an enemy Crow. If only I knew what Sisoka learned that provoked her death, I could have him slain or banished. Help us, Great Spirit, for evil lurks within his body and he still seeks my husband's life.*

Macha recalled a short talk with Two Feathers following her beloved's Sun Dance Ritual last summer when the evil man continued to mistrust and to speak against Cloud Chaser. He had told her, "When he is here no more, Dawn, you will turn to me again." She had responded, "No, Two Feathers, I will not, for I do not love or desire you." The very next day, he had joined to Sisoka, shocking not only them but also many of their people with the unexpected event. Then, not long afterward, she had found Sisoka facedown in the river with a head wound and clutching a Crow wanapin. Suspecting who was to blame for that evil, she had concealed the necklace before exposing Sisoka's death, which was accepted as an accident. Macha was not convinced that was true, and she still mistrusted Two Feathers.

Caroline furtively watched Macha for a few minutes and surmised that her friend was intimidated by Two Feathers. That deduction strengthened her resolve to thwart the man's evil intentions, whatever they might be. She had promised Cloud Chaser she would help and protect his wife and son, and she would do what she must to honor her word. She was relieved she was allowed to wear a weapon and she would use it against any threat to them. Yet, she hoped Two Feathers would not provoke such an incident, as it could cause trouble for her when she was making excellent progress with most of the Red Shields and with her heart's desire. Wasn't she?

On the following day, War Eagle watched soldiers as they worked near the road and river to build long and high sod walls with firing and observing holes in them. The site contained what Cloud Chaser said were two bastions for repelling the enemy during an attack and a sod structure where the men would eat and sleep and keep warm in the winter. He had been relieved when Cloud Chaser finally returned from Ash Hollow where his brother had sneaked close enough to overhear the soldiers receiving their orders and talking amongst themselves. His brother had learned the site was to be called Fort Grattan in honor of the lieutenant whose death had initiated this current conflict. It would be manned by the 2nd Dragoons and was being built "to provide protection for wagon trains, payroll shipments, and mail stages between Forts Kearny and Laramie." While spying, Cloud Chaser also had learned that General Harney and his forces were heading for the latter location in two more days. That told War Eagle it was time for his brother to carry out his important part of their quest, to part with them and to go there to scout the enemy up close, as a white man. To reach that destination and renew past acquaintances with people there before Harney arrived, Cloud Chaser would have to leave at first light tomorrow. War Eagle listened as his half-white brother related his plans.

"I brought everything I need with me: my white garments, weapons, supplies, and saddle. I must prepare to enter their world once more as Chase Martin." After that statement, Cloud Chaser withdrew his sharp knife and began to cut off his long hair to the length and in the style that his adversaries wore. He left to go upriver to bathe, to remove any Indian scent from his hair and body. He dressed in a cotton shirt, pants, and boots. At last, he was ready to meet his next challenge, which could be a lethal one.

Shortly before sunrise but as soon as there was sufficient light to see the trail ahead, War Eagle embraced Cloud Chaser and cautioned, "Stay alert, my brother, for the white man is sly and dangerous. They are many and you are one. After we have tracked and spoken with our Brule allies, we will camp at the chosen spot near Fort Laramie to wait for word from you."

Cloud Chaser then clasped wrists with Swift Otter, his cousin Broken Lance, and River's Edge, the twin brother of Macha. To the last man, he urged, "If I do not return and my spirit rejoins the Creator, take care of my beloved wife and son. Let no man or force harm them." After River's Edge nodded, Cloud Chaser warned the others, "If I am taken captive at the fort, do not try to rescue me. I will find a way to escape them. I go now. May the Great Spirit protect and guide all of us in our journeys."

"Heyapi," the other men voiced in unison as they agreed, *It is said.*

On Tuesday, September 11, Cloud Chaser reached his target, five days after he left his brother and companions at Ash Hollow. It was evident the military post was strategically positioned atop a lofty and almost flat bluff overlooking the Laramie River, eastward of the Laramie Mountains and the vast stretch of the Rockies. The wisely chosen site provided well for the troops, trappers and hunters, traveling peddlers, adventurers, prospectors and explorers heading farther west, and for passing homesteaders. The river offered an ample water supply; the grasslands, grazing for their stock; the North Platte Road and two emigrant trails, a connection to forts and trading posts in both directions; many animals for fresh meat; assorted birds and fish for additional sustenance; and nearby forests for lumber.

As with his last visit, there still was no stockade encompassing its structures and cannons, as if the army did not fear an Indian attack and was evincing its bravado and confidence. Some of the structures included barracks, stables, bakery, sutler's store, smithy, lumber shed, saddlery, magazine, guardhouse, supply storages, and officers' quarters. He noted there was more housing for soldiers and remembered that construction of them was in progress late last summer. Most of them had two stories, many windows, railed porches, and high-pitched roofs with multiple chimneys jutting from them. They were situated around an enormous parade ground with a tall staff, from which the American flag danced about in a strong wind.

Fort John, a big adobe building that had first served this area and now belonged to the American Fur Company for trading with trappers and Indians, sat close to the river bluff. Unlike the new fort, John had two guard towers and an adobe-enclosed yard for protection against "hostiles," as well as two brass cannons and—he recalled—weapons within the workers' easy reach.

On a grassy area below one section of the extensive bluff, Cloud Chaser glimpsed a few homes, no doubt for officers, and other unknown structures. Beyond them was a cluster of Indian tepees where the *waglukhe* camped and lived year-round as beggars. The "Loafers," outcasts or deserters from various bands, were viewed by the Indians as being "lazy" and "worthless" because they had become dependent upon the white man for survival and no longer practiced and honored "The Old Ways." The men seemed satisfied to allow their wives and daughters to do laundry, to clean quarters and homes and offices, and to prostitute themselves to the soldiers and fur company men. While their women were busy earning meager amounts of money or trade goods, they either sat—alone or in small groups—on tattered rush mats or lay around on worn and dirty and smelly buffalo hides sleeping, or drinking, or gambling. A few of the women were said to be squaws of some soldiers, but those men were not allowed to marry Indians under white law or to make a home with them. All those unfortunate bluecoats could do was "visit" their females while off-duty and support them to keep them nearby.

Not so, Cloud Chaser thought, where the other and larger Indian camp was situated along the river a short distance away. That was the camp of Red Cloud of the Bad Faces Oglala band, a chief who was respected and liked by Indians, white men, and soldiers. Red Cloud endured the whites' presence and travels across Lakota lands. He traded with them, but did not accept handouts; nor had he given up "The Old Ways." He believed it was wise to learn all he could about the intruders, and to retain peace with them for as long as possible, though he also believed that a great war would come between the two cultures in the future. He had made certain the army knew he and his band were not involved in and did not condone the Grattan slaughter. He was considered a great thinker, speaker, leader, and warrior.

Cloud Chaser hoped their paths did not cross while he was at the fort, as Red Cloud knew him to be Rising Bear's son from parleys last summer and autumn, so the chief could unintentionally expose him to the soldiers.

Cloud Chaser knew his way around the site from a visit there in May of last year before he traveled to the trading post called Fort Pierre, now truly a fort, and then made contact with his family and people. As he attempted to earn their trust and acceptance, he had visited this fort several more times during the summer and fall to gather information about the enemy. As he got closer to the setting, he smelled bread being prepared in the bakery, animal droppings from the stables and stock corral, and that indescribable but noticeable scent that only plains grass, dust, and the late summer air seemingly possessed.

He saw men unloading wagons, soldiers checking or repairing their gear, men tending the stock, a few standing guard, and the brilliant sun reflecting off windows and the river's surface. He heard saws as those tools sliced through wood at the lumber shed, the combined voices and intermingled laughter of many of the post's inhabitants, horses neighing and cows mooing, the shrill cries of a hawk overhead, the American flag popping in a strong breeze, the smithy's hammer as he shod army horses, and the prairie wind whistling past his ears. He felt calm yet tense, assured yet skeptical, ready for and yet dreading the hazardous challenge ahead. No, his keen mind refuted, not dreading the challenge, but dreading what he would discover and how it would affect his and his loved ones' lives.

He reined in his horse and dismounted at the sutler's store, having decided to make his first stop where he could renew a past acquaintance with its owner and perhaps glean important information. He stroked the sorrel's neck to reassure Red in the strange setting and to let him know it was all right to drink from the water trough. He strolled into the store, approached the long wooden counter, smiled, and said, "Been a long time, Ben, way last year. Do you remember me? I'm Chase Martin."

The sutler grinned and nodded. "Sure do, Chase. Where you been since you passed through here last summer? Git any trappin' done?"

Cloud Chaser casually leaned against the counter, removed his hat, and cocked one booted ankle over the other. "Nope. Just been riding around the territory doing odd jobs here and there, enough to keep me supplied with grub and ammo. I figured I'd better stop by and see what's happening, 'cause it sounds like there's gonna be trouble in these parts again. I heard the army's getting ready for a big fight with them Lakotas over that Grattan mess last year. Is that what you've heard?"

"Lord come Sunday, I done heard plenty about it, and none of it sits straight with me. From what they're spoutin', Old Harney should be here soon and bringin' more troops than a woman can shake dirt from a rug. It's all them soldiers talk about these days. Half of 'em is ready and champin' at the bit for a fight; the other half is seared pissless to face them Indians on their huntin' grounds. If you ask me, Harney ain't got no idear what he's about to come up against. Them Indians ain't gonna run and hide from him and his boys and they ain't gonna surrender their land without a fight. He's plain and simple crazy to order them out of their territory. Lord come Sunday, the army signed it over to them in that treaty. Now, they want to shove 'em out of it? Crazy, just plain crazy. He'll have us in an all-out bloody war before winter drops its first snowflake. He'll probably take ever' spare man here with him on his wild hunt. Atop no emee-grant travel come winter, I'll be doin' good just to survive half starvin' with so little bidness."

To delude the sutler and learn all he could from the talkative man, Cloud Chaser smiled and said, "Sounds as if you have it reasoned out right to me. In my way of thinking, there's no guessing what the Lakotas and their allies will do if Harney challenges them to war. It could even draw some of their enemies into a conflict that size. You can bet your store some of those Pawnee and Crow bands will try to take advantage of the situation while the Lakotas have their eyes looking elsewhere, or if they offer to scout for the army so the soldiers can destroy or weaken the Sioux for them."

As Cloud Chaser shifted his position, he said, "Yep, Harney can stir up a hornet's nest if he isn't careful. He could have whites fighting Indians, and Indians fighting Indians again, and have this territory in an uproar. I don't know how much Harney knows about Indians in these parts, but by now they've finished their buffalo hunts and are getting ready to settle in somewhere for the winter. They'll be well supplied with food and may be eager for a diversion. You know how warriors like to practice their fighting skills and take on big challenges, and they haven't been given many chances to kick up dust since they were ordered not to raid longtime enemies."

"Word around here is Old Harney has tangled with Indians afore. He took on Apaches and Navahos durin' the Mexican fracus, and Seminoles and some others over Florida way some years back. I'm a-guessin' he's fairly good at goin' against their tricks and skills. Leastwise that's what his boys think."

Cloud Chaser found that news disturbing. Yet, he reasoned, "I haven't been down Florida or Mexico ways, but from what I've learned about those places and ruckuses, they're nothing like this area or the Lakotas."

"You could have the right of it, Chase, and I guess we'll know soon."

"I'm afraid so, Ben, but I'm dreading it. I kinda like this territory, so I hate to see it spoiled and dangerous to travel 'cause of a misunderstanding over a dumb cow. From what I've heard, there's been little trouble around here since last year, so Harney would be smart to leave them be, especially this late in the year. Sounds reckless to provoke them so close to winter on ground they know well and he doesn't." He saw the older man nod in agreement, then scowl before the sulter revealed why.

"They surely ain't helpin' themselves prevent it. A band of 'em rode right up to the quartermaster's corral and made off with fifty or more horses just yesterday. You can bet the last coin in your pocket that ain't gonna sit straight with Old Harney when he gits here."

"I didn't notice any heavy guard when I rode in. That seems a mite strange since there was a raid yesterday." He could not help wondering if that theft was committed by Spotted Tail's and/or Little Thunder's depleted bands either in retaliation for the Blue Water Creek massacre or to obtain horses to use for escape and for hunting to replace their lost meat and hides. Both chiefs had promised Sitting Bull last autumn they wouldn't make any more raids after the Grattan incident unless they were provoked, so yesterday's theft—he reasoned—must have been the result of Harney's challenge. "Did anybody recognize any of the raiders?"

"Nope, it happened too fast and it was almost dark when they struck. Major Hoffman has a troop out lookin' for tracks now, but it ain't likely they'll git them horses back. I'm a-bettin' them Indians are long gone from around here, and Hoffman don't want his boys ridin' too far away. He has lookouts posted, but they're stayin' hid. And he's got his boys on alert while they do their duties so they can act fast if another raid is attempted. That's why I ain't busy today. Lord take Sunday, it's as quiet as a snowfall in here."

With soldiers scouring the area for renegade Indians, Cloud Chaser was glad War Eagle and his companions weren't already waiting for him nearby. He also was glad that Ben wasn't busy so they could have this enlightening exchange. "The more we talk, Ben, the worse it sounds to me."

"That ain't the all of it, Chase. Mr. Cummin', he's the Superintendent of Indian Affairs, he spoke hot and heavy against punishin' all Sioux for what them renegade Brules did. Cummin' said Capt'n Garnett—you might recall he was in charge here durin' the Grattan fiasco—anyways, Garnett claimed the massacre wasn't—let me think how he said it. . . . I believe it was 'the result of premeditation on the part of the Indians.' But a few of the others talked stronger, so Cummin' lost the vote. Those other men said too much had happened since that bloody event: robberies of fur companies and mail carriers, stages and way stations attacked, army horses and mules stolen, payrolls stolen, homesteaders attacked, and settlers and soldiers have been kilt. The renegades convinced them-in-power no peace is possible."

Cloud Chaser's mind refuted, *It would be if the American government did right by the Indian and stopped trying to steal their lands and punish all Lakotas for the misdeeds of a few!* Yet, he assumed that was unlikely. "What about Agent Twiss? Which side of the battle line is he standing on?"

"Twiss sent messages to all of the tribes and warned 'em the area designated as Lakota territory would be Harney's target for reprisals, so all friendlies should move across the Platte River until this fracus is settled. Anybody who stays put is gonna be marked as a hostile and be attacked. Last month, Twiss told the Secretary of the Interior 'the Sioux difficulties have been magnified by false and malicious reports. There is not, as I can find, within this agency, a hostile Indian. On the contrary, all are friendly.' You think Harney and them-in-power are gonna believe that bunch of words and call off their plans? That's about as likely as it bein' hot here in January. I guess Twiss forgot about them raids and deaths since The Grattan Massacre the Army knows about. Even if most of 'em happened last year right after that sorry fight, the horse stealin' yesterday will prove him wrong and show Harney them Indians are still kickin' up their heels and doin' mischief."

"That's a shame, a real shame," Cloud Chaser muttered as two soldiers entered the store and began looking around for wanted items. "I best be going. I need to get my horse reshod over at the fur company's smithy. I'll be here a day or two, so I'll be back for supplies before I ride out. Good seeing and talking to you again."

As he left, Cloud Chaser concluded that Ben was right: it wouldn't matter to Harney and the army that most of the charges against the "Sioux" had taken place last year after Grattan's unprovoked and lethal assault on the Brules and that recently no attacks had occurred at posts, homesteads, or companies; nor had any stages or wagon trains been attacked. No raids, his keen mind corrected, except for yesterday's theft, which may have been in retaliation for Harney's lethal and cruel assault on the Brules downriver. It also wouldn't matter that some bands—like Red Cloud's—were camped near Fort Laramie to assert their peaceful intentions, and for protection against the army's unjustified retribution on them. He was aware that a few of the smaller bands were still hunting on the vast stretch of grasslands, but most were scouting for or setting up their winter camps at prechosen sites.

At least, Cloud Chaser sighed in relief, his wife and son had Bent Bow and Wind Dancer to hunt for and defend them during his necessary absence from home. For now, they were safe, since General "The Butcher" Harney was far from their location. He could not envision—nor did he even want to try to imagine—his existence without them to share his life, but he knew beyond any doubt it would be a dark and cold one if his beloved Dawn and Casmu were lost to him forever, just as his father had suffered agony when Winona was lost to him for two years. He also knew with absolute certainty that he would fight Harney and any number of soldiers or other foes, even to his own death, in order to protect them from harm.

Cloud Chaser looked upward and sighted an eagle after a large shadow traveled across the ground before him. The majestic bird made him think of his younger brother. He hoped the impending conflict would not cause problems for Caroline, as a few among them like Two Feathers might blame all whites for it and try to create hostility and rejection toward her. With good luck and hard work, perhaps she was earning acceptance and respect from more Red Shields during their absence, as the genial and obedient female already had made friends with many members of their band. He assumed that little would please War Eagle more than for Caroline to become attainable to him. Knowing what it was

like to win the woman one loved and desired, he hoped War
Eagle was victorious in that enormous challenge.

He could not help wondering if his brother's party had
found the surviving Brules by today, and he prayed they
were safe and alive. For now, he needed to get his horse shod
to support his false identity and story. Besides, his mount
was not an Indian pony and truly did need to have its iron
shoes changed. That duty had not been done since last year,
but the cherished animal had been neither trained nor used
for swift and surefooted buffalo hunting, only for riding.
After that responsibility was handled, he would seek a secluded spot at the bluff's base and near the river to camp for
the night where his horse could graze and drink, and he
could keep an eye out for Red Cloud. He worried that if he
bumped into that well-known chief and Red Cloud showed
recognition of him, it would damage his pretense. He had to
keep alert to make certain their paths did not cross there. . . .

Almost two days later, Cloud Chaser observed in near-
trepidation as General Harney and his massive force of men
and wagons approached that setting. It looked as if soldiers
stretched out in multimen lines into the vast forever. He realized his heart was thudding, he was staring wide-eyed, and
he was breathing fast at he watched the galloping throng
cover the distance between them and their destination. He
had to admit, this was the closest to panic he had ever come,
and that reaction shocked and dismayed him. He had seen
this group of bluecoats in Blue Water Canyon and camped at
its mouth, but they had been scattered out in those places
and had not looked as countless and formidable as they did
riding as one unit. Watching them in this manner revealed
their imposing size and power. He did not want to imagine
that horde swooping down on his people's camp and using
their new long-range rifles and canons, which could take
down warriors before the Red Shields could get close enough

to fire arrows or fling lances or swing war clubs. Even with the Great Spirit's help, he worried, how could they battle and defeat such a large and mighty swarm of murderous beings?

Cloud Chaser focused his now narrowed gaze on the detested leader who rode at the front of the seemingly endless multitude. Harney's white beard, mustache, and hair implied he was advanced in years. Yet, the encroacher appeared tall, sturdy, and vigilant; and Cloud Chaser knew from the massacre at Blue Water Creek that Harney was smart and had no qualms about the sex or age or how-to of the targets he slaughtered. He wished the raiding party had not stolen horses there yesterday, as it would only enrage the heartless beast when he learned of that daring incident, but that reckless event could not be recalled.

After the first line of soldiers reached a row of buildings that included the Post Trader's Store, Magazine, and Bedlam Bachelor Officers' Quarters, Cloud Chaser saw them veer left instead of riding to the enormous parade ground. From where he was camped and studying their commander in the forefront, he felt as if he was staring at the epitome of The Enemy, the embodiment of Evil, and perhaps the controller of the Lakotas' fate. Those perceptions made him cringe in dread of discovering if they were accurate. He wished he could use the field glasses to see Harney's expression and gaze up close, but exposing them might bring unwanted attention and suspicion.

Help us, Great Spirit, for we are as a fawn being chased by a grizzly. If we are to escape his sharp teeth and claws and not feed his large hunger for our lives and lands, You must guide us to the path of safety and wisdom. Remove this fear and doubt from my body, for I must trust in Your will.

Cloud Chaser saw the throng ride to a large open space to the rear of the scattered structures of the fort. After they dismounted, the men began setting up their tent encampment there. He saw Major Hoffman, whom he recognized from a past scouting visit, waste no time going to greet the new arrivals. He assumed Hoffman invited Harney to his office to talk away from the noise, dust, and sun's glare, as the two men headed in that direction, a location Cloud Chaser remembered well. He had sneaked inside last year to take the fort's three-page double of the Laramie Treaty and letters from or replicas of those to important people so he could copy them to read that information to his people. Afterward he had returned those items to what was then Lieutenant Fleming's office, who had been removed as commander ensuing the Grattan fiasco. He put aside those thoughts to observe again.

He saw groups of men tending horses, fetching water, and taking wagons toward the Laramie Mountains to cut and haul in wood for cook fires from an abundance of pine, spruce, and other trees growing there. He knew that somewhere in the crowd was Caroline's brother. Yet, it was doubtful he would encounter David and, if a chance meeting occurred, it might not be wise or harmless to slip him a message about his sister. That was a decision to make at the time of the incident. Even so, he would prepare a note that revealed she was alive and safe and would contact him as soon as possible. For now, he must focus on carrying out his crucial reason for being there.

Shortly before dusk and after people appeared to be settling down following a long ride for the newcomers and a busy day for most there, Cloud Chaser walked his horse to the sutler's store to see what he could learn. He left the sorrel at the hitching post and went inside to find the man alone.

Ben looked up from his closing tasks, grinned, and said, "Good to see you again, Chase. Lord come Sunday, this has been a wild day."

"I saw all the commotion from my campsite near the river. I guess you weren't talking too tall when you said Harney had a big force coming with him. Maybe they'll stir up some business for you while they're here."

"I surely can use the sales, 'cause they're gonna be down low after Harney takes off on his 'Sioux Campaign,' that's what he's callin' it."

Cloud Chaser leaned against the counter. "What did you hear?"

"Plenty, but from the usuals around here. Seems Harney is keepin' his boys close to their encampment. I guess he don't want 'em minglin' with the friendlies around here and goin' soft on Indians. He was sure hot in the temper about them stolen horses on Monday. Him and Major Hoffman and Agent Twiss, and some others rode over to Red Cloud's camp this afternoon. Charlie and Jim told me he spouted them same orders we already know about. He told 'em all friendlies should stay out of their territory and avoid any hostiles whilst he's chasin' 'em down so they won't git mistook for the enemy and git shot. He sent out braves from Red Cloud's band to take his messages to their allies. He said the Brules—Oh, I guess you ain't heard about the fracus down the road yet. Have you?"

Cloud Chaser faked ignorance and shook his head. "What happened?"

"Old Harney took on Spotted Tail's and Little Thunder's bands over near Ash Hollow last week and near wiped 'em out. Some got away, 'cludin' them two chiefs, so he's eager to git the rest. I heard his boys took down women and children durin' the fight, if you can call a surprise attack with more men and better weapons a fair fight. They even kilt babies in their mamas' arms, and captured a whole bunch more of 'em. Sent the lot to Fort Kearny to be held there until they're wagoned on to Fort Leavenworth."

Ben grabbed a quick breath before continuing. "I sure am glad I ain't no soldier and had to obey them sorry orders. No mama's son should be forced to kill women and surely not children and babies. Anyways, Harney said the rest of them Brules and whoever else has been in on them raids and was in on Grattan's Massacre has to surrender within two weeks.

If they don't, he's gonna find their camp and attack every poor soul in it, just like he did on Blue Water Creek. He said if any of the other bands are hiding those guilty ones, he's gonna attack them too. Fact is, he's plannin' to attack any camp he thinks is hostile. Lord only knows how he's gonna judge who's good and who's bad, 'specially since he's got it in his head all Lakotas are bad. I doubt even Red Cloud, and that chief's a good talker and well liked in these parts, even Red Cloud won't be able to change his mind. From what Charlie and Jim told me after that parley in the Bad Faces camp, Harney's plannin' on ridin' right into the enemy's mouth and out his tail and yank out his heart whilst he's doin' so. Onest he invades 'Sioux country' as he's callin' it and tries that trick, a long and bloody war is sure to get started. I'm a-bettin' you agree with me on that."

Once more, Cloud Chaser experienced those unwanted sensations of near panic and soul-trembling intimidation as he realized that massive army's march would include the Red Shield camp, which would imperil all of his loved ones. His beloved wife and son and family . . . To think of the same type of vicious assault he had witnessed last week taking place on their camp flooded his entire body with hatred for Harney and his blindness to right and wrong, to good and evil. He took a deep breath, exhaled the spent air, straightened, and said, "You're right, Ben; such a challenge would make war inevitable." *But what can I do to prevent it? What can even the Creator do to prevent it?* He had no answers. . . .

Chapter Thirteen

Late in the afternoon of the following day, Cloud Chaser went to check the southwestward location downriver where War Eagle and the others were to come and wait for him after completing their task. Finding they had not arrived and knowing two patrols had galloped out this morning but toward the east and the north, he prayed his brother and friends either had caught up with the Brules or were still tracking their fleeing allies and that all of them were hidden and safe. Although he wished for the Brules to survive, he hoped they did not seek a haven with the Red Shields, which was certain to endanger his people and camp if those guilty of crimes were found there. If the remnant of Harney's attack tried to seek refuge among them, surely his father and the council would convince them they must leave. Since he could not give advice from that distance, he pushed aside the troubling thought and returned to the fort to see if Ben had learned anything new today.

Cloud Chaser looked eastward as he saw one of the patrols galloping up the road, kicking up dust and making a lot of noise as the soldiers neared their destination, no doubt in a hurry to obtain rest and nourishment. After they bypassed his location and rode into their huge camp, he went into the store and was elated to find the genial sutler alone again, but busy putting out more items from his stockroom. "Evening, Ben. Hope I'm not intruding on your time too much these days while I'm resting up before leaving. I just got back from giving my horse some needed exercise and thought I'd stop in to talk before I make camp and eat and grab some sleep."

"You're no bother at all, Chase, and I can use some rest for a while. Fact of it is, I enjoy jawin' with you. It's about the onliest time I can speak my true mind around here. What little I got of one," Ben added and chuckled.

Then, he waxed serious. "With all that's goin' on, it would seem like I been out in the prairie sun too long or I'm be-damned if I say anythin' bad about Harney or anythin' good about the Lakotas. Fact of it is, I've traded with plenty of 'em over the years since I came here, even Brules, and never had no problems. They learned fast. After they sold their furs and hides over at the big man's company, I give 'em fairer prices on goods. I surely do hate to see Harney and his boys slaughterin' most of 'em. If the army and government treated 'em only half as fair as I do, wouldn't be no trouble in these parts and we wouldn't have no war starin' us down the throat."

"I agree with you, Ben. I know some of those Brules and their friends have done some bad things, but it doesn't jus-tify challenging and punishing all Lakotas for those raids and killings. I'm like you, I've met and dealt with plenty of good men among them. They've never shot a single arrow at me or stolen anything from me. It's gonna be—" Cloud Chaser halted as he heard boots approaching on the store's porch. He and Ben turned and looked in that direction. He concealed his surprise and elation as a soldier entered the door and walked toward them.

"Can I help you with somethin'? I'm the owner here. Name's Ben."

"It's a pleasure to meet you, Ben. I'm David Sims."

Cloud Chaser saw David smile as he extended his right arm and shook hands with the sutler before relating his intention for coming there.

"I want to purchase writing supplies: paper, two envelopes, and a pen and ink or several pencils. Do you have everything I need here?"

Cloud Chaser watched David pause for Ben to nod.

"If I pay extra, can you post and mail a letter for me after it's written? It's personal, so I don't want to stick it in my company's mail pouch."

Cloud Chaser deduced from David's speech and behavior that the man was about his age and was educated and possessed manners. He had sandy hair, no visible scars, and was good-looking to a woman's gaze. His eyes were darker blue than his sister's and their color was enhanced by that of his uniform, one still dusty from today's duties. He noted that David did not give a military rank when introducing himself and appeared a little nervous about being there or about his purchase. . . .

Ben told him, "Won't be no trouble at all, and no extra charge for mailin' it for you. I'll git what you need. You just wait here awhile."

"Thank you, Ben; that's very kind of you."

As Ben went to fill David's order, Cloud Chaser seized an opportunity to glean facts. "You're one of Harney's men, right?" He watched David half turn and look at him before responding.

"That's correct, stranger."

Cloud Chaser tried again to illicit information. "What you troops did down Ash Hollow way has folks in this area plenty worried. Name's Chase Martin," he said as he offered to shake hands, and David accepted the gesture. "Does Harney realize a massacre like that will stir up the Indians against all whites? I mean, killing women and children, destroying their winter supplies, and taking some prisoners. It's been mostly peaceful around here since the treaty in fifty-one, but he's challenging them to war. What man of honor wouldn't do all he could to protect his family, home, people, and lands? In those ways, Indians aren't any different from us whites. Yep, what Harney did to those Brules and their friends has us locals worried plenty."

After he saw the sutler close and the lock the door, David said, "It has me and some of the others worried, too, but we had to obey our orders. Most of us didn't mean to hit women and children, but they got in the cross fire or we couldn't tell their sex and age in hiding or at that distance. I surely do hope and pray none of my bullets were to blame for such deaths."

Cloud Chaser was pleased by David's admissions and feelings. He read distress in the man's gaze and detected it in his voice and mood. Although he knew David had spared Brule lives, he perceived that Caroline's brother felt guilt and anguish over that tragic incident. Perhaps if he didn't probe too hard and too fast, he could extract more information about Harney and his plans, and David himself. "Did you ride in from back East with Harney?"

"No, I was at Pierre under Major Cady until we were transferred to Kearny in June and the major was put in charge there. After General Harney arrived last month, you could say he confiscated us to help in his campaign."

As he set three metal cups on the counter and filled them with hot coffee, Ben motioned with his head for them to take one while he joined in on the talk. "We heard Harney built a fort at Ash Hollow and named it for Grattan. I doubt it'll sit well with the survivors of his attack last year to have anythin' in their territory with his name on it. I also doubt it's sittin' well with 'em about the tradin' post at Pierre becomin' a fort a few months back. Seems to them the army's tightenin' its grip on their assigned territory. I guess a big show of superior power and numbers is supposed to scare 'em into doin' whatever the army and Harney have to say. I'm afraid Harney and a lot of innocent folk are gonna find out them Indians don't scare easy."

David said, "I confess I don't agree with how the general handled the assault at Ash Hollow, but in his defense, he was obeying orders, too. He was commanded by his superiors and the leaders in Washington to ferret out the Indians guilty of raids, and killings, and the massacre of Grattan and his unit. We found letters from a mail robbery last November and items belonging to Grattan and his men in those joint Brule camps we attacked. Doesn't that prove those were the culprits we were after and they were responsible for those crimes? Harney ordered them to surrender, but they refused."

Cloud Chaser refuted in a genial tone, "All it proves is the Brules kept those soldiers' possessions after they defended themselves against Grattan's reckless attack." He could not argue the point on the mail raid, as most knew or suspected Spotted Tail was to blame. He delayed more talk on that matter to relate the facts about the treaty four years ago, who had and had not been present, what it was supposed to achieve, the assignments of territories to friend and foe, the promised annuities and vows of nonencroachment, and how the treaty's terms had not been honored by the whites.

He explained about the three different branches, many tribes, and numerous bands of the Dakota Nation; and pointed out that one band should not be punished for another's misdeeds, nor should the entire Lakota branch be held accountable and punished for the crimes or retaliations of a single or several allied groups. He went on to disclose what happened the day of Grattan's attack on Brave Bear's camp, who was involved, and why that incident was critical to both sides. He noticed how attentive and uneasy David was about that news, and he was glad it troubled the man.

"Ben and I have lived here for a long time and we've learned a lot about the Lakotas, what most whites call the

Sioux. I told you all of that so you'd understand what you're facing out here, 'cause Harney hasn't taken the time to get any hard facts on these people and this territory or what's really been going on here. I guess enlisted men aren't allowed to read officers' reports. But we know for a fact—don't we, Ben?—that conflicting information was sent in. Our leaders in Washington just chose to believe the ones that blamed the Indians. That's a real shame, David, a deadly mistake."

"I suppose you have a valid point, Chase, because some of the officers don't agree on what or how it happened at Ash Hollow. Lieutenant Warren, he's a topographical engineer traveling with Harney, said it was unnecessary slaughter. He told me some of the Indians sought protection in the bluffs, but 'seven women and three children were found dead' in one cave alone. After the melee, I saw children shot in the back, head, arms, and knees. One girl even had bullet wounds on the bottoms of both feet. I saw dead mothers with dead babies in their arms. But I have to tell you, Colonel Cook, Engineer Warren, Doc Ridgely, and others tended the wounded."

Between sips of cool coffee, Ben remarked, "Sounds to me like those Indians never stood a chance against them new long-range rifles we heard you boys were usin'. I doubt them Indians could get close enough in most cases to land an arrow or throw a lance or knife at you boys. Sounds like a one-sided battle to me. That Warren called it right: pure slaughter."

Cloud Chaser witnessed how that dark truth affected Caroline's older brother. The man took a deep breath, lowered his gaze, and slowly released the spent air. It appeared to Cloud Chaser as if David needed and wanted to unload or at least lighten the heavy burden he was carrying. If David possessed an evil heart and mind, Cloud Chaser reasoned, he would not be feeling guilt and shame. Those, he decided, were good signs.

David lifted his head and gaze. "An interpreter said the

Indians are calling the general 'The Butcher' and 'Squaw-killer.' I suppose if I'm honest with you two and with myself, he earned those names on Monday. I saw with my own eyes when Chief Little Thunder held up a white flag and came out with others to talk, but the general thought it was a trick and wasn't in the mood for mercy or peace."

Cloud Chaser asked, "What were the death and capture counts?"

"A hundred and thirty-six killed in Little Thunder's camp. At Spotted Tail's, eighty-six, mostly women and children. I heard one of the casualties was the chief's wife and another wife was captured. We captured seven wounded warriors and took about seventy women and children prisoner. The two chiefs and some warriors fled with the rest of the women and children. Harney ordered the dragoons to pursue them, but Steel's company came back empty-handed after chasing them for six miles or more. Afterward, Cook reprimanded Heth for his failure to prevent the Indians from getting past his line of assault because Heth was positioned at the north end of the valley. Harney sent the prisoners to Fort Kearny, but they'll be heading on to Fort Leavenworth soon. Probably some of them won't make it there alive because they were seriously wounded. The day following the battle, Harney sent units to their camps to confiscate anything valuable or useful and had the rest of their belongings burned in a huge fire. If any of them return, they won't find anything left."

Ben asked, "What about the general's force? Any dead and wounded?"

"Our side sustained seven serious wounds and five dead. The injured were sent to Kearny, and the dead were buried near the river. There's one man unaccounted for; he could have deserted during the attack. Lord knows I was tempted to do the same because of such unwarranted atrocities."

Cloud Chaser saw how shocked David was about voicing that admission aloud before the embarrassed man rushed on to excuse his outburst, or perhaps to explain the motivating feelings behind it.

"It's hard for a man of honor and decency to accept taking part in such repugnant and cruel events. Even if I weren't bound by my sworn oath to obey orders, I couldn't have deserted because I would have been hunted down, arrested, and executed. I suppose I should hate the Indians and not mind attacking them because they abducted my sister while she was en route to join me at Kearny. At least that's what the army believes. I have to stay alive to find her and I'm praying she's safe out there somewhere."

"What do you mean by the army thinks she was taken by Indians?" Cloud Chaser asked.

"As I told you earlier, I was assigned to Major Cady at Fort Pierre, but we were shifted to Kearny in June. After our parents died and bankers took over the family property, my sister left Georgia to join me at Pierre. Since she was en route west, I couldn't contact her about my transfer. I told the officer left in charge at Pierre to relate that news to her upon her arrival. Caroline left Pierre on August first under the escort of the last troops being relocated to Kearny. They never reached the fort. Major Cady sent out a search patrol that tracked the wagons to a grassland site a few days out from Pierre. Then, it was as if the ground opened up and swallowed them. The wagon and horse prints just stopped and the patrol couldn't find any sign of them anywhere in the area, and they searched in every direction. All they saw were thousands of buffalo tracks and new grass from recent storms; I suppose those things obliterated any trail the enemy made. Major Cady believes the Indians attacked, stole everything, killed the soldiers, and captured my sister; then, stampeded buffalo back and forth to destroy the evidence of their crimes. Something happened to that troop because men, wagons, and cannons just don't vanish like morning fog after the sun rises."

Cloud Chaser empathized with the man's confusion and anguish, but felt it was necessary to mislead the army through David. "Indians might not be to blame for that mystery. Last summer there was a gang of white men dressing as Indians, right up to using full-head scalps they had lifted, and attacking military shipments and stages. During one of their raids, they killed an entire escort of soldiers bringing weapons and supplies here and stole their load. They shot arrows into those soldiers' bodies and took scalp locks to point the army's eyes in the wrong direction. They were killed while trying to rob a mail stage and their identities as white men were exposed. Probably some of those other raids the Indians are being blamed for were committed by that gang before it was destroyed. Could be some of its members escaped and have formed a new gang and they're responsible for your sister's disappearance, or maybe another gang is at work in this territory now. Ask Major Cady to check Lieutenant Fleming's reports for last August if Major Hoffman still has them in his office. It would be a smart idea for Harney to do the same; he might learn he can't blame Indians for every misdeed carried out in these parts. Best I recall, it was toward the first of the month, but most of us don't keep up with day numbers out here."

Ben added, "I remember that fracus. Flemin' got big praise for it, but it didn't save his butt after that Grattan mess. Besides, seems to me, if my recall is right, Grattan handled that trap 'cause Flemin' was at Kearny."

"That does sound familiar to me," Cloud Chaser concurred in a casual tone, though he possessed the truth of the entire matter. He knew from checking out that report later that his name and involvement in it had not been recorded. Since Grattan and those soldiers had been slain in that so-called massacre, no one was alive who could expose his part in it. He was glad Grattan had wanted all of the recognition for uncovering and resolving that matter. Yet, learning about such deceptions by his own kind had not changed Grattan's mind about "ignorant and uncivilized" Indians needing to be subjugated or slain or driven into the wilderness far away from this desired territory. That man's feelings, blindness, and arrogance had gotten him and his soldiers killed, along with many innocent or provoked Brules.

David smiled and said, "Thanks for the information, Chase, and you could be right. I'll ask Major Cady to check out those reports from last August. Maybe Fate is being kind to me and she brought us together today to give me hope about Caroline. At least you've given me a clearer image of the Indians and history here. I'll be sure to include those facts in the letter I'm writing to Secretary Davis. I mean,"— David halted and scowled—"there's no need to lie to you two, but I hope you won't mention to anybody what I said and intend to do. I just thought I should send the Secretary of War a detailed and honest account of what happened at Ash Hollow because I'm doubtful the whole truth will be told in our officers' reports, and I think the secretary, president, and Congress should know what's really going on out here. I'm hoping they don't want to be a party to such atrocities and will order them stopped."

"Don't worry, David, we'll keep quiet, won't we, Ben?"

"Sounds like a good and brave deed to me," Ben said. "And it surely needs to be kept quiet or it'll cause you plenty of trouble."

"I'm not signing my name to it, and that's why I asked you to mail it for me, Ben. Thanks for keeping my secret."

Cloud Chaser responded for them, "You're welcome, David. I'm glad we got to meet and talk. Good luck with finding your sister. While I'm traveling around, if I hear anything about a white woman being with Indians, I'll send word to you at Fort Kearny. Ben will keep his ears open, too."

"I'll be grateful for anything you can do to help locate her, and perhaps you've already pointed me in the right direction. She's hard not to notice if you sight her: nineteen, slender, blond hair, blue eyes, beautiful, and a real southern lady. She's intelligent, brave, and kindhearted; so maybe those traits will keep her safe until I can rescue her. It's getting late, so I need to get back to my company. How much for those writing supplies, Ben?"

After the charge was paid and the men shook hands, David departed with his purchases concealed beneath his coat. Shortly afterward, Cloud Chaser left to make camp near the clear mountain-fed Laramie River.

The next day, Cloud Chaser struck up a conversation with a teamster named William Chandless who had passed Ash Hollow en route there to deliver goods and was preparing to head back for another haul. Chandless related that when he had camped overnight at the hollow some soldiers had told him General Harney made an "inflammatory speech" laced heavily with obscenities against the Indians to get his men worked up into the "killing mood" before the recent attack there.

Chandless voiced his opinion as "I'm sure Harney will take a beating from Christians and northerners because of what he did and being a southerner, but I guess he had no choice except to set them Indians straight. He surely had the upper hand with rifles that can kill at half a mile. 'Course, I had to feel a little sorry for them Indians who didn't get buried; wolves and ravens were working hard on their bodies."

Following a few more minutes of talk, Chandless had to leave, so Cloud Chaser thanked him for the news and bade him a safe journey. Afterward, he rode to the site where his brother and companions were to meet him, but they still had not arrived. He hoped and prayed they were safe and would join him soon so he could reveal all he had learned and they could make plans for their next move, for which he had a daring idea. . . .

*   *   *

Far northeast of the fort on "the river that lives," War Eagle and his party were greeted by their allies in the makeshift joint-camp of Little Thunder and Spotted Tail. While allowing their four weary mounts to rest, drink, and graze, they sat down on the grassy surface to speak with the two leaders and their remaining warriors.

As they did so, somber women busied themselves with their tasks while small children clung to either their dress tails or their legs, still visibly frightened from their recent clash with terror. It was sad to the visitors to see that all the survivors possessed were the garments they wore, weapons, and some horses. They had no tepees, sleeping or sitting mats, winter rations, or other personal needs for doing their chores. Yet, the women were making the best of a grim situation as they roasted freshly slain antelope and large plant roots over carefully controlled flames to avoid telltale smoke in the air. Without water bags and horn holders, drinking was being done at the river. Shelters had been made by laying branches across crevices in the lower bluffs, beneath which they could escape the sun or any bad weather. Upon arrival, they noted the men were busy preparing more arrows and sharpening other weapons to be ready for hunting and defense.

The Red Shields were told about the fierce battle and that the Brules and their friends had fled through the north end of the Blue Water Creek Valley. As with the escapees, they had traveled across rolling grass-covered sand hills or around barren dunes and over flat-lying plains to the hilly section of high and low bluffs, some with sharp ridges. It was a good place to camp, as trees and scrub brush were numerous. That and the broken terrain would provide concealment from enemy eyes and wood for cook fires. The river would supply them with water; and the location, with ample game for food.

After Little Thunder finished his revelations, War Eagle

disclosed how he and his companions had witnessed the attack and explained why they could not join in on the battle. With great reluctance and empathy, but out of necessity, he told the two chiefs and the people what they had observed for the remainder of that dark sun and during the ensuing three days. He related how his party had tracked them to that location to enlighten them to those terrible events.

He addressed his first words to Spotted Tail. "We ask Sinte Galeska and his friends to forgive us for staying hidden, but there were too many bluecoats with firesticks to battle. It is not the Lakota way to make a challenge a warrior cannot win, to sacrifice his life in certain defeat, for our people need us on coming suns. We could not free those taken captive or tend to your dead, for the bluecoats remained alert for such deeds."

Spotted Tail said, "It is good the slayers of women and children do not have the eagle's eyes and skills or we would be dead, for we would not have surrendered on that sun. Our hearts and minds were too full of hatred and anger. You did not dishonor yourselves, son of Rising Bear and good Red Shields, for a Lakota victory on that sun could not be. You were wise not to challenge such a large and powerful force, for you must live to help defeat this enemy when they challenge Lakotas again, for they are sure to do so."

After he waited for War Eagle to nod agreement and gratitude, Spotted Tail went on to say, "The bluecoats chased us for less than half a sun. They do not know the Creator's land as we do. We hid from their evil eyes and ears until they gave up their search and returned to Mad Dog's camp. We have few warriors among us, but we rode as the wind and took horses from their fort. The others hid until we returned and used them to come here to rest and tend to our wounds. We sent braves to the camps of our allies. They rode as the wind and returned fast with the new messages from Agent Twiss and Mad Dog. I lost two of my wives, one to a bluecoat's firestick and one to capture. One of my children also fell to the enemy's firestick, as did other members of my larger family. It is wrong that they feed the Creator's creatures and do not lie upon scaffolds for their spirits to return to His side. Two of their bullets pierced my flesh and two bluecoats cut me with their long knives, but I live and heal. Our hearts are sad. Our bodies are weak, and some are injured. Our spirits no longer soar high and free as the sky birds."

After he repeated the harsh demands of General Harney, Spotted Tail said, "If we do not surrender to Mad Dog, he will hunt us down and slay us, no matter how many suns or seasons he must chase us to do so. We cannot seek help from our allies, for Mad Dog will attack them as he attacked us at Blue Water. Without our possessions and with our number so few, we cannot survive the coming winter. If we remain free, Mad Dog will believe others help us hide from him to survive. He will attack all Lakota camps searching for us. We must not endanger the lives of others. Long Chin and Red Leaf say I speak wise and true. The Cheyenne among us left to join their allies far away, for their chief Tseske Vosototse was slain during the attack. The son of my sister will not surrender at my side. Crazy Horse will leave us soon to join another band to live in freedom while he waits for the sun to challenge the white man. He does not trust them and says his vision told him he must do a great deed for all Lakotas when he is older. I accept his words."

War Eagle knew that Long Chin and Red Leaf were the brothers of Chief Brave Bear, who had been killed by Grattan's unit. He also knew that Little Butte was an ally of his friend Red Wolf's Cheyenne band. After he returned home, he must take that sad news to Red Wolf's people.

Little Thunder said, "We did not believe Mad Dog would attack for we were camped peacefully and have done no raids since the last hot season. I will not surrender to the butcher who attacked us and dishonored their own white flag of truce. Surely I would be tortured and slain, and my body left to feed the scavengers. I will lead my people far away where we will be safe. I will no longer challenge the blue-coats and whites, for they are too many and too strong. We will ride in two suns. Little Thunder has spoken."

Following more talk, War Eagle said they had to leave to join his second brother, who was scouting at Fort Laramie. He told Spotted Tail, "You are wise and brave and possess a good heart, Sinte Galeska. We will pray for the white war chief to show you and your people mercy. Farewell, my Brule friends. May the Great Spirit go with you and guide you."

"Pilamaya, Wanbli. *Wakantanka nici un."* The chief thanked him and echoed his last words.

As they galloped away, War Eagle dreaded to learn the fates of Spotted Tail, Long Chin, Red Leaf, and their band members. He surmised that Harney would not be wholly satisfied with their surrenders since that event excluded those of Little Thunder and the remnants of his band when it was well known that Little Thunder was responsible for some raids and involvement in Grattan's defeat. To War Eagle, it was selfish and cowardly of Little Thunder to imperil all Lakotas and their territory so he could remain free and alive. He prayed that the white leaders would show mercy to the submissive Brules. If they were slaughtered after yielding, it would be taken as a show that the white man was utterly evil, could not be trusted in the slightest, and no truce was possible, ever.

Anxious to join his brother and hear what Cloud Chaser had learned, War Eagle ordered them to a swifter pace, while staying alert for any threat. He could not help thinking that as soon as their duties were completed, he could ride for home to help protect their people, and Caroline. Calling her image to mind and knowing she would be near him again soon caused his heart to beat faster, his desire to enflame, and his spirit to soar. *It will not be long before we are together again, Kawa Cante. I quiver with eagerness to look upon your face, to hear your voice, to touch you. Somehow I must find a way to make you mine, for I am filled with love for you.*

Three days later and concealed amidst trees growing along the riverbank, War Eagle and his companions sat with Cloud Chaser and listened to all he had learned during their separation. As soon as Cloud Chaser completed his revelations, War Eagle told him the shocking news about the imminent surrender of Spotted Tail, his remaining band, and few others. He related the refusals and intentions of Little Thunder and Crazy Horse, and the northwest departure of the surviving Cheyenne following the death of their leader and some band members. "We will wait here to see if Sinte Galeska and others do as they told us; then we will ride fast to our camp."

Cloud Chaser shook his head and urged in a gentle tone, "No, my brother, you must ride for our camp on this sun to tell Father and our people all we have seen and heard and done. Our camp must be moved before The Butcher continues his brutal journey in our territory. I will remain here to watch for the surrenders of our allies and learn what will be done with them. While I do so, I will scout the enemy and will ride with or near the white war chief to study him and to learn his plans. I was told he will soon head into the heart of our country and make his way to Fort Pierre. After I do so and when I am near the sacred hills, I will leave The Butcher and return home. Our people must move deeper into the Paha Sapa for concealment from this fierce enemy. Lead them to the place of the river canyon where we hunted last winter; it will be a safe location and will provide for our needs and shelter during the cold season. I will join you there later."

War Eagle smiled and said, "That is the same place my mind chose. We will ride out after dark when the bluecoats are on their sleeping mats. The moon wears her full yellow face, so she will give us plenty of light for our journey. Take no risks, my brother; guard your body and life well. Stay ready to flee if Mad Dog gives a sign he does not trust you. I will protect and hunt for your wife and son"—*and Caroline*— "until you are among us again."

"That is good and generous; my heart thanks you. There is one last matter I must reveal to you," Cloud Chaser began, then related his meeting with David Sims and his intention to pass along a message to David about his sister since he had spared Indian lives at Blue Water Creek and was sending a truthful report to the white leaders about the cruel events in this area. "You must tell Caroline such news, for it will make her happy and will repay her for her good deeds among us."

"I will speak with her, and your plans are wise ones."

After they locked gazes and clasped wrists for a few moments, War Eagle watched Cloud Chaser mount and leave. He knew his second brother had carried out successful scouting there in the past and recently, so he should be safe to continue doing so. His heart and mind were filled with pride, love, and respect for Cloud Chaser. His heart and mind also were filled with those same emotions toward Caroline, and they were charged with elation to be heading home today. *Soon, Kawa Cante, soon. . . .*

That same day in the Red Shield camp, as she did her daily chores with Dawn and Hanmani near the river, Caroline noticed how Hanmani kept stealing glances at the warrior who was speaking with Wind Dancer as her oldest brother watered his horse a short distance away. She had seen Dawn grin at Hanmani and had overhead Dawn whisper the man's name—Red Wolf of the Fire Hearts Cheyenne—which told Caroline he was from the family that War Eagle had been taking her to long ago before he changed his mind. All of them had heard the Cheyenne brave say that he came to visit his good friend and close ally War Eagle, and was being told by Wind Dancer of War Eagle's absence. At least, she thought with a smile, she could grasp much of the men's conversation from the amount of Lakota she had learned during the almost two months she had lived among the Red Shields.

From the seventeen-year-old girl's behavior and expressions, Caroline surmised that Hanmani was enchanted by the handsome Indian but was dismayed by those romantic feelings. When she realized that Red Wolf not only was from another tribe and culture but also was half white, she decided it was best not to mention her observation and conclusions. *So,* she mused, *he is the son of Sparrow, and Hanmani desires him. . . .*

It was almost dark when Caroline slipped into the forest. She was hidden behind bushes when two people neared her location and began to talk. She froze in place and stayed silent as she listened to them devising a horrendous and lethal plot. . . .

Chapter Fourteen

When she first heard the twosome coming, Caroline remained still and quiet. She assumed the intruders would stroll past her location and she could slip away unseen, as she did not want to encounter either offensive person. When they halted within a few feet of her and began to talk, she was horrified by what they said.

"Do you still desire Wind Dancer as your mate?"

"It cannot be, Two Feathers, for he belongs to Dewdrops."

"Do you still desire Wind Dancer as your mate?"

Caroline heard him persist in a stern tone for a response. She dared not peer through the bushes to study their expressions, as any movement or noise surely would seize the warrior's attention. She listened as Wastemna exhaled as if annoyed or frustrated before the woman finally answered him.

"Yes, but I cannot have him. Why do you pain my heart this way?"

"If Dewdrops is dead, Wind Dancer will be free to take another wife. He will be forced to make a choice fast, for he will need a mother to tend his children and tepee. There is no female among us more beautiful and skilled than Wastemna. Do you fear you cannot lure him into your arms?"

"He looked upon me long ago with desire, before Dewdrops stole his eye and clouded his mind. But she is young and unsick. She will not die."

Caroline grasped disappointment and hatred in the female's voice. She was doubtful that Wind Dancer had ever desired such a vile creature, as Chumani had told her about the wicked things Wastemna had done to drive her away or have her banished or murder her.

"She will die if the knife of an enemy enters her body while she is in the forest alone."

"There is no hope of an enemy getting so close to our camp or, if one does so, there is no hope Dewdrops would be slain by him. Do you forget she was a female warrior before she came to live among us and she rode at Wind Dancer's side during the vision quest? She is skilled with weapons and in fighting, so no enemy could take her by surprise."

"There is hope if I am that enemy and do the deed for you."

Caroline tensed during a span of silence that seemed much longer than it was. She did not know if she had been detected or if Wastemna was stunned speechless by the man's evil offer.

"What do you mean by such words, Two Feathers?" the woman finally asked.

"I will slay Dewdrops for you if you will slay Cloud Chaser for me. With them dead, Dawn will be mine once more and Wind Dancer will be yours. That is a good trade, is it not?"

"How can I slay a skilled warrior? I remember little of him when we were children and I was banished when Cloud Chaser came back, but I have learned much about him since my return fourteen suns past. How can a small woman slay a warrior of his size and prowess?"

"Follow the half-breed when he leaves camp alone and when he turns his back to you, beat his head with a rock or limb until he lives no more."

Half-breed? Caroline's mind echoed in astonishment and curiosity.

"If I am caught, I will be tortured and slain. I can not do it."

"You can do it, Wastemna, for you are cunning and brave, and you desire Wind Dancer. Do you forget the many clever tricks you played on Dewdrops long ago? You were exposed because you talked with your mother while others listened. You will not make that slip again."

A full moon was rising and there was little daylight left. Caroline had been gone for a long time, so Macha might come look for her or send someone else to search for her. Yet, she was trapped until the two sinister conspirators departed.

"It is reckless; two deaths in our chief's family with few suns between them will be suspicious to others. We would be caught and slain."

"Will you be happy to live among us and see Dewdrops in your place? Watch her be with the man you desire? Watch her with children who should be yours? Watch her treat you with scorn? Is that the existence you want?"

"No, but I am too weak and afraid to seek what my heart desires."

"It is a good challenge and will be a glorious victory. If we are sly and careful, no one will look in our direction."

"Why do you not slay Cloud Chaser yourself?"

"There has been much conflict and many bad words between us since his return. I must not be near him or even in camp when he is slain and his body is found, or many will believe I took his life. No one will think a 'weak and afraid' female could do such a brave and daring deed. You will be safe."

"I must think long and hard on this matter, Two Feathers."

"No, you must speak your choice to me this moon. I warn you, no Red Shield will accept your words if you betray me to them. You will be sent away again, to live alone, in great need, in peril. Summon your courage and wits, Wastemna. Seize the war prize you crave. Will you join me in battle?"

Caroline awaited the woman's answer with bated breath, and grimaced when it was spoken.

"Yes, but I must decide when we will strike our first blow."

"It is yours to choose, if you do not wait long to do so. Go now before you are missed and we are seen together. We must stay apart until we can sneak another meeting."

"I will do this deed, Two Feathers, but do not betray me or refuse to carry out your part of our trade after he is no more."

"We must trust each other, Wastemna. Wind Dancer will belong to you soon. Return to camp and do not come near me until I signal you."

Caroline heard the menacing creature leave, but Two Feathers stayed where he was. She tensed again, fearing he knew she was lurking nearby and had waited for Wastemna's departure before dealing lethally with her. She struggled to control her breathing as her heart beat fast, then faster, within her chest. Her body ached from remaining motionless for so long. She prayed her protesting knee joints would not go *pop* or her shaky ankles make a cracking sound. She heard Two Feathers laugh faintly, the tone frigid and fiendish. Then, she soon discovered why the warrior was still standing there and was so distracted. . . .

"Foolish woman, you will not enjoy Wind Dancer for many suns and moons, for I will slay him and claim the next chief's bonnet for myself. War Eagle will never wear it. He will be unworthy of taking that rank after his father and brother are dead, for he will soon be the dishonored captive of his captive. After I slip my knife into your heart, foolish woman, it will look as if you were so sad and wild with grief you killed yourself. I will not have to place a foe's *wanapin* in your hand to trick others as I did with Sisoka after I took her life. Rising Bear is too old to lead us in the great war ahead and his spirit will be destroyed by the deaths of his two sons and the dishonor of his third in the arms of the enemy. I no longer love and respect you, Rising Bear, and I hunger for your death to end your weakness and shame. You tainted yourself by mating with a white woman and placing your man seeds within the captive enemy's body and bringing forth a half-breed who stole my woman and scorns me before others. I will be the next chief and I will have Dawn as my wife. So I have spoken, so it will be."

Caroline cringed at the icy tone of the warrior's last sentence. She was relieved and exhausted when he finally walked away. As she waited for a while to be certain he was gone and not hiding nearby to ensnare her, she thought about those two misguided and black-hearted people, and what she should do about their insidious plot. Although she had not grasped every word spoken, she had understood most of what was said and was positive she was not mistaken about what she had overheard.

She still was shocked by the truth about Cloud Chaser. Why had he not told her his own mother was a white woman, a captive to his father? After he had made his slip ensuing the Naming Ceremony, she had suspected he was part white, then convinced herself that was ridiculous and he must have meant he was a mixture of two different Indian tribes. Had his mother really "died" or had she escaped, been sold or traded, or slain for some reason? Somehow she believed the woman had died of natural causes.

She recalled how Wastemna had treated and spoken to her since the woman's return two weeks ago. The despicable creature had been sly and careful with her insults, but it was evident Wastemna hated her and detested her presence among them. She could imagine how that offensive woman would treat her if she were only a captive.

What she had learned about War Eagle knifed her heart. The man she loved and desired would dishonor himself if he laid claim to her and could not become chief if anything happened to Rising Bear and Wind Dancer, which was his right and duty, and retaining his honor meant so much to him. Yet, his father had taken a white captive to his bed and created a son with her. How and why had Rising Bear done so? And why would it be so wrong and shameful for War Eagle to do so since his father—guilty of that same deed—had remained as chief, loved and respected and obeyed? She needed those answers to decide if she was only pursuing a futile dream or if there was hope for a glorious victory. Was she like Wastemna, "too weak and afraid to seek what my heart desires" when her goal seemed so unattainable?

At least she had discovered what Two Feather's goals were: Dawn and the chief's rank. Although she knew he was evil, it still shocked her that he so deeply hated his uncle and cousins and would murder them to achieve his desires. She must not permit him to carry out his plot. She must not allow Chumani and Cloud Chaser to die, to be cold-bloodedly murdered. She must not allow War Eagle, Dawn, Wind Dancer, Hanmani, and Nahemana to suffer such losses and anguish. She must not allow Two Feathers to become chief of the Red Shields, as he would surely war fiercely with the whites and soldiers, which would bring about the band's defeat and deaths.

She had worked with the shaman recently by sharing their healing skills and knowledge. She even had been allowed to stitch a severe cut on a warrior's arm, while Nahemana and others observed, and praised her skills and generosity afterward. She had done daily chores with Dawn, Chumani, Winona, Hanmani, Zitkala, Little Turtle, and other females. She liked these people, and most appeared to like her and to treat her fairly. But would they believe her grim allegations? A white captive accusing one of their elite warriors, a close relative of their chief, of a lethal conspiracy? If she was doubted, would she be slain, or perhaps tortured beforehand? Or maybe just sold or traded or given away to another band, an unkind one?

As she left her concealed position and hurried back to Dawn's tepee, staying alert for a threat the entire way, Caroline told herself she must not make a hasty and hazardous deci-

sion. She had to expose the culprits, but first she had to figure out the best time and safest way to do so.

*So, whom should you tell? When? Where? How? Whom
can you trust and who trusts you that much?* The answers
came fast and easy. . . .

After entering the tepee, Caroline watched Dawn turn
quickly, look at her with near-panic in her dark brown gaze,
and say she had been about to come look for her. Caroline
forced a smile and thanked her.

Dawn set down Casmu's cradle-board that she had been
about to place on her back.

Later as Caroline lay on her buffalo mat and awaited her
destiny, her mind was tormented and her heart was pained by
the possibilities she might never see War Eagle and her
brother again if no one there believed what she must tell
them. She loved both men and longed to be with them, at
least one last time. She yearned for War Eagle's company,
his smile, the sound of his voice, his strong embrace, his
powerful protection. She did not want to perish before she
shared at least one passionate and fulfilling experience with
him. It would be blissful to hear him tell her that he loved her.
It would be ecstasy to . . . Yes, right or wrong, she wanted,
needed, craved to make love with him. If he were there,
Caroline conceded, she would be tempted to surrender to her
desires before she risked her life to save the lives and to prevent the sorrows of her friends.

She was amazed that these carnal feelings did not shock
her, though they did surprise her a little. Had she changed so
much since captivity, the deaths of her parents, and the loss
of her family's possessions?

While Macha was breast-feeding Casmu the next morning, Caroline asked if she could visit Chumani for a short
time, acting and looking as casual as possible. Macha smiled
and gave her permission to leave.

As Caroline walked the short distance to Wind Dancer's colorful tepee, her anxiety mounted and she trembled, but she did not slow her steady pace, turn back, or change her mind. At the closed flap, she called out for permission to enter, as one did not do so when it was not secured open. After she heard Chumani invite her inside, Caroline joined her. She found the older woman alone and feeding her almost-four-week-old infant, the reason for the privacy signal. She was relieved to discover that Wind Dancer and Tokapa were gone, at least for now.

"Psa'owinza akan yanka." Chumani told her to sit on a rush mat nearby.

In English, Caroline said in a low voice after she took a seat, "I did not want to disturb you, Dewdrops, but I need to speak with you."

Chumani noted a worried expression on the white girl's face and in her blue gaze. She also noticed that her visitor was not speaking Lakota as usual and was using a hushed tone. She softly asked in English, "What is wrong, Caroline? You look afraid and uneasy."

Caroline intentionally used English in the event someone arrived and overheard her accusations. She nodded as she almost whispered, "I am, Dewdrops, but I will wait for you to finish feeding Inunpa before we speak."

Chumani looked down at her daughter—alive because of Caroline—and said, "She eats no more and she sleeps. I will put her in her cradle-board."

As the baby was being secured there for her nap, Caroline asked, "Will Wind Dancer and Tokapa return soon?"

"No, for they have eaten and go to walk in the forest," Chumani said as she sat down before the white woman, their knees almost touching. "Speak of what troubles your heart and head," she coaxed, curious and concerned.

Caroline lowered her gaze for a moment as she took a deep breath. When she looked up, she murmured, "Where and how do I begin my story?"

Chumani leaned forward, placed her warm hands over Caroline's cold ones that gripped her knees tightly, and smiled to encourage and relax the tense female. "The first step of a hard journey is the worst, but take it, my friend. I will help you travel and finish it, as you have helped me live to make my life's walk on Mother Earth."

"Do you trust me, Dewdrops?"

"I do not understand your meaning, Caroline."

"Will you believe me if I swear to you that evil—*sica, wastesni*—is living and plotting in your camp and threatens the lives of my good friends here?"

"What evil sprit attacks our camp? How does it do so, Caroline?"

"In the bodies of Two Feathers and Wastemna."

Chumani straightened and stared at Caroline. "What do you say?"

Caroline related how she had overhead a shocking talk last night in the forest and what was said between those two people. She saw Chumani's gaze first widen in astonishment, then narrow in anger.

"I swear upon my life and honor I speak the truth," Caroline said. "I did not misunderstand their words and meanings. I feared no one would believe such a terrible story from a white captive about a great warrior, one who is a member of the chief's family, and a man I fear and dislike and who scorns me. I feared I would be punished and slain or sent away to another band who might mistreat me. Even if that happens, I could not allow them to harm you and Cloud Chaser and cause your loved ones and people to suffer from your losses." She revealed her temptation to leave Cloud Chaser a warning message and escape, but told why she could not handle the perilous plot in that manner.

Caroline was glad when Chumani remained quiet and attentive so she could finish her difficult task and had not accused her of lying or of being mistaken. "I came to you,

Dewdrops, because I think you are the best one who might believe me and you can find a way to thwart them. I hoped we could set a trap for him to prove to all Red Shields I speak the truth: I thought I could lure him into the forest, tell him I overheard his talk with Wastemna, and ask him to let me be the one to slay Cloud Chaser in trade for my freedom while Wind Dancer and others hid and listened. But I realized Two Feathers would not believe me, for he knows we are friends. He would suspect I was tricking him and would reveal nothing. I do not know how I can prove I speak the truth, but I do, I swear it."

"I believe you, Caroline." Chumani saw and heard her sigh in relief, then smile in joy. "You are a good friend, a brave woman, to take such a great risk with your life. You did the same when you saved me and my child and helped War Eagle defeat a foe and tended Red Feather's cut. You have done many good deeds among us. You have not viewed or treated us as the 'savages' and 'hostiles' most whites believe us to be. Surely the Great Spirit sent you to us and He works His will through you. Remain here with Inunpa and guard her while I go to bring my husband, our chief, and the shaman to talk. Zitkala will keep Tokapa while we do so. We will plan our action before we speak with Dawn. Did you tell her of this evil?"

"No. I did not want to frighten her too soon."

"That is good. We must be careful our enemies do not learn we know of their evil before we entrap them. I will return soon." Chumani started to rise to leave, then sank back on her folded legs. "There is one thing you should not reveal to others, Two Feathers' words about you and War Eagle. Tell them Two Feathers' plots to destroy my husband and his youngest brother so he can become chief, but do not say how he planned to do so. It does not matter about Cloud Chaser, for all know the truth of his birth."

"Are you saying I should lie to Wind Dancer and the others?"

"No, just hold back that tiny part about War Eagle's secret feelings for you, for it could cause him trouble if it is true and is revealed too soon. I will tell my husband later when we are alone, but our chief and shaman do not need to know that secret at this time, for I do not want them to view you as a threat to War Eagle's honor and rank. It is enough to say Two Feathers plots to destroy all three sons so he can become the next chief."

"Would it dishonor War Eagle if he . . . wanted me as his woman?"

"I do not know, for I cannot see into the future. I will return soon."

Caroline watched Chumani make a hasty departure and wondered if the "secret" disturbed her and the woman was escaping any discussion of it. Or perhaps Chumani was only distracted by her own worries or wanted to handle the grave matter fast. Surely they would discuss it at another time.

She moved to Chumani's sitting mat after the woman departed and gazed at the sleeping infant. She reached out a hand, and lightly stroked a chubby cheek with the pad of her forefinger so as not to awaken Inunpa. Caroline was pervaded with elation and pride and she smiled as she watched the small miracle she had delivered. *You will not lose your mother, little one. She will be safe from their threat, as will your uncle. Perhaps one day I will have a daughter or a son or both. Perhaps he or she will have dark eyes and hair like yours if I can win the man I love.*

Caroline closed her eyes and prayed. *If You truly sent me here to live and to do good things, Great Spirit, allow me to become as a Red Shield and make me worthy of becoming War Eagle's wife without it dishonoring him. Bring peace to this territory. Guide and protect each of us.*

Caroline looked up when Chumani returned, alone. . . . Where, she worried, were the three men? Had she been distrusted and deluded by her friend? No, that could not be

true! Had the men disbelieved Chumani's allegations and refused to come and speak with a lowly slave? Were they deciding on her punishment at that very minute? Would it be—

Chumani joined Caroline and whispered, "The others
will come soon, one by one, so our people will not think it
strange and wonder why they rush here to meet. Two Feathers
has gone hunting and Wastemna is in the forest gathering
wood, so they will not see them come."

Caroline murmured in awe, "They believed you, believed
me?"

"Yes, but it was hard for them to accept. I only told them
Two Feathers and Wastemna are plotting evil and I must expose them."

"What will happen to Wastemna and Two Feathers?"

Chumani admitted, "I do not know. It is hard for us to slay
a band member as punishment, and we do not have a wooden
tepee to hold evil ones captive as the whites and soldiers do."

"But if they are only banished, the could sneak back one
night and try to slay you and Cloud Chaser or others for revenge."

"That is true, but their fates must be left in the Creator's
hands. He—" Chumani halted her explanation as Wind Dancer
arrived and gazed back and forth between them. "Come, my
husband, sit with us."

Wind Dancer took a place beside his wife and said in
Lakota, "We will not speak of the trouble until Father and
Grandfather come to meet with us. Such evil does not need
to fill your mouth many times."

Chumani translated his words for Caroline to make certain she understood his request, and her friend nodded.

Caroline focused her attention on the baby so she would
not have to look at the powerful warrior who was seated in
front of her and was studying her intently. In many ways,
War Eagle favored his older brother, but he had scant resemblance to Cloud Chaser, who probably took part of his looks

from his white ancestors. Yet, all three males were handsome, tall, and strong. From what she had observed and learned of their past exploits and characters, any one of them would make an excellent Red Shield chief. All three were brave, perhaps utterly fearless to a certain degree, cunning, intelligent, and skilled in hunting and warfare. They were loved, obeyed, and esteemed by their people, except for the two evildoers. They were fiercely loyal to their families, people, customs, and lands. They were men of great honor who practiced their beliefs daily and lived by their Four Virtues. How could she not admire and befriend such men of quality and high rank? How could she not love and desire War Eagle? It was impossible. It was—

Caroline halted her musings as the chief arrived to join them and Rising Bear took a seat beside his eldest son. As she watched him enter and take his place, she gave him a rapid scrutiny. His strength, agility, and near-regal bearing disguised his fifty years of age. His long dark hair exposed only a meager amount of silver or white near his temples. The top and sides of his black hair were drawn back and secured behind his head with a leather thong, an eagle feather dangling from the lock. His features were prominent, but not unappealing. He was a nice-looking man, but not handsome like his three sons. He was clad in a deerskin vest, leggings, breechclout, a tie belt with a knife sheath, and well-made moccasins. He wore no chief's bonnet or eagle-bone breastplate in camp. but there was a leather medallion with symbols painted upon it suspended around his neck.

Caroline realized that Rising Bear was studying her, while Wind Dancer's attention was focused on his wife and daughter. She presumed the younger warrior was angered by his cousin's threat to his family. Although he had his emotions under control, there was a chilling gleam in his eye and a slight tautness to his jawline that suggested he was riled by the insidious scheme. As for the chief, his expression and gaze told her nothing, as both were stoic, probably from years of practice to dupe enemies or mislead troublemakers. Yet, a man of his rank and with such a strong sense of loyalty to his family, surely Rising Bear was inflamed by the treachery and hatred of his nephew.

Nahemana came forward to join them. He was different from the chief and his grandson. He gave off an aura of reverence, inspiring veneration, and evoking awe. He was wise and serene and gentle, but had great strength of character and purpose. It did not seem as if the kind shaman ever had possessed a warrior's spirit or even could, as he was the guardian of their emotional and physical well-being. He was a man of honor and peace, a teacher, a healer, a ceremonial leader, and intercessor to their Creator. The sage had convinced her he had inexplicable mystical powers, so—if he sensed her feelings for War Eagle, and his for her—what did Nahemana think and feel about such a possibly forbidden relationship? She pushed those ponderings aside as everyone appeared ready to take on the problem at hand.

Caroline sat still and quiet as the men listened while Chumani spoke. When questions were asked afterward, Chumani either answered them from what she had told her friend earlier or queried Caroline in English for clarity, then passed along her responses. She noticed how the men kept glancing at her while Chumani was speaking to them or querying her about certain points, as if to make sure they understood her correctly and/or to assess her honesty.

Then, Caroline heard Wind Dancer say he wanted to question her grasp of their language to be reassured she was not mistaken. She tensed, and prayed she could pass his test of her knowledge and skills. What if he asked only things she didn't know? What would happen to her and her endangered friends if she failed his challenge? Would they believe it was easier to understand another language when one heard it spoken than it was to speak it? Or that one could catch words here and there and grasp the gist of a talk?

Since so much depended on her success, she listened carefully to his first question, which was about how she had learned their language, and was told to respond in Lakota. . . .

Chapter Fifteen

"Yutokeca Mahpiya he oiekicaton ta unspemakiye." Caroline replied that Cloud Chaser had taught her his language.

"How do you say *to kill* in Lakota?"

Caroline repeated his query, not just those two words, *"Kte toske Lakotiya eyapi he?"*

Wind Dancer realized she had used *he,* the female ending to a question and not the male's *hwo. "Tuktel yati hwo?"*

"I live in Cloud Chaser's tepee," she told him in English.

"Nituktetanhan hwo? Speak Lakota," he instructed in a gentle tone.

In response to his "Where do you come from?" Caroline told him, "Paha Sapa *itehanyan,"* to relate *far away from Black Hills.*

"Taku eniciyapi hwo? Speak English this time."

"My name is Caroline Sims."

"Tanyan ecanun yelo."

After he told Caroline, "You did well," relief and joy surged through her and she thanked him. *"Pilamaya."* She comprehended when he told the others she must have overheard those *"wicoie sica"*—*bad words*—correctly, for she spoke good

Lakota. Caroline realized the smiling Chumani already knew she had passed that test and was pleased. Since Rising Bear and Nahemana did not speak English, they had not known she was victorious until Wind Dancer told them. Both leaders looked at her and nodded, which she took as gratitude for her discovery and praise for her skills. Afterward, she saw the men exchange many glances as if they were communicating without words as the gravity of the matter settled in on them and/or they were seeking to learn how that insidious news was affecting the others. She grasped most of their words as they discussed the conspiracy and the two people involved in it and how they planned to deal with all three. . .

Later in Cloud Chaser's tepee, Chumani related the grave scheme and how it would be handled to Macha, whose wide gaze kept traveling back and forth between Chumani and Caroline. Afterward, all three were silent for a time as Macha absorbed the shocking news. As she did so, it was apparent to the other two women that she did not doubt their honesty.

Macha said in her language, "It is good the Great Spirit sent you to us, Caroline, for you save lives in many ways. I could not bear to lose my beloved husband and our son. It is good the Great Spirit sent you into the forest, that He guides you along a path of true friendship and help to us. I would never become Two Feathers' mate for any reason. His hunger for me is wicked. He wants to steal me from Cloud Chaser out of hatred and jealousy toward my husband. I thank you, my friend."

Caroline nodded her gratitude and replied in Lakota, "I did not want to tell you such bad things on the past moon and bring much fear to your heart. I needed time to think of how to speak such words. I hear and grasp more Lakota than I can speak. I went to Dewdrops, for she speaks my tongue, and such talk was hard and long. I prayed she would believe me, to save her life and your husband's. Forgive me for hiding their threat from you on the past moon."

Macha smiled and told Caroline she believed her just as she and Cloud Chaser believed Two Feathers had killed his wife, Sisoka, last year and tried to blame her death on an enemy. They had surmised Sisoka had discovered her husband's evil and was going to expose him, so she was slain to prevent it.

Macha concluded that Two Feathers had hidden his evil behind a faked truce with Cloud Chaser until he thought it was safe to bring it forth again to obtain his goals, and Wastemna's return had given him what he must view as the perfect opportunity to go after them. They had known Two Feathers craved her as his wife and hated Cloud Chaser, but could not guess what evoked his hostility toward her husband. Now, the truth was revealed, thanks to the brave and kind Caroline.

"I saw Two Feathers return from hunting as we entered your tepee. Soon, they will summon us to gather and he will be entrapped there."

After those words left Chumani's lips, all three heard a loud voice as Blue Owl walked through the camp and shouted, *"Omniciye ekta u wo!"*

Caroline had heard those words before: "Come to the meeting." She looked at Chumani, then at Macha, then back at Chumani. Her adversary and his accomplice were certain to deny the perilous accusations against them. Perhaps other Red Shields might not accept a white captive's claims and she would be caught in the middle—the instigator of a grievous split between band members.

"Winyeya nanka he?" Chumani asked if they were ready to go.

"Han, winyeya," they replied simultaneously. Then Macha and Caroline looked at each other and smiled in amusement.

After Casmu and Inunpa were placed on their mothers' backs in their cradle-boards, the three women joined the crowd outside.

It did not take long for Two Feathers to sight Caroline amidst the gathering and to narrow his gaze in anger. He almost shoved his way past many people to reach her. He glared at her and demanded she leave the meeting. "You are a slave, a captive; you do not belong here. Go, white dog, and do our tasks before you are punished for such an offense."

Nahemana had seen Two Feathers' reaction and surmised his intention. The shaman placed a gnarled hand on the young warrior's arm and said, "Speak no more bad words in a bad voice, Two Feathers. I say she can remain here. She is a friend to us."

Caroline was relieved by Nahemana's hasty and gentle defense of her, but she cringed at the blatant enmity in Two Feathers' gaze and tone. She was astonished when he defied the shaman.

"She is one of the enemy. She is only a captive. She is not a friend. She speaks and acts false to trick us, to stay safe among us. Send her away."

Nahemana noticed how Two Feathers jerked his arm from his light grasp and glared at him while protesting his decision. "Why do you challenge my words, flinch from my touch, and speak bad to your shaman, son of Runs Fast and Pretty Meadow? Why do you hate and fear a harmless white woman who has done much good for our people? What evil spirit dwells within you and provokes you to such wickedness?"

Caroline saw Two Feathers glance around and see that all eyes were on him, including the stunned gazes of his parents and closest friends. She surmised he perceived his slip in behavior and tried to amend the damage when he apologized— falsely and cunningly, she presumed—to the shaman.

"I am sorry, Wise One. I speak and act bad. I do not agree with your words and feelings about the captive, but I will obey your command."

Before the warrior could retrace his path, Nahemana halted him. "Do not go, Two Feathers, for we have gathered here to speak with you."

"What words do you have to share with me, Wise One?"

"Why do you seek to take the lives of Cloud Chaser and Dewdrops?"

Caroline saw the warrior's gaze widen in surprise as he was taken off guard by that unexpected and fast-spoken query. Wastemna was urged forward by Wind Dancer's grip on her forearm. Caroline saw her shake her head ever so slightly, as if sending her partner a signal she had not betrayed him. Two Feathers seemed to grasp her sly message and relax before he attempted a bold bluff.

"What is the meaning of your words, Wise One? For they are untrue. I do not draw my knife against members of my family. If I did such evil, the Great Spirit would expose me and slay me."

As the astonished and confused Red Shields edged closer and closer to hear and see better, Nahemana disclosed, "One among us overhead your evil plans to slay them." Then, he repeated the sinister talk that had taken place between Two Feathers and Wastemna last night. "You have plotted such evil, Two Feathers, and the Great Spirit found a way to stop you."

"It is not true! He speaks false!" Wastemna shouted. "I am no threat to them. I will bite the knife and swear those words."

Caroline had been told of the custom to prove one's honesty by saying the words or deed in question while holding a knife between one's teeth. If the knife was dropped or it cut that person, it was a sign of lying. No doubt, she supposed, Wastemna had practiced that action countless times in the event such a hazard as this one occurred.

"We did not talk of slaying others. We met in the forest to speak of a joining between us. I did not want to ask

Wastemna to become my mate before others if she would reject me. Who speaks false against us? I will fight him for truth. I challenge him to a death battle; that is my right."

Caroline froze in trepidation. No one had told her—warned her—about that custom. There was no way she could defeat such a skilled and strong and large warrior in a competition to the *death*.

Nahemana refuted, "It is your right if the Great Spirit's helper is Red Shield. She is not, so you cannot challenge her to the *kicizapi wiconte*."

Caroline watched Two Feathers stare at the shaman in confusion for a few moments; then, his narrowed and chilled gaze settled on her as he apparently guessed the truth. She forced herself to lock gazes with him, though his was potent and intimidating. She feared that to look away and refuse to face the accused would imply weakness and deceit on her part. She saw gleams of what she assumed were arrogance and satisfaction in his eyes and he almost grinned—no, sneered—at her. It was as if his invidious gaze said, *So, it is you, white dog; you are no match for me; you are a dead woman.*

She prayed for the strength and wits to thwart him. He was the first to look away as he turned to address the shaman and his people.

"The white captive speaks false. She hates me and wants to see me slain or exiled, as does Cloud Chaser. My cousin told her to do this wicked task while he was gone; he told her of Wastemna's past troubles here. I say the white enemy must be beaten and slain for her false tongue."

As he glared at the insolent man, Wind Dancer argued in a sarcastic tone, "How could my brother evoke such mischief when he did not know of Wastemna's return before he left camp to help save our people? Caroline did not know of Wastemna's existence until you brought her to our camp. I tested Caroline's skills with our language before Father and Grandfather, and she grasps it well. I believe Caroline heard you and Buffalo Hump's daughter plotting against my wife and my brother. Caroline would not know such things if she did not hear them from your mouths. I say it is Two Feathers and Wastemna who lie and must be punished."

"I challenge you to prove I speak false in the ring of fire."

Wind Dancer told him, "You do not deserve that honor and right. You must die. What say you, my people?"

"It can not be true!" Runs Fast shouted before a vote could be taken. "You can not slay my first son before giving him a chance to prove himself; this is our way, our law, our custom."

Nahemana said, "He has betrayed all of them and us, Runs Fast. He is unworthy to be a Red Shield and to breathe the air of the Great Spirit."

"Banish him, but do not slay him," Pretty Meadow begged her brother.

Rising Bear said, "If we did so, sister, he would sneak back to camp for revenge. He must die. What say you, my people?"

Caroline observed as the other men agreed with their chief, all except the man's father, who tried one final time to obtain mercy. Runs Fast glared at her as he spoke to the somber gathering of his people.

"The white captive lies. You must not slay him. He is the grandson of Ghost Warrior. He is a Sacred Bow Carrier. She lies; slay her."

Nahemana told the distraught and riled father, "Your first son has dishonored that rank and brought shame to his bloodline. He is unworthy—"

Caroline was almost knocked down as Two Feathers shoved her aside, raced toward his horse, and leapt on its back. He galloped away while the stunned crowd's gazes followed his swift and desperate movements.

"He proves his guilt by showing fear and trying to escape. I will go after him, Father, for he must be punished," the future chief announced.

"No!" Runs Fast shouted. He seized Wind Dancer's arm to halt his pursuit. "I will go after my son and speak with him. I will learn why he flees our camp and does not defend himself against such false words, for he is not evil. We will return soon to tell all the truth."

Nahemana shook his head and reasoned, "No, Runs Fast, for your father's heart and pride cloud your eyes and mind to his wickedness. They would not allow you to force him to return to face his punishment."

"Why must you slay him? Why can he not be banished?"

Before Rising Bear could respond to the distressed father, Red Wolf urged his way forward and entreated, "Let me go after him, my friends and allies, and do that task for you so his blood will not be on family hands. This is why the Great Spirit guided me to your camp at this dark time."

Rising Bear nodded permission as he took a deep breath of gratitude, and Red Wolf hurried to mount his horse and pursue the fleeing man.

Caroline glanced at Hanmani, whose expression suggested fear for the Cheyenne warrior's survival, as it was well known that Two Feathers was a skilled fighter. Too, a desperate man was unpredictable and dangerous. In a split second, Caroline's mind told her she was glad War Eagle was not there to go after her enemy.

While everyone was distracted, Wastemna seized a knife from the sheath of Runs Fast and plunged it into her own chest with great force, screaming as she did so. The startled crowd parted as the wild woman collapsed to the ground, bleeding and writhing in pain.

"For-give me, Cre-ator. . . . Two . . . Feathers . . . blinded me . . . to what . . . is . . . good . . . Sum-mon . . . my spirit . . . to Your . . . side . . . and . . . pro-tect . . . it . . . from . . . harm."

Wind Dancer knelt beside her and asked in a rush, "Did Caroline speak the truth about my cousin's evil plans? If you lie or do not answer me and cleanse your soul, the Creator will reject you and your spirit will roam forever, alone and in darkness. Did Caroline speak the truth?"

"Yes. For-give me . . . my . . . love. I . . . wanted . . . to be . . . your—"

All observed in astonishment—many in relief—as Wastemna drew her final breath on earth, trying to reach out and touch Wind Dancer's face. Many dark eyes settled on the white female's pale face and somber blue gaze as they realized she had saved the life of Cloud Chaser—son of their chief and doer of many large and glorious deeds last summer—and once again the life of Chumani, wife of their next chief and the Vision-Quest Woman of four years ago. Many murmurs of approval and praise for Caroline's bravery and generosity were heard, as well as countless words of gratitude, especially by Rising Bear and his family.

Caroline barely saw and heard what the Red Shields did and said; her gaze was locked on Wastemna's bloody body and her mind was trying to convince her she was not to blame for that tragedy.

Chumani placed an arm around her waist. "Do not feel bad, my friend, for evil must destroy itself or it must be destroyed. You did what is good and right. We thank you."

After Hanmani and Wind Dancer confirmed Chumani's words, Caroline nodded acceptance of them; yet, her heart remained troubled. She grimaced as she saw Wind Dancer extract the knife from Wastemna's chest and return it to Runs Fast, who stared at the blood upon the metal blade—a white man's weapon, one perhaps stolen during a raid or taken from an enemy during a battle, perhaps by his traitorous son. She saw Runs Fast shift his narrowed gaze to her and glare at her in hatred and derision, as if she were to blame for his offspring's malice and impending death. Yet, she realized he was a loving father in torment, a self-deluded parent. For a few moments, she had a longing to apologize for causing his anguish and to offer him sympathy, but knew that was unwise and would be scorned and rejected.

As Macha coaxed her away from the grim scene and the man's rancor, Caroline wished War Eagle were there to give her comfort. She needed his strength and gentleness, his infusion of courage, and his persuasion of innocence. She needed to know if her "bravery and generosity" had changed anything in her existence. Yes, the Indians appreciated, respected, and accepted her as an obedient captive. But would they ever accept her as more, as War Eagle's woman, his wife? Would her beloved ever desire and accept her in that role? What if Rising Bear and his people offered her freedom in payment for her good deeds? Could she leave, return to her brother and the white world? Could she plead to stay? If she left, she would lose War Eagle forever. *How can you lose,* her mind challenged, *what you do not possess?* Then her heart replied, *But there is no chance of winning him if you are gone. Stay, even if you must insist on it, at least until he returns and rejects you.*

One of those same thoughts had entered Rising Bear's mind. He asked Wind Dancer inside his son's tepee, "Should we release the white woman? For she has done many good deeds among us and has a good heart."

"I do not know, Father. What do you say, my wife?"

Chumani, who suspected romantic feelings between Caroline and War Eagle, told them, "I say it is bad to free her in this season when danger and war threaten us and our lands," *and before War Eagle returns and can speak a claim on her, if my perceptions are true.* "If her brother rides with the white war chief to challenge all Lakotas, she would be alone at the fort and have no protection from the cravings of wicked soldiers. If he is slain in battle, the same is true, for she has no other family. She could face much peril and even death if our allies attacked the fort where she is taken. She is our friend and helper, so we must protect her until peace comes and she can be freed to join her brother if he still lives," *and if she so desires and does not become the mate of your brother and son.*

Rising Bear nodded. "Dewdrops speaks wise and true, my son."

Wind Dancer added. "It is so, Father. I say we wait until the Great Spirit sends us a sign that it is time to free her. We will honor her with gifts and praise to show our gratitude for her deeds."

"When should the ceremony take place?" the chief asked.

"After Red Wolf returns in victory. We will honor both at the same feast."

"So it shall be. My wife and three daughters will plan the feast. Nahemana will do the ceremony. We wait for Red Wolf's return."

Chumani smiled and nodded in agreement, knowing the chief referred to her and Macha as daughters because they were joined to his sons. She was filled with elation and plea-sure, and knew what her gift would be. . . .

Shortly before dusk, one of the lookouts galloped into camp and alerted the chief and band to Red Wolf's advance. A crowd gathered fast to meet him upon his arrival. The Cheyenne warrior—one of the Fire Hearts' elite Dog Men— halted his mount before the large group. In one hand, he held the leather thong of Two Feathers' horse, the Red Shield's body lying across the animal's back.

"It is done, Rising Bear. I did not attack him from hiding; he was slain in a fair fight with hands and knives. He rode fast and hard until his horse could travel no more. He halted for my challenge, for he knew I chased him. I bring his body home for his family to tend and his passing to mourn. Do you want me to leave your camp and wait for War Eagle's re-turn in another place nearby? I want to hear what he has learned of our white enemy so I can take those words to my father and people."

"You have done a brave and kind and generous deed for us, Red Wolf of the Cheyenne, friend of my third son. Stay, eat, sleep in my tepee. Allow us to honor you and Caroline on the next moon with a feast and ceremony."

Red Wolf—who also carried *vehoe* blood from his mother—glanced at the white woman nearby, and noticed War Eagle's sister, who was standing close to her, and out of his reach forever. . . . He looked at the chief and said, "You have spoken, Rising Bear, and so it shall be. I thank you."

Caroline lowered her head slightly to sneak a peek at Hanmani's face. She surmised that the girl was trying to behave as if the visitor was nothing more to her than her brother's friend.

As if Hanmani realized her gaze was lingering too long and intensely on the Cheyenne Dog Soldier, she focused on her father. If she wasn't mistaken, Caroline mused, War Eagle's sister was enchanted by his good friend, but feared to reveal those feelings. Caroline sympathized, as she knew how it felt to have a man out of reach.

As a somber Runs Fast and Pretty Meadow guided their son's horse toward their tepee to prepare the body to place upon a death scaffold at sunrise for the forces of nature to reclaim, Caroline returned to Macha's tepee to eat and sleep. Tomorrow was an important—and intimidating—day for her, perhaps a fate-changing or destiny-fulfilling one. . . .

As she lay upon her buffalo mat, Caroline had difficulty getting to sleep. Her mind kept going over recent events and trying to place them in their proper perspective. She could hardly believe she was to be honored by the Indian band that held her captive.

What should she wear to the ceremony? The blue cotton dress was simple but pretty, and was clean though wrinkled from the lack of an iron and a little faded from use. At least her hair and body were clean since she and Macha had taken care of those tasks this morning in a mountain stream whose water was becoming chillier by the week as autumn progressed toward winter.

She wished War Eagle were there to observe this special occasion, this vindication of his past decision to capture her. Although she had spent little time with him, she missed him terribly. She missed her brother, too.

Oh, David, if you could see me now, what would you think and feel and say about these enormous changes in me? Would you be understanding or disappointed and angry? Please, Heavenly Father, let him be safe and alive, and find some way to let him know I am too. He lost Mama and Papa without having the opportunity to say good-bye to them, so don't let him suffer because of my disappearance. He's probably wishing I had stayed in the South and blaming himself for asking me to come here.

As that last thought entered her head, Caroline could not suppress a grin in the darkness, though the light of a full moon overhead was beaming down from the ventilation spread. She easily could imagine what the rich, arrogant, and aristocratic William Crawford would think, say, and feel about the changes and situation. Surely he would believe, no matter what she swore on a Bible, that she had been defiled and was unworthy of him. Undoubtedly he would reject her even as a social companion, though probably not as a sexual dalliance. He probably would tell her it was her fault and she deserved an awful fate for refusing his marriage proposal and coming to a "wild and godforsaken land of savages."

That couldn't be further from the truth, you vain and lustful dandy. Even if I were still at home or somewhere close by, I would never marry you. I could only marry a man who makes me feel as War Eagle does.

Caroline closed her eyes and scolded herself for her wishful thinking. *Go to sleep,* she ordered herself, *or you're going to look terrible tomorrow. You can't change anything tonight, if ever. Just count your blessings for now.*

* * *

Two hours before sunset on the following day, the Red Shields and the honorees gathered in a large open area between the forest and river. Before the ceremony began, a great feast was held, prepared by the chief's family and numerous female helpers. Many foods were served: roasted or boiled camas bulbs and tasty tubers of other plants, various soups of meat or wild vegetables or a combination of them with wild onions and herbs for added flavor, breads made from willow or acorn flour with dried nuts and berries, dried fruits such as prickly pear and the egg-shaped buffalo berry, mature stem cores of fireweed, and assorted cooked or raw greens. Many hunters had provided the meats to be eaten— deer, antelope, turkey, and grouse—which were either roasted on wooden skewers or gently boiled in a small amount of water in trade kettles. Naturally buffalo was part of the meal, most of it in either dried strips called *pa-pa* or large rolls called *wakapanpi.*

Caroline was familiar with most of the items offered, as she had helped gather and cook them on past days, but not on this one as an honoree. She also had helped prepare *wakapanpi* during the summer, the major source of their winter food supply. Sun and wind-dried strips of buffalo meat were pounded into a near-powder, mixed with dried berries and hot fat and sometimes dried nuts, allowed to cool, formed into rolls, and stored in leather parfleches. She had been told by Chumani that *wakapanpi* would last for years without spoiling if made and kept properly.

Caroline couldn't help wondering what they would think about wheat flour, cornmeal, pork, chicken, coffee, tea, Crosby's canned tomatoes, Winslow's canned sweet corn, Reverend Graham's crackers, Russell's ice cream, cheese, rice, potatoes, homemade or store-bought canned goods, stoves with ovens, iceboxes, gaslights, and other discoveries of her people. She knew from Chumani that some had tasted sugar and liked it, but honey was their sweetener.

If they were not nomadic and determined to live in the old ways and resolved not to trade with her people, she could teach them how to plant, tend, and harvest vegetables; and how to raise and use domesticated animals and fowl. She could teach them how to store potatoes and onions for long periods, how to dry peas and beans, to can vegetables, and to dry fruits. She could teach them how to pickle, smoke, and salt-cure items. She could teach them how to use wood-stoves for cooking and baking, which would be easier in the winter and would also warm their dwellings. Yet, she was certain they would not agree and her offer might insult them by falsely implying that her ways were better and theirs were primitive. Still, as more whites advanced on this area and settled in it and the Indians' food supply was depleted, they would be forced to change or perish. When that day or year came and if she was still among them, she would make the offer.

Caroline halted her rambling thoughts. The women were finished spreading out the feast and it was time to begin.

After everyone was satisfied, Red Wolf and Caroline were called forward by the shaman. The people sat either on mats or on the grass in ever-widening circles to observe the event. First, Nahemana prayed to evoke the Great Spirit's presence.

"We call to You, Creator, to look down and see us, to hear our words. We gather to honor two friends who have done good deeds for us. We thank You for Your many blessings and for giving them breath and for sending them to our camp. Guide and protect them in the suns and moons to come. Guide and protect all Red Shields in the dark season ahead. Hear us and see us, Great One, for we are Your children and we do Your will."

Wind Dancer was called forward to do the "telling of Caroline's coups" since she had come to live with them, which he did with ease and respect. Afterward, the war chief

Blue Owl related the coup of Naehonehe, son of the war chief Mahahkoe—Badger—of the Fire Hearts Cheyenne.

Then, Nahemana stood before Red Wolf and said, "We thank you for your good deed, Naehonehe." After the warrior nodded, the shaman stepped before Caroline and said, "We thank you for your good deeds among us. From this sun forth, you will be called *Wahcawi,* for your yellow hair."

Caroline was astonished to receive the Indian name of Sunflower. Her heart filled with joy and pride. She smiled and nodded to the elderly man whose gaze and manner were gentle, though there was an odd gleam in his age-beclouded eyes and a half grin that implied concealed amusement.

Rising Bear came forward and presented Red Wolf with gifts from his band: a bow, a quiver of unmarked arrows, and several prime hides and furs.

The warrior slowly turned in a circle as he told the group, "Thank you for these gifts and for honoring me on this sun, my friends and allies."

Rising Bear turned to his wife and nodded a signal to her. Winona stood before Caroline and secured a small quilled rosette in her blond hair, with a red-tailed hawk feather, which dangled to her shoulder. The chief said, "It is a medicine wheel with a sky warrior's feather; it is a sign of your coup for saving the lives of my son and second daughter."

Caroline was speechless. She knew the significance of the item, an almost sacred symbol, for Chumani possessed one for her past deeds. She looked at the parents of her secret love and said, *"Pilamaya,"* in a voice hoarsened by deep emotion, pride, and joy. Those emotions increased as Hanmani presented her with a lovely Indian dress worn only once, as they were about the same size. Zitkala, Chumani's best friend and one of the vision-quest riders, gave her a belt for saving Dewdrops' life. Dawn gave her a small drawstring pouch to suspend from it, an Indian purse. Nahemana gave her a medicine pouch containing many healing herbs and "magic tokens." His wife, Little Turtle, gave her a scraper of buffalo bone with a leather-wrapped handle for removing fat from hides and furs. Others gave her hides and furs for making garments, wristbands, a sitting mat, two blankets, several storage pouches for her belongings, teeth and claws from animals to use as decorations, and other items. As people handed her gifts of gratitude, she smiled and thanked them.

Caroline was surprised when Pretty Meadow came forth and offered her a necklace. Caroline smiled and thanked the chief's sister, mother of Two Feathers, whose defeat had prompted this ceremony.

Last, Chumani stepped forward and presented Caroline with a flesher, the female's counterpart of a male's coup stick. She pointed to the small dots painted upon its surface and related the meaning for each color: one red—*fought an enemy,* as she did with War Eagle on the trail; five green—*saved a life,* the lives of Inunpa, War Eagle, Cloud Chaser, and hers twice; three yellow—*healed or tended a seriously sick or injured person,* as with the warrior's cut arm and the medicine skills used on her and Inunpa; one large black—*hides tanned for others after a buffalo hunt.* Chumani smiled, embraced her, and thanked her for all she had done for her and for others.

Almost overcome by heartfelt emotions, Caroline smiled, hugged the woman, and thanked her. "You are a good friend and woman, Dewdrops."

As the shaman was announcing what would happen next, Caroline gazed at the flesher and remembered what Chumani, Macha, and Hanmani had told her about the treasured object. A girl was given an elk-horn flesher at her celebration into womanhood; then, it was up to her to fill it with colorful dots for doing good deeds; deeds such as for hides tanned and robes made, for winning a sewing or quilling contest, for helping others construct their tepee, or for performing a generous or brave deed. Macha had told her that a man often asked to see a woman's flesher before he asked for her hand, to decide if she would make a good wife, especially if passionate love and desire were not his motives for seeking her out. Her owner's wife had laughed and whispered that Cloud Chaser had not asked to examine hers, as his motives were indeed love and desire, and the Great Spirit had shown her to him in a sacred vision before he returned home, just as the Great Spirit had sent Nahemana a vision about Chumani and Wind Dancer.

How wonderful it would be, Caroline thought, if the Great Spirit would send the shaman a sacred vision about her and War Eagle being destined to marry. But that was unlikely to happen, so she pushed that wish aside. As she gazed at the flesher one last time, she remembered that to an Indian woman, counting the dots on her flesher was comparable to the counting of coup for a warrior on his *can woyustan*. It was exhilarating to see how many she had earned in only a few months and she wanted to add more. Surely it would be beneficial to her for War Eagle and his people to notice her numerous accomplishments and to think they made her worthy of him.

Caroline placed the prized item atop her other gifts and followed her friends to the beginning of a long human fence to her right and to her left. Red Wolf stood in front of her, and Caroline noticed how Hanmani gazed at him before taking a place in the row to the left, as did Macha. Caroline realized the Cheyenne warrior's skin and hair were not as dark as a full-blooded Indian's, and she recalled the same was true for his eyes, no doubt the results of having white ancestors.

Chumani whispered to her, "I will touch your back when it is time for you to follow Red Wolf down the line. Hold out your arms as he does, with your hands open in friendship. As you pass our people, they will reach out and touch your palm with their fingers to show they honor and thank you."

Caroline awaited her turn to carry out the hand-tag ceremony. She heard the large kettledrum send forth rhythmic beats as eight Big Bellies sat around it and struck its taut surface with sticks as they chanted melodious vocables. She watched Red Wolf extend his strong arms, palms down, but fists balled, as was the custom for an elite warrior. With head held high and his body straight, the Fire Hearts Dog Soldier walked the lengthy distance as his fists were touched by the Red Shields, except for Runs Fast, whose head and arms were kept lowered. It was understandable to her, and no doubt to Red Wolf, that a grieving father could not praise and thank his son's destroyer. As soon as the Cheyenne finished his stroll, he lifted his arms upward in a salute to the Great Spirit, and took a place at the end of one line.

After Chumani touched her on the back to signal she was to begin her journey and hurried to the end of one line, Caroline extended her arms with palms facing forward and started her walk. She held her head slightly downward to prevent appearing boastful by lifting her chin too high. Though she kept her gaze on her destination as advised, she knew when her friends and esteemed band members tagged her hand. Runs Fast did not, though his wife did.

Three-fourths of the way to completion, her arms protested their strained position and her legs felt weak and trembly. *Please, Heavenly Father, give me the strength to finish this important task. Please do not let me shame myself and insult these people by lowering my arms or stumbling. Just a little farther, Caroline. . . .*

With renewed determination, she came to the end of the long lines and the last two people. As Red Wolf touched one hand, Caroline darted her gaze to Chumani and smiled as her friend tagged the other one. She did not raise her arms as the Cheyenne had done, as that was not the action for a woman to do. While she and the other women talked, the men built a large fire. When it was ready, they took seats on sitting mats in the inner circle, and ever-widening rings were made by the throng who sat on the ground.

Before long, dances were being performed around the center blaze in step to the kettledrum's beats and occasionally the Big Bellies' chanting. Some performances included only men; some, only women; and some, couples.

Although Caroline did not dance, her friends did, always returning with smiles, flushed faces, and glowing eyes. She noticed that people laughed and talked amongst themselves in harmony and serenity, as if the threat of trouble were either nonexistent or far away. Children played or pretend-danced beyond the last loop, the small ones being tended by older siblings. The camp guards were changed, so that those on duty during the prior events could join in on the festivities, which would go on until bedtime. A full moon made its way higher and brighter in the darkened sky. Nocturnal insects and birds and frogs at the river sang their own songs, as if joining in the merriment.

As the celebration continued, Caroline thought, *How different their music and dances are from those I heard and did back home. I wonder if it would be all right to ask my friends to teach them to me and if I would be permitted to join in next time. I suppose I should be thankful I've made as much progress as I have, considering the circumstances. But is it so wrong of me to want more from life than I have now, to want to improve my situation, to have the man I love? Yet, I can't push too far and too fast. I have to be patient, obedient, respectful, and helpful to achieve my goals. I can't allow my desires to destroy me as they destroyed Wastemna and Two Feathers. I must not get caught in a similar trap of craving a mate out of reach and doing reckless things to win him. Just be yourself and bide your time. . . .*

Two days later, Caroline watched Zitkala brushing Cikala's hair while Chumani and Macha tended the babies and Tokapa played nearby with Hanmani. Caroline was flooded by yearning for her own children, her own home, her own husband. For War Eagle to be that man. If only—

Caroline's daydreaming was interrupted as one of the

lookouts rode into camp, shouting that War Eagle and his companions were approaching. *He's coming home! He's coming home!* her jubilant mind sang merrily. *He's alive and safe. He's almost here. How do I look? How should I behave? What will he say about the events that happened here during his absence?*

Her mind scolded. *Listen to you prattle on, you selfish woman! What if he's returning with bad news? What if General Harney and his troops are heading here to attack? What if David is riding with Harney? What will happen if your brother is among that threatening force and many of these people are slain in battle? Please, dear God, don't let that be true. . . .*

Chapter Sixteen

Caroline tried to conceal her anxiety about possible bad news and an intense longing to see War Eagle. She told Macha to go meet her husband, his brother, and their friends while she tended to Casmu. "I will carry him into the tepee so the noise will not disturb his sleep. I will wait for you there. Go fast, Dawn, for you have been parted for a long time."

"Thank you, my friend, for I am eager to see my love again."

As Macha hurried toward a crowd gathering near the edge of camp, Caroline lifted Casmu's cradle-board and carried the slumbering infant inside. She was concerned that if she joined the others, she might expose her fervent emotions. Too, she did not want to overstep her lingering role as a captive, as that could be frowned upon by some if she behaved as one of them when she had not been given that particular privilege.

She placed the baby nearby where she could grab quick glances at him while she furtively observed the arriving party. She stood to one side of the opened entrance and peered toward the excited group, hoping the interior was too dim for anybody to see her. She was glad Cloud Chaser's abode was angled perfectly and the people had collected where they had for her to be able to witness his return undetected.

As the men halted and greeted their families and people, Caroline's smile faded, her body stiffened, and her breath caught in her chest. As her gaze had touched on Broken Lance, she realized he soon would learn of his older brother's treachery and death, and of her involvement in the man's shameful defeat, as would War Eagle. She prayed Broken Lance would not hate her and speak against her as his father had done.

She spotted her beloved on the far side of the scouting party, then realized Cloud Chaser was not among them. Dread filled her. Had he been captured or slain? To lose her husband would torment Macha deeply. *Please, dear God, make him only late in arriving.*

Then, another reality—or hope—struck her: the men did not look or act as if they were mourning a companion's loss. But as she watched their expressions and demeanors wax serious and sad and saw many heads bow as if receiving terrible news, her mind shouted, *No! No! If only I could hear what they're saying,* but she could not at that distance.

She glanced toward Casmu to make sure he was still sleeping, and he was. She searched the throng for Dawn and found the woman near Chumani. Yet, with Dawn facing the other way, she could not see her expression. Had she received bad news? Where was her husband? *Surely I will leap out of my skin if I do not learn the truth soon!*

She saw War Eagle's gaze roam the large group, then drift toward his second brother's tepee. She stepped backward to make sure he could not sight her spying on him. Or had he seen her or perceived her potent stare? Was he wondering where she was and what she was doing? Had someone just told him about her new deed and honoring ceremony? She waited for a minute or two before risking another peek, and found the crowd dispersing. She saw men heading toward the river and surmised that a council meeting was going to take place there, as if often did. With War Eagle now dismounted and immersed in the group, she could not get a good look at him. Besides, people would be passing her tepee shortly, so she had to leave her spot.

She lifted Casmu's cradle-board and went to the center of the tepee and sat down on her own sitting mat to await Macha's return. When she arrived Caroline asked, "Is the news bad, my friend?"

"Yes, Wahcawi, it is bad."

Caroline gently probed the distracted woman. "What is wrong?"

"My husband did not return with the others, so my heart is sad."

Caroline tensed in dread. She did not want to torment her friend, but she had to discover the truth. "Was Cloud Chaser captured or . . ."

"No, he lives and is free. He stayed at the fort to scout the soldiers and white war chief." She heard Caroline's sigh of relief. "I did not mean to frighten you, Wahcawi, but my thoughts roam to where my love endangers his life trying to save us from the bluecoats' evil. I do not know much, for War Eagle said little before going to meet with the council and warriors. But he spoke of a massacre at the camps of Little Thunder and Spotted Tail. Most were slain or captured, for they were given no warning of an attack."

A shocked Caroline gaped at Macha. "They rode into camp and killed people without talking first?" Surely David would not do such a horrible—

"That is true, my friend. Soldiers surrounded the camps of our allies and struck at dawn while they slept. Women, children, babies, old ones, and warriors are gone forever, their bodies left to feed the scavengers. Few escaped and they have nothing with them but the garments they wore. They can not survive winter without food, tepees, and warm robes."

Caroline murmured in distress, "How could anybody,

even an enemy, do such a wicked thing? Surely the Great Spirit will punish them."

"I pray that is true, for only He can protect us from such large evil. Soon, the bluecoats will ride deep into our territory to attack other Lakotas, for they seek to find and slay those who fled and any band who helps them. My husband will ride with the soldiers or will trail them to scout their path and actions. When he nears our new camp, he will return to us."

"New camp?" Caroline asked, her mind in a near-daze after hearing about such atrocities committed by her people.

"Yes, we must move deeper into the sacred hills to a place where the bluecoats might not find us, for we are not strong enough to battle such a powerful and cruel force alone. When the new day comes, we must ready our possessions to strike camp when the second sun rises from this one."

Caroline nodded, panicked by how the malicious event could change her life since *her* people were to blame. . . .

At the river, War Eagle stood in the midst of the gathered men and related all he and his companions had learned since their departure. His family and many others nodded agreement to his decision to remain hidden to live to fight another day, as the odds had been too large in the enemy's favor. He saw that many were astonished by the discovery that some soldiers had tended wounds and fed the captives. All were angered and saddened to hear the slain ones were left where they had fallen to be devoured by the Great Spirit's creatures and that their possessions had been either stolen or burned beyond use. He told them about their visit with the survivors and what those leaders intended to do, probably had done by now. He saw that many had difficulty believing Spotted Tail would surrender, but murmured words of praise for his courage and sacrifice in order to save others. Since Red Wolf was allowed to join them to hear the news that he could take to his people, War Eagle related the death of Cheyenne Chief Little Butte.

No one interrupted as War Eagle continued his revelations. "Before we left that area, we spoke with Red Cloud, who is camped near the fort. He gave the harsh words of the white war chief and Agent Twiss to us." He repeated those that the famed Oglala leader had spoken, the same ones that Cloud Chaser had heard from the sutler at the fort. "Red Cloud is guiding his band to the Powder River area to be far away from the bluecoats' threat of attack on all who remain in our land. He does not plan to battle them this season, but says he will be forced to do so in those to come."

War Eagle went into further detail about the facts Cloud Chaser had gleaned at Fort Laramie and what his second brother planned to do before returning home. "The white war chief will soon ride through our territory to seek those who escaped him at Blue Water Creek and all others who are hostile to whites. He is angry over the theft of many horses at the fort after the surprise attack on the Brules and their friends. He seeks to destroy any band who gives the Brules help and hiding. I do not believe the surrenders of Spotted Tail and his people will quench Harney's thirst for Lakota blood, for Little Thunder and his remaining band are a challenge to him. We must move our camp far into the sacred hills where we will be safe from winter and from the bluecoats, for the great snows will keep them away."

War Eagle finished his report with the news about Caroline's brother. He told how David Sims had spared many Brule lives, pretended to fire at fleeing allies, and was sending the truth to the white leaders far away. Before he sat down, he said that Cloud Chaser had met David at the fort and David had told him many things about Harney's actions and impending plans.

"That is good," Rising Bear concluded, "for his sister has done many good deeds for our people and it will please her to learn her brother acts as she does. While you were gone, my son, the woman you captured saved the lives of Dewdrops and Cloud Chaser, and we honored her with a feast, gifts, touching of hands in friendship and gratitude, and a Red Shield name. She is called Wahcawi now, for her hair is the color of that flower."

War Eagle wondered if he had heard his father correctly. His heart drummed in elation and hope. "I do not understand. How could the white woman save Cloud Chaser's life when he is far away?" He watched Rising Bear smile and explain.

"You have not forgotten the vision message Nahemana shared with us after we made camp here. Our shaman said a betrayer walked among us but his face and body were hidden by wolf's garments. That betrayer was Two Feathers and the prey he stalked were my sons and my rank. An evil force returned Wastemna to our camp seventeen moons past, and from the good within us, we allowed her to remain with us if she was changed in heart and mind, as her parents were slain by Crow and she was alone. Two Feathers found her injured and brought her to our camp. A few suns past, they made a trade in the forest: she would slay Cloud Chaser for him and he would slay Dewdrops for her so they could steal their mates. But Two Feathers planned to trick her, to slay her after her wicked deed was done. He planned to slay Wind Dancer and destroy you so he could become the next chief."

War Eagle was stunned by that news. His gaze darted to Wind Dancer, who nodded confirmation, then to the equally shocked Broken Lance, who gaped at their chief, and to Runs Fast, whose head was lowered no doubt in shame and grief, before returning it to his father, who continued his talk.

"Wahcawi, as we have named her, heard their dark talk while hiding in bushes nearby. She revealed it to Dewdrops, who revealed it to me, Wind Dancer, and Nahemana. We challenged the evildoers with the truth, but Two Feathers escaped and Wastemna killed herself with the knife of Runs Fast. Red Wolf pursued and battled Two Feathers for us, so we honored him at the same feast and ceremony two suns past."

War Eagle glanced at his Cheyenne friend, smiled, and nodded thanks. He was astonished that his family and people had believed Caroline over Two Feathers, for surely his cousin had sworn innocence and probably tried to have her beaten and slain. She must have been frightened, and he had not been there to offer her protection, help, and comfort. She had shown great courage, and he was proud of her.

Nahemana said, "The Great Spirit sent Wahcawi to us for many good reasons and He guided you to her path to bring her to us. It was the evil force within Two Feathers that sought to destroy her before she could carry out the will of Wakantanka. That is why he spoke against her and why he sought her in trade, to slay her as we believe he did with Sisoka."

Rising Bear added, "His evil has been defeated. He lives no more, so his name will be forgotten and not spoken by us again. It is good that Runs Fast and Pretty Meadow have another son, one with a good heart and spirit. Broken Lance will heal their wound and bring honor to them once more."

"I will do so, my chief and my father," Broken Lance told the two men.

"On the next sun, we will rest and prepare for our journey," Rising Bear said. "We will move our camp on the following sun to the place War Eagle has chosen for us."

The men talked for a while longer, then went their separate ways or gathered in small groups to speak with friends.

After his youngest brother visited with Red Wolf for a short time, Wind Dancer summoned War Eagle for a private talk. He told him everything Two Feathers and Wastemna had said in the forest and how he had tested Caroline's skill with Lakota to verify the grim incident.

A shocked and worried War Eagle asked, "Will I be weakened and shamed by her?"

Wind Dancer answered, "When Dewdrops related the evil talk to us in my tepee, she did not say how Two Feathers planned to defeat you. Caroline was afraid to deceive us, but Dewdrops told her it was not the time to reveal such feelings if they were true or false. Dewdrops held silent for she feared Father and Grandfather would view Caroline as a threat to your honor and rank, and might send her away by freeing her for her many good deeds."

So, War Eagle reasoned, that was what his cousin had meant by destroying him: he would be debased and rejected if he became the "dishonored captive of his captive." He asked, "Did they want to free her?"

"Father asked us if she should be freed, but Dewdrops spoke against it. She said Caroline would not be safe at the fort while her brother was gone and if he was slain in battle. After she told me all she had concealed at those two meetings, I believe she was wise to hold silent. Does love fill your heart for her?"

War Eagle's troubled gaze locked with his brother's probing one. "Yes," he admitted. "You also are wise, so what must I do?"

"Be strong and brave and do not speak for her until the threat from her people is past. I had to battle many forces to win and keep Dewdrops, but my challenges were unlike yours. The same is true of our brother with Dawn, though he also carries the blood of a white-eye. It is different and harder with you, for you hold the ranks of Sacred Bow Carrier and the next chief if I am slain. Wahcawi has won the love and acceptance of our family and our people, but I do not know if all would accept her as the mate of the Red Shield chief, if that sun rises. Do you love and desire her enough to risk losing those ranks and honors?"

War Eagle was compelled to respond, "Only a selfish and weak man would choose to please himself at such sacrifices.

We are at war, so I must put the survival of my family, people, and land before my heart's desire."

Wind Dancer smiled, clasped his brother's wrist, and lightly squeezed it. He said, "You have spoken wise and true. Great pride and love fill me toward you, for such words and actions cause you much denial and pain. Do not forget, Wakantanka guided you to her, sent her to us, and has worked many good deeds through her. Perhaps He also created her for you. If that is true, wait for His sign to claim her."

"How will I know that sign?" War Eagle queried in rising hope.

"Grandfather will help you see and grasp it, as he did with me."

"I will watch and wait," War Eagle vowed, praying he could do so.

"There are other things to speak of," Wind Dancer said. "After we move to our new camp, we must choose another Sacred Bow Carrier to replace Two Feathers. Whom will you speak for to take that rank?"

"Bent Bow, son of our war chief. He removed the stain from his face when he rode at our brother's side three seasons past. He showed great courage and stamina when he did his second Sun Dance and our brother traveled that hard journey with him. He is a good choice and will bring honor to that rank as Raven and Talks Little did before our cousin stained it. The Sacred Bows of Broken Arrow, Swift Otter, and my own, have remained in our possessions for over four circles of the seasons, but the fourth has passed through the hands of three warriors during that same span of time. I pray Bent Bow will carry it for many circles of the seasons, as have we."

"I also will cast my vote for him to be tested for that rank. Come, let us return to camp."

* * *

That night in Cloud Chaser's tepee, Macha told Caroline
what Chumani had related to her about the council meeting
that afternoon, the details of what her husband and his companions had done and learned during their journey. Afterward,
she revealed that War Eagle had been informed about his
cousin's treachery and death, and about Caroline's role in the
man's defeat and how she and Red Wolf had been honored
afterward.

"What did he say about such news and events?"

Macha replied, "I do not know, for Dewdrops did not tell
me. Surely he is pleased that the woman he captured has
done so many good deeds for us. My husband will be
pleased with you when he returns. Two Feathers was evil and
the Great Spirit punished him. That is how it should be."

"Will Cloud Chaser be angry I learned his secret and was
forced to remind others of his birth by a white woman?"

"No, if you promise never to tell other whites or the soldiers."

"I would not betray him to my people, if I ever see them
again."

Macha knew about her husband's meeting with Caroline's
brother. Since she and Chumani felt that War Eagle would
want to share that happy news with their friend, she withheld
that revelation. But there was another secret that troubled
her, one she decided to expose tonight. She pulled a locket
from beneath her garment and said, "This belonged to my
husband's mother. He gave it to me as a sign of his love and
bond to me. Her name was Omaste, which means Sunshine,
for her hair was the color of yours. She was a good and kind
woman, an obedient and respectful captive. She was given to
Rising Bear by a Cheyenne chief, so Rising Bear could not
refuse to accept her. She was treated well and she came to
accept us as her people."

"But she was never joined to Rising Bear, is that not
true?"

"Long ago when Rising Bear had only one son, Winona was stolen by our enemy, the Pawnee, and was lost of us for two circles of the seasons. Most believed her dead or gone forever. Rising Bear suffered much over her loss. Only one time did he turn to Omaste for comfort, and my husband came from that mating. Later, Winona escaped and returned to us. She forgave Rising Bear for his one weakness, as did our people. After Omaste died from winter in the chest, Winona cared for Cloud Chaser until he was lost to them at ten summers old and was raised by whites far away. After they died, he returned to us and we joined, for he had been told our band had been attacked and slain. Before his white parents died, he was told the truth of their false words. He has done many great deeds for us. He is much loved and respected by his father and our people."

"That is good, Dawn. I am happy for all of you."

"Cloud Chaser helped me learn some English," Macha divulged while she had the courage, and saw Caroline stare at her. "I speak some, I hear and grasp more, but not as much as you do with our tongue. When you first came to us, my husband asked me not to reveal that secret to you so I could hear your words and learn if you could be trusted. You are my friend, so I tell you that truth this night."

"You speak English?" Caroline asked, dismayed and disappointed she had been deceived for so long and by someone she viewed as a good friend.

"I speak a little English and know more. Forgive me for hiding that skill from you. I can no longer do so, for we are friends. Since I had kept it hidden for so long, I feared to tell you, for I feared it would hurt you and cause you to believe Cloud Chaser and I cannot be trusted. That is not true. We are your friends. Now, you know all things about us. If you cannot forgive us, I will ask my husband to let you go live with Dewdrops."

Macha's expression, tone, and words touched Caroline

deeply. She smiled and said, "I forgive you, Dawn. You have proven your friendship and trust by telling me the truth. We will remain friends."

"That is good, Wahcawi, and fills my heart with joy."

"As it does mine, Dawn. Tell me, how did Cloud Chaser win you and his people's love and acceptance since he also carries enemy blood?"

"You ask because of your feelings for War Eagle?"

"Yes, for he steals my eye and heart more each sun. Is that bad?"

"I do not know. I believe War Eagle sees you as a friend and ally to us, but I do not know what other feelings live in his heart and mind for you."

"If he shares the same feelings, could we ever . . . I mean, is it forbidden or dishonorable for us to . . . to become close?"

Macha did not need an explanation to grasp the meaning of Caroline's last word. "In my heart, it is not, but I cannot speak for him or others. If War Eagle were not Rising Bear's son, second in line to become chief, and a war were not coming fast between our peoples, it might be possible to become mates. But such things are true and stand tall between you."

"Does War Eagle's being second in line mean Cloud Chaser could never become chief because of his mixed blood?"

"Yes, for that is our way and law. Only one who carries Oglala and Red Shield blood can lead our people."

Caroline deduced that if the chief's beloved and esteemed second son would be denied that rank due to his mixed heritage, surely her full-blooded white lineage would prevent her from marrying the man second in line to assume the leader's place if anything happened to Wind Dancer. Since it was possible for Wind Dancer to be slain during the impending battle, War Eagle would never—in her opinion—take the risk of having the chief's line lost to his family. Too, he was a Sacred Bow Carrier, one of the most important and elite warrior ranks in the band, in the Oglala tribe itself. Surely he would do nothing to stain his face when a great challenge loomed ahead for him.

"It makes you sad to think you can only be friends with him?"

"Yes, Dawn, it makes me very sad. But I will do nothing to injure War Eagle in any way. I will not attempt to ensnare and dishonor him. If we are destined to become more than friends, the Great Spirit will show us."

"That is true, for He did so with me and Cloud Chaser, and with Wind Dancer and Dewdrops, and with Rising Bear and Winona. Perhaps the Creator will bind you and War Eagle together one sun."

"Perhaps, but I doubt it. Too much stands between us." Caroline took a deep breath and said, "Let us speak of happy things. Tell me about your adventures with Cloud Chaser before you joined to him."

As Macha began to relate their feats of last summer, War Eagle slipped away from his vulnerable location near the tepee. He was lucky not to have been caught listening to the two women talk. He had been unable to resist the urge to hear Caroline's voice, as he had gotten only a glimpse of her since his return. He wanted to see and speak with her, but he had decided that to approach her too soon could arouse suspicions of his deep feelings toward her.

Following the long council meeting and his talk with Wind Dancer, he had visited with Red Wolf in his parents' dwelling and they had eaten the evening meal there. Afterward, he and Red Wolf had left the family tepee to camp beneath a large tree near the river so they could speak privately.

* * *

Now as the two sat near a small campfire and beneath a waning full moon, Red Wolf asked, "Do you want me to take Wahcawi to my camp on the next sun? Will it not be dangerous if a white woman is found in yours when War Chief Harney rides across your land seeking his enemies? She has done many good deeds for your people, so she will be safe with mine."

War Eagle related how he had attempted to take Caroline to Red Wolf's mother many weeks past, but the Great Spirit had sent a sacred sign that told him not to do so. "Grandfather believes she was sent to us to help us, and she has done so many times. If I had not turned back from taking her to Sparrow, my second brother and Dewdrops would be dead soon. I do not know if her work among us is finished, so I must not send her away until the Great Spirit says that sun has risen. If the white war chief finds our new camp, we will hide Wahcawi from his eyes, as lookouts will watch for him."

"There is more to wanting her to stay nearby, is that not so?"

"Do my voice and looks reveal such things to you, my friend?"

"You kept them hidden until I asked to take her away. Your voice and gaze looked troubled and sad as you spoke. She means much to you?"

"I fear that is true, but no bond can be made between us."

Red Wolf asked, "Why is that so? Your second brother is part white, but he joined to a Red Shield."

War Eagle related the obstacles between them. "It is different for me and Caroline. Cloud Chaser can never become our chief, so he was allowed to join with Dawn. I cannot endanger my rank when war approaches."

"The Great Spirit guided you, not another, to Wahcawi. Perhaps He did so because He chose her for your mate. Perhaps that is why He uses her in many good ways, to evoke your people's love, respect, and acceptance. That is how the Fire Hearts feel about my mother."

"Cheyenne laws and customs are different from the Red Shields'. If I were only a band member and warrior, I could lay claim to her. I am more, so I cannot act selfishly and cause harm to my face, family, and people."

Red Wolf realized his friend was caught in a strong snare, just as he was. He was convinced there was no way Chief Rising Bear would allow him, "a half-breed," to join to his only daughter who had stolen his eye and heart many years ago. To permit a union between him and Hanmani and between War Eagle and Caroline would mean that two of his children were bonded with a white and a half white, while a third carried enemy blood himself. Surely Rising Bear and the Red Shields would think that was too much *vehoe ma-e* mingling with their chief's Oglala bloodline. As with War Eagle and his secret love, ". . . no bond can be made between" him and Hanmani. As he had done for years, Red Wolf concluded, he must keep his feelings hidden, even from his friend.

"What deep thoughts fill your mind?" War Eagle asked.

"That love is sometimes a hard, painful, and perilous path to walk when forces work against a victory in that journey."

"That is true, my friend, and I hope you never have to travel it as I do."

"What will be your next step?" Red Wolf asked, *for I can take none.* "Do you halt and wait, turn back, or continue onward with caution?"

"Since I know the coup that lies ahead, I will stand my ground and pray for the Great Spirit's guidance, help, and protection."

"That is wise and brave and generous. Do not leave your battlefield until defeat is certain. May the Great Spirit answer your prayer soon."

War Eagle nodded his gratitude, then spoke of other matters. "Will the Fire Hearts and other Cheyenne join the war against the bluecoats?"

"I do not know. We will choose our path after the white war chief chooses his. If he challenges us, we will fight him."

"As will the Red Shields and most Lakotas," War Eagle responded before they continued their talk on that serious possibility.

After the morning meal, Red Wolf said farewell to his friend and allies before he mounted and headed for home to relate all he had learned there.

As soon as he was gone and while others were busy with preparations to strike camp, and a few small parties left in search of fresh game or to scout the surrounding area, War Eagle sat on a rush mat near the entrance to his family's tepee and worked on his weapons, restringing his hunting bow and sharpening his knife and making new arrows. He wanted to be within sight of Cloud Chaser's tepee so he would know when, or if, Caroline left it and went into the forest alone. . . .

Caroline peered outside and saw War Eagle laboring before Rising Bear's tepee, the autumn sun shining on his dark hair. Muscles bulged in his arms and shoulders as he secured a new string on his daily bow. His skin looked smooth and firm, and her fingers yearned to stroke it. It would be so enjoyable to sit next to him and talk and laugh together. It would be blissful to experience his touch and kisses. *So close, my love; and yet, so far away from my reach. If only we could court and marry, I would be happy.*

Macha whispered from behind her, "Go into the forest to gather wood and see if he follows to speak with you away from the eyes and ears of others. Put on the garment Hanmani gave you, and your moccasins."

Caroline turned, looked at her, and asked, "Should I do so?"

Macha grinned and said, "Yes, for you must learn of his feelings."

"What if they do not match mine?"

"Cross that deep stream only if you approach it. Change and go."

"What will others think and say if I dress as one of you?"

Macha laughed softly and teased, "If they did not want you to do so, they would not have given you such gifts at your honoring ceremony."

She smiled and said, "You are wise and kind. I will obey."

War Eagle joined Caroline as she gathered wood in the forest, assured no one was close enough to see or hear them. *"Hau,* Wahcawi," he greeted her, then watched her straighten and turn toward him.

"Hau, Wanbli," she responded, aware he had used her Indian name. "I am glad you returned safe, for it makes your family and people happy. It will be good when Cloud Chaser returns to his wife and son, for Dawn loves and misses him much. I am sorry you brought bad news about the Brules and General Harney. My people are wrong to do such evil acts."

"It is good to be here, and soon my second brother will join us. Father and Wind Dancer told me of your brave and generous deed while I was gone. I am happy they honored you and Red Wolf. Surely the Great Spirit guided me to you. Do you also believe He sent you to us?"

Caroline selected her response with care. "I believe the Creator often works in strange ways to help and bless His people. I am honored and awed He chose me as His tool for good use. I also am honored and pleased your people trusted me and thanked me with gifts, a Red Shield name, and their friendship."

"It is good you can be called a friend and you call us friends."

"I can do so with all except Runs Fast. He blames me for his son's defeat and death, though Pretty Meadow does not seem to hate me."

"After his heart heals and his mind clears, he will not feel that way. I bring you a gift of thanks," he hinted and watched her reaction of surprise. "I bring you words of your brother."

"David? You saw him? Is he alive and safe?" she asked in haste.

"My eyes looked upon him from far away. He rode with the white war chief at Blue Water Creek during the battle with the Brules."

Caroline's heart pounded in dread and dismay. "How did you know it was David? Did he . . . Did he battle them?" she asked in reluctance.

"Cloud Chaser knew his face and revealed his presence to us. He is like his sister and possesses a good heart. He did not slay Brules with his firestick and he helped some escape the attack, though he hid his actions from other soldiers." He paused while she sighed in relief, then smiled in joy. "Cloud Chaser spoke with him at Fort Laramie. He did not tell your brother you live in our camp. He sends what you call letters to the white leaders far away to give them the truth about the massacre and Harney's evil. Before Cloud Chaser leaves the soldiers, he will let your brother know you are alive and safe, but not where you are. Does that please you?"

"Yes, if fills my heart with happiness and pride. I am glad David does not obey the evil orders of General Harney. That news is the largest gift I could receive. I thank you, Wanbli."

"Do you hate and blame me for capturing you?"

How, she wondered should she answer? With the truth, she decided. "I do not hate or blame you, Wanbli. A force more powerful than you urged you to . . . act as you did that day. Much good has come from your . . . capture of me, so how could it be wrong?"

"Your words and feelings please me, Wahcawi."

"As yours please me." *As your smile weakens me all over.* "May I give and take a gift?"

"I do not understand. What gift can I give to you?"

"A kiss."

Caroline stared at him in confusion, astonishment, and delight. She did not move or break their locked gazes as he closed the distance between them. She quivered in desire and pleasure as his mouth met with hers.

The first kiss was long and tender. His arms banded her upper back, and hers encircled his waist. They clung to each other and savored each other's touch and taste. The kiss soon waxed intense, swift, urgent, probing. It sent their spirits soaring.

War Eagle's fingers drifted into her sunny locks and stroked her hair, relishing the way the curls encompassed his hands and tickled the flesh on them. His questing mouth left hers for a short time to rove her face, then returned to her willing lips.

Caroline's hands sneaked beneath his leather vest and adored the firm and soft surfaces she discovered there. His body was warm, appealing, and enticing. She loved him. She desired him. She was enslaved to him. She felt her breasts grow taut and a strange tightening in her womb.

Sensing a slight and sudden tension and hesitation in Caroline, War Eagle surmised it was their rising and perilous passion that was alarming her. He also realized a union of bodies was impossible on this sun, for the same reasons that no doubt troubled her and cooled the heat of her response. He ended the kiss, gazed down at her, and smiled. "When we touch in this way, strange feelings claim us. They are good, but dangerous while we are only friends. We must halt them for this sun and wait to learn if they return and grow."

"You are kind and wise, Wanbli." To change the subject,

she asked, "Should you not overtake Red Wolf and send me to his camp? With Harney riding in your territory, it is dangerous for me to be with the Red Shields."

"Do not fear, Wahcawi, for he will not find you among us."

Caroline misunderstood his meaning and murmured in sadness, "You are sending me away? To the Cheyenne camp?"

"No, we will hide you if he finds our new camp. Do you hunger to leave us? You want to go live in the Fire Hearts camp?"

"No, but I do not want to be a threat to you and your people. I like Red Wolf, and his mother must be a good woman." To test his reaction to the topic of marriage and to see if he would give her only a clue about his intention toward her, she asked in a casual tone, "Do you think Red Wolf will ask for your sister's hand in joining?"

"He is my friend and ally. He does not seek my sister as a mate."

"I think they are drawn to each other."

"Your eyes trick you, Wahcawi. If such were true, Red Wolf would tell me. He would not seek a prize out of his reach."

"Why is Hanmani out of his reach?"

"Father would not allow her to join to him and live far away."

Caroline did not ask him to explain further. She believed it was because Red Wolf was part white, and War Eagle would not want to reveal that to her. If that union was impossible, she reasoned, surely there was no hope of one for her. Her heart and mind in torment, she needed to escape this forbidden temptation. "Then, it is good my senses tricked me about their feelings. I must finish my tasks and return to camp. Dawn will worry if I take too long. Thank you for the good words about my brother. I must hurry now." She turned and retrieved the half-full sling and headed for camp, praying she would not weep.

War Eagle perceived a change in her mood and gaze, but

he could not guess what had provoked it. He yearned to halt her swift departure to ask her not to reject him while he waited to see if the Great Spirit would clear their tangled path for them so they could join as mates, but it was too soon. He dared not confess his love and desire aloud, but he had given her signs of them to try to bind her to him. Had he failed in his attempts? Was she resisting such feelings for a "savage"? Had she been pretending with him only to trick him into sending her away? Did she have feelings for Red Wolf, as his friend had been in camp with her for many days and they were honored together? Was that why she asked about Red Wolf and Hanmani, to see if he mentioned another woman in the Cheyenne camp?

What truly lives in your heart and head, Kawa Cante? You will not become the mate of Red Wolf or another, for you are mine. Soon, I will learn if you share my feelings or only seek to trick me. . . .

Chapter Seventeen

The next morning, the Red Shields were busy striking camp at the edge of Paha Sapa to move deeper into the sacred hills. The people worked fast so they could make a good distance before nightfall. War Eagle and others scouted the way as the lengthy processional evacuated that site. A rear guard used pine limbs to brush away their tracks and used other debris to conceal old fires before taking up their positions to protect the band's flank. The large group headed southwestward toward the Cave of the Spirit Winds to set up a new village along the banks of a tranquil sylvan lake. Black spires and pinnacles of various shapes and heights were used as markers to guide them. Soon, an abundance of ridges, evergreens, valleys, and slopes would conceal them from the enemy's view, be it Indian or white.

While Macha—with Casmu on her back in his cradleboard—rode the animal that pulled the loaded tag-along, Caroline walked nearby, holding the tethers of Cloud Chaser's buffalo horse, as that special creature was only ridden during hunts. She recalled how War Eagle had joined them at dawn to take down his brother's *Huyamni* and pack the three-legged stand and weapons, as women were never to touch them, and Cloud Chaser could not carry them at the fort. They had exchanged looks several times as he did those tasks, but were careful with their behavior while so many people were scurrying around the area. At times, it was almost as if his probing gaze was asking her questions she could not grasp. If a serious relationship was impossible for them, she fretted, what did he want and expect from her? She could not continue to dally with him in the forest. They could be caught, and she dreaded to imagine the result of that exposure.

Worse, Caroline worried, their rising desires could lead to a hazardous and uncontrollable surrender to passion. Yes, she loved him, wanted him, craved him intensely, but she had been reared as a Christian who believed people should be married before consummating their bond. Too, she could become pregnant. If that happened, would War Eagle marry her or would their child be born a bastard, a captive like its mother? Rising Bear had not joined to Omaste, but he had accepted and reared Cloud Chaser as his son, and Macha's husband did not suffer from his misbegotten birth. Even so, that was not a stigma she wanted to give her child.

After a longer midday break to eat and rest, Caroline glanced around as the sometimes arduous walk continued. She had not even glimpsed War Eagle since their departure because he was riding as an advance scout, as other Lakota bands could be camped along their route or bold enemies could be encroaching for raids or stealthy whites could be trapping or hunting in the forbidden hills. Their pace was steady, but it was the undulating landscape that strained their stamina and energy. The weather was mild and the sky was clear of ominous clouds. So far, no trouble had struck.

The journey became more difficult when gently rolling hills rose to higher ground that they could not skirt, then took sharp turns downward into canyons. The dense forest and scattered woods were filled with deer, turkey, elk, and other creatures. The majority of the trees and bushes were evergreens, but in some places, numerous hardwoods were present, changing colors at that season. The meadows they crossed or viewed displayed mainly yellow to brown grass and many late summer to fall wildflowers, and were dotted by grazing buffalo and other creatures. They encountered streams and creeks along the path to their destination. Although most of the rock was in shades of ebony, some was a pale gray. In craggs or on narrow shelves along the sides of high and rugged cliffs, mountain goats and sheep were sighted, but not hunted during their rush. On occasion, a rambling bear, skulking wolf, or curious coyote was seen, but none challenged their passing.

Caroline found the vast location beautiful, the terrain sheltered in winter, and very serene, at least for now. It was apparent to her why the Indians loved and frequented this area that seemed to leap from the earth amidst an enormous prairie as a gift from their Great Spirit to sustain their lives. She could imagine the awesome changes wrought upon it with white settlement. She hated to think of this land falling into the hands of her people for trapping, hunting, home-steading, farming, and lumbering. But it was not within her power to prevent that. If it were, she would do so.

At last, the first day came to an end and the band halted to rest, eat, and sleep, to repeat the same actions for many days. . . .

Far away at Fort Laramie on that same morning, Cloud Chaser stood within the shadows of the sutler's door as he watched Spotted Tail, Long Chin, Red Leaf, and others ride to the camp of General Harney to surrender to him. He noted that the chiefs and warriors were clad in their finest array and were singing and chanting their death songs as if they were certain their executions awaited them. The surviving members of their band rode or walked behind their leaders, their heads lowered in shame and sorrow.

Cloud Chaser grieved with them and feared for their lives, though he recalled no mistreatment of the past prisoners. He noticed that Little Thunder and his band were not with them as War Eagle had told him last week. He wondered if Harney would be satisfied with the event in progress and with the report of Little Thunder's move from the territory and promise never to raid whites or challenge soldiers again. Having witnessed Harney's crushing intent and bad feelings for the Lakotas at large, he doubted it.

The next morning, Cloud Chaser watched as a troop of soldiers left to escort the prisoners to Fort Leavenworth via Kearny. Ben had told him one of the Fort Laramie men had disclosed that the chiefs and elite warriors were to be hanged there and the others would be imprisoned. He prayed the army would change its mind, as that incident would provoke more hostility, distrust, and warfare from other bands and tribes. He knew that Harney planned to leave on his "Sioux Campaign" on Saturday, September 29, three days from this sad one. The general's plan, according to what he had learned, was to take the old fur trade trail that snaked its way across their territory to Fort Pierre, checking every camp for "hostiles" and "escapees" along the way and attacking any party that challenged him. But what worried Cloud Chaser was the map a Crow scout had made for Harney, one with large X's where Lakota camps were said to be situated. Somehow and some way, Cloud Chaser plotted, he must steal and destroy it. . . .

When Cloud Chaser saw David walking toward the store later that day he palmed the note he had prepared about

Caroline. He headed out the door fast as David—with his head lowered—was about to enter it, causing them to bump into each other with force. Cloud Chaser grabbed David's arm to steady the soldier's balance and, while doing so, stuffed the note into the man's pocket to be found and read later. He shook his head and apologized, "Sorry about that jolt. Guess my thoughts were elsewhere."

"So were mine, and the accident was half my fault, so I apologize, too."

"I suppose you boys are getting ready to ride out soon."

"At sunrise on Saturday, but I'm not looking forward to the journey."

"Where you boys heading? Heard it was straight into Sioux country."

"That's General Harney's plan, stalk right through the heart of it."

"Sounds as if you don't want to go with him, and I can't blame you. By now, all Lakotas know about the Ash Hollow incident and will be prepared for trouble. Harney won't be able to pull any more sneak attacks, and he'll be challenging them on their terrain, something they're familiar with and he isn't. Fact is, I'm heading for Fort Pierre, so I might stick close to you boys for protection in case the Indians get riled by his encroachment and start attacking every man they see. You think General Harney will object?"

"I don't see why he would. If he refuses to let you ride with us, you could just stick as close as possible so you can join us if trouble strikes."

"How much longer you got in the army's confines?"

"Two years, and then I'm out, permanently. After I find my sister, I plan to head to California and start fresh there. It's been good talking to you while I was here and you taught me plenty. I'm grateful to you, Chase, and it might help me stay alive while I'm searching for Caroline."

"How can you search for her while you're riding with Harney?"

"As soon as we reach Fort Pierre, I'm requesting a leave to look for her. Maybe the general will send a troop with me since he has men and weapons missing. If not, I'll figure something out. You'll have to excuse me now. I have to mail a letter and return to my area. I guess I'll see you later."

"I hope so. Good luck."

"I'm sure I'll need it, and thanks."

Cloud Chaser left the store to return to his campsite. Soon, he would be heading home. That day could not come fast enough.

After David gave Ben a letter to mail to Washington and thanked the sutler, he headed to rejoin his unit. As he pulled out his handkerchief to dab blood from a scrape, the dislodged note fell to the ground. A gust of wind seized it and blew it away without him noticing it. . . .

"Lacetkiya, Wanbli. *Wociciyaka wacin."*

When his grandfather called out for him to "Come this way. I want to speak with you," War Eagle halted his task and looked at Nahemana. He surmised something was afoot but could not imagine what it was. He headed to obey, his curiosity aroused. . . .

They walked a short distance from their new campsite so they could speak in private. When they halted, they sat on large rocks amidst trees.

"What troubles you on this sun, Grandfather?"

"A dream was sent to me on the past moon. I saw a glowing hand come from the sky and push Wahcawi toward you. But it halted her before she reached you and would let her approach no closer. I believe the Great Spirit has chosen her to become your mate, but the sun has not risen when that truth should be revealed to others. I saw the shiny hand return and take her far away before she was returned to your side and you were joined. The Great Spirit has given her many chances to prove she is worthy of you, and she has grasped victory each time. But more challenges are ahead in the shadows for her to meet before all accept her and you lay claim to her."

War Eagle was astonished and elated by that news. Yet, he also was worried by some parts of it. "What remaining challenges stand between us? Where will she go, Grandfather? Why must she leave? For how long?"

"That was not shown to me, but I saw a white blanket on the land and ice in the water when you joined. The moon before her honoring ceremony, another message was sent to me; it revealed I was to give her a Red Shield name. While you were scouting at the bluecoat fort, we talked much and shared healing skills. It is good she knows such things, for she can tend those injured by bluecoat firesticks and those sickened by their diseases. Is it not true you love and desire her?"

"It is true, Grandfather. But I feared I could not have her."

"Has the Great Spirit placed those same feelings within her?"

"I believe he has. Surely He would do so since she was chosen for me. My spirit soars as my name. Much joy and pride fill me."

Nahemana cautioned the happy man, "Do not forget, War Eagle: you must not reveal your feelings to others or lay claim to her before the right sun rises. To do so could bring great harm to the Creator's plan."

"It will be hard to do so, Grandfather, but I will walk the path you pointed out to me," he promised. Now that the Great Spirit had given him the long-awaited sign of victory, he could calm his fears of never having or of losing her. But he must be careful not to do anything to prevent that dream from coming true. He yearned to run to Caroline's side to reveal his love and share this good news. Yet, he must avoid her today, as his joy could make him careless. Just seeing her while knowing the truth could cause him to expose his feelings before others when the Great Spirit commanded secrecy for a while longer. Even if he could control himself, perhaps she could not. *Soon, Kawa Cante, all will know and you will be mine.*

The next day, the Red Shield Band of the Oglala Lakotas gathered as they awaited the start of the Sacred Bow ritual, which was believed to yield powerful medicine for war and for peace. Despite the anxiety of impending war, all knew that each person's existence traveled in a circle as with the Sacred Hoop of Life, and death was a part of it, though a fallen one's spirit dwelled with Wakantanka and that fact was soothing.

The Sacred Medicine Bow Society's meeting lodge had been set up in a forest clearing early that morning, with a sweat lodge erected beside it. The three other Bow Carriers—War Eagle, Swift Otter, and Broken Arrow—were to participate in the event to prove that Bent Bow's skills were equal to theirs and that he possessed the prowess to join their high rank.

Following purification in the *initipi* of the four men who were clad only in plain breechclouts and moccasins, special words were spoken in private in the members' meeting lodge. After they joined their people near the lake, the ceremony began with a prayer sent forth by Nahemana to the Great Spirit and other powerful forces of nature—wind, lightning, thunder, hail, snake, and bear—to evoke guidance and assistance with the challenge ahead.

Four posts, which represented the four directions of the wind and Medicine Wheel, were already in place in opposing positions and were decorated with sacred symbols. The runners' bodies were painted red, the color of Mother Earth where the buffalo wallowed, the main provider of their survival. Other Medicine Bow colors and designs were added.

Yellow lines to depict lightning snaked across their faces, and their cheeks bore blue hailstones. A yellow quarter moon was painted upon their bare chests. Other sky-blue lines drawn on arms and legs evoked the powers of the four winds.

The four runners faced the west, their expressions serious, their moods reverent. After the signal was given, Bent Bow displayed his stamina and determination by matching the pace of the other three participants, necessary competition to evince his worth and compatibility. Since it was not a contest between several hopefuls, no token was collected at each post to determine the winner. Each man simply touched the post in passing. All reached Nahemana at almost the same time. More tests quickly followed to expose weapons skills, prowess, endurance, and intelligence.

As Wind Dancer observed, great love and pride filled his heart for his brother. He knew that if anything happened to him and his father, War Eagle would make a good chief and leader. All he had to hope for was his brother's survival and for him to also meet a woman well matched to him. But he worried, could Wahcawi be that woman? He liked and respected her and was grateful to her for all she had done for his family and people, but could she make a good chief's wife, a good Red Shield?

As Caroline watched the ritual, her gaze was constantly drawn to War Eagle, whose attention seemed entirely centered on the action. He looked mysterious and appealing with his body painted in various vivid colors. Surely those depicted forces were no more powerful than he was, at least where she was concerned. He was such a strong, virile, handsome, and honorable man that her heart pounded with love and desire, and it was difficult to keep focused on the stirring event. She was glad that no one, except Runs Fast, from his glare earlier, objected to her presence near Macha and Chumani. She watched as War Eagle rapidly fired many arrows upward, suspending them all in midair before the first one plummeted to the ground. She feared her heart would stop when he stood motionless as the sharp arrow-heads plunged toward him and stuck up straight in the earth within a few feet of him. She saw him hurl lances through willow circles of varying sizes and at different distances, succeeding every time. She saw him fling war clubs at targets, striking each appointed spot on his goal. It was evident to her that he possessed superior skills with all weapons. There was no doubt in her mind that he was an elite warrior, protector, and hunter. A surge of pride filled her body and warmed her very soul.

After the demands were met, everyone observed as their war chief's son strung his new bow, one that was longer and heavier than a regular hunting weapon and exposed a lance point on the top end. It now would be the man's duty to help bring about peace for his band and to fight fiercely for it in times of war. He was presented with a hanger, a staff for supporting the sacred object when not in use, as it must not lie upon the ground or be propped against anything that might drain or taint its special powers.

With Two Feathers' replacement chosen, the Sacred Bow foursome was once again complete. The other members— four club bearers and four staff carriers—joined their society brothers in a ceremonial dance and chant.

Caroline watched War Eagle step and whirl in time to the beating of the kettledrum. Despite the mild weather, she saw perspiration glistening on his face and body. At times, his eyes were closed as if in reverence of the ceremony. During swift twirls and leaps, his long ebony hair seemingly performed a dance of its own. He had great strength and agility in his muscled legs. He was an awesome sight.

Afterward, the four reentered the *initipi* for a final purification rite where their bodies were washed clean of paints and were rubbed with sweet and sage grasses in symbolic gesture to the land that fed the buffalo.

Caroline returned to Cloud Chaser's tepee to do daily

chores with Macha, as both talked about the woman's absent husband and wondered what he was doing at that moment.

On the morning of that same day, Cloud Chaser rode behind the seemingly endless rows of well-armed soldiers as they left Fort Laramie, with David positioned somewhere amidst them. To the rear of the troops were supply wagons and cannon bearers. He hoped his people had moved their camp and it was far from Harney's path. He prayed the general would not ride into the sacred hills in search of villages. If The Butcher did so, he would gallop ahead with a warning. If only there were some way he could disable the cannons, but there was none to his knowledge. At least the ones War Eagle had dumped into the Badlands could not be used against them or their allies.

Soon, my beloved wife, I will be at your side again.

As Caroline gathered scrub wood while Macha washed garments in the lake with other women, she halted and stiffened as she heard a strange noise that sounded like the deep-throat purring—no, rumbling—of a large cat. Using caution, she straightened at a near snail's pace and looked beyond her. She froze and her blue gaze widened as she sighted a large and sleek mountain lion poised on a rock ledge about twenty-five feet beyond her. His golden eyes were fastened on her, his ears were erect, his whiskers were drawn back, and his long tail was swaying slightly as if in anticipation and suspense. His stance—bent knees—implied he was ready to spring forward at any given moment. Why he hesitated there, she did not know, unless he enjoyed stalking and intimidating his prey. If she screamed for help or turned and fled, it would bound off the ledge, pursue, and attack her. She had no doubt she could not outrun the tawny beast. Yet,

Caroline decided she could not stand there and stare it down, and it probably would not lose interest in her and leave. With her hand on the knife handle at her waist, she began to take short and slow steps backward. Then, she heard a low voice behind her tell her to stop, to remain still and quiet, a voice she knew well. Her beloved's. Now she understood why the creature had delayed his attack, as a threat to his success and survival was close by.

War Eagle eased up beside Caroline, relieved he had come looking for her to steal a few words in secret. Upon his stealthy approach, he had heard the animal's throaty sounds and sighted it on the ledge, watching his love, its swaying tail revealing its intent to leap at her soon. When he had stepped from behind the large pine, he knew the beast also sighted him, though it did not flee, just studied him. He had readied an arrow in his bow before exposing his presence. He was proud and happy that Caroline had not panicked, screamed, or run, or been startled by his arrival. He knew the sleek, powerful, and swift puma could have overtaken her with ease. Even if it had not slain her, its slashing claws could have injured her badly. Since there was an abundance of game in the area and pumas did not usually attack people, he wondered why this one was tempted to do so. He hated to slay the majestic animal, but it could be a threat to children playing or women working nearby on another day.

War Eagle took aim on the creature's golden chest and re-leased his feathered shaft. The arrow's flight was true, and upon its impact, the beast staggered, tumbling off the precipice with a heavy thud. In the blink of an eye, another arrow was sent into its body, striking its heart. A short time later, it lay still. He hurried forward and knelt to make certain the animal was dead, and wondered why it had not let out a piercing scream upon its first wound or fall. He was glad it had not, as that sound could have carried to camp.

War Eagle looked up from his position as Caroline joined

him. She was staring at the puma with wide eyes, her face pale, and her body trembling. He stood and said, "You safe, Kawa Cante."

Caroline almost flung herself against his hard body, her arms banding his waist and her cheek pressed to his chest. "I was so afraid. You saved my life," she murmured in English, just as he had done. "Thank you, Wanbli."

He grasped her chin and lifted her head so he could gaze into her blue eyes. "Pain would fill me if you were harmed or slain," he said in Lakota.

"Pain would fill me if you were harmed or slain," she echoed. *Just as it would if you chose another woman to marry.*

"It is good our feelings match, for we are close. I feared it would not be so for the one who captured you and keeps you from your people."

Do our feelings truly match, my love, or do I misread your meaning? "I am safe and happy with the Red Shields. That would not be true among my people, for many do evil things to yours in past seasons and during this one. I am sorry that is true, Wanbli, for it brings shame and sadness to me."

"It must not do so, Wahcawi, for you are good and kind. Will you hate and scorn us when we are forced to battle with your people?"

"No, for you cannot yield to their wicked demands. To protect your people and land, you must seek peace if it is possible. If it is not, you must fight for them. But I pray at least a truce can come between the two sides."

"That is for War Chief Harney to make happen, for he is the one who attacks even those who do not want to battle him."

"You said my brother was sending a message to the white leaders far away. I pray David's words will touch their hearts and change their plans. I fear war will come one day, but I hope it does not come for a long time." She saw him nod in agreement. "I watched you in the Sacred Bow ritual. You have many skills and much prowess. Fear leapt into my heart when you stood beneath the rain of arrows. You found victory in every challenge."

"Those deeds were to prove Bent Bow is worthy of his new rank and to prove that Swift Otter, Broken Arrow, and I remain worthy to keep ours, for Sacred Bow Carriers lead in big battles and are last to leave a fight."

With Harney on the move and with fierce war perhaps imminent, that reminder alarmed Caroline. "Does a Sacred Bow Carrier ever . . ."—how to explain *retire?*—"give up his rank?"

"Wind Dancer did so when he became a Shirt Wearer and to guard his life, for he will become our next chief. Others have done so when their seasons on Mother Earth were many and their skills weakened. There is no shame in doing so, but few give up that rank until they must."

An idea entered Caroline's mind and she shared it with War Eagle. "Do you know which path Harney will ride into your territory?"

"He has many wagons and rolling thundersticks. There is an old trail between the two forts that fur traders used. We think he will travel it."

She saw him eyeing her strangely at her odd query and abrupt change of subject. "If you send out pairs of scouts and place them at different locations between the camp and trail, one can watch for Harney's approach while the other carries a message to the next man who carries it to the next until it reaches our camp. That will tell you where he is and rides next."

War Eagle grinned in pleasure. "Your plan is good and cunning. I will tell Father and we will use it when the sun rises again." His gaze roamed over her lovely features, her expression and mood now calm with the danger past. He lifted one hand and caressed her soft cheek, and saw it suffuse with color to almost match that of the sunset. He felt her hands flatten against his lower back, and saw her swallow as her gaze was bound to his. He could not stop himself from lowering his head and sealing their mouths in that much-needed contact.

Caroline responded with eagerness and joy as the first tender kiss gradually fused into a near-feverish one as their smoldering passions were kindled into roaring flames of desire. Her fingers pressed into the firm flesh of his back as she urged him closer to her body, and she felt his embrace tighten, the bow release from his grasp to free his hands. Her heart sang merrily and her wits were dazed by his enchanting presence and stimulating touch, his irresistible reaching out to and for her.

A muffled groan escaped War Eagle's throat as his mouth shifted to place kisses on her face and neck. He was elated and enthralled by the way she surrendered to his enticements and how she coaxed him for more. He had no doubt she was the perfect woman for him, that he loved and desired only her as a woman. He could imagine the ecstasy he would obtain from a complete mating with her. Gone were any doubts of her feelings for him and any suspicions that she had been drawn to Red Wolf. The Great Spirit knew they were well matched and He would bond them together soon.

Caroline was thrilled by the way War Eagle caressed and kissed her, as she sensed the depth and honesty of his emotions. She was convinced he wanted her as his woman, and his only delay in revealing his goal to her and others was in waiting until he removed any obstacles between them. If making love was all he wanted from her, she reasoned, he could have taken her or tricked her into submission before now. He must love her and want to join—

War Eagle and Caroline jerked apart as Macha hurried forward and whispered, "Others walk this way to hunt. You must part before they come."

Caroline stared at her smiling and amused friend who had come to warn them of impending intrusion. "Thank you, Dawn."

"I must talk fast. After the passings of five suns, the moon's face will be dark. You can sneak to your brother's tepee and visit with her without others seeing and knowing. Is that good?" she asked him.

War Eagle grinned and nodded. "It is good and kind, Dawn. Take Wahcawi with you. I must skin the creature that tried to attack her," he said as he motioned to the mountain lion. "Go quickly, for I hear voices."

Caroline and Macha rushed into the concealment of trees and rocks as they took a roundabout way back to camp, avoiding the three hunters who would soon encounter War Eagle as he labored with the golden creature.

Inside Cloud Chaser's tepee, Caroline asked, "How did you know we were in the forest together?"

"I saw War Eagle walk the same path you had taken. I looked around and made sure no one had seen him, then entered the edge of the woods and watched for others to come that way. When I sighted hunters walking nearby, I came to find you."

"How did you know we would be . . . would need to be warned?"

Macha laughed softly. "I believe much love and desire lives within Wahcawi and Wanbli. I reasoned that those feelings would break free when you were alone. After Cloud Chaser's return to us, we were drawn together as you are this season. Before he became a Red Shield again, it was forbidden for us to reach out to each other, but our love and needs could not be denied. We sneaked meetings in the forest to speak and kiss, and Hanmani stood guard for us. That is what I do for you."

"You are a good friend, Dawn, and I thank you. I love him and I want to join to him, to live among the Red Shields. I pray that will happen."

"Do not worry or fear, Wahcawi. I believe the sun will rise."

*   *   *

Six nights later, Caroline sat on her buffalo mat with War Eagle beside her, their thighs touching and their fingers interlocked, just as their adoring gazes were. She wished they had total privacy, but that was impossible for now. Macha sat on her sleeping mat on the opposite side of the tepee, her back to them as she hummed softly to Casmu as if trying not to overhear their softly spoken words. The tepee flap was laced, so no one would disturb them, unless trouble struck. A small fire burned in the center of the cozy abode, warming and lighting its confines, the smoke drifting upward to escape through the apex opening.

War Eagle raised Caroline's hand to his lips and kissed it before he used his cheek to stroke its back, which caused her to smile and to sigh in contentment. He savored their contact, this stolen time, her glowing gaze, her acceptance of him. He leaned forward and whispered into her ear, "My heart beats with love for you, Heart Flower. When the Great Spirit clears our path one sun, will you join to me?"

Caroline leaned away slightly so she could look into his eyes. His dark brown gaze was tender and evocative; his seductive smile, enticing. Yes, she had heard him declare his love and propose to her, and he was serious. She freed her fingers and clasped his head between her hands so she could draw it close to whisper for his ears alone, "I love you, Wanbli, and yearn to become your wife. What if your family and people refuse to allow our union?"

With their lowered foreheads touching, he told her, "The sun will rise when they learn you have been chosen for me by the Creator. Seven suns past, Grandfather told me of a sacred dream he had." He related the wise man's words to him in the forest and their ensuing talk.

Whether or not, Caroline reasoned, the shaman possessed genuine mystical and prophetic abilities, Nahemana believed it was true, as did War Eagle, as did his people. She did not doubt such powers existed in holy men, as the Bible was filled with stories about them. She was delighted the shaman approved of her and would help her. "I wonder what challenges lie ahead for me, for us. I do not want to leave you. Do you think the snow and ice mean we will join this winter?"

"I do not know, Heart Flower, but I hope that is true."

"When did you know you loved and desired me?" she asked.

"I think it was the first time I looked into your sky eyes and heard your voice. It was as if my heart opened up and you walked inside it."

"Long ago, before I came to your land, I dreamed of you. I could not see your face, for your back was to me. But your hair was long and black and your skin was this color," she murmured as she touched his hand.

"Before Cloud Chaser returned to us, he dreamed of Dawn. Perhaps your dream of me is why I did not frighten you much, though you have big courage and many wits," he said, smiling at her before he kissed her.

Caroline returned the kiss: then they shared several more before the time came for him to leave, too soon to suit her.

"I must go, for it is late. Father and Mother will wonder what halts my return. Until we are one, we must be careful with our looks and actions as Grandfather warned, for we must not injure the Great Spirit's plan for us."

"That is true, but it will be hard to hide my love and to avoid you. Much harder now that I know you feel as I do."

He nodded in agreement. "I love you, Heart Flower, and we will become as one on a future moon. You will be mine forever. Now, I must go."

Caroline stood with him, looked into his eyes one last time, kissed him, and said, "I love you and will wait for you to become my husband."

War Eagle thanked Macha before he unlaced the flap, glanced at Caroline and smiled, then slipped into the darkness.

Caroline relaced the flap and told Macha, "Thank you, my good friend, for my heart is filled with joy and my spirit soars as my love's namesake."

Macha smiled and said, "Sleep now and have good dreams of him, as I will have of my husband. I pray he is safe and will return soon."

"Do not fear or worry, Dawn, for he is brave, cunning, and skilled."

Five nights later and about forty miles away, those skills failed Cloud Chaser as he took an enormous and daring risk to steal the map of Lakota camps and was captured. . . .

Chapter Eighteen

Cloud Chaser sat bound to a tree near the Cheyenne River. He had traveled and talked with the soldiers from Fort Laramie to the headwaters of the White River and journeyed along its bank to the Badlands, which were cut into the surrounding grasslands. In a narrow center section between two larger areas of rugged mudstone ridges, buttes, and spires amidst canyons and ravines, they had crossed the river to ride northeast beside it, then switched to the Bad River to follow it to Fort Pierre. Being close to home and his beloved wife, he had gotten too eager to finish his task. After dark, when the fatigued troops had taken to their bedrolls and while guards were posted at intervals around the perimeter of the encampment, he had sneaked into Harney's tent to steal a Crow-made map of the Lakotas' winter camps. Unfortunately, the general had proven to be a light sleeper.

Since the Red Shields surely had moved their camp by now and were concealed within the Paha Sapa's interior, a dark mountain range within sight on the western horizon during the day, he should have slipped away and returned home. He recalled that along their route, Indians in all camps they had encountered had vowed they were honoring the peace treaty and had proven—with searches—that they harbored no "escapees" or "hostiles." To Cloud Chaser's surprise, Harney had not attacked a single village so far. The now-feared white war chief—The Butcher—had simply intimidated their inhabitants with his show of force, twelve hundred strong and armed with superior weapons. Harney had warned all bands that any display of aggression would be dealt with promptly and lethally, and the Indians believed him, aware of the Blue Water Creek Massacre nine weeks ago.

Now, Cloud Chaser fretted as he raged against the tight bonds; he feared and dreaded that the scouts would find the Red Shields' tracks and pursue them into the Black Hills, and take their move as a sign of guilt and a need to hide from him. Also, there was a possible threat to the remaining camps of allies or any hunting parties that Harney encountered from this point onward to his destination.

He had failed, Cloud Chaser admitted, and here he sat, secured by ropes and waiting to be sent to Fort Leavenworth via Kearny tomorrow to be jailed. Unless he escaped, which would be difficult when surrounded by a troop of twenty soldiers, men ordered to be alert for problems. He was to be escorted under guard along the same trail they had taken to this location, as Harney felt it was safer and faster not to travel overland, which was the shortest route. Yet, they were not to stop at Fort Laramie.

To make matters worse, he had drawn David Sims into his trouble. David had attempted to sneak over and free him and had been caught. Now, Caroline's brother—who was being held captive in another area—faced an impending trial and prison. He recalled how a cunning David had tried to convince Harney—who was irritated at having his rest interrupted twice tonight—he was only trying to release him in exchange for helping to find and rescue his sister who vanished months ago while en route to join him. The sad tale had not affected Harney's decision. How, Cloud Chaser worried, was he going to get out of this?

He came to full alert and listened again, closer that time. Yes, it was a Red Shield signal in the form of a certain bird-call. But how did they know he had . . . No doubt, he reasoned in elation, Nahemana had been enlightened to his imminent trouble in a vision and the shaman had sent scouts to check on him. He had to get a message to whoever was out there, and not far away. Thankfully, Harney had chosen to have him secured to a large tree near the river, placing him at the boundary of the large encampment, though two guards were nearby.

Cloud Chaser lowered his head and pretended to chant softly as he revealed the grim news to one of his fellow warriors on the other bank. He did his task with haste and finished relating the needed information just as one of the guards kicked the bottom of his boot and ordered him to be quiet or he would gag him. He looked at the scowling soldier and said, "It is a Pawnee Death Chant, for I will be hanged when I reach Fort Leavenworth. I must prepare my spirit to join the Creator when that day comes soon."

"Well, think that Injun talk, mister, but keep your mouth shut. The others are sleeping and you'll wake 'em. If it was me giving orders instead of the general, I'd had you shot tonight for turning against your own kind."

"Shot for only trying to prevent a bloody and unnecessary war?" Cloud Chaser scoffed. "Shot for trying to save lives on both sides, including yours? Shot for trying to stop this territory from becoming a fierce battleground for years? If General Harney attacks any innocent camps, and most of them aren't to blame for what's been going on here, every tribe in this area will band together and swarm down on you boys to retaliate for such an injustice. By the time you realize the Indians are there, you'll be surrounded by thousands of skilled warriors who know how to fight on this kind of terrain. You won't have time to ready and use those cannons or long-range rifles before at least half of you are dead, or wish you were. You're lucky they haven't united against you already after you pulled that sneak attack near Ash Hollow and murdered so many Brules, most of them women and children and old people, even babies. There isn't any honor in or cause for committing such atrocities."

"You mean like the massacre of Grattan and his unit?"

Cloud Chaser exhaled and shook his head in mute scolding. "It's a shame you men don't know the truth about that incident and a lot of others the Indians have been falsely accused of doing. Grattan attacked a friendly camp and killed the head chief of all Lakotas, all because an emigrant's cow wandered into their camp, was slaughtered, and eaten. As I told Harney, I figured if he lost his map, he'd head on to Fort Pierre and stop this foolish challenge in every camp. I tried to tell him the Indians had settled down for the winter, so it's rash to ride around provoking and insulting them. I live and trap in this territory like a lot of other white men, and a lot of settlers pass through here, and you are endangering all of us."

"The Injuns have to be punished for that massacre and other stuff."

"Punished for trying to protect their lives and lands?"

"That ain't how the general and others see it."

"I know, and that's the stupidity and tragedy of the situation. A lot of people on both sides are going to die when a truce is possible if the Indians are treated fairly and honorably. They don't want to war with the whites, but they'll be forced to do just that if Harney continues with his plans to humiliate and conquer them and to punish innocents for the wrongdoings of renegades or acts committed by white gangs dressed as Indians."

"White men raiding as Injuns? That's pure nonsense. Hush up now and git to sleep. I ain't listening to no more crap."

Cloud Chaser surmised that the truth was getting through to the man and troubling him, though he was resisting it. "Do as you please, soldier; stay ignorant and keep on mur-

dering Indians and see what happens." He saw the soldier
scowl and grit his teeth, then put a short distance between
them. He leaned his head against the tree, hoping to sleep
and dream of Macha.

By sunrise, Bent Bow entered the Red Shield camp, weary,
hungry, thirsty, and worried about his good friend who was
in big trouble far away. He had ridden for most of the night,
changing horses at each scouting point, as he felt he must be
the one to relate the bad news to the chief and council. He
dismounted and rushed to Rising Bear's tepee where he called
out to be allowed to enter and speak about an important matter.

War Eagle, along with his parents and sister, stared at the
agitated brave who hurried inside as soon as they were
aroused from slumber and permission was granted to join
them. "What is wrong, my friend?"

"Cloud Chaser and Wahcawi's brother have been captured by the white war chief. They are to be sent to a fort far
away and be punished. Soldiers are to leave with them on this
sun from where they camp on the river near the Badlands."

"How did you learn such things?" Rising Bear asked in
dread.

Bent Bow told them what he had witnessed with the field
glasses and the sly message that Cloud Chaser had passed to
him after he had sneaked close to where he was bound to a
tree and signaled him with a birdcall. "Soldiers guarded
him, so I could not free him. We must go after them and save
my friend. I will help challenge the soldiers for his return."

Rising Bear reasoned in dismay, "If I send a large party of
warriors to rescue my son, our camp force will be greatly
weakened when the enemy is nearby with powerful weapons
and many soldiers."

"Twenty will ride as guards on their journey," Bent Bow
revealed in anxiety. "If you send only ten warriors, that will

be two targets each, an easy defeat using stealth; and it will not lower our camp defense too much."

War Eagle injected, "Bent Bow speaks wisely and cunningly, Father. We must save Cloud Chaser and Wahcawi's brother, for he is a good white man."

"How will you take the soldiers by surprise, my son? For they will be on alert for trouble. I cannot lose two sons to the enemy."

War Eagle said, "We will think of a cunning plan while we ride toward them. We will not risk our lives if a rescue endangers us."

Rising Bear took a deep breath and asked, "Who will ride with you?"

"Bent Bow, Swift Otter, Broken Lance, River's Edge, Red Feather, Black Wolf, Yellow Tree, Calls-the-Buffalo, and Tall Mountain."

"You choose three of our four Sacred Bow Carriers?"

"If trouble comes to our camp, Broken Arrow will ride at our war chief's side, as will Wind Dancer. I need good bow men to find victory since our number will be smaller than our enemy's. Do you wish me to leave my society brothers behind and choose others to ride with me?"

"No, my son, you have picked wisely. We must summon your brother and our men to reveal this dark news to them."

"I will go speak with Dawn, for she should hear these words from me and not before the presence of others, as it will bring fear to her heart and tears to her eyes," *as it will with my love.* "Bent Bow will summon the others while you go tell Wind Dancer what has happened. Mother, will you prepare food and water and my sleeping mat for my journey while we talk?"

"Such things will be ready for your departure," Winona responded, her heart thudding in fear and her thoughts panicked for her youngest son.

A short time later in Cloud Chaser's tepee, War Eagle related the grim facts and his impending actions to the two women, who looked shocked and frightened. "Do not worry, for we will return soon with them."

"What did they do to be captured and punished?" Caroline asked.

"I do not know, for Cloud Chaser did not tell Bent Bow. We will learn that deed from their lips after we take them from the soldiers."

"They will be expecting a rescue attempt, so how can you surprise them and succeed? You could be injured badly or slain."

War Eagle caressed Caroline's flushed cheek and said, "The Great Spirit will show us how to save them. We will be careful."

"I can help carry out a surprise raid. I can—"

War Eagle touched his forefinger to her lips and said, "You are not a warrior, Heart Flower, so you cannot challenge the soldiers. You must stay here and wait for me, for I will return to you."

Caroline grasped his hand and lowered it. "Hear my words, my love. If the soldiers sight an injured white woman on the road, they will halt to tend and assist her. While they are distracted by me, your party can surround them. You can choose a location where rocks are near the road, then leap upon them from hiding."

"What if you do not trick the soldiers and they capture you? I cannot endanger your life, for mine would be sad without you to share it."

Caroline was warmed and touched by his concern and love, but time was short. "If I am dirty, my dress is torn, and I have injuries you can place upon my face and body, they will be tricked. I will tell them I was attacked by white men dressed as Indians or by Crow or Pawnee, but I escaped. While they tend me and we speak, their senses will be dulled."

War Eagle was moved and impressed by her cunning and her brave offer, but he could not allow her to take such a large risk, one with a big flaw. "Your brother will know you and will shout your name."

"Not if he is held captive in the middle or to the rear of their group and my face is turned away from them. I can cover my yellow hair with my sunbonnet. Before David knows it is me, you can entrap the soldiers and disable them. Do not forget your grandfather's sacred dream. I am to go far away and face more challenges. Does this evil time not match his words?"

War Eagle gazed at her as he considered her suggestion and reminder. Perhaps she was right. "We will go speak with Father, Grandfather, and the council. If they think your plan is good, you will come with us. If they vote against it, you must remain here and wait for me. Do you agree?"

Caroline smiled and nodded that she would obey him.

"But it is dangerous, Wahcawi," Macha fretted in alarm.

Caroline grasped her hand, looked at her, and said, "I must help save my brother and your husband, who is my friend. While we are gone, pray we will find victory. I must do this deed for both of us."

"I will pray on every sun and moon. Thank you, my friend. May the Great Spirit ride with you, guide you, protect you, and return you to us."

Following the council meeting and together in Cloud Chaser's tepee, War Eagle grimaced time and time again in empathy and emotional torment as he pinched and struck Caroline, who winced but did not scream or ask him to halt his necessary infliction upon her for their pretense. Both, as well as the others, knew her injuries could not be fresh ones when they reached their destination, so aging them forced the reluctant man to do the arduous task before their departure to prevent suspicion and peril later. She had donned a torn dress that she had rubbed on the ground first to get it filthy. She had sprinkled dirt on her head and worked it into her hair, already made oily with animal fat. A leather thong was placed around her neck and wriggled back and forth to make marks upon her pale skin; the same was done to her wrists, to imply she had been bound, a captive.

War Eagle halted and said, "I can give you no more pain, Heart Flower. Surely these injuries are enough to trick the soldiers."

"Do not blame yourself, my love," she whispered as she stroked his jawline. "It is my people's evil that forced us to do this to me."

War Eagle wiped the blood from her lower lip and pulled her into his arms. He held her tightly for a few moments, then loosened his grasp and leaned back his head to seal their mouths. He kissed her with tenderness, enormous pride, and unrelenting love. "We must go. We have far to ride."

They joined the others, who looked at Caroline and also winced at what she must have endured, in silence and willingness. Many nodded approval of her courage and prowess. All seemed to believe she was doing this difficult task as much for Cloud Chaser as for her brother. Chumani, Macha, and Hanmani embraced her in friendship, gratitude, and affection. Wind Dancer, Rising Bear, and Nahemana rubbed the back of her hand to show those same feelings. Little Turtle, the shaman's wife, gave her a soft rabbit pelt to keep her hands warm during their journey. Even Pretty Meadow, the mother of Broken Lance and the deceased Two Feathers, gave her a leather pouch of nut and berry bread.

Caroline thanked all of them for their kindnesses, her throat too tight with heartfelt emotion to say anything more.

After the party of eleven mounted to leave, War Eagle bound her wrists snugly before her, then nodded in encouragement and pride.

Caroline returned the gesture, knowing the emotions behind it.

As soon as farewells and hopes of good fortune were spoken to them, the eager group rode away to head overland at a rapid pace to reach the selected attack point first, with her on a horse belonging to Rising Bear.

As they traveled through canyons and hills of the Paha Sapa, Caroline glanced down at her arms with their discoloration and felt her swollen lip, deciding they would be perfect and misleading bruises by the time the soldiers saw them. She realized she must look terrible, but this sorry condition was needed to carry off her ruse. It had been Nahemana, she recalled, who had persuaded the others to use her plan, disclosing that it had been revealed to him in a sacred dream not long ago.

Please, God, she prayed as she snuggled in the confines of a warm buffalo robe, *let this scheme work. Let us save David and Cloud Chaser. And, if at all possible, don't make it necessary to slay the soldiers.*

For over three days, War Eagle, Caroline, and the others traveled fast and for long hours after leaving the concealment of the rugged Paha Sapa. They traversed open plains of vast grasslands and rolling hills; rode through valleys; skirted steep slopes; crossed the Cheyenne, White, and Niobrara Rivers and many streams and creeks; and entered an area of awesome buttes and scattered foothills at the Platte River. They halted to camp and await the soldiers' arrival near what emigrants called Scotts Bluff—a tan-colored promontory eight hundred feet high and a landmark on the trail. The site was about ten miles east of Horse Creek, where the peace treaty had been signed in 1851. This was about twenty miles east of the place where Grattan and his troops had attacked a Brule camp and been slain, an event that had provoked the current conflict and Harney's presence.

While the others made camp following the arduous journey, though most of the terrain had been easy and swift to cover, one man was posted eastward to watch for their targets' approach and to bring them a message as soon as the soldiers were in visual range. Since they did not know how far in advance they had reached this area, though they were certain they had done so first, all they could do was sit and wait while the men took turns with the observation task from an elevated point up the road.

After tending their horses and allowing the animals to drink and graze while their companions talked and/or played games with marked stones of a near-flat surface on both sides, War Eagle and Caroline took a walk. He said it was to loosen sore muscles from days on horseback and to calm their restless spirits, but it was to have privacy to talk and kiss before confronting peril—possible death or capture—within the next day or two. As soon as the couple was out of their companions' sight, but not hearing range if a threat struck, they embraced and melded their mouths in sweet bliss.

They kissed many times and thrilled to the love and passion between them. Some kisses were long, slow, and tender; others were short, intense, and deep and exposed their enormous cravings and pleasures. Their eager hands roamed each other's face, arms, and back as if exploring and mapping new terrain. Their questing fingers drifted through contrasting strands of hair and over susceptible flesh and aroused each other to ardent longing to unite their bodies as one force seeking victory and contentment.

Soon, they were breathless from their tantalizing actions and inflamed by rampant desire. They realized they must halt their fervent journey, as they could travel no further at that time and place. They hugged with her cheek pressed to his chest and with his jawline nestled to her head. They drew in deep lungfuls of chilly air to cool the heat assailing them, to clear their clouded wits, and to relax their taut bodies.

Finally War Eagle broached a dreaded question. "After we save your brother, he must flee to far away or the white war chief will send soldiers to search for him and punish him. He will ask you to go with him. I want you to stay with the Red Shields and join to me, for I love you and need you in my Life Circle. What words will you speak to him?"

Caroline lifted her head and locked gazes with him. "I will tell David of our love and plan to be joined. He will be sad for us to part, but he will understand and accept my feelings for you and my need to remain with you. As long as we are both safe, we will be happy for each other. In the seasons ahead when peace comes and Harney is gone, he can return to visit us."

"You will be happy in my life and tepee, is that not true?"

"That is so, Wanbli, for I love you and need you as my husband for my Life Circle to be complete. We are destined to be together, to live here."

"That is what I believe, Heart Flower, and it will come to be, for the Great Spirit has chosen us for each other," he said with confidence.

They kissed once more before they returned to their companions, again pervaded by suspense of what loomed before them. . . .

Nearing dusk the next day, Red Feather—best friend since childhood to Wind Dancer—joined his companions and related that the soldiers were nearing their location. But, the elite warrior continued, the two prisoners were riding close to the front of the group of twenty bluecoats who looked alert and whose rifles were at the ready as if they expected trouble and were prepared to challenge it. He did not have to point out the beginning of bad weather, which included chilly winds, dark clouds, and heavy humidity.

"Soon," Red Feather reasoned, "they must halt and camp, for the sky and air warn of a storm this moon. When it strikes, they will lower their alert and be weakened, for they will not think that enemies ride in one."

Caroline stood and said, "I will get ready to trick them."

"No," War Eagle countered, as another ploy filled his thought and he changed his mind about her perilous participation in a rescue attempt after learning of the captives' positions amidst the enemy and upon hearing Red Feather's clever last words. "Our brothers ride to the front and might see and know you. Your brother might shout your name in joy to find you alive and nearby. Or shout in worry at thinking you badly harmed or slain. It is too dangerous to use your cunning trick. The Air Spirit's breath thickens into a white blanket. Soon, they must camp. We will sneak there when most sleep and the guards can not see us in the mist. We will strike their heads, free our friends, leave Pawnee possessions, and slip away. What do you think, my friends? Is it a good plan?"

The other warriors voiced agreement to the change, so Caroline sat down and nodded obedience. If fog engulfed them, she surmised, her beloved's idea should work, and it was a safer one considering the odds of two to one and the unexpected circumstances. Too, it meant the soldiers would not be slain, just as she had prayed for during their departure from the Black Hills. She was glad War Eagle decided against their deaths, though tribal foes would be incriminated by the false clues they had brought along and would leave behind. If all went well tonight, she would see her brother again soon and David would learn she was alive and safe, and those realities delighted her. *Please, God, guide and protect all of them.*

Swift Otter returned to their hiding place and revealed that the soldiers were asleep, except for two guarding the camp. Using the light of a match obtained last year by Cloud Chaser at Fort Laramie, he drew a sketch upon the soft ground of the attack area and their targets' positions in it.

Using another match, as he motioned to the scratchings on the earth, War Eagle made the assignments. "Red Feather will sneak up on this soldier. Tall Mountain will disable this one. Calls-the-Buffalo and Black Wolf will gather the horses of Cloud Chaser and Wahcawi's brother. Bent Bow, Broken Lance, and Yellow Tree will watch the others for trouble and give the night bird's call if any awaken. River's Edge and I will free the captives. Swift Otter will protect Wahcawi and our horses while we are gone. We must move slow and careful, as we cannot see far into the mist and must make no sounds. Carry only your knives and the Pawnee tricks. Try not to slay them, for they must take blame on our enemy to the fort. We must not allow it to fall upon the head of any Lakota. Come, we go now."

War Eagle exchanged smiles with Caroline before he and the others left her and his best friend behind and were swallowed up fast by fog.

Caroline sat on the moist ground on the buffalo robe she had been given at her honoring ceremony. Her knees were hugged to her chest where her heart thudded in worry, and it was difficult to calm her labored breathing. Her blond hair and tattered dress were damp, her body chilled by the crisp night air since a warming fire was hazardous. She noted that Swift Otter stayed on constant alert, ready to react to a threat, ready to save her just as his best friend had planned by leaving that elite fighter behind. All she could think about was the peril her loved ones and friends were facing at that moment, too aware that lethal defeat was a grim possibility. . . .

War Eagle and his party used their superior prowess and the familiar landscape to their advantage as they sneaked toward their goals. In spite of the vision-obstructing fog, they moved along covered by dark buffalo hides, making no noise in passing and finally reaching their assigned destinations.

War Eagle and Macha's twin brother slipped to the tree where Cloud Chaser and David Sims were bound, one on each side of it, no doubt to make certain the captives could not reach each other's bonds to untie them. As planned, each rescuer placed a hand over his objective's mouth to silence any shriek of surprise at being startled by their arrival, doing their tasks simultaneously as other Red Shields incapacitated the two guards.

Cloud Chaser struggled to see and made out the grinning face of his wife's brother as River's Edge moved away his hand and cut his restraints.

War Eagle whispered to David, "You safe, No speak, I free you. I Chaser's brother. We come to save. Must hurry."

After David nodded, War Eagle severed the ropes confining the man. "Walk slow, careful."

David saw Chase Martin follow another Indian into the shadows, so he did the same with the one who had freed him. He could not remain a captive heading for a trial and prison or a hangman's noose. He had to stay alive to find his beloved sister, which meant trusting Chase and his friends. He used caution so he would not awaken the soldiers, surprised and grateful they hadn't been slain. He kept close to the warrior ahead of him, wondering where he was being taken.

Caroline threw aside the warm robe, leapt to her feet, and hurried to greet her shocked brother. "We have to be quiet. Noise travels easily and far over this kind of terrain."

Cloud Chaser said in a low voice, "She's fine, David. She's been safe with my people. You two must talk later. We have to ride now. Hello, Caroline, it's good to see you again."

"It's good to see you again, Cloud Chaser, my friend. Dawn and your son are fine."

Cloud Chaser smiled. "Let's go, but be quiet. We'll walk for a ways before we mount. Stay close and tight in this fog. We don't want anybody getting lost or stumbling into another soldier's camp."

David nodded compliance, then glanced at his sister in rising intrigue.

Chapter Nineteen

In the Wild Cat Hills nearby, they wound their way single file amidst numerous eroded pale gray bluffs and scattered rocks of various sizes and through forests of mainly pine with intermingled juniper, cottonwood, box elder, and willow. At last, they halted to camp in a secluded and sheltered area of rugged formations and dense trees. They had walked their horses for a time until it seemed safe to mount and ride into that region to camp for the remainder of the night. Yellow Tree had stayed hidden near Scotts Bluff—which was visible from elevated locations—to observe how the soldiers reacted to the discovery of the missing prisoners and to see which direction they took to report that strange incident to others.

The Red Shields thought it was divine intervention when the threat of bad weather vanished during their short journey. The fog had dissipated, the sky had cleared, the winds had lost much of their strong force and even some of their chill, and a half-moon glowed overhead to give them sufficient light to see the ground and each other.

After they dismounted and embraced, David asked Caroline, "Where have you been, Caro? What happened to you? I've been worried near to madness over your disappearance. What are you doing here with these . . . men? Are you all right? You look terrible, little sister."

"I'm fine, David, honestly; and my appearance was a ruse to dupe the soldiers. I was gong to lie in the road and feign injury to get them to halt so my friends could rescue you and Cloud Chaser, but the plan was changed when you two were riding up front and the weather took a bad turn."

"Cloud Chaser? Is he the one named Chase Martin?"

"That's the name he uses when he roams in the white world. His real name is Cloud Chaser; he's the son of the Red Shield chief; they're Oglala Lakotas. I've been living with them since I vanished en route to join you."

"He's a chief's son? He's an Indian?"

"Yes, and so is the man who rescued you. They're brothers."

"I met Chase, Cloud Chaser, at Fort Laramie, but he didn't mention you were with his people when we talked several times. I'll have to question him about that deception. How have they treated you?"

"I have endured no abuse from them. They're good people, truly."

"How did you come to be with them? A search party couldn't find any clues as to what happened to you and your escort."

"It's a long and complicated story, big brother, I'll—"

"Reveal everything to him in the morning," Cloud Chaser interrupted her in a gentle tone. "It's late and we need to sleep. We'll need our rest and strength if trouble strikes soon and we have to leave fast."

"But she's been missing for months. I want to know what hap—"

Caroline injected, "Cloud Chaser is right, David. We need to get to sleep. We'll talk in the morning, I promise. Don't worry, I'm fine."

David looked at the man beside Caroline and persisted, "I have one question that has to be answered tonight, now. You knew how worried I was about her, so why didn't you tell me at Laramie she was alive and safe?"

"From atop the canyon bluffs, we witnessed the surprise attack at Blue Water Creek and saw you try to help our allies in secret. When I talked with you at the fort, you were sending letters to the white leaders far away to tell them the truth of the grave offenses being committed here against Indians. Before I left my camp to scout the enemy at the fort, Caroline told me much about you and showed me your picture; that is how I recognized you at the battle scene. I believed you were a good man and could be trusted, but much was at stake to risk being wrong. If I had told you where she was and you did not believe she was unharmed, you could have sent soldiers to my camp to attack my people to rescue her. They could have done the same evil things we witnessed at Blue Water Creek. Did the note I gave to you not ease your fears and worries about her?"

"What note?"

"The note I slipped into your pocket when we bumped into each other the last time at the fort. It told you she was alive and safe and would get a message to you when the time was good."

"I never found a note in my pocket."

War Eagle observed the interaction, grasping most of their words. It was late, but he did not halt or intrude on the necessary talk. He was glad to get this chance to scrutinize his love's brother up close and to learn how the two related to each other. He was aware that Caroline also was watching them, too focused on their talk to notice his presence and his keen study.

"Then, it is still there or it fell out when you withdrew something and was lost. I speak the truth, David; I stuffed a note in your pocket that day."

David eyed the man closely and decided he was being honest. "I believe you, Chase, but I never found it. I wish I had, to ease my worry."

"I thought you had guessed it was from me and that was why you tried to help me escape before your capture."

"No, I was trying to help you because I thought if you had connections to the Indians you could help me find my sister and rescue her. I was planning to desert and leave with you if we could strike a deal."

Caroline asked, "You were arrested for trying to help him escape?"

"That's right. I hoped if I helped him he would help me find you. In a way, he has. Thanks, Chase. She's all the family I have left and I love her."

"It is good we can be friends. Now, we must sleep. We can have more talk tomorrow. Come and I will show you where to lie down for the night."

"You, too, Caro. Heaven be thanked, it's good to see you again."

David hugged Caroline once more before he retrieved his bedroll and followed Cloud Chaser to a sheltered spot near a large gray bluff, assuming his sister would be close behind.

War Eagle came forward from the shadows and said, "He is a good man from what my senses tell me."

"Yes," Caroline concurred, "he is. And so are you," she added as she locked gazes with him and exchanged smiles.

"We will speak on the next sun after you talk with your brother again. You have much to tell him and he has much to hear and accept."

Caroline whispered, "Do not worry, Wanbli, for I love you and my life is here with you. David will understand and accept that truth."

"My heart is filled with love for you, Kawa Cante. Come, we must sleep, for there is much to be done and said soon." *I pray he will not change your mind about remaining here with me, for I can not lose you.*

Caroline spread her buffalo mat between David's and War Eagle's, her heart rejoicing in the fact that both men she loved best were nearby. Yet, sensations of dread and suspense gnawed at her as she realized what loomed ahead tomorrow: she must explain to one of the two most important people in her life why she was choosing the other person over him, and convince him she knew what she was doing. . . .

After they had risen, eaten, and prepared for a swift escape if one was necessary, Caroline and David secluded themselves a short distance away to talk. He asked the same questions he had voiced the night before, and she began answering them, slowly and carefully so he could absorb the news.

"I'm sure you know by now that a terrible conflict is raging here, much of it based upon misunderstandings and a lot of it upon deceits and greed from our people. I've witnessed and learned a great deal since I came to this territory, and I must say I'm ashamed of how our government continues to view and treat the Indians." She related the things she had been told, had observed, and had overhead at Fort Pierre, during her ride across the grasslands with the soldiers, and in the Red Shield camp. She repeated the things Cloud Chaser had told her about past and recent events, including the incidents with white gangs posing as Indians, the Grattan episode, and the problems with inferior and scant annuities. "The settlers and soldiers have been led to believe the Indians are savages and hostiles who attack whites without provocation."

Caroline was glad he did not interrupt during her lengthy disclosures and as she refuted those allegations. "That isn't true, David. Most of them want to live in peace and in their ancestors' ways, but they keep being harassed, insulted, challenged, and deceived. They see their lands being stolen, gradually gobbled up by homesteaders and forts and roads and businesses. They see their game being hunted or trapped into extinction or driven far from their treaty-assigned territories, creatures they depend on for supplying food, clothes, tepees, and other necessities. They see their very survival at stake. But whenever they protest or defend their rights, they're told to accept such offenses or they'll be slaughtered and their possessions will be destroyed. You saw what General Harney did to the Brules at Blue Water Creek, all because a few of them killed and ate a cow that strayed into their camp and Grattan demanded a blood payment. The soldiers fired first on the Indians and murdered their leader, the very man the army had appointed as head chief of all the Lakota tribes. If our land and family were being attacked, we would have defended them."

"Chase, I mean Cloud Chaser, told me some of the history and trouble of the Indians and this area and I saw what happened during that massacre, so I understand their fears, distrust, and retaliations. But how did you come to be with these Indians? What happened to you, Caro? You're a mess."

"A small party of Red Shields attacked the soldiers escorting me to Fort Kearny. They were all slain, but not tortured before or mutilated after death like the rumors I heard at Fort Pierre. They were hauling cannons and weapons to be used during imminent attacks on Indians, so the Red Shields believed they had to destroy them. The soldiers were slain because, if they had been allowed to live, they would have reported who was responsible for that raid and the Red Shields would have been attacked and slaughtered like the Brules were for the Grattan incident. The soldiers were buried in a secret place, not left to rot or feed scavengers like Harney did with his victims; and the weapons were dumped where they can't be recovered and used against any Indian camp. The had no choice, David. I wasn't harmed in any way. I was captured and taken to their village. I've been living in the tepee of Cloud Chaser and his wife. I help her with chores and with tending their infant son. I've also taken care of sick or injured band members; I even delivered the future chief's daughter when a hazardous problem arose. I have Grandfather's medical kit with me and you know how I used to work with him in his office. The Red Shields like, respect, and accept me among them because I've done those and several other good deeds for them."

"Such as?" David prompted, intrigued by her astonishing tales.

Caroline revealed the things she had done in their camp and how she had been honored by them, even given the Lakota name of Sunflower and a coup feather. She saw her brother stare at her in amazement, then smiled in love and pride. "The reason I look so terrible is a ruse," she began and explained the initial rescue plan, her preparation to take part in it, and why it was changed. "I've made many close friends there, and I've been fine."

"I'm very proud of you, little sister. You've shown great courage and intelligence and kindness. I was worried about you and I blamed myself for allowing you to come here and be endangered. I would never have forgiven myself if you had been slain or injured."

"We made the right decision about my coming. Besides, we had no choice after the bank took everything following Mama's and Papa's deaths. At least they went fast. Merciful heavens, I still miss them terribly."

As they comforted each other with an embrace, David murmured, "So do I, Caro. I guess it seems less real to me because I was so far away. It's hard to believe I won't ever see them again. I should have been there."

To get his mind off of undeserved guilt and to assuage his anguish, she said, "I'm sorry you couldn't come home for their funerals and burials, but I handled everything properly. I never expected to lose our home and land and possessions. I imagine that's what helps me understand the Indians' feelings and reactions so well. I suppose the bankers told the truth about Papa's debt to them. If they lied, there was no way I could prove it."

David clasped her hands in his and said, "I'm sorry you had to face those ordeals alone, Caro, but the army refused to grant me a leave."

"You would have been there if possible, so don't blame yourself. I was lucky our letters got passed along so quickly. I certainly didn't want to become a beggar and burden to any of our friends. I would have sought out a respectable means of support, but you know what kinds of jobs single women are offered and how sorry they're paid. And I certainly couldn't marry that William Crawford to get myself out of dire straights."

"I'm glad you didn't turn to him. I never liked that arrogant dandy, and you deserve better. We can't stay in this area, not with the army sure to search for me soon. How does heading for Texas sound to you? I think we would like ranching. Of course, I'd have to work until I earned enough to buy a little land and stock. You think you might enjoy becoming a cowgirl?"

Caroline reached the moment and subject she had dreaded; it was time to reveal her secret plans and she prayed he would take the news well. She selected her words with great care and used a gentle voice to speak them. "I think it sounds wonderful for you, big brother, but not for me. I want to stay here." Noticing his confusion, she hurried on. "I've met a man and we've gotten close, very close. We love each other and want to become man and wife. I'm sure you'll meet a woman in Texas, get married, have a home and lots of children, so you don't need to have me around," she jested to lighten the heavy situation, but David neither smiled nor laughed.

"What man, Caro? You've only been here for a few months. Your stay at Fort Pierre was brief and you've been with the Indians since . . ."

When David halted and stared at her, she resolved the mystery for him. "It's the man who rescued you, Cloud Chaser's brother. His name is Wanbli. He's the chief's youngest son. If anything happens to his older brother, Wind Dancer, he will become the next chief when their father dies. He's a good man, David. I love him and want to become his wife."

"And he loves you? He's told you so? He's already proposed to you?"

"Yes, yes, and yes to your three questions. We're perfectly matched."

"But you haven't known him very long."

"We've spent a lot of time together during the last few months, so I know him well. Are you disappointed in me? Do you think he's unworthy of me because he's an Indian?"

"I'm deeply concerned because you two are from different cultures. I know you're a good judge of character, but are you sure you know what you're doing? Marriage is serious, Caro. Besides, this area and his people will be at war soon if things don't settle down and reverse."

"I understand the risks I'll be taking to marry him and remain here. But I love him and want to spend my life with him. Don't forget, I've been living in their ways and village for months, so I know I can fit in there. I wouldn't be happy and complete if I left with you, and I can't forget him."

David realized that arguing could cause a breach between them, and that wasn't how he wanted to leave matters before their separation. "You have a good head on your shoulders, Caro, so I'll have to trust you and your decision. But will you promise me you'll come to Texas to join me if things get too bad here? I can leave word at the Dallas post office where I'll be."

Caroline surmised the situation was difficult and sad for him and she was elated by his reaction, his generous—if reluctant—concession to her wishes. "If I need you, big brother, I'll get in touch with you. Thank you, David, for understanding and having faith in me. I love you and I'll miss you. Please be careful and take excellent care of yourself."

"I love you, little sister, and I'll miss you. At least I know you're alive and safe before I leave and I'll know the general area where you are. When things settle down here and General Harney is gone, I'll come back in a few years and locate you for a visit."

"That would make me happy," she said as she hugged him. "Would you like to speak with Wanbli to appease your worries about me, about us? He speaks some English and Cloud Chaser can translate anything else. Oh, yes, I've learned their language, so we communicate just fine."

David chuckled and teased, "As I said, I have an intelligent sister. Yes, I would like to meet him and speak with him, if he doesn't mind."

"He won't. I've told him a great deal about you, and he saw for himself I was being honest. He was the leader of the party that witnessed the Brule attack, so he knows what you did there and his brother told him about the letter you were sending to Washington. He's most impressed by you. Just as you'll be favorably impressed by him after you get acquainted."

David grinned, amused by her expression and tone and touched by her confidence in both of them. It was obvious to him that his sister was truly in love. "Then I guess we're off to a good start at being family members."

"I'm glad to hear you say that. I'll go get Wanbli and Cloud Chaser." As she headed toward the two men, Caroline almost scolded herself for one tiny deception; by intention she had not used her beloved's name in English as she did not want her brother associating him with *war*.

When she did not return with them, David surmised that Caroline was allowing them privacy to talk man-to-man and out of their friends' hearing range since the matter was personal. He looked at the stranger and said, "I guess you're Wanbli, the man who captured my sister's heart?"

"I Wanbli," War Eagle replied in English, having grasped those words. "You Caroline brother, David. We speak, make friends. Yes?"

David extended his right hand and said, "It's an honor to meet you, Wanbli. Caroline told me a lot about you and your people."

War Eagle knew of the handshaking custom, so he returned the gesture. He noticed David had a firm and assured grip, though the man did not squeeze hard as if to prove that his strength and worth were superior. He realized the siblings favored each other in appearance and traits, so David's looks and genial manner calmed his apprehensions of the unknown. Caroline had told him everything had gone well with their talk, and he sensed nothing in David's expression and mood to indicate a problem would arise.

"I want to thank you and your people for sparing my sister's life and for taking good care of her. I also want to thank you for saving mine. To show my gratitude and to help prevent trouble that could ensnare her, I'll tell you all I know about the military's plans and opinions. First, I'd like to ask if you truly love my sister and want her to marry you and if you believe you can make her happy and keep her safe from harm."

To be certain his brother understood everything David had said, Cloud Chaser hurriedly translated his message into Lakota for War Eagle.

War Eagle decided it was best to be honest and direct. "Caroline good, brave woman. She capture Wanbli heart. Creator guide Wanbli to her and give sign we become one. Wanbli love Caroline. Wanbli want her as wife. She be happy, be safe. Wanbli give life to protect her. You no take Caroline away?"

David respected him for being forthright and for providing answers he needed to alleviate his concerns. The subject was serious; yet, he could not help chuckling, and said, "I doubt I could bind her and drag her away from you and your people. She wants to stay here with you as your wife. My sister is a kind and brave woman, and she's smart, so I trust her decision."

After Cloud Chaser translated again, War Eagle smiled and nodded appreciation as his spirit leapt with joy and relief. "David be Wanbli brother after we join. We be friends. You safe in our lands. You good white man."

"Thanks, and I'm honored to be your friend and brother-in-law. As to another matter, we all realize I can't stay in this territory because General Harney won't stop searching for me until he's convinced I've left the area. I'm heading for Texas today. You know where that is Cloud Chaser?" After the man nodded, David continued, "I'm going there to work until I scrape enough money together to buy some land and cattle for ranching."

Cloud Chaser said, "That sounds like a good choice, David. Two of our companions will escort you to the Sante Fe Trail so you won't get lost and you'll have protection. We don't want you to run into any of our allies or enemies alone. After you're on the trail, just ride it to the end and head on down into Texas. We'll give you some supplies to use along the way."

"That's generous of you, Cloud Chaser. In a year or two after things settle down here and Harney's gone and the army's forgotten about me, I'll come visit Caroline and your people, if that's all right."

"You're welcome in our camp any day," he responded, then told his younger brother what they had been saying.

War Eagle said, "It good plan. You come back one season."

"I will, and you take good care of my sister. Now, I'll tell you what I know about Harney and his plans," David began and related those facts. As he finished his revelations and conclusions, the scout who had been left behind arrived, and their talk ceased as they went to hear his report.

Yellow Tree told them he had seen the soldiers heading

toward Fort Laramie after they awakened, found the captives missing, and freed the two guards. The bluecoats had gathered the Pawnee clues that they had left behind, then mounted and galloped away without even eating.

War Eagle deduced the soldiers had headed westward because that fort was closer to them than Kearny and no doubt they had feared another attack. "It is good they ride away from our next target."

"What does he mean by that?" David asked after another translation.

Cloud Chaser explained what he and Caroline intended to do at Fort Kearny to prevent future trouble for a search for her and the missing escort and weapons. "Do you agree with our plan?"

"It sound like a clever idea to me and should end the matter. You're lucky those soldiers headed in the opposite direction so you two can carry it out. Please do it fast because they might return with reinforcements to search this area and continue on to Kearny afterward. You wouldn't want to be sighted and captured again, and I don't want Caroline imperiled by her ties to you and your band."

Cloud Chaser urged, "Don't worry, David, I'll protect her while we're there; and we'll work fast like you said. We'll be long gone before they have time to arrive. I hate to rush you, but we all need to get moving. You should say any final words you have for your sister and mount up."

While the brothers and their companions talked and made preparations to leave, David took his suggestion and joined Caroline a short distance away. "Well, little sister, it's time for me to go. Cloud Chaser is giving me supplies, and two of his friends are riding a ways with me as guides and protectors until I'm out of this territory."

"That's wonderful news, David, so I won't worry as much about you. I'm going to miss you and I hope—I know— you'll succeed there. I'll keep looking for you to come visit us one day."

"I'm going to miss you, too, Caro. Our reunion was too short and full of complications. I promise you I'll be fine and I'll return one day. Be safe and happy, Caro; you deserve it."

"I will be, I promise. The same goes for you, big brother. Find a good woman and marry her, have lots of children, and build a prosperous ranch."

"I'll try my best to follow your advice." He glanced toward the others before he locked gazes with her and said, "I like Wanbli and Cloud Chaser. If the rest of their family and people are anything like them, you've done well with your choice of a husband and decision to stay here."

Caroline hugged him as she replied in an emotion-constricted voice, "Thank you, David; it means so much to me to hear you think and feel that way. I love you and I'll miss you something fierce."

"Good-bye, little sister. You take excellent care of yourself."

"Good-bye, David, and I'm so glad we had this time together."

"So am I. Mama and Papa would be so proud of you. I am."

"They would be proud of you, too. I'm glad you're out of this conflict. No soldier should have to obey such wicked orders."

"You're right, and I couldn't. I'm no murderer. I—" David halted as Cloud Chaser and War Eagle approached them with his roan.

"I'm sorry, Caroline, David, but we have to ride. Your horse is ready and loaded. Black Wolf and Red Feather will travel with you until you reach the Sante Fe Trail." He motioned to one of the men and said, "Red Feather speaks some English; he's my older brother's best friend. If trouble strikes, just do as Red Feather says and you'll be safe."

David shook hands with Cloud Chaser and War Eagle. "Good-bye, my friends, and I'll pray for the best with what's ahead for your people." To War Eagle, he added, "I have a

feeling you and my sister will be happy together. I'll be seeing you again. Good-bye, Caro, and be careful at Fort
Kearny."

"Good-bye, David, and I will." She watched him mount
and gaze down at her for a minute, then smile and leave with
his companions. *Please, God, protect him and help him with
his new life in Texas. Let him find a woman who's a perfect
match for him. And help us in the dark days ahead. Please
don't let anything delay or prevent my marriage to War
Eagle.*

"Are you ready to ride, Caroline? I mean, Wahcawi. I'll
have to get used to your new name, and it suits you perfectly.
I'm glad things worked out for you with my family and people. You'll be good for us."

"Thank you, Cloud Chaser, and so am I. But don't get
used to my new name until after we finish our task at Fort
Kearny," she jested.

"You're right. Let's go get it done."

Caroline exchanged smiles with War Eagle, aware this
was not the time or place to sneak off to talk and kiss and
celebrate their victory.

Over two days later, Caroline and her group reached Ash
Hollow where soldiers' graves were visible near the river
and road. She could not help thinking those men would be
alive if General Harney had not viciously attacked the Brules
nearby. After using his field glasses to study the landscape,
Cloud Chaser told her and the others that Fort Grattan looked
abandoned, as there were no dragoons or other soldiers or
horses in view. They also had been fortunate, in her opinion,
that they had not encountered anyone so far. It almost seemed
as if the region was deserted by both Indians and whites.

Following a rest and eating break, Caroline and Cloud
Chaser left to head onward to their destination, with War
Eagle watching them until they were out of sight. He prayed

they would stay safe and would find victory, and would be at his side again soon. Surely everything was going as the Great Spirit planned, and he had deep faith in the Creator. Even so, he would be apprehensive until they were reunited.

Far away, Wind Dancer and two other braves were shadowing General Harney and his massive force as they traveled toward Fort Pierre. The weather had become cold and damp, and some snow and rain had fallen during their long journey. As far as he knew all "hostiles" had moved north beyond the upper Cheyenne and Heart Rivers or ventured into the Powder River area, which was Crow territory, and the white war chief was not heading in any of those directions. To Wind Dancer, it seemed as if the soldiers and their fierce leader were eager to reach the fort ahead. As soon as he was convinced that was true, he and his companions would return to their camp. The one small Oglala party they had encountered ensuing their meeting with Harney had told them Harney intended to hold a big council after winter passed, and all tribes would be ordered to attend it. That implied to him the army would winter at the old trading post, and he hoped that was true, for it meant they were safe from his threat until then.

After traveling the Mormon Trail amidst flat grasslands where brisk winds gusted constantly, Caroline and Cloud Chaser sighted Fort Kearny, which was situated between a mail road to Fort Leavenworth and the Platte River where many cottonwoods and spruces grew along its wide banks. A stage depot and stable sat on the road's south side and provided mail and passenger service from Fort Leavenworth to Fort Laramie. It had taken them over three days of long and fast and bone-chilling riding along the well-worn road to reach their destination, as they wanted this matter settled in a hurry so they could rejoin the others and head for home.

Beyond them, wood or adobe structures—officers' quarters and two homes, a small hospital, company quarters, workshops, several storehouses, stables, a smithy, a guardhouse, and kitchens—were scattered out on the plains landscape. Under construction, they noticed, but far enough along to ascertain their purposes were a magazine, a bakery, additional stables, an adjutant's office, and laundresses' quarters. The new magazine was secluded, probably as a safety measure. A slaughterhouse was set apart perhaps for odor and summer insect control. Corrals also were a good distance away from living quarters probably for that same reason. As usual, most of those places were positioned around a huge parade ground.

Since dusk was approaching fast, they noted that few soldiers were outside and those who were scurried in haste to complete their chores and escape the frigid air. They rode to the stage stable and dismounted. Within minutes, Cloud Chaser—clad and acting as a white man—obtained permission for them to sleep inside. Although no fire would be allowed, which might endanger the hay, the stable would be warmer than camping outside tonight.

Caroline joined Cloud Chaser in the stage station where they were given a hot meal by the generous attendant, who was sympathetic to the false tale Cloud Chaser had told him about her abduction and release.

Caroline savored every bite of the meat and potato stew and large biscuits, and every sip of the steaming coffee with sugar. The man even opened and shared a precious jar of canned peaches from the South. Many times as they ate and chatted, she thanked him for his kindness in providing them with a delicious meal and shelter.

Afterward, to repay his good deed, Caroline washed and dried the dishes and helped store the leftovers. The food, house, furnishings, chores, and use of English made her suddenly tense and sad. They reminded her of those or similar things from her life at home, a happy life with her family, her lost parents, her missing brother, the sacrifices she must make to have War Eagle and a future with him. She did not want to appear impolite and in a rush or falsely grateful, but she was eager to leave the cozy structure and the attendant's company. She did not want to continue making small talk, so she feigned fatigue and drowsiness to imply she needed to be excused to rest following a long and hard journey and an alleged ordeal with villains.

Cloud Chaser took her hint and said, "We enjoyed our food and talk, Mr. Bean, but it's time for us to turn in for the night. Miss Caroline has been through a terrible time and she's bone tired. We're plenty grateful to you."

"Been my pleasure, folks. You're welcome to join me for breakfast. I eat about seven after I tend the stock and do other chores. You won't be able to see Captain Wharton till after eight. He just got here two days past, so he's been busy getting settled in. He's happier than a flea on a fat dog since General Harney released him from that Sioux Campaign he took off on over two months ago. I bet Major Cady wished he was the one sent back. Harney just rode in and confiscated him and his five companies of the 6th Infantry. The word is they been doing some awful fighting with Indians. Anyways, I got fresh eggs to toss around in a skillet and cured ham to fry. They'll taste real good with some biscuits and coffee. I bet you two could use another hot meal after being on the trail so long. What do you say?"

Caroline assumed Cloud Chaser wanted her to answer for them, so she felt obligated to smile and say, "We would be honored to join you again, Mr. Bean. Thank you for the invitation. Good night. We'll see you at seven."

"I'm afraid I'll have to disturb you folks around six; there'll be things I'll need out of the stable for my chores.

You're more than welcome to wash up in here, Miss Caroline, where it'll be warm and private."

"Thank you again, sir, and I'll do so. Good night."

"Good night, Miss Caroline. Night, Jake."

"Good night, Mr. Bean. See you in the morning, and I'll be happy to help with the chores. Just give me a holler when you're up and ready."

"Thanks, Jake, I'll be much obliged for the help."

At eight o'clock the next morning, Caroline and Cloud Chaser were seated in Captain Wharton's office before his plain wooden desk; introductions had been made upon their entry.

After Captain Wharton asked how he could help them, Caroline used an exaggerated southern accent and southern belle behavior as she alleged she had been abducted by a band of horrible and vile-talking white men while en route there in early August to join her brother, who was serving under Major Cady's command. She told him Mr. Bean had informed her last night that the major was gone and a Captain Wharton was in charge at the present.

When he did not interrupt with questions as she had expected and he merely gazed at her, she went on to tell him the crude villains had slain the soldiers who were escorting her there, stolen the cannons and weapons they were delivering, and had kidnapped her. Again, Caroline was surprised and intrigued when the officer remained quiet after hearing those grim *facts,* though she appeared to have his full attention.

She claimed she overheard the assailants say they intended to sell the stolen supplies, wagons, weapons, and teams at trading posts farther west where owners would pay big sums of money for such items. She said she had been sold to an Indian tribe as a slave, but the chief released her after hearing about the Harney massacre at Blue Water Creek. She had been given a horse and supplies and been set free. After wandering about in the "wilderness alone and terrified," she had encountered the trapper with her, a "Mr. Jake Hardy," who took pity on her and agreed to guide her there to join her brother and report those incidents.

That time, Caroline did not pause for the officer to speak, just hurried on to make certain points. "I am most fortunate the Indians did not harm me, since I was at their mercy. They gave me food, which was unfamiliar and bland, and allowed me to sleep in a tepee with an old man and woman. For a bed, I used the hide of one of those massive furry beasts I saw on the grasslands. Buffalo, I believe the soldiers told me. But the Indians made me work all day, every day, usually for that old couple where I was staying."

She lifted her hands and frowned at them as she fretted. "My poor hands are so chapped and rough, they'll never be soft and pretty again; I even have calluses on them. And those appalling men who attacked us took all of my possessions, everything except for what I'm wearing, and it's in awful condition. All of my lovely dresses, gowns, and slippers, gone, in the hands of those wicked criminals. Mr. Bean at the stage office also took pity on me and provided me with supper, breakfast, and a place to sleep in his stable. He is most kind, sir, an asset to your post. He also allowed me to repair my appearance as much as possible in his station, but I still look a frightful sight. You must forgive my appearance and agitation, sir, but I have been through a ghastly ordeal for months."

After Captain Wharton told her how sorry he was about her troubles, he explained that Major Cady and his troops were serving somewhere in the Sioux territory and would probably winter at Fort Pierre.

Caroline frowned in dismay, pretended to think for a few minutes, and said, "I do not want to stay here during winter.

I think it's best if I travel on to Omaha and find a place to stay there until spring. I'm sure I would like living in a town with families better than on a post with so many men. I'm familiar with Omaha from a stop there while en route to Fort Pierre, where my brother was supposed to be assigned according to his last letter before my departure. Yes, I am certain I would prefer to spend the winter in Omaha. I can sell the horse I was given and use the money to rent a room and buy food. I can find some type of proper employment to support myself until David comes for me. Will you give my brother a message about my situation and location when he returns here next spring?"

"I could send a letter to Fort Leavenworth by stage to be forwarded to Private Sims on the next boat to Fort Pierre. I doubt the Missouri's become impassable this early in the winter. Or you can send a letter to him after you reach Omaha. It would ease his mind more if the message came from you."

"You're right, sir, so I shall handle the letter matter myself. Thank you for your wise suggestion. I suppose I'm still not thinking clearly."

"Since the army knows about the strange disappearance of that troop and those wagons, I'll mention your safe return and explanation in my report to Major Cady and General Harney when they return next spring. I do have a few questions for you, Miss Sims, on some confusing points."

Caroline had been rising to leave, but she halted and resettled herself in the seat, as did Cloud Chaser in his. "What are they, sir?" she asked, trying to look undisturbed by his words and action. Had she made an error, she worried, and aroused his suspicions? *Stay alert, woman!*

"Do you know the names of the men who attacked your party, the name of their destinations, and the Indian chief's and his band's names where you were held captive?"

"The white villains were careful not to use names in front of me and they did not mention those of their destinations.

As to the Indians, since I do not speak their language, I could not understand them; nor could they understand me. We communicated by hand signals and gestures and such."

"Then how do you know why they released you?"

Caroline had prepared herself for that question, as she had for his previous four queries, so she did not hesitate or flush with guilt or tremble in tension when she answered, "I assumed the reason I gave you earlier from what happened the day I was released. Another Indian rode into their settlement. I heard the name Harney mentioned many times, and the Indians looked worried by what they were being told. After the visitor left, I was given the horse and food, and shoved out of their village. After I encountered Mr. Hardy in the wilderness, thank the Good Lord for placing him in my path, he told me about the massacre. I concluded I was released to prevent a similar attack on their camp, and Mr. Hardy agreed. I suppose I could be mistaken, but it does not matter since I'm free now."

Cloud Chaser alleged, "I found her wandering about with hazy wits near Heber Springs, west of the Medicine Bow Mountains. I was planning to guide her to Fort Laramie, but she wanted to come here. Since I'm heading to Independence for the winter, I had no reason to refuse her request. I didn't come across any Indians in the area where I found her, so I have no guess about who was holding her captive. Best I could tell, there aren't any tribal or band markings on the horse or food pouch, and she said she'd been by herself and riding for at least four or five days. Naturally I didn't try to backtrack on her trail and learn where she'd come from. After she told me her sad tale, I figured the Indians were spooked by General Harney's defeat of the Brules and didn't want her found in or near their camp."

"I agree you two reasoned it out correctly. Besides giving you folks some trail supplies, anything else I can do for you, Miss Sims?"

Caroline sent him a smile of feigned gratitude. "No, sir.

You've been very kind and understanding. I am most appreciative of your help, as my brother will be when he learns of your assistance and generosity."

While Captain Wharton was telling a soldier at his door to fetch trail supplies for them, she looked at Cloud Chaser and—to finalize their ruse within the officer's hearing—asked, "Will you please escort me to Omaha, Mr. Hardy, before you continue your journey to Independence? After I sell that horse, I shall pay you all I can spare to do so. Or you can give me your address and I shall have my brother send you payment for your assistance."

"It'll be many miles out of my way, Miss Sims, but I guess it never harmed anybody to do another person a good turn. Let's get moving fast as we can and it'll help me reach my destination sooner."

"Thank you, sir, and God bless you for being such a good man."

Within a few minutes after leaving Wharton's office, Caroline and Cloud Chaser headed northeastward on the Mormon Trail toward Omaha, in the event they were being watched. After the Oregon Trail split off and veered southeast toward Independence, they stayed on the Mormon route until they found a good spot to circle back to join War Eagle and the others.

Caroline's heart rejoiced in their success and leapt in excitement of seeing her beloved, her future husband, within three or four days, if nothing happened during their return trip. . . .

Chapter Twenty

In a cozy cave in the bluffs at Ash Hollow, Cloud Chaser recounted their adventure to War Eagle and the others. He also told them what he had learned from Mr. Bean, that Fort Grattan had been abandoned for three weeks and that Spotted Tail and the other prisoners had stayed at Fort Kearny for a short time before they were sent to Fort Leavenworth, where they would be confined until their fates were decided by the army.

Afterward, plans were made to spend the night there away from the wind's knifing assault and to leave for camp at dawn tomorrow. The horses were left in a protective ravine that was not visible from the road, nor was the cave entrance, in the event anybody was traveling it this late in the day, though they thought it was unlikely this time of year. Yet, as a precaution, they built only a small fire to provide scant light but insufficient heat, using their buffalo robes to ward off the chill that crept inside the opening.

As their companions talked about current and past events that had influenced their lives, War Eagle and Caroline sat as far away as possible in the dim enclosure so they could talk for a short while.

War Eagle leaned close and whispered, "My head sings with pride and joy for all you have done for me and my people. My heart beats with love for you. My spirit soars with eagerness for us to join and fulfill our destinies."

Those wonderful thoughts and emotions matched Caroline's and she almost echoed his words to share them with her beloved. She watched him smile as his dark gaze seemed to roam over and adore every inch of her face. Her gaze did the same over his handsome features, and that action almost stole her breath as a powerful flood of ardor and desire surged through her. He was everything she wanted and needed in a man, in a husband, in a soul mate, a protector, provider, and the father of her children. Yes, he was as near to perfect as a man could be, and totally ideal as her life partner.

They yearned for more than the brief touch of an arm or a hand, more than a visual or auditory one, delightful as those were. Since others were present, they could not kiss and embrace, but they exchanged looks and words that exposed their feelings to each other. What helped them endure their physical denial was the reality that its time was limited.

Many long and tiring days passed as they journeyed toward the Black Hills, ever watchful for any sign of a threat from the army or Indian enemies. As they did so, the air became colder, the unrelenting wind blew stronger, and most of the area's game sought warmer refuge elsewhere. Hardwoods were shedding their last leaves. Flowers and many plants were gone. The blades on the grasslands were tan and withered. It was obvious winter was making its harsh arrival known more each day.

Soon, Caroline thought, they would reach camp. Snow was falling and ice was showing itself in the rivers and streams. She had gone far away and had faced and defeated more challenges. All seemed to have come true as Nahemana had predicted from his dream before she and War Eagle could marry in Indian fashion. But what would happen, she could not help wondering, after they reached their destination? Was there anything or anyone who could prevent her from achieving her most coveted goal? Surely not, she reasoned, for she had been told the shaman was never wrong. Yet, she prayed Nahemana's divine powers were real and accurate.

When they reached camp after journeying beneath a gentle snowfall, War Eagle's family and most of their people left their cozy tepees to greet them, to rejoice in their safe return, and to praise their victories.

An ecstatic Macha ran forward and flung herself into her husband's arms the moment he dismounted. A laughing and equally exhilarated Cloud Chaser hugged her in an open and unembarrassed display of joy and love.

Caroline was amused and delighted by their actions. Now, her friend could relax, for Macha's perfectly matched partner had returned to her.

While the reunited couple talked in whispers and the other members of the party were embraced by their families, the noticeable absences of Black Wolf and Red Feather were questioned by the chief.

As the falling snow slackened its pace and amount, War Eagle described the rescues of his and Wahcawi's brothers, and said their two companions were escorting David out of the territory to safety since it was too perilous for all concerned for their white friend to seek refuge with them or to stay in their territory. He was pleased to reveal David's brave attempt to rescue Cloud Chaser, though David had been captured while trying to do so. He told what Caroline and Cloud Chaser had done at Fort Kearny, and other news they had gathered, such as about Fort Grattan and their Brule allies.

Wind Dancer spoke of his journey in the shadow of General Harney to Fort Pierre and of his return two days ago.

Cloud Chaser disclosed that Harney had over twelve hundred soldiers with him, too many for a band or tribe to challenge without the aid of many allies, if a victory over that force was possible even with help. Since Harney—according to Wind Dancer—had reached Fort Pierre and—according to Captain Wharton—intended to winter there, it seemed as if they would have peace or at least be safe from attack until spring.

Nahemana, his gray hair covered with a trade blanket and his body by a buffalo robe, told War Eagle, "I have revealed my dream to our people about you and Wahcawi. No one spoke against your joining, for she has done many good deeds for us and is worthy to become your wife. Little Turtle, Winona, Hanmani, and other women have prepared a tepee for you. If it pleases you, my grandson, we will hold the joining ceremony on the next sun."

War Eagle glanced at Caroline and smiled, but did not think he had to ask if that suggestion was acceptable to her. He already knew she was just as eager as he was for that event to take place, and her smile confirmed it for him. "It brings much joy and pride to my heart to lay claim to her as my mate. I believe it is the plan of the Creator for us to join, and Wahcawi feels and thinks as I do. We will become one family on the next sun."

Although his grandson had spoken for them, Nahemana wanted their people to hear the truth come from her mouth and heart, so he asked Caroline, "Do you think and feel as Wanbli does?"

Her blue gaze met the shaman's age-clouded one and she responded, "Yes, Wise One, I love Wanbli and want to be his wife and a Red Shield."

"So it will be. Winona," Nahemana addressed his daughter, "you will prepare for the happy event for your son and Wahcawi."

"It is good, Father. I am honored for her to become a daughter."

* * *

As if the Great Spirit and Mother Earth and other good forces showed their approval of the impending event, snow and fierce wind had ceased the previous evening; and today's weather was sunny and unseasonably warm beneath a lovely blue sky and with gentle breezes swaying the trees.

With the help of her three closest friends, Caroline finished getting ready in Cloud Chaser's tepee. She was wearing the dress that Hanmani had given to her, and the younger female praised her beauty in it. With her—a white woman— joining to War Eagle, she mused, perhaps there was hope after all for a union between Hanmani and the half-blooded Cheyenne Dog Soldier, but that was something to be decided in the future. . . .

The sacred Medicine Wheel with a coup feather attached from Rising Bear was tied around a lock of her long blond hair. The belt from Zitkala, Chumani's best friend, was secured around her waist. The purse pouch from Macha was suspended from it, a lacy handkerchief tucked inside in case it was needed to dab away tears of joy. The necklace from Pretty Meadow was around her neck, and Caroline hoped Runs Fast would accept the truth one day and cease blaming her for his son's grim fate. The moccasins she was wearing were from Chumani, an old pair but still in good condition and they fit as if made for her. She had donned those garments and items to show her gratitude to their presenters and her acceptance of Indian ways.

During the long winter, she would use the furs, hides, and pelts from others to make herself more Indian garments and a new pair of moccasins. For a minute or two, she thought about the new dot on the flesher that Chumani had given to her, and pride surged through her to be so honored and accepted by War Eagle's family and people. Soon, he had told her yesterday, the Story Catchers would paint her deeds upon the Tribal History Hide, added to those of his two brothers and their wives.

The only people missing were her family. She hoped that somehow her parents were watching from heaven. She hoped her brother was safe and far away, and would come to visit them within the next few years.

At last, Caroline and the three females left the tepee and gathered with War Eagle, his family, and their people in a clearing surrounded by evergreens and barren hardwoods beneath a warming sun and clear blue sky.

Nahemana invoked the Great Spirit to observe the ceremony and bless the couple. He looked at War Eagle and asked him to say the proper words.

War Eagle's gaze locked with Caroline's and he smiled and said, "I join to Wahcawi before the eyes of Wakantanka and the Red Shields."

After Nahemana told Caroline to do the same, she smiled at War Eagle and said, "I join to Wanbli before the eyes of Wakantanka and the Red Shields." According to their custom and laws, all that was required was an announcement before the band and beneath the eyes of the Creator for them to be considered joined, married. It was not the wedding she had imagined for herself long ago, but it was perfect and she was elated soul deep.

Nahemana proclaimed, "Wanbli and Wahcawi are mates. It is as the Great Spirit willed when He created them and crossed their paths."

Rising Bear said, "I am blessed by the three women who have joined to my sons, for they have done many good and brave deeds for our band. As I prayed long ago, War Eagle has found a wife as brave, cunning, skilled, and kindhearted as Dewdrops and Dawn are. Come, my sons and daughters, we feast with our people to honor War Eagle and Sunflower."

Caroline and War Eagle sat in places of honor on rush and willow mats as they were served food and water by the women, many of the same items she had enjoyed at the feast for her and Red Wolf. Yet, it was hard for them to enjoy the meal, talk, and merriment when they wanted to be alone.

They listened and tried to conceal their anticipation as some of their people sang, chanted, and played the kettledrum and flutes.

Later, while War Eagle and the other members of the Sacred Bow Society danced around a glowing fire, Caroline observed them. As she did so, many thoughts raced across her mind. Next summer, she and her husband would go to the Badlands during the annual buffalo hunt to recover some of her possessions. Afterward, perhaps she and Cloud Chaser could go to one of the trading posts to sell the fancy dresses and trunks, and use that money for supplies. In days past, she and Cloud Chaser had offered to teach the Red Shields to farm and ranch, and might be allowed to do so in the future, for the Indian world was changing each year. They had peace for now, but they didn't know what spring or summer would bring. She knew some of the reasons for matters settling down for a while. Little Thunder had resigned from the warpath and had moved far away. Crazy Horse, Spotted Tail's nephew, had joined another Oglala band that camped somewhere northward with Red Cloud's Bad Faces. Sitting Bull also had guided his people far away. Spotted Tail and his followers were imprisoned at Fort Leavenworth, but Nahemana had predicted they would live and be freed before Mother Earth renewed her face again and the next season of grass was born. But if war or more encroachment came, she would work with the shaman to doctor any gunshot wounds and white man's diseases. She halted her mental roamings as he husband joined her and the celebrating continued.

As the late afternoon moved toward dusk, the sun began to set in the west and the air cooled at a rapid pace with its warmth gone. Shadows of trees, rocks, and dwellings lengthened upon the hard ground as daylight gradually vanished. The large fire had been allowed to devour its last pieces of wood, and only glowing coals remained inside the rock enclosure.

Nahemana stood and said, "It is time to return to our tepees. Gather your family and possessions, for the sun goes to sleep soon. Go, Wanbli and Wahcawi, to live in your new tepee as mates."

As they stood inside their tepee with the flap laced tightly, their first home, they glanced around in pleasure and happiness, but each knew they would examine it later. At the present, other desires called out to them. They stood near the abode's center, close to a low-burning fire. For a time, all they did was gaze at each other and mentally count their blessings.

It had been three weeks since Caroline's physical preparations for the rescue attempt, so her injuries had healed. Even so, War Eagle kissed every spot he had been compelled to wound, and he had not forgotten a single one. "Do they still hurt, my beautiful wife?" As he asked his first question, he nibbled upon her lips. After she shook her head, his mouth drifted across her cheek and brushed over her ear. After many kisses, with each waxing deeper and swifter, one of his hands fondled a breast through her garment. He was eager to seek blissful rapture in her arms and body, but he did not want to rush this special event, their first union.

For Caroline, it was as if when he kissed her and touched her, she lost all will to think clearly, and craved to answer his seductive summons. She loved him and wanted him urgently, so she let her emotions soar away with her eagle to seek pleasure and fulfillment.

War Eagle felt her body loosen and knew she was willing and eager to proceed with their sensual adventure as his lips met with hers and he kissed her with great hunger. He felt her arms encircle his body and rove his back as her mouth feasted on his.

They kissed and caressed each other until passions were inflamed and their carnal urges could not be denied. A flood of anticipation washed over them. They found it exciting to kindle each other to fiery heights as they imagined the quest and victory looming before them. They shed their outer garments so their naked flesh could make heady contact; then, their fingers drifted over their mate's bare skin as their mouths clung and worked magic on each other. Soon, they sank to their knees on the buffalo mat and each removed the undergarments that stood between their bodies. They eased to the furry hide to kiss and stroke for a while.

Caroline relaxed as much as those blissful sensations would allow and surrendered fully to his possession. She quivered when he nibbled her earlobe and spread kisses over her face, neck, and breasts. His hands roved lower and lower until she was almost dazed by rapturous sensations.

War Eagle gazed into her blue eyes with their glow of enticement. Her beauty and allure were so enormous that his breath caught in his throat and his pulse quickened. With tenderness, he moved atop her and gently made them one. He remained motionless for a short while as he simply savored the special moment and allowed her to relax after his entry, for she was pure of body. Slowly and carefully he began to move within her. He was thrilled when her arms clung to him, her legs gripped him snugly around his buttocks, and she melded their mouths. He could barely maintain his self-control and struggled to do so, as he knew the objective he strove for was worth his best effort and she must reach that destination first.

Caroline kissed his neck and her hands clasped his shoulders as she listened to his ragged respiration near her ear as his cheek pressed against her temple. Exhilarating and wonderful emotions charged through her body as he whetted her appetite and gloriously fed it when a powerful release burst upon her and warmed her skin from head to toes. She moaned in triumph and murmured her love of him over and over.

War Eagle realized she had captured her goal, so he reached for his and found sweet ecstasy. After his triumph, he sealed their lips as he embraced her with tenderness and fulfillment.

Caroline was engulfed by love, happiness, and contentment. She smiled into his tender gaze and trailed her fingers over his strong jawline. "You gave me much pleasure, *mihigna,*" she told him, thrilled the brief discomfort had been mild and she could now call him *my husband.*

War Eagle grinned. "As you gave me, *mitawin.* It is good we have the same thirst and hunger for each other."

"Will it always be this wonderful way between us?"

"*Ohinniyan,* Kawa Cante. *Waste cadake.*"

She felt aglow with elation as her dreamy mind echoed his words: *Always, Heart Flower. I love you.* She gazed into his dark eyes and said, "Always, Wanbli, for I love you. I pray for peace to fill our hearts and lives."

A happy War Eagle murmured in her ear, "As Macha said last summer, 'Peace often is as short as the night flower's life. Yet, while it blooms, it gives much beauty and joy.' It also will be that way for us, Kawa Cante, my beautiful Lakota Sunflower, but our life together and love will not be short."

As they kissed and talked, passions were rekindled and soon they were making rapturous love again, their fates sealed as one forever. . . .